PRAISE FOR D. E. BECKLER

'A dark and gritty read set in the homeless community with a real sense of authenticity and a sure touch. The setting is superbly drawn, the characters real and complex . . . A cracking read.'

—Trevor Wood, author of the Jimmy Mullen and
DCI Jack Parker series

'Tense and gripping, with a likeable down-at-heel detective. Beckler knows these streets, and it shows.'

—Antony Johnston, award-winning
New York Times bestselling author

AF513801

TRAPPED

ALSO BY D. E. BECKLER

Missing

Hunted

Writing as David Beckler

Antonia Conti Thriller series

A Long Shadow

A Stolen Memory

A Nuclear Reaction

Mason & Sterling series

Brotherhood

The Profit Motive

Forged in Flames

The Money Trap

Anthology

The Road More Travelled: Tales of those seeking refuge

A CITY STREETS MYSTERY

TRAPPED

D. E. BECKLER

THOMAS & MERCER

This is a work of fiction. Names, characters, organizations, places, events, and incidents are either products of the author's imagination or are used fictitiously. Any resemblance to actual persons, living or dead, or actual events is purely coincidental.

Text copyright © 2026 by D. E. Beckler
All rights reserved.

No part of this book may be reproduced, or stored in a retrieval system, or transmitted in any form or by any means, electronic, mechanical, photocopying, recording, or otherwise, without express written permission of the publisher.

Published by Thomas & Mercer, Seattle

www.apub.com

Amazon, the Amazon logo, and Thomas & Mercer are trademarks of Amazon.com, Inc., or its affiliates.

EU Product Safety Contact:
Amazon Media EU S.à r.l.
38, avenue John F. Kennedy, L-1855 Luxembourg
amazonpublishing-gpsr@amazon.com

ISBN-13: 9781662528323
eISBN: 9781662528316

Cover photography and design by Dominic Forbes

Printed in the United States of America

I've been very lucky with the editors I've worked with and have learned something from each one. David Downing, who has edited six of my books, including this one, has taught me the most. I've appreciated his insightful, intelligent and sometimes uncompromising feedback, knowing it was all to improve my often-scruffy manuscripts. I shall miss his wisdom and kindness and wish him a long and happy retirement.

CHAPTER 1

The streetlights had either given up the ghost or been smashed on this stretch of road, and Harry relied on the bright moonlight to show the way. He tripped over Cleo in the gloom and only just regained his balance. 'Look out, girl, you almost had me over.'

She wagged her tail and looked up at him with her big brown eyes.

'What's got into you?' She'd been jumpy since they'd left the main road. He clipped on her lead. 'Come on, let's get home.'

Home. Harry almost laughed at that. At least they had somewhere dry. They'd been okay over the summer, but now they were sliding into autumn he should look for somewhere with heating.

As should his brother. John seemed to have tumbled disastrously back into the drink when Harry had bumped into him outside the cathedral earlier that day. As usual, John had been in the company of Craig, his hulking sidekick.

Harry shouldn't have said anything, but he couldn't help himself.

'You drinking again, John?'

'What business is it of yours, Brother?' The slurred 'bushnessh' confirmation of how much he'd put away.

The fact that his brother used that title to address all men made it feel like an insult. 'How could you? You promised me on our mother's life.'

John jabbed a stubby finger at him. 'You're not my keeper, Harry. Don't forget that.'

'No, I'm not.' He glanced at Craig. 'But someone needs to look after you. You're a disgrace.'

John's already red face darkened, and he clenched his fists. 'That's rich, coming from you.'

Craig, who'd observed the exchange impassively, stepped between them. 'Time we went, John.' He guided his friend away. 'See you later, Harry,' the big man called back. 'Don't forget my offer. Anytime.'

Harry had watched him lead John away, an exaggerated care in placing his feet the only clue his brother was drunk. The fact that both brothers had ended up on the streets because of their addictions filled Harry with sorrow. John, first in their family to go to university, had seemed so together while Harry's addiction to gambling had led him into a spiral of debt and despair.

He'd rebuffed John's offers of help, until one day John's life imploded. He often wondered if John would have kept things together had Harry accepted his help. His brother had always had a well-developed sense of responsibility. And now here was Harry, trying but failing to reverse their roles. Too late now for such transformations, no doubt. Or for regrets.

Harry and Cleo reached the junction with Palmerston Street and would soon pass Pin Mill Brow. That place gave him the creeps, especially at night. He checked for traffic, even though at this time of night there was rarely anyone around.

The low burble of an engine came from behind him. A boxy vehicle, like a pickup or SUV, seventy metres away, crawling towards them. Or was it stopped? It didn't have any lights on.

He crossed the road and hurried along Palmerston Street, glancing across at the thickets on the opposite side. If it were daytime, he'd cut through there, but not at night, especially after last week.

Cleo whimpered again and stopped, pulling him backwards. 'Bloody hell!'

Behind, the car had pulled out onto Palmerston Street but kept its distance. A chill slid down his back. Were they the two men he'd seen last week? They'd been on foot but must have had a vehicle. Feeling exposed, he cast about. A few cars passed on the main road, out of sight, but none closer. Across was the path into the Brow he could take to get home, and would if it weren't dark. He'd got to know it in the ten days he'd stayed at his latest squat. *Come on, you're a grown man, you shouldn't be scared of the dark.* He swallowed his fear and crossed the road.

With a growl, the car accelerated. His heart jerked and, filled with panic, he pulled on Cleo's lead and ran, plunging between two metal bollards, through the undergrowth and onto the overgrown path. The road had been dark enough, but now he saw nothing. Brambles tugged at his clothes, and branches smacked him in the face. Cleo, sensing his panic, pulled on the lead. He ran to keep up, almost tripping on the uneven path. The stench of rotting leaves, dumped rubbish and worse made him gag. The noise of his headlong rush hid any sounds of pursuit.

They burst out of the undergrowth onto the tarmacked waste ground in the centre of the trees. The moon gave him enough light to show the path towards the bridge over the Medlock. He paused to listen. Voices came from the right. It couldn't be the men chasing him; they wouldn't have got that far so fast. Or would they? He headed away from them, back into the undergrowth.

Harry's lungs were on fire, and his legs felt like jelly. In his panic, he'd left the path he knew, and he ran blind, relying on Cleo to get him through. The rush of water came from his right. Where the hell was the bridge? Then he glimpsed the pale coping stones and rushed towards them. Which way was home? He paused to get his bearings, but Cleo didn't. He followed her, stumbling on a step. With a sense of relief, he grabbed the metal railing and forced his legs up the first flight of steps leading out of the waste ground.

At the top, he hesitated and listened. What if they'd driven around and were waiting for him? His breath rasped, and a stitch stabbed his side. The hot meal he'd got at the church hall – the reason he was out so late – churned inside him. Once through the Brow, he forced tired legs onwards, moving faster the nearer he got to 'home' – the derelict pub he'd found last week.

The owner had barricaded the downstairs doors and windows, but someone had pried one of the security screens off the back door and ransacked the place. He'd found it empty and set up his base. He used his phone light to check the entrance. It looked like it had when he'd left it.

He unclipped Cleo and pulled the corner of the screen back. It opened with a screech, and she shot in, her reaction reassuring him nobody waited inside. He followed her in, pulled the screen shut after him and dragged an old door across the opening before jamming a piece of timber against it as a lock. It wasn't the most secure, but it had to do.

They went upstairs, where he'd set up a bed and stored his meagre belongings. He'd cleaned up what had been a kitchen and laid an old mattress along the back wall. He turned off his phone to preserve the battery and got under the covers.

Despite his exhaustion, sleep eluded him as the old building made its random noises, settling for the night.

A tongue in his ear woke him, or had he heard something? He pushed Cleo away and huddled against the wall, listening intently. Cleo licked his hand and let out a low whine.

'Ssshhh.' He stroked her thin body, which trembled beneath his hand.

A crash came from the floor below. There was no doubt now, someone else was in the building. He told himself it was just another person in his position, looking for shelter, but his thoughts locked upon the vehicle he'd run from. And the two men who'd followed him to Pin Mill Brow a week earlier.

He'd told John about them, and he'd offered to help, or Craig had, but Harry found the ex-soldier intimidating. And Cleo hated Craig's little Yorkshire terrier with a passion, greeting it with frenzied barking whenever she saw it.

She'd better not bark now, but she rarely did unless she saw another dog.

The noise from downstairs continued, now a rhythmic banging. To quell his terror, he pictured the room below, trying to work out what they were doing. There wasn't much left down there. Looters had emptied it, taking anything worth selling. Previous occupants had ripped up floorboards to burn. Is that what they were doing? That would be a vote for their being just someone like him. But although wet and cool, the early October weather didn't justify a fire.

What if it were the men he'd seen? They'd have even less reason to be tearing the place up beneath him. And it had been a week ago that he'd seen them. If they'd had evil designs on him, why had they waited to carry them out?

Once they'd taken up residence in his mind's eye, there was no shaking them. The thought that they'd been thinking about him for a week chilled him. They'd only do that if they seriously meant to harm him. He'd come across people who resented the homeless, though he wasn't sure why they would. Was it anger at the reminder that their lives could also unravel? Most made do with hurling abuse, 'get a job' being a favourite. Some even spat at you, or threw the odd punch and kick if there was someone for them to put on a show for. Following you for a week and tracking down where you lived was another level.

Despite his wariness of Craig, Harry now wished he'd taken him up on his offer. He had John's number and powered up his phone. The screen lit up with a warning that he had less than 10 per cent power. He found John's number and pressed the green button. The voicemail kicked in.

'Shit!' He waited for the greeting to cycle. 'John, it's Harry. There's someone downstairs—' *Was that a step on the stairs?* He killed the call and put the phone on his bed, realising his stupidity. Even if he got hold of John, what could he do? It wasn't as if he could drive over, and even if he had a car he'd be too late. And thinking back to their encounter that afternoon, he realised his brother was probably still too pissed to do anything.

Maybe he should call the police? But his experience of them since being on the streets didn't give him much confidence. Anyway, what would he say? *Someone else has broken into the squat I broke into?*

No. He had to deal with this himself. He'd been a competent and able man before the tide had turned against him and washed him out onto the streets. *Come on, think, man, what would the old Harry do?* Cleo whimpered, and he shushed her, stroking her head, then made his way to the door. A previous occupant or intruder had smashed the top panel nearest the lock. Harry had pushed the damaged timber together in a flimsy attempt at repair, but it had left a scar a centimetre wide, and he placed his ear against it. A breeze kissed the side of his head. Was that a light flickering beyond the door?

A creak of floorboards made his pulse jump, then the sound stopped. Someone whispered. There had to be two of them. His mind froze. How to stop them from getting in here? The battered kitchen unit someone had detached from the wall stood near the door. But they'd hear him dragging it across the floor. He should just keep quiet and hope they left. Then Cleo barked.

Shit! After a panicked moment he shouted, 'I've called the police, you bastards!'

He stepped towards the unit, gripped it by the gap a drawer had left, and pulled. Outside, steps pounded on the stairs, no pretence at stealth now. He heaved, muscles screaming, but his fear trumped the pain. The cupboard resisted, then with a jerk it slid. Timber screeched as the base traversed bare boards. When his abused muscles gave up, he'd heaved it halfway across the doorway.

The door slammed in and bounced off the unit, then came to rest against it, leaving an opening a hand's width across. He shoved the door into its frame, then tried to ram the unit against it. It didn't move, but even where it was it should stop them getting to him.

He looked for a weapon but just found one of the lighter wall cabinets in the corner. He dragged it over and added it to his barricade.

Panting with the exertion and panic, he managed to say, 'The police will be here any minute!'

A nasty laugh greeted his threat, and the men held a whispered conversation. Then silence and footsteps. Were they looking for another way in, or searching for a battering ram? He'd scoured the entire building and remembered nothing they could use. The footsteps faded. Had they gone, or was it a trick to lure him out?

He stood by the barrier, waiting. Then the familiar scrape of the metal screen, and again when they pushed it back into place. But why bother doing that? Why were they doing *anything* they were doing? Car doors slammed, and an engine roared into life. He reached the barred window in time to see brake lights flare and the vehicle turn left at the T-junction.

'They've gone, Cleo.' Or had just one of them left to make Harry think he was safe?

Cleo's high-pitched whine suggested the latter.

His heart racing, Harry made his way back to the door and listened. A crackling sound he couldn't place, followed by a smell he could. *Fire!* He had to get out.

He pulled the small cupboard away and grappled with the heavy base unit. Panic gave him strength, and he pulled it free, then dragged the door open. Smoke poured in, attacking his throat and making him cough. He crouched down and crawled along the landing. Flames danced at the bottom of the stairs, blocking his exit.

Fear froze him solid, but Cleo's yap roused him, and he hurried back to the sanctuary of his room, where she waited. He slammed the door, but smoke had infiltrated the room. He retreated to the window. Outside, the flat roof offered a way down, but bars across the window blocked his way.

The frame had been nailed shut, so he couldn't even reach the bars. He picked up a broken drawer and used it to smash the glass. Cool, clean air rushed in, and he took a gulp. He cleared the broken shards, sharks' teeth in the wooden frame, and grabbed the metal rods. Although rusty, they were solid. He tested each one, but could move none of them. With a frustrated grunt, he slapped the nearest one.

'HELP!' he bellowed into the night. He listened, but apart from crackling behind him he heard only the rustling of the leaves from the trees opposite the back of the pub.

Despite the door being shut and the window open, the smoke grew thicker. He lowered himself to the floor, where it seemed clearer. Cleo nuzzled into him and let out a bark. He had to get her out. He picked her up and stood, coughing as he hit the smoke barrier. His eyes streamed, and he held a wriggling Cleo in both hands. He squinted and guided her between two of the bars.

'Sorry, girl, it's only a few feet to the roof.' He released her, and she yelped before landing with a dull thud. 'Cleo!'

A growl and a yap let him know she was okay. Now that she was safe, he remembered his phone. *Where the hell is it?* Of course, on his bed. He crawled across the floor to where he thought it was, but just found bare boards. Where was his bed? He thrashed about looking for it, breathing in smoke and coughing.

'Think, man!'

He pictured the room. From the window, the bed was on his right. *Why the hell did you go left?* He returned to the window. A gust of cold, fresh air stroked his cheek as he reached it. He paused for two breaths and then continued, reaching his bed in seconds. But where was the phone? In a panic, he searched for it, but couldn't find it.

He lay on the bed, frustrated and terrified and fantastically weary. Downstairs, the crackling had grown to a roar. Something heavy fell with a crash, then with a whoosh a wave of heat struck him like a physical blow.

A coughing fit seized him. Through it all, the thought that he had to get to the window, but disorientated by the heat and smoke he crawled the wrong way before collapsing in the corner.

CHAPTER 2

Judy Novak punched the screen of her phone, cutting off her dad. The sooner he came to terms with the fact that she was now running things, the sooner they'd get back on an even keel. Although it had been almost six months since he'd ended up in a wheelchair after being shot, he'd finally agreed to let her take charge three months back.

She counted and had reached twenty-seven before her door slammed open. 'Come in, Dad.'

'I am in – thanks.' He spoke through gritted teeth. He wedged his chair in through the door, shoved it closed behind him and rolled up to her desk. 'Why not?' he demanded, continuing the conversation she'd cut off.

'Because, Dad, the guy's corrupt.'

'Yeah. Of course he is. That's why he'll do what we want. As Shakespeare said, "Corruption wins more than honesty."'

'Are you sure, Dad?' She'd inherited his gift for hoarding quotations – though not, thankfully, his compulsion for sharing them – and her gift was in better repair than his. She was positive Shakespeare had said quite the opposite.

'Of course I'm sure. It's my legs that don't work, not my brain.'

'And it's me who has to work with him. The guy gives me the creeps. I feel like I need a shower every time I meet him.'

'He's not touched you, has he?' Alex Novak's fists clenched and his forearms, developed by his obsessive exercising, bunched like twisted roots.

'No, Dad, I'd kick him in the nuts if he tried anything. I just don't want to deal with him, full stop.'

Alex exhaled and relaxed. 'You're in charge.' He looked around the office and at the pile in the corner. 'You've taken down Marko's stuff.'

She'd been expecting this argument. 'Yes, this is *my* office. You've still got Milan's, so why don't you put all Marko's stuff up there? I don't want a load of signed football shirts and his other junk in my office.'

'Nah. It would be a reminder every day that they're not around.'

'Yeah, but it's fine for me to be reminded?'

'Yeah, okay, you've got a point.' His forearms swelled, signalling another irritation. 'We still haven't found the bastards who did it. We mustn't forget.'

'Isn't it time we let that go?'

'And let people think they can walk all over us?'

She saw his point, but her eagerness to move away from their past and into more legitimate channels overrode it. An obsession with avenging his two sons wouldn't be profitable. 'Didn't Gandhi say, "Forgiveness is for the strong"?'

'Yeah, and Elizabeth I said, "God forgives, but I can't."'

'She also said, "Forgiveness is a gift you give yourself."' She wasn't sure that was Elizabeth. Although she could recall most of the quotes her dad had made her memorise when she was at that posh school, she didn't always remember who'd said them.

'And she also said, "Nothing inspires forgiveness like revenge."'

She didn't think the latter quote was from the queen either, but knew better than to correct him again. 'Let's not get sidetracked.' Her phone buzzed, and she glanced at it. 'I need to take this.'

He didn't look like he was going anywhere.

'Dad, it's a personal call.'

'Oh, right.' He spun his chair and wheeled out.

Judy waited until he'd worked his way back through the door and rattled it shut, hoping the voicemail didn't kick in. 'Mr Robertson, thanks for calling back.'

'No problem, Judy – and don't forget, it's Archie.' His rich, educated, Scottish voice made her imagine an Edinburgh lawyer in a kilt and tweed jacket.

'Have you considered my offer?'

'It is of interest,' he said. 'But I must warn you, I've already taken extensive steps to acquire the land, so would want that reflected in any deal we agree.'

Of course you have. If that were true, he'd have rebuffed her offer. 'I'm sure we can come to an equitable agreement. We haven't been idle, and being local we have the contacts needed to ensure the project runs without a hitch.'

'Of course, Judy. Why don't we meet? I much prefer dealing face to face.'

'Good idea. Why don't I come up to Aberdeen?'

'I was thinking of coming to Manchester. I've always fancied staying at the Midland.'

That would not do. She had to make sure her dad didn't get wind of the deal until she'd agreed everything. If Robertson plonked himself in the centre of Manchester, there was no way she could hide his presence. 'How about Edinburgh, neutral ground?'

'As I say, I am keen to stay at the Midland.'

'You'll have plenty of opportunities once we're working together. The build will take two years at least.'

'Verra well. You're a persuasive young woman. We shall have to welcome you to Scotland.'

They agreed on a date and venue and ended the call. A friend had just returned from a visit and raved about the small hotel she'd stayed in. Judy hated lying to Dad *and*, worse, going behind his back. He'd be furious, but she couldn't help that. The project was too big for her to handle alone.

A knock on her door announced her father's return.

'Come in, Dad.'

'Yeah, you're right,' he said as he wheeled himself to her desk. 'We should distance ourselves from our past and the people we dealt with.'

'Oh. Yes, you're right, Dad.'

He looked at her empty mug with an eager expression.

'Shall I get you a drink?' She stood.

'A whisky, if it's not too much trouble.'

She poured him one, wondering what he wanted. His easy capitulation suggested he desired something else. He waited until he had his drink before coming down to business.

'So, who's going to be our go-between with the planning committee on the Rochdale Canal project?'

'We're not having one.'

'Is that wise? Someone needs to liaise with them.'

'Yes. The architect and me.'

He sighed. 'I'm not trying to mensplain, but that's not how things work.'

'That's how they should work. You were trying to short-circuit the process—'

'We have to, otherwise we won't get anywhere. People like us, our family, aren't part of the establishment. We're seen as outsiders, no better than gangsters.'

She snorted. 'The man you were using is on remand for involvement in the murder of a senior council employee.'

Alex waved that inconvenient fact away. 'Yes, but he was working for another developer.'

'You think that makes it better? He was playing you for a mug. He—'

Alex slammed his hand on the arm of his wheelchair. 'He was *not* playing me for anything!'

She took a breath. 'Sorry. What I meant was that you couldn't trust him. This way, I'm directly involved.'

'Okay, but don't let them take advantage of you.'

'I'm your daughter, don't forget.' She smiled, relieved when he seemed to relax. 'Now, leave it to me to get it sorted. I'll keep you posted.'

'Sorry, but you know how much the project means to me. It will be a monument to the boys.'

What the hell had they done to deserve a 'monument' apart from bully people, humiliate women, including her and her mum, and get themselves killed? 'Aren't we calling that place on Beswick Street after them?' The project, a fraction of the size of the one on the Rochdale Canal but eating money, was one reason she was being forced to look for partners.

'I think it's small time, and that was one thing the boys weren't. This project is a more fitting tribute.'

She suppressed a snort, deciding to leave this argument for a later date, and present the results of her plans as a fait accompli. As her dad would quote, 'It's easier to ask for forgiveness than for permission.'

He checked the time. 'I'll get off. Don't stay too late.'

'Goodnight, Dad.'

She'd stay until one. The casino would be quiet tonight, so she'd get some work done. She ordered an omelette and salad from the kitchen and cracked on with the paperwork. Before a maniac trying to take over their business shot her dad in the spine, she'd been happy working as a reporter. *Well, perhaps not happy*, she thought, recalling her slimy boss, but she'd enjoyed going out and meeting a variety of people.

Now, she seemed to spend time either stuck at a desk, or meeting dodgy 'businessmen' in expensive restaurants. Even though they were moving away from the core activities of her father and brothers' days – the unholy quartet of drink, drugs, sex and gambling – she still had to mix with people she wanted nothing to do with. Almost always older men who didn't take her seriously.

With a knock at her door, her omelette arrived, served by a tall, balding, hollow-cheeked man wearing a tailored three-piece suit over his underfed frame. 'Jerry, you working in the kitchens now?'

Jerry Sweeny gave a weak smile and placed the covered tray on the corner of her desk. 'Still running things, but—' He cut himself off and gestured at the visitor's chair.

That didn't sound good.

She nodded and waited for him to continue.

He sat, folding himself into the chair, his limbs sticking out like the legs of a spider crab, and cleared his throat. 'But not for much longer.'

Her insides dropped. 'Why, Jerry? What's wrong?' He was the one solid presence she'd been relying on.

'Things have changed. You know, with you taking over . . .'

'You don't want to work for me? It's still Dad's operation.' But Jerry was too shrewd an operator not to know that was bullshit.

'No, it's not that.' Light glinted off his silver-framed glasses as he shook his head. 'But you weren't here when that gang of thugs from Birmingham turned up. Your dad saw them off. What would happen in a case like that now?'

'That's the old way, Jerry. We're moving away from that side of the business.'

'Yeah. *Moving*, but not moved. Anyway, what would you need me for once you get rid of the casino? I'm the manager.'

'We're keeping the casino.'

'How long for?'

She wasn't sure, and didn't want to lie to him. 'You're also an excellent accountant.'

He shrugged. 'That's what I told the guy at the accountancy firm in Ardwick.'

'You taken another job?'

He shrugged again. 'Monday to Friday, nine to five and no gunmen.'

'When?'

'I wouldn't want to drop you in the lurch, but he wants me to start in December. At the latest.'

Her thoughts raced. 'That's just seven weeks.'

'Sorry.'

'Right.' How the hell was she going to replace him that quickly?

He stood and gestured at the tray. 'Don't let it get cold.'

When he'd gone, she pulled the tray to her and removed the cover. The aroma of the chopped parsley and the butter they'd cooked the omelette in made her feel sick. She covered it again and pushed it away. Not only did she have to find someone to replace Jerry, but he knew all their secrets.

CHAPTER 3

The alarm woke me at seven, and I silenced it before sliding my legs out of the bed. The van rocked as I stood and stretched in the cramped space. My left hand thumped the kitchen cabinet above the tiny sink with a hollow clunk.

You're awake, then.

'Morning, Oscar.' My dog had first spoken to me after six months on the streets, perhaps spurred by me going for days on end without human contact. But then he'd carried on even after we'd got a flat, and I now suspected it would be a permanent state of affairs.

You going to let me out?

'You're grumpy this morning.'

I pulled my dressing gown around my shoulders, slid my slippers on and stepped outside. After a year of sleeping fully clothed, I'd got back into the habit of wearing pyjamas. A pleasure within the van's confines, but the chill October wind knifed through the fabric as I opened the passenger door of the van that had been our home for almost six months. Oscar jumped out and disappeared into the bushes that surrounded our pitch.

'One or two?' I shouted.

Can't I go to the toilet without you announcing my movements to all and sundry?

I looked around. 'All and sundry?'

Since the end of September, the site we occupied, in a converted pub car park on the eastern edge of Manchester had been almost empty. The only people using it now were a few hardy walkers and the four other households who lived here, although they occupied static caravans several times the size of my micro-van.

How would you like it if I announced it every time you used the toilet?

'You're doing it in public.'

It's the principle. Sheesh! I don't know why I bother. What's for breakfast?

'How about dog food, for a change?'

Great. Where is it? Oscar reappeared from behind a hedge, wearing an eager expression.

I pointed into the bushes. 'Will I have to clear up after you first?'

No. Just get the food, will you?

'Give me five minutes, I need to put the bed away—' From inside the van, my phone rang. I reached in and retrieved it. 'Morning, John. Everything okay?'

'No, Brother. I got a missed call from Harry. He— Can you get here, and I'll tell you?'

'Sure. Where are you?'

'I'm at his place.' He gave me an address and ended the call.

'Come on, Oscar, we're needed.'

What about my breakfast?

To keep him quiet, I filled his bowl with food and placed it outside, then tidied my bed and folded it away, put the kettle on, and washed in the toilet block next to our van while my coffee brewed. He was still eating when I returned, dressed and ready to go. I filled my insulated cup, secured the kettle and stepped outside. Oscar lay beside his bowl chewing, and I reached for it.

I've not finished.

'You'll have to do that in the van.' I picked up the bowl and placed it on the floor in the back.

You'll give me indigestion. He clambered into the vehicle and continued eating as I slammed the door behind him.

I clipped my cup into the holder and started the van. John had sounded uncharacteristically shaken. Something must have happened at Harry's place. I didn't know Harry well, although I'd learned he was somehow related to John. Although a good friend, John was tight-lipped about his background. Harry had come on the scene after I'd got housed – well, stuck in a grotty flat and then this tiny van, which passed for a home. Keen to find out what had happened, I pushed the van, accelerating at its maximum rate. Just above that of a ride-on mower.

Whoa, take it easy, will you? I'm being thrown about back here. Bloody boy-racer.

We hit a bit of traffic but did the journey in half an hour. The presence of two fire engines, an ambulance and several police cars told me something serious had happened. I looked around for somewhere to park, keeping an eye out for John while I did so. In the event, Oscar spotted him or, more accurately, he noticed Trixie, who was with Craig, and as usual he was at John's side.

I parked the car and attached his lead to a protesting Oscar. 'You see that van there?' I pointed to the police dog van. 'That's the dogcatcher.'

Chastened, he let me clip the lead onto him, and we walked towards our friends. They stood on the pavement beside an area of woodland looking at the burnt-out shell of what had once been a pub. Steam floated out of where the roof had been. A single-storey flat-roofed section looked to be the only part of the building intact. The firefighters had finished, with just one line of hose laid into the building.

White-suited police officers and technicians drifted in and out of the doorway, their names being noted on a clipboard by a uniformed officer. I guessed what that meant.

'Right, Victor, and you, Oscar,' John called to us. Craig nodded a greeting, and Trixie, his Yorkshire terrier, today wearing a black ribbon, yapped a hello.

I pointed at her ribbon. 'Is that in honour of Harry?'

John replied. 'Yes, Brother. It's a sad day. Thank you for coming.'

'Do you know what happened?' I let Oscar off his lead, and he joined Trixie.

John produced his mobile, started the voicemail and handed it to me. Harry's tinny voice came out of the speaker. 'John, it's Harry. There's someone downstairs—' The message ended.

I returned his phone. 'Why did he ring you?' John acted as an unofficial leader and mentor to many people who lived on the streets of Manchester, but this sounded like an emergency, and seeing the burnt-out building, I knew it wasn't a false alarm.

'He's – was – my little brother.'

'Oh!' I swallowed. 'I'm so sorry, John, I didn't realise.'

John's eyes glistened. 'Yeah. Well, you weren't to know.' We stood in embarrassed silence for a moment, and then John continued. 'He'd mentioned two men followed him through Pin Mill Brow last week.' He gestured towards the thicket behind us. 'We offered to escort him home, check them out, but he declined.'

Craig bent down and ruffled Trixie's ears. 'His dog didn't like Trixie.'

I studied the steaming building. 'You sure he's in there?'

John pointed at a black van with 'private ambulance' printed on the side. 'They're here for him.'

The mention of his dog had got me thinking. 'Did Harry say what these men looked like?'

'They were both big. Not quite Craig's size. One had a posh voice, and the other had a shaved head and a red tattoo on his neck.'

My mind went back to a posh thug who'd attacked me and a tattooed bald one I'd fallen foul of. 'What kind of tattoo?'

John shrugged. 'He only glimpsed it.'

'Do you remember the Airedale I found after a fire—'

Who found him? Oscar had paused his discussion with Trixie.

'It was a team effort. You saw him, and I rescued him.'

John, used to my conversations with Oscar, said, 'Yes, what about him?'

'You recall there were two men who attacked his owner and set fire to the building he was in. If Oscar hadn't found him, he'd have died.'

Thank you for giving me my deserved credit.

I ignored him and continued, 'They chased me in a van, and I'm pretty sure one had a red tattoo on his neck. Someone attacked another homeless man with a dog a week later. I'm certain it was them.'

'Yes, I do recall,' John said. 'Craig moved off the streets for a week to avoid them. But that was months ago. You think these are the same people? Why haven't they attacked anyone in the meantime?'

I wasn't sure. 'We should let the police know.'

'Rather you than me.' Craig nodded towards the steaming building where a large, bald figure, squeezed into white coveralls, exited the back door of the pub.

My heart sank. Grimes.

Detective Chief Inspector Grimes was a terrifying figure, but his sergeant, Bowling, was a different proposition. I'd find her and give her the information.

'Can you let me have the recording?'

John gave his phone to Craig, who stabbed the screen with sausage-like fingers until my phone beeped. Craig returned John's handset. 'I've messaged you the voice file.'

I waited for Sergeant Bowling to appear but couldn't see her tall, elegant form leave the building. She was probably still inside. A pair of uniformed officers walked past, and I called to them. They approached us wearing suspicious expressions.

'You guys live around here?' the older one asked.

'No, but—'

'So what are you doing here?'

Before I could reply, his colleague pointed at my van. 'Is that yours?'

'Actually, it belongs to a mate, who's lent it to me.'

'Oh yeah. You're not camping here illegally, are you?'

'Of course not.' I gave her the address of the campsite I stayed at.

The first one continued. 'Why are you here?' His gesture included John and Craig.

The coppers were both annoying me. 'Our mate Harry was in there. I've got some evidence I want to give to the detective sergeant.'

They exchanged a look, and the woman left. She returned two minutes later with a man in his mid-thirties, about ten years younger than me, wearing a one-piece coverall, his hood pulled back. Soot marked the sleeves and legs and ash coated the feet. His prominent forehead creased as he studied me with protruding eyes.

'You got sumfink for me?' He had a pronounced southern accent.

'I wanted to speak to Sergeant Bowling.'

'Temporary Inspector Bowling, you mean? She ain't here, as you can see.'

'Oh, right. Are you her replacement?'

'Yeah' – he grinned at the uniformed officers – 'you could say that.'

I didn't like him. 'What's your name, Sergeant?'

His smile vanished. 'DS Lambert. Now, you got something for me, or are you wasting my time?'

I told him about the message and played it to him.

'What time you get that?'

'He sent it to John.'

John stepped forward with his phone. 'Eleven forty-two, Brother.'

'First of all, I ain't your brother. How come you derelicts all have smartphones?'

A surge of anger made my shoulders bunch. 'First of all, we're not "derelicts". Just because you're temporarily homeless doesn't mean you haven't got friends and family to keep in touch with. How the hell are you supposed to take part in modern society without one? Carry a laptop with you?'

'Whoa! Keep your hair on.'

'Are you interested in our evidence?'

He turned to the older constable. 'Take these' – he paused and looked us up and down – '"gentlemen's" statements.' He strode back towards the building, stiff-legged.

'We'd have been better off talking to Grimes,' I said to John.

'If you think I'm fetching *him*, you can forget it.' The constable produced a notebook.

Half an hour later, he'd taken John and Craig's statements and given me an email address to send the voicemail to. They looked sceptical when I mentioned the previous attacks but assured me they'd look into it.

The activity at the entrance had increased, and two dark-suited men wheeled a stretcher from the private ambulance towards it. Two firefighters backed out carrying one end of a black body bag;

another two at the other end followed. They placed Harry's body on the stretcher. Even though I didn't know Harry well, I could see how much his death affected John, and even Craig.

After watching him being wheeled into the van, Craig cleared his throat. 'What's happened to Cleo, his dog?'

The woman officer pointed to where the police van had been. 'K9 team will have taken it for disposal.'

'What?'

She took a step back. Craig could intimidate, even without trying. 'It will probably be diseased. It's for the best.'

I stepped between her and Craig. 'You can't put a healthy dog down.' I'd met Cleo once and remembered a lively spaniel-whippet cross who looked like a slim pharaoh hound, hence her name.

She shrugged. 'Not my decision. Speak to the dog unit.'

Her colleague stepped forward. 'Right, gents, I've got your numbers if I need you.' They watched us walk towards my van.

Oscar trotted towards me. ***You can't let them murder Cleo.***

'Don't worry, I won't let that happen.' I wasn't sure how, but I had to try.

CHAPTER 4

Zofia Dąbrowski waited at the table in the back room of a remote pub in the wilds of Derbyshire. She'd driven there on a narrow lane, which clung to the side of a steep valley. She could imagine it being delightful in the summer when you could enjoy the spectacular views from the garden. Not so much in wet and windy autumnal weather, and she was glad of the log fire crackling in the stone fireplace and scenting the room.

She was checking the time again when a figure swathed in scarves and a huge coat bustled into the room carrying a large cup of coffee. Liquid slopped into her saucer as she placed it on the copper-covered table before unwinding her scarf and throwing it onto the chair on her right. She undid her coat but kept it on and slumped into the seat opposite Zofia's, half turning it so she faced the fire. The aroma of her drink made Zofia wish she'd ordered one instead of the tea she'd just finished.

'Sorry I'm late. Traffic . . .'

Zofia returned her smile. 'No problem. You said you had something urgent for me.'

Her expression darkened. 'Yeah. Not good news, I'm afraid. I can't give you any more information about' – she looked around the empty room – 'you know who.'

Zofia, who'd feared as much when the woman had requested this urgent meeting, didn't hide her disappointment. 'You promised me the name of the policeman who's protecting him.'

'Sorry, Zofia. I can't risk it.'

'As a whistleblower, you'll be protected.'

She laughed. 'In theory. But that's not what I'm worried about. The people involved are really nasty.'

'We knew that before we started.' Zofia, despite being certain they were the only two present, did the same scan of the room. 'Not only is your boss linked to a contract hit, but you're talking about a policeman who might be covering one up.'

'Yes, and he knows somebody's investigating him.' She slugged half of her coffee. 'Someone's been blabbing.'

Zofia's heart lurched. 'The policeman?'

'Glass has heard he's being investigated. But if he knows, he'll have told the copper.'

'He's not got our names?'

'Not that I've heard. Not yet, anyway.'

'There you are, then. We need to expose him before he does.'

'I'm sorry, Zofia.' She finished her drink and stood.

'Is that it? You're just going to let him get away with it?'

The woman's eyes narrowed, and she refastened her coat. 'It's not you he'd be targeting. I've got a family.' She picked up her scarf. 'Don't contact me again.'

Zofia watched her leave, her anger ebbing as she realised the risk the woman had taken. They were pretty sure the woman's boss, Rudy Glass, had colluded in the murder of a council employee and paid off a senior police officer to escape the consequences. Either or both would probably take extreme measures to avoid exposure.

A startup news outlet had broken the story when the police refused to investigate and were paying Zofia and her brother to gather more evidence, but it was a job she probably should have turned down, especially as they were giving the startup a favourable rate.

She returned to her car and drove into Manchester, relieved to be leaving the narrow lanes behind. She'd have to tell the reporter she'd been liaising with that she had nothing for her. The thought that she might be the source of the leak hit Zofia. In which case, it made sense to walk away, much as she hated the thought of letting Glass and whoever was helping him get away with it. She'd tell the editor they'd done all they could and send a final invoice.

She pulled into the small car park behind the office on Cheetham Hill Road that she shared with her brother Kasper. He'd had an appointment with a client, and his car wasn't back. A gust of wintry wind greeted her exit from the car. She waved at the guys in the fried-chicken shop below their premises as she passed on her way to the office entrance.

A wodge of post sat in the basket behind the door, and she gathered it up before making her way upstairs. The smell of burnt cooking oil from the neighbours didn't seem as intense as usual, or maybe she was getting used to it. She dumped the post on her desk and put the coffee maker on in their small kitchen while her desktop woke up.

The envelope from the Society of Private Investigators grabbed her attention. She was sure they'd paid their annual licencing fee, and an inspection wasn't due for at least another six months. The content of the envelope made her sit, and she read it again.

Dear Mr Dąbrowski,

As a result of the serious allegations against your company, KZD Investigations, we have no option but to temporarily suspend your licence pending an investigation. Our compliance team will carry this out, and any costs incurred will be passed on to your company. In the meantime, you must stop using our logo, and your company will be removed from our website.

If you choose to continue practising while suspended, your insurance will not be valid, and it may hinder your ability to rejoin the organisation.

Yours sincerely . . .

Zofia checked the envelope to see if there was another sheet stuck inside, but that was it. Did Kasper know anything about this? She pulled up his number but decided not to call him. If he knew what it was about, he'd tell her. If he didn't know, no point in worrying him before she had to.

She read the letter a third time. The insertion of *the* in 'As a result of *the* serious allegations' suggested both the letter writer and Kasper knew what the allegations were, so they must have already contacted him.

She crossed to his desk and searched his in-tray, but it contained nothing older than three days. One thing you couldn't fault Kasper for was his filing. She checked the hanging file for the Society of Private Investigators, but there was nothing since the renewal letter nine weeks earlier.

She rang the number at the bottom of the letter and gave their reference number.

'As you're not Mr Dąbrowski, I can't discuss—'

'I told your colleague, I'm Ms Dąbrowski, his sister. I'm also a partner in the firm and the Z in our name.'

He tapped some keys, huffed and came back on the line. 'I suppose I can discuss this with you. We received a complaint that you have been working for known criminals.'

They must mean Novak, but how would they have found out? Her neck grew warm. 'Have you any evidence?'

'Are you denying you've worked for criminals?'

'Of course I am. I'm also asking you to provide evidence of the accusation.' She'd checked Novak's background when he first approached them. Although they knew he was a major criminal, she couldn't find any unspent convictions in his name. Men like him had others to take the heat.

'We've received extensive evidence, which we will check—'

'But you won't be sharing it with us.'

'Ms Dąbrowski. In cases like this, people usually know if they've been working with a criminal. You wouldn't be much of a detective if you didn't. You can either come clean now, and speed things along, or wait until we finish our investigations. If you did it inadvertently, we may be able to overlook it.'

Although she suspected that to be a lie, she felt an urge to confess, to tell them Novak had given them no option but to work for him. But that would open another can of worms.

'Ms Dąbrowski?'

'Sorry. We'll wait to hear from you, then.' She ended the call, her heart thumping and hand sweaty.

'That doesn't sound good.'

She spun in her chair. 'Victor.' A dejected-looking Oscar trudged towards her. 'What's up?'

'I could ask you the same.'

'You first. I'll get you a coffee.'

Oscar had gone straight to his bed under the printer, and Victor sat at his desk. She placed a steaming mug in front of him and returned to hers.

Victor spoke first. 'I got a call from John first thing. Two men had harassed Harry, his brother, last week. He rang John and left a voicemail saying someone was in the derelict pub he was dossing down in. In the early hours, someone set it on fire. He didn't survive.'

'Oh, Victor. I'm so sorry. Poor John. What about you? Were you and Harry close?'

'I knew him to say hello to. He arrived in Manchester after I got the flat, so we weren't on the streets together. But obviously John's devastated.'

Victor looked like he wanted to add something. 'There's something else?'

He looked uncertain. 'They sound like the two who chased me after Oscar and I rescued that homeless man from a fire. That man had a dog as well.'

'Have you told the police?'

He held up his phone. 'I gave a statement to a uniformed copper and emailed the voicemail to a detective sergeant. I mentioned the earlier attack in the email.'

'It wasn't Colette?' She had a good relationship with Sergeant Bowling.

'No, Grimes has a new sidekick. Colette's a temporary inspector now.'

'Good for her. I've got her mobile number, and I'll see if she can find out if they're taking it seriously.'

'Yeah, okay.' Victor swallowed a mouthful of coffee. 'What about you?'

She told him about the letter.

'What does that mean?'

'Obviously, the insurance is an issue. We can still practise as private investigators, it's pretty unregulated. But we've been emphasising the fact that we're members of the SPI, and it's been bringing us business, especially corporate work.'

'But Novak didn't give you any choice.'

'He didn't, but that was partly our fault. We put ourselves in a vulnerable position by working for Robertson.' Or Kasper had.

'You said Novak had no unspent convictions. Could Robertson be the one they're talking about?'

She'd considered that. 'I don't think his name is in our books. He paid in crypto and contacted us – Kasper – using encrypted channels.' It all sounded so stupidly shady to her, now that she said it aloud. 'Anyway, he hasn't any convictions either.'

Victor expelled air through his lips. 'Did they say who complained about you?'

'They didn't even say what evidence there is against us. It just seems unfair.'

'Yeah.' He checked the time. 'I need to make a call.'

A surge of irritation at his seeming to dismiss her concerns dissipated as she listened to his end of the call.

'What do you mean you'll have to leave it to a vet to decide?'

Victor's hand tightened on the handset.

'Of course she's malnourished and has parasites. She's been living on the streets.'

He swore to himself.

'I will. Thank you.' He jabbed the call button.

'Harry's dog survived?'

'Yeah, the police dog unit took her. They're assessing her to decide what to do.'

'You mean whether to put her down?'

Victor nodded, then looked at Oscar and said, 'Of course I will.' He returned his attention to Zofia. 'I'll be ringing once the vet has examined her this afternoon.'

'What will you do?'

'I took the Airedale we rescued from the fire six months ago to a vet in Ancoats. They patched him up for free. They don't charge for treating street dogs.'

'And what happens once they've treated her?'

Victor shrugged. 'We'll deal with that later. I want to make sure she's okay first.'

'Good idea.' Could they take her in? Kasper, after at first taking a dislike to Oscar, had grown fond of him, and they'd even had him live with them for a short while.

Victor got down to some work, and Zofia tried to do the same, but her thoughts kept returning to the investigation she was now forced to abandon. Rudy Glass was a nasty piece of work and deserved to go down, but she needed to find a link between him and the senior police officer. One powerful enough to direct a murder investigation away from the crooked property developer.

Victor cleared his throat. 'About the SPI business. I saw Kasper with a letter last week. He hid it when I arrived.'

That was just like her brother. 'Do you know what he did with it?'

'I think he locked it in the bottom drawer.' He pointed at Kasper's desk.

She removed the key from hers and took it to Kasper's desk. It fitted but wouldn't turn. She wiggled it until it bent.

Victor joined her. 'Do you want me to have a go?'

The main door opened, and Kasper stood in the entrance. 'What the hell are you two doing?'

Zofia removed the key and held it up. 'I'm looking for the letter from the SPI.'

Kasper reddened. 'What letter?'

Despite her irritation, she couldn't help laughing, and Kasper frowned.

Victor said, 'Never play cards for money, Kasper.'

He scowled at Victor but looked at his sister and sighed. 'Okay. I didn't want to worry you.' He took his jacket off and made his way to his desk.

Zofia stood aside to let him sit, but stayed near him. 'Let me see it. We got one today.'

Victor collected today's letter from Zofia's desk and brought it to Kasper while he unlocked the drawer and retrieved the first one.

Zofia read it. 'It's not either of them.'

'What do you mean?' Kasper looked from her to Victor.

'We were speculating if it was Novak or Robertson we were being accused of working for. I've never even heard of a' – she checked the letter – 'Nirmal Casin.'

Kasper looked even guiltier. 'I know him. He . . . He came in one day asking if we could carry out background checks on two people. I gave him a standard engagement letter, and he left, promising to send the details.'

'Didn't you check him out?' She returned to her desk.

'He never sent me the details of the job, then I found out he'd paid a deposit when I checked the bank account.'

'What? How did he manage that? And what did you do with it?'

'It's still in our account.'

She gave an exasperated sigh. 'I'm going to check him out.' She opened the criminal records database they used. 'I can't get access.'

'Yeah,' said Kasper. 'That's through our SPI membership.'

'It would be.' She closed it and opened a database they rarely used, as it cost each time they used it, and wasn't as accurate. It delivered, though. 'Here he is. Fraud and obtaining money under false pretences.'

'You think he was working a scam on us?'

She was trying to work out what scam it could be when Victor spoke up. 'What date did he approach you?'

Kasper checked his screen. 'Early September, ninth. Why?'

'Wasn't that about the time you got the dirt on Rudy Glass?'

Dirt was right. She'd uncovered his links to a contract killer who'd taken out a corrupt council planning officer. Zofia checked her emails. 'I emailed the police on the fourth, but they did nothing.'

Victor said, 'Yeah, but the press did, and he's been blacklisted by the council.'

Kasper gave an exaggerated sigh. 'Well, either the police or the paper you sent it to tipped him off, and my money is on the cops. It will be why they've done nothing.'

Zofia shook her head. 'It was definitely the police. I didn't contact the press until the sixteenth.'

'There you are.' Kasper gave a triumphant smile. 'He must have a copper in his pocket.'

And she'd been hoping to get the name of which one. 'Are you suggesting that Glass put Nirmal Casin up to paying us so it looked like we'd worked for a criminal, and to get us struck off by the SPI as payback because we exposed his criminal activity?'

Kasper said, 'It's the sort of spiteful thing he'd do.'

The reality of what else he might do if he thought they were still investigating him hit Zofia.

CHAPTER 5

I finally got hold of the police vet who was examining Cleo, Harry's dog. He listed her ailments, most of which were minor and a result of having lived on the streets with an inadequate diet.

'You can treat all of those,' I said. 'There's no need to have her put down.'

'But someone has to pay for it. And the kennels won't take her until we've treated her.'

'Can I pay for it?' I needed little myself, especially while I lived in my friend's van, although I sent a good amount to my ex for my daughters. I could pay the vet from the money I was saving for a deposit so I could rent a house.

'It's not that simple, Mr . . .'

'Timothy. Peter Timothy.' I used my real name when dealing with the police.

'Okay, Peter. I can only bill the police. If you sort out how to pay them, I'll do it. Although she would need to be rehoused.'

'That shouldn't be a problem.' I remembered a thin, but happy and affectionate dog.

'I would normally say yes. Although she's not a puppy, someone would probably fall in love with her. But there's a huge number of strays in the area, and it depends if the kennels the police use will keep her long enough to find a home before . . . you know.'

To find a home before they kill her. 'I'll worry about that later.' He gave me the number of the police finance office.

After half an hour on the phone, I was only avoiding swearing by reminding myself we were talking about Cleo's life. 'You're telling me there's no way I can pay for this dog to be treated?'

'Not through us. Sorry, sir, we don't have any mechanism for taking funds from members of the public.'

I almost screamed in frustration. 'What happens to other dogs in this position?'

'Well, sir, they're usually euthanised.'

Murdered. Just say it.

The woman on the other end coughed. 'Sometimes family members take them.'

An idea took root. 'So, Harry's brother could take her?'

'I wouldn't see why not. If he could prove it, and had the wherewithal to care for her.'

I ended the call with a sense of optimism. All I had to do was claim I was Harry's brother. And prove it. I could ask John, his actual brother, to do it, but that added more complications, and I could just get him to brief me. But how stringent would the police checks be? They would surely just welcome someone taking a healthy dog off them.

'Everything okay?' Zofia asked me.

I told her what I'd found out.

'What will you do if they let you take her?'

'First, I'll take her to the vet in Ancoats and get them to sort her out. Then, I'll see.'

'Would you take her on?'

I looked at Oscar, asleep in his bed. I'd need to discuss it with him. 'It might be difficult.'

She followed my gaze and raised her eyebrows. I felt she was going to offer, but she glanced at her brother and said, 'Okay, why don't you go off and rescue her from the police.'

Kasper reminded us he was listening. 'We have got a lot on, you know.'

'It's lunchtime. Don't be mean, Kasper.'

He took the warning, and I rang John, telling him what I intended and pumping him about Harry. John told me all he could but seemed embarrassed by how little he knew of Harry's recent life. After waking Oscar, I put my jacket on and set off. In the car park, I let him up onto the front seat and started the van.

Where are we going?

'To see if we can get the police to release Cleo.'

Why doesn't her owner do that?

'He's dead.'

He considered this for a few moments while I drove onto the inner ring road. ***So, who's going to feed her?***

'I'm not sure. Let's not worry about that.'

Okay. He laid his head on the seat and closed his eyes.

I found the police K9 unit on a leafy avenue to the south of the city and parked in a visitor's space. The stiff wind of the morning had died down, but a miserable drizzle fell. I cracked the window open and got out.

You can close it, you know.

'And get done for leaving you locked in a car?'

Leave me a rug if you're going to insist.

I ignored him and found the way to the reception, where I told them why I was there. The receptionist asked me to wait and directed me to three hard chairs arranged along the wall opposite his desk. A uniformed officer a few years older than me came through to meet me, dog hairs on his dark trousers and carrying the odour of wet dog.

'Mr Timothy.' He held out a nicotine-stained hand.

I stood and took it. 'I believe you've got Harry's dog, Cleo.'

'Yeah. Sorry for your loss. Did you say you were his brother?'

I had to remember not to trip myself up. 'Half. Same dad, but he grew up in Norwich and me in Bristol.'

'Your dad must have been keen to get away from your mum. Sorry, I just meant—'

'Yes, it was a long way, so we had little to do with each other.'

'How well do you know Cleo?'

'I met her twice. I've got one of my own.'

'Oh yeah, what's she or he?'

'A standard Schnauzer.'

'They can be temperamental. I've got a miniature.'

'Tell me about it.'

He hesitated for a moment. 'We're supposed to get yours and your brother's IDs verified, but from what I understand, they found nothing of his after the fire.'

'I've only got a bank card on me. Will that do?'

'What was your dad called?'

'Harold.' That was one thing John knew for certain.

'Oh yeah? So was mine.' He hesitated again and seemed to come to a decision. 'You got your dog with you?'

'He's in the van.'

'Can I see him?'

'Sure.' I led him to the car park and opened the passenger door. 'This is Oscar.'

Oscar lifted his head.

'Hello, Oscar.' He offered a hand for Oscar to sniff.

Doesn't he know smoking kills?

'Don't be rude.'

The officer frowned and then decided. 'Right, he looks well looked after. And I bet he wears the trousers.' He winked at me. 'Let's get the paperwork done.'

Twenty minutes later, I returned with a long-legged spaniel-whippet cross who looked very sorry for herself. I opened the rear doors and coaxed her in.

I hope she hasn't got fleas.

'Don't be mean, Oscar.' The vet had told me she had mange, so I put an old towel down for her to lie on. The pungent odour of wet, dirty dog filled the van.

If I get them, you will.

'Just behave yourself. Don't take any notice of him, Cleo.' I gave her a reassuring smile.

I rang the vet in Ancoats, who agreed to examine her. Oscar insisted on coming in and trailed us into the waiting area. The surgery occupied what had once been a corner shop, complete with a bell above the door. The nurse took one look at Cleo and fussed over her. The intense aroma in the waiting area confirmed Cleo wasn't the first animal in need of a wash there today.

The nurse noticed Oscar. 'He doesn't seem too bad.'

I'm in prime condition, I'll have you know. Despite his propensity to neglect me.

'That's Oscar, my dog.'

'Hello, Oscar.' She bent to face him. 'I'll take them both through, it may settle Cleo if she has her friend with her.'

Friend! We haven't even been introduced.

'Oscar. Behave.'

The vet, a young woman who looked like she spent a lot of time outdoors, examined Cleo. She listed her ailments, the same ones I'd heard from the police vet.

'I'd also suggest you have her spayed, or get him done.' She nodded to Oscar.

What does she mean, get me done?

'Although they could make beautiful puppies.'

What makes you think I want to make puppies with her? Hang on, do you mean . . . ? You're not going to let her touch my crown jewels.

'Nobody's going to touch you.'

'It would be cheaper,' the vet said.

'She's a street dog. I thought it would be free.'

'You said her owner is' – she looked at Cleo – 'D.E.A.D. Aren't you going to keep her?'

'Well, I wasn't planning to. We've got a tiny place, and Oscar's not good with sharing.'

Blame me, I'm used to it.

'Well, *do* you want to share with Cleo?'

Why not have me put down? Then, you and Cleo could have a lovely time.

'Nobody is talking about having you put down.'

'Of course not, silly boy.' The vet crouched down to his level.

You could adopt me instead, he said to her.

I rolled my eyes. 'Can you treat Cleo?'

'Sure. I'll sort her out and get her spayed. You can collect her tomorrow. No charge, but feel free to donate.'

'Could you put the feelers out, see if anyone can take her?'

'I'll ask around. She's a lovely dog. It's an unusual combination, springer and *galgo*—'

'A what?'

'*Galgo español*, a Spanish greyhound. They're smaller than ours, but bigger than a whippet.'

I thanked her, paid her nurse a hundred and took Oscar back to the office.

Oscar sulked all the way back.

'I never intended to get your . . . you neutered.'

Using fancy terms won't change the barbarity of what you were planning to do. How can I ever trust you?

'Stop being dramatic.'

A large black SUV blocked the pavement opposite our office, sending a trickle of unease down my neck. Dark tint on the back windows hid the occupants, but two large lumps filled the front seats. Out of habit, I memorised the number plate, pulled around the back, parked up and led Oscar to the pavement. The front of the SUV was now empty. The two men stood on either side of the opening to the car park.

'Victor?'

'Yes?' The pitch of my voice rose.

'Come with us.' The nearest one grabbed my arm with a fierce grip and propelled me across the road with them.

CHAPTER 6

'Hey, what about Oscar? My dog.' I tried with absolutely no effect to free myself from the implacable grip on my bicep.

The two men ignored me and dragged me across Cheetham Hill Road. I twisted around to see Oscar watching me from the pavement. Before I could say anything, we reached the SUV on the other side, and one of my captors pulled the back door open.

'Hello, Victor.'

I peered into the dim interior at the woman on the opposite side. 'Jodie?'

'It's Judy now. Welcome.' She gestured at the seat next to her. 'I'd like to show you something.'

'I can't leave Oscar on the pavement.'

She frowned and studied the immaculate pale grey carpet.

'I need to get him into the office,' I said. 'Zofia can look after him.'

She gestured to the lump still gripping my arm to release me. I snatched my arm away once he did and, checking the traffic, returned to Oscar, determined not to massage the muscle where he'd crushed it.

'Thanks for helping me.'

I was memorising the number plate.

'Were you?'

No, I can't read. But I sensed they didn't mean you harm.

I couldn't tell if he was having me on, and led him to the office door. I pressed the bell and unlocked it, ushering him in.

'Victor, you forgotten your key?' Zofia's voice came over the intercom.

'I've let Oscar in. Can you let him into the office? Judy Novak is outside and wants me to go somewhere with her.' I recited the number plate and said goodbye without giving her a chance to follow up.

Judy's henchmen watched me cross the road to them, and one held open the back door while the other got into the driver's seat. I clambered in, inhaling the aroma of new carpet and fresh upholstery. I sank into the soft leather seat and fastened my seat belt while studying Judy. She looked her age. I'd first met her playing the part of a homeless urchin and had mistaken her for a teenager. She was in fact twenty-four and wearing what even I recognised as designer clothes. Not flash, but understated quality. She could afford it, as her father, Alex, ran one of the most successful crime families in Manchester.

'You're looking well, Victor.'

'So are you.' *Cliché 101, well done, Victor.* 'What did you want? Your phone not working? You forgotten our email address?'

She gave a polite smile at my weak jokes. 'As I said, I want to show you something.'

'Okay, will it take long?'

'No.' She sat back and, producing her phone, messaged and emailed on it while I enjoyed being chauffeured into the city centre.

We approached the bottom end of Deansgate, and light glinted off the towers sprouting almost daily. The car pulled off the road and parked on the pavement. The door-heavy jumped out of the passenger side and opened Judy's, leaving me to manage my own. I joined her on the pavement. A glass-and-concrete tower loomed over us, and she approached the entrance, which opened before she reached it.

She spoke over her shoulder to the door-heavy. 'I'll let you know when Mr Mitchum needs a lift back.'

Mr Mitchum. That made a change from bruising my bicep.

I followed her into a marble-lined entrance area, narrower than I expected. A uniformed security guard greeted her by name from behind a desk as we made our way to a pair of lifts.

As we shot up to the forty-second floor, she spoke to me for the first time since telling me our visit wouldn't take long. 'There's a swimming pool and gym downstairs. The hotel on the lower floors has a restaurant, and residents get priority booking. You can also order food to be delivered.'

I'd lost the thread. 'Is this the new business you're moving into – estate agency?'

Her steely glare reminded me of her father's, and I shut up.

She led me through too-warm corridors to a varnished mahogany door and inserted a key. Locks clicked, sounding substantial, and she swung the door inwards. It must have been over six centimetres thick and had a steel core with several bars retracted into it.

The smell of wood polish and incense filled the room. She closed the door behind us with a click, and I imagined a prison cell.

Although furnished, the flat had the air of a show home or a short-term let. She led me through it in silence, and we ended up on an enclosed balcony. The cars on Deansgate looked tiny on the shiny wet tarmac, as did the trams on the nearby tracks. In the distance, beyond the serried ranks of glass towers, I made out smudged hills. They probably looked great on a clear day.

'Very nice,' I said, thinking I should say something. 'Is this your flat?'

'It was, but they put that up.' She pointed to another tower to the side of the balcony. 'Spoilt my view.'

'So, what, you're selling it?' Her refusal to tell me why she'd kidnapped me had begun to irritate me.

'It's going to be where my new general manager lives. If he wants the job.'

'Very nice. So why am I here?' She must have known my situation. Was she taunting me?

'What do you think of it?'

'It's bloody great, especially compared to where I live.' I pointed to the streets below. 'Hundreds of people down there would give their right arm to live in the airing cupboard of this place. And I don't mean figuratively.'

'So, you'd consider the job?'

'What?'

'As my general manager?'

Was she taking the piss? I looked around into the upper corners. 'Where are the cameras?'

'Cameras?'

'Yeah, so you and your mates can have a good laugh when I say yes and you tell me it's a joke.'

'No joke, Victor.' She gestured towards the living room. 'Shall we go back inside? It's quieter.'

I noticed the low hum of the wind for the first time and followed her to a kitchen table. If this wasn't a joke, could that mean that I could *live* here? I imagined bringing Helen and Em here. I'd been on the streets for over a year, then in a disgusting flat before ending up in my van. Almost two years without seeing my daughters for more than a few days in the holidays. And Em loved swimming. Having a pool downstairs would be heaven for her.

Judy's invitation to sit made me jump. A large envelope lay on the polished surface, and she slid it to me.

'Open it.'

Inside were several sheets of paper. The top one was a job description, which I leaned over and read. 'This isn't me.' I tapped the paper. 'I can't do half of those things.'

'You'd be surprised what you can do, Victor. The most important attribute is that I can trust you. I can't say that about many people.'

'You barely know me.'

'I know enough.' She tapped the sheet. 'Read on.'

I got to the remuneration and swallowed. 'Is that on top of the flat?'

Her smile made me uneasy, like she'd trapped me. 'It is.'

My mind raced. This had to be a joke, a cruel one. But what if she'd discovered my part in her brothers' deaths and this was her way of humiliating me before getting her revenge?

'I couldn't live somewhere where Oscar wasn't welcome,' I said, grasping for a way to extricate myself.

She laughed and pointed out of the floor-to-ceiling window and across to the block that had stolen her view. A golden retriever stood in a window studying us. 'No problem with dogs.'

Maybe she wasn't winding me up. I had saved her father's life, but he'd been planning to torture me just before it happened. I'd be a nervous wreck being around people like that.

But good God, with that salary, I could save enough to get away from here and start again. Go back to Bristol to be near my girls.

'Did I mention the car?'

'Car?' I said, like an idiot.

'You'd have a car, like the one I brought you in.'

I imagined myself drawing up outside our old house in Redland in such a vehicle and collecting the girls, to bring them here.

'So that's a yes, Victor.' A flash of irritation showed in her tone.

I remembered what her brothers had done to Zofia. The job description mentioned managing the family's casino – a place I'd slept outside for months. I'd seen women leave it, some never to return – and later discovered why they hadn't. The brothers, again.

How could I live with myself if I worked in that world?

'I know what you do, Judy.'

'You don't.' Her irritation became more palpable. 'You know what my father and my brothers did. But they're gone.'

'Your father isn't.'

'No, he's still around. Thanks to you. But he's taking a back seat. I'm in charge, and I'm changing things.' She tapped the envelope. 'That's my business plan. Read it, think about it, and get back to me. Imagine living here, having Helen and Emily to stay.'

I was thinking of little else, but something snagged me: I was sure I'd never told her about my daughters. Was she telling me they knew about my family? One of her brothers had tried that when he'd wanted me to give him some incriminating evidence. Was she making me an offer I dared not refuse?

CHAPTER 7

Zofia put down the entry phone and let Oscar into the office. The camera they'd installed covering the front door had a small motor enabling them to control it. She rushed to her desk, opened the app and manoeuvred it to cover the traffic on the road outside. A large SUV pulled off the pavement in front of a bus, but she caught the registration. That was the one containing Victor.

What could Judy Novak possibly want with him? Zofia had not told her brother, but Judy had given her some of the dirt on Rudy Glass. Zofia had known Glass was a business rival of Judy's dad, Alex, so had been careful to double-check the information she got before passing it to the news outlet paying them to investigate Glass.

Oscar nudged her leg.

'Hello, boy, didn't Victor feed you?'

He shook his head, or she imagined he did. She really mustn't anthropomorphise him. It was just hard not to, so often did Victor do so. Maybe it was because he was lonely. He didn't need to be.

'Come on.' She stood and led Oscar into the kitchen, where she'd set up a feeding station after Kasper complained about having bowls in the office.

She left him, tail wagging as he tucked in to a bowl of feed, and returned to her desk.

'Was that Oscar?' Kasper said.

'What are the attributes of a detective? Isn't observant on the list?'

'Sorry, I've been distracted. Thinking about the letter from the SPI. I've drafted a response. What do you think? I'll email it to you.'

She opened her emails and read the attachment. 'We'd be on stronger ground if we'd returned Nirmal Casin's retainer.'

'But I never asked for one. We never invoiced him.'

'How could he possibly have got our bank details?'

'I think I know,' Kasper said. 'I've been looking into him to find out what he does and if he has any links with Glass.'

'And?'

'I found some details of the fraud he was convicted of. He persuaded people to transfer their funds out of their bank accounts to "protect" them. Which I suppose might give a bright fellow an inkling of how to go about discovering our bank details.'

'But no link to Glass?'

'Not yet.' Kasper heaved an exasperated sigh. 'So, this letter. What do you suggest I say about why he paid us that money?'

'If we can explain his actions, give a plausible motive, we'll have a stronger defence. Tell them how our investigation into Glass led to him losing a valuable business opportunity and say we suspect he sent Casin to us in revenge. We do need to find a link between him and Glass.'

'Okay, but I've got to finish the investigation for the guy I saw this morning.'

'You do that, and I'll start a workflow to search for links between Casin and Glass.' She opened a new page on their project management app and filled in the details.

They'd investigated Glass, so had plenty of information about him. Casin was a different matter, and she made a start. Not being able to get into the databases they accessed through the Society of Private Investigators slowed everything down. She searched news outlets for reports on his crimes. Eleven years back, she found several reports in local papers and two in the nationals. The judge had considered the crimes serious enough to hand him a six-year sentence.

She read the details and accounts of the suffering and distress he'd caused his victims. 'Bastard!'

'What?' Kasper and Oscar looked at her.

'Casin. He stole people's life savings and spent it on booze, prostitutes and gambling.'

'And the rest he squandered?' Kasper cracked, paraphrasing a George Best quote.

'Ha, ha. The guy is a real bastard.'

'Yeah, I didn't like him much when I met him last month.' He shuddered.

The six-year sentence plus the seven until it would drop off his record meant he had two more years until that conviction no longer showed up on background checks. Not good news for them. An account of the trial made her pause. Despite overwhelming evidence, one of the investigating officers from the fraud squad spoke up for the accused. Mulberry, the sergeant's name, provoked a memory. She found the email from the police confirming they weren't going to investigate Rudy Glass after she'd sent evidence implicating him in the murder of the corrupt planning officer. Signed by Chief Superintendent Gavin Mulberry. She'd been working on the assumption that the police officer protecting Glass was senior to Mulberry and would keep in the background. What if he was so confident he didn't care if people linked him to Glass?

Her hands tingled. 'Kasper?'

'Yeah?' He got up, alerted by her tone, and joined her.

'Look at this.' She pulled up the report of Casin's trial and then the email from Mulberry. She opened her browser.

'You looking for photos from the trial?'

'Yes.' She entered the name, and her excitement grew as a series of photos came up. 'It's the same guy.'

'Duh! Of course it is. How many Mulberrys in the police force?'

'It's best to be sure.'

'What do you think?' Kasper sat on the corner of her desk.

'I think Mulberry is dirty and is in Glass's pocket. I suspect Glass asked him to find someone who could compromise our licence, and he came up with Casin.'

'And how much of that can we prove?'

'None. But I will. And . . .' She hesitated before telling Kasper the worrying news she'd received. 'I think Glass might have heard someone's still investigating him.' She told him what her contact had said at their meeting.

This revelation made Kasper shrink. 'And if he thinks it's us, he'll be back. Someone linked to a murder won't be happy with just inconveniencing us.'

Zofia had already worked that out, although he would surely be wary of going too far as he'd already been linked to a killing, even if the police hadn't taken it further.

A disconsolate Kasper returned to his desk, and she picked up her mobile and rang a stored number.

'Zofia, how can I help you?'

'Hi Colette, can you talk?'

'I'm in my new office attacking a pile of boring paperwork, so yes, please, whatever trouble you want to bring to my door, I welcome.'

'Victor said you were a DI.'

'Just an "I", I'm afraid. I have to do six months in uniform before I can go back to plain clothes. I'm hoping they count the temporary spell I'm doing now. Anyway, how did Victor find out?'

'He spoke to your replacement.' Zofia explained what had happened.

'Hmm. Good luck with him and watch your back.'

'Victor said something about preferring to deal with Grimes.'

Bowling laughed. 'Is that why you called?'

'No, I just want some background on an officer. Chief Super Mulberry.'

Bowling didn't reply for many seconds. 'You remember I said I'd welcome whatever trouble you bring? I didn't mean it.'

'Bad news?'

'I crossed his path a few months ago and wished I hadn't. It almost cost me this promotion. If it wasn't for Darren, DCI Grimes, stepping in . . .'

'Would you know if Mulberry were dirty?'

Another laugh, but no humour in this one. 'Nothing I or anyone else can prove. What's your interest?'

She told Bowling about their troubles and her suspicion about Mulberry's part in it, driven by Glass's vendetta against them.

'It wouldn't surprise me, but be very careful. He's probably the most vindictive person I've ever met, and that includes the worst of the lowlifes I've put away.' She hesitated. 'I shouldn't tell you this, but rumours suggest he's got links to a network of serious criminals who do his bidding.'

'Why doesn't someone put him away?'

'Many have tried. And some of us haven't given up yet.'

Zofia thanked the policewoman and ended the call, more certain than ever that she'd found the link to their troubles.

'What did Colette say?'

While she considered how to word her reply, the front door opened, and Victor returned.

'Hello, Victor.' She stood. 'Coffee?' It would give her time to think.

'Yeah, thanks.' He looked stressed.

'Everything okay?'

'Not really.' He removed his jacket and hung it up.

'Where did you go?' Kasper demanded.

'Let him sit down before you interrogate him. Do you want a coffee as well?' She left to make the drinks.

She wouldn't let the business with Mulberry go, but she didn't want Kasper to blunder in and stir things up. When she found the moment, she had to tell him what Bowling had told her. First, she'd find out what was worrying Victor. Dealing with the Novaks, even Judy, was enough to worry anyone, but they had a soft spot for Victor since he'd saved Alex's life.

The tense atmosphere told her Kasper had tried to press Victor on what he'd been doing. Victor was studying some sheets of paper from the envelope he'd brought with him. She put one mug of coffee in front of him and took the other to Kasper.

'What did Judy want?'

'She offered me a job.'

Her shocked 'What?' overlapped with Kasper's 'You're joking!'

'I wish I were.'

Zofia was quicker with the follow-up. 'What does she want you to do?'

Victor brought the top sheet of paper to her, and she read it while he returned to his desk. The job description was for a senior management post. At first she dismissed Victor's suitability, but that was because she knew he'd been homeless before he came to them. She told herself to dismiss her prejudices. He'd since shown abilities she knew she and Kasper weren't paying him for. They couldn't afford to, especially if they didn't sort out their SPI membership.

Kasper came and stood at her shoulder. 'Is that the salary?' He pointed at the sheet.

Trust him to focus on money. Zofia hadn't and looked again. She whistled.

'And she's offering a flat in that fancy tower on Deansgate,' Victor said.

'How big?' Kasper said.

'Three bed. Plus a car. A big SUV, before you ask.'

This time, Kasper whistled. 'When do you start?'

Zofia waited with bated breath.

'I don't want to work for gangsters.'

She could have hugged him and would have done if they'd been alone. An interesting realisation. She should probably keep an eye on her impulses.

'Even for that money?' Kasper sounded surprised.

'You know what they did to those women?' Victor asked. 'I've got daughters.' He swallowed. 'Speaking of which, did either of you mention my daughters to Judy?'

Zofia thought back to her meeting with Judy when she gave her the information about Glass and felt her stomach tighten. 'Why?'

'She mentioned them by name when she said I could have them to stay if I took the flat. It sounded like telling me, "Nice family you've got there. Shame if anything happened to them."'

Kasper strolled back to his desk. 'I've not even seen her since that uncomfortable meal we all had with her and her dad.'

Zofia's face grew hot. 'I have.'

They both looked at her.

'She gave me the intel on Glass a few weeks ago, when our investigation into him stalled. I remembered she'd found out something about Glass while she was working for that news site, but her editor spiked it.'

'Did you mention my family?'

She bit her lip. 'I might have. Sorry, Victor.'

He took a breath and settled himself. 'Yeah, well, you weren't to know she intended to use it against me. At least she hasn't been stalking them.' He tapped the other sheets he'd retrieved from the envelope. 'She's moving into property in a big way. It looks from this that she's developing the site Glass was interested in. I'm sure your intervention didn't harm her project. On the contrary, the exposure of Glass removed him as a rival.'

He gave her such a look of disappointment she almost cried out.

Kasper came to her rescue. 'That's not fair, Victor. We were trying to bring Glass down, and wouldn't have done it without Judy's help.'

'Yeah, I suppose so. Anyway, wasn't Robertson interested in the same site?'

'A good reason for not taking that job. We've seen what he does to people who get in his way.'

'Yep. I'm not inclined to take it.'

'Then why have you brought those with you?' Kasper pointed at the papers on Victor's desk.

He looked uncomfortable. 'I told her I'd consider her offer, but I can't see myself telling her yes.'

Zofia felt dizzy. It was too good an opportunity for Victor. He had to think about his family. Worry about their safety if he said no, or secure their prosperity if he said yes?

CHAPTER 8

The offer from Judy swirled round my head as I slept, waking up twice in the night to make my way to the chilly toilet block. The thought of doing this in the depths of winter didn't appeal, especially if I could be in a warm bedroom with a luxury ensuite. I woke and lay in bed listening to the dawn chorus.

I took Oscar over the field, which formed the campsite, passing the solitary tent pitched by a brave hiker and to the field beyond. As I looked at the old farm buildings we passed, I wondered, as I often did, how the occupants felt about the encroaching housing estates.

Like me, Oscar seemed deep in thought, and we returned to breakfast in silence.

His first words apart from ***Where's my breakfast?*** arrived as we turned off Oldham Road.

This isn't the way to work.

'I'm trying a new route.'

Why?

'Just fancied it.'

He seemed to accept my explanation until we crossed the Rochdale Canal.

This is the way to the horrible place we used to live, isn't it?

I hoped he'd not notice. He hadn't yesterday, but Cleo's presence had distracted him. 'It's near there.'

Why are we going back? Panic had entered his voice.

'We're not. We're collecting Cleo.'

Why didn't you say? Do you enjoy tormenting me?

'I didn't intend to. Sorry.'

He sulked until we pulled up outside the clinic.

Where are we taking her?

'Haven't decided yet.' I was hoping the vet would have found someone who could give her a home. 'Do you want to come in with me?'

What do you think? The nurse had given him a treat last time, so I let him out and locked the van.

Among the people in the waiting room were two men who looked homeless, one with a dog and the other holding a cat. Oscar ignored them all and made for the nurse.

'Hello, Oscar. Do you want a treat?' She produced a strip, which he gobbled.

'Say thank you.'

He mumbled something, his jaws working, as the nurse showed me through into the surgery and he followed me.

The vet looked up from Cleo, who wore a cone and had a strip shaved in the fur of her flank. 'Ah, it's Oscar's dad. Well, she's ready for you. You'll need to keep this on for about a week, and here are her meds.' She held up a paper bag before removing the contents. 'As I mentioned, the poor thing has mange. We've washed her once, but you need to use this shampoo on her again in a day or two, and use it to clean any bedding she's been using.' She then explained what doses Cleo needed of the other drugs.

I felt bad, realising how little my donation would have helped. 'I live in a van, so I can't wash her.'

She looked at me. 'How do you wash yourself?'

'There's a toilet block at the site, but they don't allow dogs.'

'What about Oscar?'

I'm exceptional.

'I sneak him in once a week, and everyone knows him.'

'Yeah, I'm sure they do. I asked a local kennel if they could take care of her and try to re-home her. They've said they will once the mange clears up, and the cone comes off.'

'Can't you keep her until then?'

Her easy-going persona disappeared. 'We're full, and you've seen our waiting room.'

'Right. Okay.' I put the contents back in the bag and picked up Cleo's lead. 'Come on, girl.'

What are you doing?

'I'm taking her with us.'

We haven't got room.

'We'll make room.'

What about me?

'Don't be a baby.'

He moaned all the way back to the van, and Cleo must have sensed it. Her reluctance to come with me filled me with shame. 'Oscar, you behave, otherwise . . .'

He knew how far to push me and shut up. I'd already bagged the bedding she'd used yesterday – Oscar had refused to use it – and found a towel she could sit on in the front where I could see her. I put him in the back and set off. Her timidity didn't improve when we arrived at the office.

Zofia saw Cleo and stood. 'Hello, who are you?'

I explained who she was.

'You *are* a cutie, aren't you?' Zofia crouched down to pet her.

What about me? I'm here, you know. Me, Oscar, your favourite dog.

'Behave.' I fetched her some food in his bowl. 'I'll get you a new bowl before lunch.'

Cleo seemed to take a liking to Zofia and slept under her desk on Oscar's sleeping pad.

I looked at Oscar, feeling sorry for him. 'I'll get you a new bed as well.'

Don't mind me. He lay on a square of carpet he'd used before Zofia bought him the bed.

Zofia focused on tracking down Casin, the architect of their troubles. I reminded myself that I was part of KZD and their troubles were also mine. I would *not* be working for Judy, however attractive the package. Meanwhile, I investigated attacks on homeless men with dogs.

As John had intimated, there seemed to be a gap in the attacks of several months. Besides the man Oscar and I had rescued, someone had attacked three other homeless men with dogs in the spring of this year – but then nothing until this week. With the dogs always in the mix, I'd assumed it had been Alex Novak's men, looking for me and Oscar, and the attacks had stopped once I'd saved his life. But the killing of Harry Sanders meant they'd started again.

But why the long gap? The men who'd chased me had used a van. It had suffered damage when they had tried to run me over. What if they couldn't fix it? Taking it to a garage would have been too risky if the police had bothered investigating, and driving around with a damaged vehicle would also bring unwelcome attention. I checked reports of vehicle fires in the two weeks after they'd attacked me.

I found one. A van with missing number plates had been driven into wasteland in Kersal and set on fire in the early hours. Fire crews had trouble reaching the site, and the vehicle had burnt to an ash-filled shell by the time they reached it.

Would the need to acquire a replacement vehicle account for the break in attacks? They could just steal one each time, but that risked discovery as they patrolled the streets looking for victims.

I checked the dates and found no reports in the press. Even if the media didn't consider such attacks worth reporting, John and Craig had close links throughout their community and would know if anyone had been attacked.

Someone else I knew had his finger on the pulse – Digger, whose van I lived in and who ran a diner for the homeless of Manchester. I rang him.

'Digger, has anyone reported being followed by two men in a large car like a pickup or SUV?'

'Funny you should mention that. I had a customer talking about just that last week. You'll have seen him around – he's got all his stuff in a supermarket trolley with carrier bags hanging off it.'

I had. 'Sid, Simon, something like that?'

'Samuel. Anyway, he said they were following him but drove off when a cop car pulled him up, wanting to search his stuff.'

'Where was this?'

'Sorry, Victor, I can't remember. He'll be in tonight. I'll ask him.'

I couldn't recall Samuel having a dog, so I asked.

'Yeah, he's got one these days. An Irish terrier. Lively thing. He found it abandoned and half starved a few weeks ago.'

An Irish terrier could be mistaken for Oscar.

I knew another person who might be looking for me and Oscar. Miles Colby. He'd used me as a urinal while I slept on the streets, then beaten me up when I objected. Oscar had bitten him when we later encountered him in a café, and he'd threatened vengeance then. But would he still be on my tail? I'd tracked him down once and knew where he worked. Time I looked into him again.

I ended the call and rang John. He knew Samuel but hadn't heard about his being followed. 'But I've got something we need to investigate,' he said.

After agreeing to meet him and Craig at Pin Mill Brow, I got up and collected my jacket.

'I'm going to meet John and Craig,' I told Zofia. 'Can I leave Cleo? I don't think she gets on with Trixie.'

Another reason not to trust her. Oscar stood and stretched.

Zofia bent down to look at Cleo. 'Of course, she'll be fine with me. She won't need any of her tablets before you get back, will she?'

I'd written the instructions the vet had given me on a sheet of paper and placed it in the bag of drugs. 'The next one will be last thing tonight.'

I took Oscar to the car, but he hesitated before getting into the front. ***I don't want to get mange.***

'Don't be silly, the nice vet deloused her, and she sat on this towel.' I kicked the plastic bin liner I'd stuffed the towel into in the footwell.

I'll blame you if I get mites.

'Feel free. Now get in or I'll leave you behind.'

He grumbled all the way to our rendezvous.

John and Craig waited on the corner of Palmerston Street next to a tumbledown building half concealed by hoarding and covered in straggly shrubs. I pulled up opposite, left Oscar in the front and joined them.

'Alright, John, what have you got?'

'Hello, Brother. This is where Harry crossed into the Brow to get home.' He pointed to an overgrown path passing between metal bollards. 'Show him, Craig.'

Craig held a creased and water-damaged piece of paper. 'This is a leaflet from Bradford Road Evangelical Church just over there.' He pointed towards Ancoats. 'Monday night they have an open kitchen, anyone can get a hot meal. That's where he was.'

'You spoken to them?'

John nodded. 'The woman serving remembered Harry. He was the last one to leave. She gave him something for Cleo once everyone else had gone.'

'Have you told the police?'

'We were going to leave that to you, if you think it's worth it.'

I wasn't sure. Lambert, the sergeant who'd replaced Bowling, didn't seem that interested. 'Have you traced his route from the church? Someone might have seen him or a vehicle following him.'

John produced his phone and opened a map. 'We think he most likely came on this route.'

I studied it and agreed. 'Have you spoken to anyone on the route?'

'We tried a few houses, but most were out or ignored us. One bloke came out and threatened to call the police. We thought you might have a better chance.'

I noticed how scruffy both John and Craig looked. 'Are you still at that halfway house?'

John gave a rueful grin. 'A difference of opinion with the management.'

Now that I paid attention, I noticed the stink of alcohol. How the hell had I not noticed my friend's deterioration? To be fair, though, before yesterday's call, I'd not seen him for some weeks.

'Where are you staying, John?'

'Here and there.'

I looked at Craig, who shrugged.

'Do you want to get in the van and we'll drive the route?' I coaxed a complaining Oscar into the back with John, while Craig sat in the front, his knees up against the dash.

We stopped at any likely premises to see if people had noticed Harry or a vehicle following him. Modern apartment blocks, marketed to landlords wanting to attract young professionals as the latest in luxury living, towered over the small, down-at-heel houses which had themselves been sold as the epitome of modern living following the slum clearances of the sixties. After two hours we arrived outside the church where Harry had eaten his last meal. I sensed the dejection of both my companions.

'I'll come back later when more people should be home,' I said. It was now mid-afternoon, and we hadn't eaten. A shop opposite the entrance to the church offered hot food. 'You guys fancy a bite?'

Nobody objected, and, after taking their orders, I crossed the road and entered the shop. While I waited for food, I glanced at a screen showing four images.

'Is that CCTV?'

'Yeah.' The owner, a balding Chinese man in his forties, pointed at the screen. 'We get damn local kids trying to rip us off all the time. YouknowhatImean.'

I studied the images. 'Is that the front?'

'Yeah. They park up in those bays, engine running, and two come in. One distracts you while the other goes for the till.'

'Do you keep a record?' I realised it was a long shot, but a jolt of excitement energised me.

He shrugged. 'Sure. I save all footage onto the cloud.'

'Have you got yesterday evening's?'

He studied me. 'Don't you need a warrant or something?'

'Only if you object to showing it to me. I'm investigating the death of that guy on the other side of the Brow.'

'Oh yeah. Poor guy. Did he live around here?'

'We think he was there last night.' I pointed to the church. 'Two men in an SUV or pickup followed him.'

'Yeah? I saw one outside, engine running. I thought it was kids scamming, but nobody got out. They stayed forty minutes, then left. It was around eleven, the time I was shutting.'

'Can I see the footage?'

'Um, yeah, okay, but your pasties are done, they'll get cold.'

Five minutes later he'd located the footage, and we watched the vehicle, a dark, double-cab pickup. We watched it arrive and leave, but couldn't see the number plate.

I exhaled in frustration.

He pointed at the frozen image on the screen. 'That's a GMC Sierra, and look at the way it pulls out of the parking bay. It's fitted with Quadrasteer. I had one about twenty years ago. They stopped making them in '04 because nobody wanted to pay the extra. YouknowwhatImean. There won't be many around.'

I rushed out with our cooling pies and the footage of the vehicle that had followed Harry on the night he died.

CHAPTER 9

Once the commotion caused by Victor and Oscar leaving had died down, Cleo relaxed and lay at Zofia's feet, the cone not seeming to bother her. Zofia had been thinking about Judy's job offer to Victor and whether he'd take it. She'd not always admitted it to herself, but she'd really miss him. Maybe she should tell him. She often thought he felt the same, but something seemed to be holding him back.

Kasper's question broke into her thoughts. 'Do you think Judy Novak was serious about giving Victor the job?'

'Why not?'

'The guy was living on the street a few months ago. Would you trust someone like that to run a multi-million-pound business?'

'He's got a degree and had a responsible job before he ended up on the street.'

'I know, but he threw it away, didn't he?'

'Until you've been in the same position, how can you judge?'

Kasper blew out his cheeks. 'I'm pretty sure that whatever life threw at me, I'd never end up on the streets.'

'That's because Mum left us the house.'

'No. Even if she hadn't, I'd always manage. It's a matter of moral fortitude.'

'I'd trust him more than I'd trust you.'

In the stunned silence that followed this, she got up and made a coffee. Although she realised what she'd said was true, she'd hurt her brother. She made him a drink and took it through, giving him a hug. He shrugged her off, then relented.

'Sorry, bro.'

He tapped her hand. 'You're right. I'm just jealous. Nobody's offering me six-figure salaries.'

She released him and fetched her drink. 'The way the business is going, we're well on the way to paying ourselves decent salaries. Not six figures, but good enough.'

'Unless it all goes tits-up with this hassle with the SPI.'

'Have you responded to them yet?'

'Like you suggested, I'm waiting until we've refunded the money to Casin, then we can refute their charge that we worked for a criminal. I should have done it straight away.'

'Don't worry, I'll do it.' She opened their banking app and checked the payment. It didn't show who'd paid the money, just a payment reference of Nirmal Casin. A chat with a bot on the app followed by a call to an actual human, and she discovered they couldn't return the money unless Casin gave them his bank details. She told Kasper.

'Can't we trace his bank details, like he did ours?'

'Possibly,' she allowed, 'but I want to speak to him. See if he lets slip who he was working for.' Although she'd emailed the editor of the news outlet that they'd investigated Glass for, to tell her they'd done all they could and sent her a final invoice, she worried more grief was on the way. At least until Glass realised his intimidation had worked, and they'd laid off him. The thought made her want to continue investigating the bastard.

She spent an hour and tracked Casin down through his wife, who owned the house they lived in. On paper anyway. She made out a receipt for a full refund and printed it off. Cleo's warm body against her legs held her in place until she eased the dog away and collected her printing. The cone on Cleo's head tracked her like a directional microphone.

'Okay, girl, I need to go out.'

The dog's tail thumped on the bedding.

'Can you make sure Cleo is okay while I nip out?'

Kasper frowned. 'What do I need to do?'

'Nothing, probably, you heard Victor. Just make sure she's not too anxious while I'm away.'

'What if she, you know . . . ?'

'Well, you know what to do – take some bags with you – good grief. I'll take her out before I go.'

'Why don't you take her with you?'

Kasper could be such a baby. She could leave her in the car. Victor had left her lead and, after attaching it to her collar, she led Cleo to the car, taking her for a walk when she stopped at a cashpoint on her way to Monton, where Casin lived in a Victorian semi on a cul-de-sac off the main road. A smart-looking car with last year's plates sat on the drive. Conning people obviously paid well.

The bell rang deep in the house, and an electronic camera observed Zofia. A woman in her forties wearing designer jeans and a frilly blouse opened the door.

'Hello, I'm looking for Mr Casin.'

The woman's expression darkened. 'And who are you?'

'My name's Zofia. Your husband paid us a deposit for some work which we never did, so I'd like to return it.' She produced the envelope she'd placed the money in from her handbag.

'Okay, give it to me.' She held out a hand.

'Mr Casin needs to sign for it.'

The woman folded her arms. 'Well, he's at work.'

'I can take it there.'

'Yeah, whatever.' She gave Zofia the address.

Back at the car, Cleo treated her return as a significant event, and Zofia felt guilty she'd left her. She checked the map. He worked less than half a mile away, across the M602, but the drive would be three times as far. Zofia turned the car around and five minutes later entered the industrial estate he worked on. Vandals had spray-painted St George's crosses onto the plan of the site so she couldn't work out where to find Casin's employer.

A forklift truck driver unloading steel bars from a lorry directed her, and she pulled up outside a vast, corrugated steel warehouse with a brick-built two-storey office attached at the side like a growth. A spiked steel fence surrounded the compound, and a horizontal barrier blocked vehicle entry. She parked on the road outside and, after reassuring Cleo, got out of the car.

The acrid chemical smell, which had crept into her nostrils as she approached, intensified. Inside the compound, large polythene cubes over a metre high lay along one perimeter fence. Signs on the metal frames encasing the cubes warned of the dangers within. She edged past the vehicle barrier and made her way to the office block.

The warehouse had two huge roller-shutters across the front, one of them raised two metres. Three men in grey overalls stood in the opening and studied her. Behind them, a heavy-duty plastic strip-curtain hid the interior. She nodded a greeting, which wasn't returned.

At the office block, the receptionist buzzed her in and waited behind a desk in a stark space containing two moulded chairs and a square coffee table piled high with industry magazines. Zofia told her why she was here.

'He's in the warehouse.'

'Can I go in and see him?'

'Not without an escort. There are a lot of dangerous chemicals in there.'

'Is there anyone who can take me?'

'You'd also need to put on protective clothing.'

Despite her frustration, Zofia smiled. 'Would it be possible to ask him to come out?'

'Can I ask what it's about?'

'It's a personal matter.' She'd be better going back to his house when he finished work, but this woman was irritating her. And she suspected that once Casin knew she was looking for him, he'd go to ground.

'I'll ask.' The receptionist picked up her phone. 'Name?'

'Zofia.' She ignored the woman's obvious desire for more and sat on one of the moulded chairs.

The woman mumbled into the handset and clicked it down. 'He's on a break in twenty minutes. If you want a brew . . .' She pointed at a machine in the corner and returned her attention to her screen.

Zofia glanced at the magazines but checked her emails instead. Twenty minutes passed and nobody came.

'Can you check what's happened?'

The receptionist stopped typing. 'He'll be in the middle of a process. They can't just drop everything.'

She suspected he'd continue to keep her waiting. 'Can you tell him it's about Mr Mulberry?' The mention of the corrupt policeman would either bring him running, or set him on the run.

In the event, it was the former, and a sweating man of about forty charged through a door on the side of the room into the waiting area, accompanied by a pungent chemical stink. He was one of the three overall-clad men who'd watched her arrival. He had conventional good looks, with even features and a tidy moustache. His expensively styled hair was awry after being shoved under a plastic hood.

'You're not supposed to come in here with those on.' The receptionist indicated his gauntlets and rubber boots.

Zofia said, 'Mr Casin?'

'Who are you?'

'Can we talk somewhere private?'

The receptionist said, 'If you take that gear off, you can use the boardroom.'

He hesitated for a moment. 'I'll use the canteen. There's nobody in there now.' He backed out through the door behind him.

Zofia leapt to her feet and followed. He strode along a plain corridor with a rubber-tiled floor to the back of the building. He stuck his head in a doorway, releasing the odour of stale food and burnt coffee, but backed out.

'There's someone in there.' He continued until they reached the end of the corridor and stepped out into a vast space full of stainless-steel tanks and piping. The chemical stink increased.

She looked around, feeling uneasy. 'Shouldn't I be wearing protective clothing?'

'What have you got to say about Mulberry?'

'Is he a friend of yours?' She plunged her hand into her bag.

He gave a nasty laugh. 'Nowhere near. But why did you mention him?'

'I wanted to return your money.' She took out the envelope.

'What money?'

'The two fifty you paid KZD Investigations.'

His expression of puzzled irritation changed to fear. 'I'm not touching that. Now sling your hook.' He gestured behind her, towards the front of the building.

'It's your money,' she insisted. 'We've done no work for you. Now please take it and sign this receipt.'

He knocked the receipt out of her left hand, his wet, gauntleted fingers touching her skin. 'Now fuck off before you get hurt.'

She stepped back and wiped her hand on her top. What the hell was on his gloves? He looked ready to attack her, and she prepared to run. Then, voices came closer.

He lowered his voice to a vehement whisper. 'Now, piss off, lady. Mulberry is no mate of mine, but I'm going to tell him you're harassing me. And you'll wish you'd never heard his name.'

She gripped the envelope and hurried back to the reception, her pulse pounding in her ears.

CHAPTER 10

Judy, convinced she'd offered Victor an irresistible package, couldn't focus as she replayed his rejection. Although he'd said he needed time to consider it, she could read a brush-off at a hundred paces. At first, she'd laughed at her dad's suggestion, but he'd been persuasive and, once persuaded, she was determined to recruit him. The most important attribute for Jerry Sweeny's replacement was trustworthiness. Victor had a sense of honesty and integrity not often found in the circles her father occupied. She had to admit, she'd seen little of it in the news industry she'd dipped her toe in.

In a way, Victor's rejection of her offer highlighted his qualities, but she wasn't a woman used to being refused. Victor also had access to a network, some of whom had skills she needed. She had a couple of alternatives to him in mind, but she considered them second best. The first was due in for interview this afternoon.

The knock on her door delivered a surprise. 'Dad? What are you doing here?'

'You're interviewing for Jerry's replacement?'

He was using the powered wheelchair, something he rarely did. Was he not feeling well today? She forgot that, although fit and vigorous, he was an old man, well into his sixties, and was still recovering from a shooting.

She checked the time. 'In half an hour. Why?' She'd guessed why, but wanted him to say it.

'I'd like to offer my experience. It's always better to have more than one pair of eyes and ears at an interview. You always miss stuff. As Jerry Lewis said, "Two heads are better than one."'

'That was C. S.'

His eyebrows slid up his forehead. 'C. S.?'

'C. S. Lewis.'

'Right, yeah, that's who I said.'

'Thanks, Dad. But Jerry – Jerry Sweeny, not Lewis – is sitting in with me.'

'Three heads are even better.'

She wanted to prepare for her interview in peace and wasn't in the mood to have a row with her father. 'Okay, you can sit in.'

'Did Jerry say why he's leaving?'

'I told you—'

'Yeah, but is that the real reason?'

She'd not mentioned to him Sweeny's intimation that she wasn't up to dealing with any rough stuff, because she suspected her father agreed. 'Ask him when he arrives. He should be here any minute.' She returned her attention to her screen and the CV of the candidate.

'You realise Jerry could sink us.'

She stopped a sigh, which had come unbidden, and returned her gaze to him. 'Don't you trust him? You picked him.'

'I did trust him, and while he'd tied his future to us I had no qualms. It's easy to be loyal when you have your fates tied together. But as Sun Tzu said, "For troops to be loyal, punishments must be enforced." It's difficult to punish someone when you have no power over them.'

She wasn't sure he'd got the quote right – he often didn't – but she could see his point. 'What are you suggesting?'

'We tie him to us in some way.'

'And if we can't?'

A knock on the door broke the long silence. 'Sorry I'm late, Judy. Oh, I didn't realise—'

'Come in, Jerry. Dad's going to sit in on the interview.' Sweeny looked even thinner than usual, and although he'd shaved, patches of grey stubble dusted his hollow cheeks.

'Oh, right.' Sweeny recovered fast. 'Good idea, having someone with your experience on the panel, Alex.'

They arranged the seating around the meeting table Judy had placed in the corner of her office. Her older brother's old office, which her dad used, would be better for interviews, being bigger, but they had enough room. Judy sat in the middle, with Sweeny on her left and her father on her right. As Keira Foley, her PA, came in to tell her the candidate had arrived, her dad's chair whined, and he rose fifteen centimetres. He now towered above them.

Judy stifled a grin and called in the candidate, Miles Colby. A tall man, a few years older than her, with a bushy black beard and cropped hair, strode in. He wore a designer suit which, although not tailored, a skilled professional had altered to fit his bulky upper body. A sharp citrus aftershave accompanied him as he took the seat Judy offered him. Her father's chair whined some more, raising him another few centimetres.

As agreed, Judy started. 'I've seen you in the casino, haven't I, Mr Colby?'

'I've got a membership.' He gestured to Sweeny. 'My company audits your books, so I know Jerry pretty well.'

'And you know what we do here?'

He grinned. 'Relieve mugs like me of their money.'

She kept a straight face. 'I meant the details of the businesses we're involved in.'

'Yes, of course. Apart from the casino, you have several pubs and two nightclubs. Neither of which makes a lot of money.' He winked at Sweeny. 'Plus, you have a property empire which you're expanding.'

She didn't like the wink, and as the interview progressed she got the impression someone had briefed Colby, and her money was on Sweeny. Despite the coaching, it became clear he'd not had much management or leadership experience.

Her father focused on that. 'Okay, imagine you're here on a Friday night and a crew from another outfit turns up, takes down two of your men and the others are ready to turn tail. What would you do?'

Judy directed a glare at her father, which he ignored, so she studied Colby, who swallowed and blinked.

He hunched his shoulders to appear bigger. 'I can look after myself, so I'd wade into them. Lead by example.'

Despite his bulk, he didn't convince, and her father's snicker made him redden.

Judy leant forward. 'Our company policy is to rely on the forces of law and order. We would withdraw all staff to a safe place, secure the premises, summon the police and wait for them to arrive.'

'Of course. That's a very sensible tactic.' Colby nodded as if he'd suggested the idea.

He had a few questions about pensions and holidays, the typical bullshit you ask at interviews, and she wound it up. She showed him out and made her way to the drinks cabinet.

'Usual, Dad?'

'Please.' He lowered his chair.

She poured his and Sweeny's drinks, took a bottle of water for herself and returned to her desk. 'Okay, what do you think, Jerry?'

'I thought he did alright. He's got a big advantage in that he knows the business—'

'How much of the business does he know?' her father said.

'Well, the bit the auditors see.'

'Are you sure you've not given him more?'

'Seriously, Alex? What do you take me for?'

'What Dad means is he seemed well versed on some of our plans, which aren't common knowledge.'

Jerry took a sip of his whisky. 'He's a bright lad with his finger on the pulse. His company audits many of our competitors. In fact, that's a bonus if you take him on. He'll know what the competition is up to, especially in property.'

Judy wasn't happy with Sweeny pushing her towards a particular candidate. 'I don't think he's got what it takes.'

Sweeny didn't argue. 'If the other guy you want takes the job, Miles could still just look after the accounts. Your preferred candidate doesn't have much accounting experience, does he?'

She'd not told Jerry about Victor's response to their offer, telling herself it was because he still hadn't rejected it. 'If we're taking someone on to work under him, he'll have to interview them.'

'So you're saying no to Miles.'

Her father leaned forward. 'We're saying he's not suitable for *this* job.'

'Right.' Sweeny emptied his glass. 'I'll let you get on, then.'

They waited until he'd left and closed the door. Her brothers had made their office doors secure, which also meant that once closed they kept prying ears out.

Judy resumed their conversation from before the interview. 'Going back to what we were discussing. How do you propose tying Jerry to us?'

'His name's on most of our paperwork. He's been doing our accounts – all of them, not just the stuff he shows the auditors – for over a decade.'

'Yeah, but most of that relates to Milan and Marko, and they're not around.' No mention of why that was, as she didn't want him obsessing again about finding their killers. It was such a waste of time and energy. They were gone, and she was in charge. That was it. 'If they want to take you and me down, they'll most likely offer him a deal.'

Her father took a sip as he considered this. 'His daughter just graduated from university. She studied accountancy and business studies but hasn't got a decent job offer yet.'

'Are you suggesting we offer her his job? She won't have the experience, let alone his other attributes.'

'Not *his* job, but a more junior role. Nothing where she'd come across material to hurt us, but if she were to put her name to some paperwork which could compromise her . . .' He winked.

'You really are a sneaky bastard.'

'Thank you.'

'Do you think Jerry would be happy letting her work for us, especially if he's leaving?'

'He won't find out. She's been living with her mum, like you did when you were growing up. But unlike you, she has little to do with her dad. She doesn't even know he works for us.'

Judy considered this. 'In that case, why would he care what happens to her?'

'She might not have time for him, but she's his world, and he'd hate anything to happen to her.' He finished his drink and smacked his lips. 'Now about Victor, what do you think would make him more amenable to your offer?'

'I don't know. I've offered him a great salary, a car and even thrown in my old apartment.'

'He's not turned you down yet.'

'No, but I could tell. He's not going to agree.'

'Unless we persuade him.'

'What do you mean?'

'I've got an idea of how we can do that. Let me make a couple of calls.'

CHAPTER 11

I rushed back to John and Craig, and once we'd eaten our pies we crammed into the back and studied the footage on my phone. I froze the image of the pickup and enlarged it but couldn't make out the occupants' features, just that there were two in the front.

Craig pointed a black-rimmed fingernail at the screen. 'Do you think the police could enhance it?'

'I'll send it to them.' I composed an email explaining where we'd found it and sent it to the same email address I'd forwarded the voice file from John's phone.

'Do you want to check they've got it?'

I didn't have DS Lambert's number, but rang the switchboard at his station. After explaining myself to three people, I finally got to speak to him and related what I'd sent.

'Yeah, okay, we'll get to it when we do.'

'The footage shows the men who followed him—'

'Does it show them following him?'

'No, but—'

'So that's conjecture. Like I said, we'll get to it when we do.'

'Was the voicemail any use?'

'No idea. I've not listened to it.'

'Why not?'

'You're beginning to piss me off, fella. We decide how to investigate. The guvnor tells me you're a private eye' – he imbued the words with contempt – 'so what say you focus on finding lost cats and let real coppers do our job.'

'If I thought you capable—' I realised he'd ended the call and stabbed the screen in frustration. 'I should have spoken to Grimes.' Although I didn't want to admit he terrified me, I was sure he'd listen. He wasn't an idiot.

Craig gave a sympathetic smile. 'Well, you tried.'

'We can check it on my screen at the office. It's a lot bigger than this phone, and Kasper loaded some image-enhancing software on all the computers a few weeks ago.'

John checked the time. 'Can we do that tomorrow, Brother? We're at the hostel tonight, and it's busier than ever. If we're not there early enough . . .'

I remembered them letting me push in the queue one night because I'd arrived late. I also recalled that the people who ran the hostel checked people for drink and drug consumption, and realised John hadn't imbibed today.

John had guessed what I was thinking. 'Not had a drop today, nor will I. The last time I spoke to my brother was to row about my drinking.' His features set, and darkened. 'And I didn't hear Harry's call that night because . . . well, you know.' His voice roughened delivering those last words.

'You can't blame yourself, John,' I told him.

'That's what I told him.' Craig gripped John's shoulder.

I swallowed. It was a huge load to carry. 'There was nothing you could have done, John. By the time you got here, he'd have been dead.'

'I could have phoned the fire bobbies.'

'You didn't even know there was a fire.'

John shrugged, a haunted look in his eyes. 'I'm his big brother. It was my job to take care of him.'

There was nothing I could say to that. 'Shall I give you a lift?'

Craig said, 'Drop us on the main road and we'll walk. It will give us an appetite.'

I wrestled with whether to offer them money for the hostel, but assumed they had enough and would find my offer insulting. It brought home to me again how lucky I was to have the van. I dropped them off and watched them walk across Great Ancoats Street and disappear into a narrow lane between two of the few original early-twentieth-century buildings left on that stretch, before heading back to the office. I was indicating to turn into the car park when Oscar piped up.

Are you getting me a new bed?

I turned the indicator off. 'We'll go now, shall we?'

And feeding bowl?

'Yes, okay.'

I drove on to the huge retail park half a mile past the office and parked up outside a gigantic pet store. I lowered Oscar's window and got out.

You not taking me with you?

'I'm getting you a bed and food bowl. I won't be long.'

Don't I get to choose?

'It's just a dog's bed and food bowl.'

Just! Like we're not important enough to be given a choice.

'You never complained about the one Zofia bought you.'

Yes, she has taste, and I trusted her. He let the implication sink in.

'Right, come on, then.' I put his lead on and, after locking the car, led him into the store. We walked up and down the aisles as he insisted we find a bed like the one he'd given up to Cleo.

'How will you tell which one is yours if they're both the same?'

He gave me a pitying look. ***But they won't be the same. One will smell of her, and the other of me.***

'They'll both smell of dog to me, so I'll probably end up giving you the wrong one.'

He glared at me and led me back to the last aisle. ***Okay, this one.***

'That's the one I was going to get you first, but you said it's too boring.'

No, it wasn't.

I didn't argue and put it in the trolley before going through the same rigmarole with a food bowl. As we made our way to the checkout, he pulled me to a display of harnesses.

Can I have one of those? Having a leather choker around my neck makes me feel like chattel. It's a symbol of my oppression.

'You what?'

My oppression is bound to and influenced by the intersectional systems of our human-centric society. By placing this collar around my neck, you're announcing that I'm your property, not a creature with free will and dreams of my own.

'Do you dream?'

That's not the point. Are you going to get me one of these?

I reminded myself not to listen to any more podcasts on the political philosophers of the twentieth century while he was in the room, and let him pick out a dark harness which contrasted with his grey fur.

Neither Zofia nor Cleo was at the office when we returned. Oscar seemed very put out they weren't there to admire his harness. He nudged Kasper's leg to get a response.

'Oi, you stupid mutt, you made me spill my coffee.' Kasper headed to the kitchen to fetch a cloth.

Next time, I'll let them shoot you.

'Oscar, there's no need for that.' Although I often shared the sentiment. I unpacked Oscar's new bed and put it under the printer table and put the bowl in the kitchen.

Kasper came back with a wad of kitchen towel, which he used to mop up the coffee on his desk. 'Hey. Oscar, that's a smart harness. Welcome to the twenty-first century.'

It's too late now. You had your chance. He lay on the bed, his back to us.

'What's up with Oscar?'

'He's upset Cleo's not here.'

'Ahh, how romantic.'

I'm NOT upset about Cleo not being here.

I chuckled, then uploaded the CCTV footage from the shop onto my desktop and opened the app for enhancing the images. Whatever I tried didn't enable me to read the number plate of the GMC pickup, but I cleaned up one image enough to tell the driver had a large beard. Miles Colby, the man who'd woken me by using me as a urinal, had a beard. Was he again attacking homeless men? If he were, he'd escalated from fists and boots.

Oscar had stolen the man's work lanyard, and we'd traced him to a firm of accountants. I entered their name on a search engine and found their website. The 'Our People' page had photos of their staff. There he was, listed as senior accountant. I enlarged his headshot and compared it to the image taken through the windscreen of the pickup.

'Kasper, do you think these are images of the same person?'

'Let's have a look.' He sauntered to my desk and peered at the screen. 'Do you mind?' He gestured at my chair.

I let him take it and watched as he manipulated the two images, overlaying one on the other. I'd done the basic course for the software, but Kasper had clearly become skilled. He used the mouse to tick boxes and then pressed Enter. A series of numbers spun across the screen and then stopped.

'What does that mean?'

'That's the likelihood of it being the same person. Eighty-one per cent.'

'Is that good?'

'Pretty high, but I doubt the police would take it forward unless they had other evidence. Do we?'

I told him my history.

'Well done, Oscar,' he said when I told him about him biting Colby at the café.

Oscar's tail thumped on his bed, but I could tell he hadn't quite forgiven Kasper.

'But you never reported the attack?'

'Not really.' I remembered my shame at what he'd done to me. 'I tried, but the cops weren't interested, so I backed off.'

'That's a pity.' Kasper made it sound like an accusation.

I wished Zofia were here, she'd have been more understanding.

'Anyway,' Kasper continued, 'what's his motive for attacking Harry?'

'After Oscar bit him, he threatened to visit revenge on me and Oscar. Someone like him probably thinks all homeless men with dogs look the same.'

Kasper frowned. 'Okay, I could possibly buy that. But what about the other guy in the vehicle?'

I'd been thinking about who that could be since I'd heard about his tattoo. I'd seen a similar marking on one of the two men who'd chased me after an attack on another homeless man. At the time, I'd suspected one of Novak's goons, but it couldn't have been him. I'd since discovered he was dead.

'I don't know yet, but I'm sure we'll find one when we know who he is. In the meantime, we need to investigate this Colby guy,' I said. 'See if he could have carried out the attack on Harry and the other attacks.'

'How are we going to do that? We can't demand alibis.'

'Not yet, but we can get a timeline together for the incidents so if we're ever in a position to take it to the police, we'll have it ready.'

'Hmm, I'm not sure. We've got a lot on.'

'I'll do most of it in my own time, and Craig and John can help me.'

'Okay, as long as it doesn't interfere with our work.'

'No problem.' The thought that we might have the identity of one of the men who'd attacked Harry gave me a boost. A call from Digger added to my elation.

'Samuel's here, Victor, but he's in a hostel tonight where he's expected to be in by seven, so he won't be staying long.'

I checked the time, quarter to six. 'Okay, I'll be there soon.' I ended the call and spoke to Kasper. 'Do you know where Zofia and Cleo are?'

'She's tracking down the guy who buggered up our licence. Do you want me to ring her?'

I could imagine our call interrupting delicate negotiations. 'I'll come back for Cleo. Digger's only on Deansgate.'

I parked on a side street off the main road, on a meter, before taking Oscar to the building where Digger helped feed the city's homeless population. The building he occupied wasn't far from the block of luxury apartments Judy had taken me to and, on the other side, a series of glass towers of empty apartments, seeming to mock the plight of the people waiting to go in. The queue stretched out to the pavement, something I'd never seen before. A few grumbles accompanied my passage as I skirted the queue and walked into the dining hall.

A cacophony of conversation and laughter greeted me. The aromas of garlic and cumin mixed with those of stale sweat and unwashed damp clothing. People I recognised from a local Indian restaurant stood behind the counter serving. Digger spotted me and waved me over to a table at the far end. Samuel sat at the end of the table focused on emptying a bowl of curry and rice. At his feet, a handsome brown dog, a bit smaller than Oscar, ate from a bowl. Oscar approached to investigate, and the dog growled.

'Easy, O'Malley,' Samuel admonished.

'O'Malley?'

Samuel shrugged. 'He's Irish.'

The dog ignored him and continued growling.

Oscar retreated and stood by the wall. ***I was just being friendly, I don't want your scabby food.***

Samuel waved a fork at his dog. 'Sorry about him, I've not trained him up yet.'

'No problem, Oscar's the same. One word from me, and he does what he wants. Can I?' I gestured at the empty seat opposite and took it when he nodded. 'Digger said you had a run-in with a couple of guys in a big car.'

'Yeah.' He chewed some more. 'An extended cab pickup.'

I retrieved my phone and showed him a still from the CCTV footage. He took it from me and stared at the image, then returned it, complete with a curry-stained thumbprint.

'That's the one. I got a good look at one of the guys in it.'

'The guy with the beard?'

'Nah. This one had a tat of a red snake on his neck.'

This sent a jolt through me. 'Are you sure?'

He pointed two fingers at his eyes. 'Nowt wrong with me sight.'

I knew one man with a tattoo like that, but I'd already dismissed him as a suspect. Kasper and Zofia had killed him. So who the hell was this one, and were they linked?

CHAPTER 12

The skin where Casin's gauntlets had touched her itched as Zofia drove back to the office after her aborted interview with him. What had he been handling with them? She attempted to recall what she'd seen on the containers in the yard outside. Various dire warnings, accentuated by orange and red symbols, had covered them. She should have checked before leaving, but she'd been so shaken by Casin's behaviour, all she'd wanted to do was get away.

The M602 ended, and she saw signs for the retail park, where she knew of several food outlets. She should wash her hands at least. As she parked up outside a coffee shop, Cleo whined. Zofia had found the poor animal distressed on her return from her visit to Casin's workplace. It was her fault for taking so long. She should have checked on her.

'I won't be long.' She stroked the back of Cleo's neck and backed out of the car, ignoring her cries.

She strode into the coffee outlet, rushed to the toilet and rinsed her hands until the itching eased.

She got a takeaway decaf and returned to the car. When she transferred the cup to her left hand, the pain from the heat made her drop it, splashing her shoes and ankles with hot coffee. The reddened skin where the hot cup had touched it felt on fire and looked even angrier. She cleared up the cup and got into her car, reassuring Cleo. Salford Royal Hospital was a couple of miles back along the motorway, and she headed for it. On her way, she rang Casin's employer.

The receptionist answered with a rushed-sounding, 'Hello?'

'I came to see Nirmal Casin this afternoon and—'

'We're just finishing for the day. If you need to—'

'I need to know what chemicals he's working with.'

'I can't tell you that. Our processes are confidential.'

'I've got some on my hands. You yourself said he shouldn't be wearing that gear in the offices. I'm sure health and safety would love to know how you treat visitors.'

After a long silence she said, 'Give me your name and number and I'll make sure someone rings you back.'

'Make it quick, I'm on my way to Salford Royal.'

Cleo picked up on her alarm, and Zofia took deep breaths to calm down. She arrived at the hospital, found a parking spot and, leaving Cleo alone in the car for the fourth time in a few hours, rushed to accident and emergency. She was speaking to the receptionist when her phone rang.

'Hello, Ms Dąbrowski.' The man introduced himself as the chief safety officer of the factory. 'The liquid on Mr Casin's gloves was hydrochloric acid. We use thirty-three per cent concentrate, but Mr Casin assures me he'd rinsed his gloves off, so you'd have been exposed to a much lower concentration.'

'What does that mean?'

'If you rinse them in cold water for fifteen minutes, you should be okay. My colleague said you're going to hospital.'

'I'm here now.'

'Okay, great, can I speak to someone there?'

She passed her handset to the receptionist and rushed to the toilets and held her left hand under the cold tap until she lost feeling in it. She returned to reception, her left hand and forearm trembling. After recovering her phone, she waited in a cubicle as directed.

Her fingers had recovered feeling when a nurse joined her. 'Let's see your hands.'

Zofia held out her left hand. 'It's just this one.'

'Hmm. Slight reddening but no blistering. You should be alright. It's removed the top layer of skin, leaving it sensitive. I wouldn't pick up hot cups with it for a few days until the skin regrows.'

'Are you going to give me anything?'

'Painkillers?'

'I meant to counter the acid.'

'You've rinsed it off, so there should be none left on your skin. If it gets worse, come back.' She pointed at Zofia's top. 'You might need a new jumper.'

The dye had faded on the spot where she'd wiped her hand. Doing so must have reduced the damage to her hand. She could stand that.

A frantic Cleo greeted her on her return to the car and Zofia took her for a walk around the car park. Her phone rang.

'Where are you, sis?'

'I'm at Salford Royal.'

'What's happened?'

'Nothing. Nothing serious. I came . . . I'll tell you about it once I get home.'

He eventually replied. 'Okay, what are you doing with Cleo?'

'I'll bring her home.'

'What about her drugs? Victor's returning to collect her.'

'Where is he? Isn't he back from meeting John and Craig?'

'Yeah, he's been in, but Digger rang him, and he's gone there.'

A wave of exhaustion washed over her. She couldn't face going back to the office. 'Take the drugs home. I'll bring Cleo and let Victor know what we're doing.'

Kasper agreed, and she ended the call. 'Come on, Cleo, let's go home.'

There was no match at Old Trafford, so she made it home in half an hour, beating Kasper. A nervous Cleo inspected the ground floor of the house but refused to go upstairs. The kettle boiled, and Kasper charged in.

'What's happened?'

She told him.

'Let's see.'

Apart from a reddening, her hand didn't look too bad, and she felt that she'd maybe made a fuss over nothing.

'We should bloody sue the bastards. I'll get a photo.' He produced his phone and studied her injured hand.

'Let's not. I just want to forget about it. Have you got Cleo's drugs?'

'And the bed from work. I'll get them. Oscar's got a new one, and a smart harness.'

She made them drinks and put the oven on while Kasper fetched the items. They'd have something from the freezer; she was too shattered to cook anything. Kasper put the bag of drugs from the vet on the kitchen table and then put the bed in the corner under the stairs, trying to coax Cleo into it. Zofia opened the bag from the vet and read the instructions. Victor would have trouble shampooing Cleo, so she'd do that tonight.

'I'll give Cleo a shower and then have one myself. Can you find something in the freezer?'

The dog still didn't want to go upstairs, and it took both of them to coax her. She must have suffered some sort of trauma upstairs in a house. Zofia could have killed whoever had done that to the poor animal. To shampoo her without damaging the cone or getting her operation scar wet took some doing, especially as Zofia was avoiding getting warm water on her left hand.

With a struggle during which she got soaked, she did it and took the clean and almost dry dog back to the kitchen and placed her in her bed. The aroma of basil and rosemary told her they were having pizza, and by the time she'd showered and returned, Kasper had served it up with a healthy salad.

Kasper asked her to talk him through everything that had happened, and they discussed what Casin's behaviour suggested. She hesitated before telling Kasper she'd mentioned Mulberry and the threat Casin had delivered on parting.

'You did what?'

'We needed to know if he was involved.'

'Did Casin say he was?'

'No! I told you, he said he'd tell him. Surely that suggests he's involved.'

'Maybe.' Kasper closed his eyes and took a deep breath. 'Do you think Mulberry will do anything?'

She knew she shouldn't have told him what Colette had said about Mulberry. 'I doubt it. We're working on the premise that Mulberry is doing what Glass tells him. I've made it clear we've finished our investigation into Glass, so he's got no reason to come after us.' But had that message got through to Glass?

'You're probably right.' Kasper looked thoughtful and chewed another mouthful of pizza. 'We should document our attempt to return Casin's money and the fact he attacked you with acid—'

'He didn't attack me with acid.'

'How about this? In his aggressive attempt to avoid taking the money, he splashed you with acid from his work gloves.'

'Can we discuss this in the morning?' She was too tired to think about it now.

Kasper shrugged. 'Okay.'

They finished eating in silence, and she cleared away the dishes while Kasper watched TV in the lounge. She took Cleo for a walk on the local streets and returned home. When she attempted to leave the kitchen, Cleo emitted such distressing cries that she took pity on her and let her sleep in her room. She fell asleep almost before her head hit the pillow.

In what seemed the next instant, her phone woke her. The display on the screen showed 3 a.m. She fumbled with the handset and put the bedside light on. Two brown eyes studied her from inside a cone as she listened to the message from the alarm company. After thugs working for the Novaks had broken into their offices earlier in the year, they'd upgraded their alarm to a monitored system.

She met Kasper on the landing. 'Did they ring you as well?'

'No, I just heard your phone. Alarm, was it?' He squinted and rubbed his eyes.

'I'll sort it.'

'What if there's still someone there?'

'With the siren blaring, they'll have long gone.'

'I'll come with you.'

Cleo had followed her onto the landing. 'We'd better take her with us.'

She didn't like being placed in the back and kept glancing between the seats to make sure Zofia was still there. At this time of night, the four miles to their office took no time at all. Zofia glanced at the front door as she pulled up on the pavement past it and parked. She'd normally park round the back, but their last break-in had been through a rear window and, despite her earlier claims, she still worried the intruders wouldn't have left. The eerie emptiness of this usually busy road added to her unease.

'You okay?' Kasper said.

'Yeah, let's do it.' She released her seat belt and got out.

On the pavement, the muffled sound of their alarm grew louder. As she retrieved her keys and made her way to the front door, a loud whoosh came from the car park at the rear of the building.

'What the hell was that?' Kasper set off to find out.

'Be careful, Kasper.'

Her brother disappeared around the side of the building. She hesitated. Should she phone the police? A shape moved near her car. A large figure detached from the shadows. As he came closer, she saw the knife glinting in his hand.

She turned to run and got two paces before he kicked her feet from under her. She crashed to the ground, smashing her head on the pavement. Dizzy and in pain, she looked up at her attacker. He lifted the knife.

CHAPTER 13

The panicked call from Kasper snapped me from zero to maximum consciousness, and I got dressed and on the road in under two minutes. Oscar, grumbling about being woken, stopped his complaints when I told him someone had hurt Zofia. Kasper's garbled account hadn't made it clear what had happened, just that someone had attacked his sister.

It was only the van's lack of oomph that stopped me getting a series of speeding tickets on the way in to work. In my panic, I ignored red lights and passed the few cars I encountered. On Cheetham Hill Road, the flashing blue lights appeared in the distance ahead of me before I passed the Manchester Oratory, three hundred metres from the office. I pushed the van to almost fifty before applying the brakes and stopping just short of the first police car.

They hadn't closed the street, which I took to be a good sign. If something awful had happened . . .

I forced myself not to think of the worst. Oscar jumped out behind me onto the road. I didn't want to take the time to get his lead or push him back, so I let him follow me. A uniformed officer watched my charge towards the ambulance, which stood on the pavement past his car.

'Hang on, sir, you can't go past.'

'My friend—'

'Victor!' Kasper's shout interrupted me.

The officer let me run past him, Oscar at my heels. 'Where is she? What happened?'

'She's fine! She's fine!' He pointed at the ambulance. 'Just a bit shocked.' The stink of acrid smoke clung to his clothes, and I feared she'd been burnt as I brushed past him to the ambulance.

The rear doors were open, and Zofia sat on a stretcher, a clear mask over her mouth. A paramedic stood talking to her, and another stood in the opening, his back to me. Zofia waved, then removed the mask and smiled. The tension that had seized my body since the call flowed away, and I staggered.

Oscar ran past me and attempted to enter the ambulance. 'Come on, boy.' I pulled him back by his harness. 'Zofia, what happened?'

'I'm okay, thanks.'

'Kasper said a man attacked you.' I noticed the red mark on her forehead. 'You're hurt.'

'It's nothing.'

'Who did it?'

'The guys from the takeaway—' She waved a hand towards the fried-chicken shop below their office.

'Bastards! Why?' I looked around for them.

'No! They scared him off. You didn't need to come, but it's good to see you both.'

A warm feeling made my heart hitch.

'Can you give us a minute?' I asked the paramedic in the doorway.

He pushed one leaf closed. 'Sorry, mate.'

I stepped back. Kasper stood on the pavement talking to the two guys from the takeaway. 'Come on, Oscar.'

Kasper waited for me to join them. 'These guys chased—'

'Yeah, so Zofia said. Thanks, guys.' I shook each of their hands.

They looked embarrassed. 'No problem, we're happy to help.'

A uniformed policeman arrived. 'I need a statement from you gentlemen. That's your shop?' He pointed at the fried-chicken takeaway. 'Let's get out of the cold.'

They led him into the shop, and I waited until he closed the door behind them, leaving us on the pavement.

'What happened?' I asked Kasper.

'Someone set the alarm off, so we came to have a look, and after last time . . .'

He didn't need to remind me. 'What happened to Zofia?'

'I didn't see. When we got here, there was an explosion at the back of the office, and I ran through to see what it was. Zofia stayed here at the front. Someone had set up a petrol bomb in the bins. I thought they were trying to burn us down, but it must have been to split us up in case both of us turned up.'

'You're okay?' I felt bad I'd not asked about his wellbeing.

'Yeah, I just walked into a cloud of smoke, then I heard Zofia cry out. I rushed back, and someone scarpered down there.' He pointed to Derby Street opposite. 'One guy from the takeaway was helping Zofia while the other chased the man who attacked her.'

'He didn't catch him?'

'He almost did, caught him a glancing blow as he got in their car. They had it parked behind the Sikh place.'

'What did it look like?' It couldn't be the same men who'd attacked Harry. How would they know about KZD, Kasper and Zofia's business?

'We heard it, but I saw nothing.'

'We'll ask the guys from the shop what they saw once the copper finishes questioning them.' I thought of the injury to Zofia with a sense of helplessness and rage. 'How did she get the mark on her head?'

'The guy tripped her up, and she hit the deck. She was woozy, but the paramedic said she should be alright.'

Added to her insistence she was okay, this made me feel calmer. 'What caused the alarm?'

'An unsophisticated half-brick sent through one of the back windows. It hit the printer, but no damage apart from a mark on the casing.'

A familiar figure approached along the pavement. As she passed under a lamppost, I noticed the uniform. 'Inspector Bowling, good morning.'

'Hello, Victor, Kasper.' She smiled in greeting. 'You've been in the wars again?'

Kasper pointed at the ambulance. 'Zofia has, but she'll be okay.'

Bowling looked towards the ambulance. 'I'll have a word with her and then speak to you two.'

'But I've just arrived,' I said. 'I saw nothing.'

'I still want to talk to you.' She crouched down to greet Oscar, then stood. 'You can wait inside. It should be warmer. Mine's black, no sugar.'

Now that my adrenaline had worn off, I shivered. Upstairs in the office, a draught blew in through the broken window at the back. Kasper and I effected a temporary repair using the cardboard from two boxes and packaging tape. We'd got the coffee on by the time Bowling arrived with Zofia, who looked around.

'Where's Cleo?'

Kasper said, 'Sorry, I forgot all about her.'

He told me where she was and, taking Zofia's car keys, I rushed down to fetch her. She was, of course, frantic when I reached the car. The ambulance had gone, but two police cars and a van remained. I opened the back door, and she shrank against the far door, so I slid onto the seat. It took me five minutes of coaxing before she let me get close, and I led her back to the office. She ran straight to Zofia and lay at her feet.

Bowling had taken Zofia's statement and recorded Kasper's and mine. 'And none of you know who might have been behind the attack?'

I wasn't sure whether to mention Miles and his oppo with the snake tattoo. Zofia looked like she wanted to speak, but the sharp ring of the bell stopped her. I was nearest the intercom and recognised our caller, so I buzzed him in.

'DS Lambert,' I announced and opened the door to the waiting room.

'Mr Timothy. This where you do your detecting?' He walked past me into the office and looked around. 'Two dogs, but neither is a bloodhound.' He smiled at his weak joke. Nobody else did.

'Inspector.' He nodded at Bowling. 'I believe this is our case.'

'A break-in and an assault. Have they redefined major crimes since I left?'

He reddened. 'I believe there was an explosive device used. Obviously, with the make-up of the local population, we're concerned there may be a terrorist angle.'

I couldn't hold back. 'How do you work that out? This business is owned by two Christians, not Muslims or Jews, which is what I suppose you're alluding to. Even though the two populations have got along fine around here for decades.'

'It's our job to ensure your safety. We decide who to investigate.'

'Why aren't you investigating who killed Harry Sanders?'

'We are.' He glared at me. 'I don't answer to you.'

'I bet you haven't even looked at the footage I sent you.'

He jabbed an index finger towards me. 'You're going the right way about getting arrested, matey.'

Bowling's voice cut through the silence. 'And what would you arrest him for, Sergeant?'

He clenched his jaw and looked around the room. 'I'll let the DCI know you're refusing to hand the incident over.'

'Don't worry, I'll tell him.'

'Are you sure you want to do this, Acting Inspector?'

'I do, Acting Detective Sergeant.'

'I'll let the boss know.'

'Great, he'll be told twice. And I'll make sure he gets a *full* report.'

Lambert's mouth formed a thin line. 'Inspector.' He spun on his heel and left.

Zofia spoke first. 'Will you get into trouble, Colette?'

'From that pipsqueak? He's a sergeant and I'm an inspector.'

'What if he reports you to Grimes?'

She laughed. 'I doubt Darren knows he's here. Why the hell would Major Crimes investigate this? I expect the local CID to take this.' She sipped her coffee. 'You were going to say something before Lambert interrupted you, Victor.'

I forgot she rarely missed anything and told her about the two men who I believed had killed Harry. When I mentioned the description Samuel had given me, Zofia let out a yelp.

Bowling studied her. 'You asked me about one of your kidnappers who had a snake tattoo. I told you then, he's dead. This can't be the same man. Why are you so sure he's one of the men who killed your friend?'

I explained my theory about them attacking homeless men with dogs, but didn't explain why I thought they might be doing it.

'I remember the one you dragged out of the fire. Didn't one of his attackers hit you over the head?'

'Yeah, and later on that evening, he tried running me over.'

'Did he now? You never reported that.'

'Your boss intimidated me.' I had only Oscar's word that it was the same man.

'He has that effect, but he's really not an ogre.' She smiled. 'Well, not too bad an ogre.' She made a note in her pocketbook.

'I'll let him know you've sent the footage and voicemail, just in case the sergeant forgets to mention it.'

Zofia said, 'That's the second time you've said something suggesting he's not on the same side as Mr Grimes. Is there something we should know?'

'No,' she said too quickly. 'And Zofia, you had something to say.'

Zofia bit her lip. 'Yesterday afternoon I went to see a man, Nirmal Casin.' She explained Casin's part in getting their professional accreditation suspended. 'He kept refusing to show himself, just went on keeping me waiting, so I mentioned' – she swallowed and cleared her throat – 'I mentioned Mulberry. That brought him out to me straight away, but then he threatened to tell him I'd been asking questions.'

Bowling frowned. 'Is that why you asked me about Mulberry?'

'We think he's involved in this campaign against us. I'm pretty sure it's because we helped discredit a property developer called Rudy Glass and, until Tuesday, we were still investigating him.'

'What happened on Tuesday?'

Zofia checked the room. 'I met an informant, and she told me Glass knew someone was investigating him.'

Kasper stood. 'You never said.'

'No, sorry.'

Bowling raised her eyebrows. 'I know better than to ask who you were working for, or the name of your informant, but what's Mulberry got to do with it?'

Zofia said, 'He knew Casin because he had arrested him when he was a sergeant. I heard Glass has a senior officer in his pocket.'

I'd been following the conversation, knowing little of the background, but trying to untangle what I could work out. 'Do you think this Mulberry could be behind the break-in and attack on Zofia?'

Bowling didn't reply straight away, but looked around the room.

I guessed her concern. 'As a matter of client confidentiality, we sweep the offices every few days.' I didn't mention we'd started the practice because we feared careless talk might betray our part in the killing of the Novak brothers.

'Have you done it since the brick came through your window?'

Kasper stood and brought the scanner from the cupboard we kept it in. We watched him scan the room, the tension building. When he'd finished, we all looked at Bowling.

'Short answer, yes. I'd put nothing past Mulberry, and' – she paused, gathering her thoughts – 'the fact DS Adrian Lambert arrived convinces me he's behind it. Lambert is his creature. It explains why he showed up here.'

'What are you going to do?' I didn't know this Mulberry, but guessed he was a senior officer.

'The local CID will take over, but I'm going to monitor what they're doing, and if they find any evidence linking Mulberry to what's happened, I'll make sure he goes down.'

I suspected it wouldn't be as straightforward as Bowling made out, however good her intentions.

Kasper obviously felt the same way. 'I'm not letting the attack on my sister go. We'll carry out our own investigation.'

'I should tell you to leave it to us. Instead, I'll reiterate the advice I gave Zofia: be careful. This is a very dangerous man.'

CHAPTER 14

'Edinburgh? What the hell for?' Alex Novak almost vibrated with irritation as he faced his daughter.

Judy knew he wouldn't be pleased, but she hadn't expected this level of histrionics. 'I need a break, Dad. It's a fantastic city, and I've got a deal on a five-star spa hotel. I'm going to treat myself.'

'Your mother behind this?'

'What do you mean, "behind this"? I'm a grown woman making my own decisions.'

'How can you think of going away before we've got a manager to replace Jerry?'

She exhaled in frustration. 'We won't get one over the weekend, will we?'

'"One test of leadership is the ability to recognise a problem before it becomes an emergency."'

'What emergency?' Sometimes, his bloody quotes got on her nerves.

'If we don't find a replacement for Jerry before he leaves, what do you think's gonna happen? Without him, we'll struggle to run the business.'

The confirmation that her father didn't really think she was up to it made her want to punch him, but she held a neutral expression. 'I've been thinking,' she said. 'Between us – you and me – we should be able to run things.'

'You what? I'm not a bloody accountant. Anyway, you may not have noticed, but I'm in a wheelchair.'

'But as you keep telling me, it's your legs that don't work, not your brain.'

He took that on board. 'We always have a manager. A front man in case anything goes wrong.'

'We used to, but we're going legit, don't forget.'

'*Going* is the operative word. How many years before the first of our projects comes to fruition? What do we live on in the meantime? My place, your apartments, both of them, cost a packet just to run.'

'Yes, I know, Dad. I've spent every day of the last three months getting to know exactly what our assets are worth and how our business runs. That's why I need a break. Anyway, I thought you were going to persuade Victor to take the job.'

'I've not had a chance.'

'Didn't Machiavelli say, "Tardiness often robs us of opportunity"?' She suppressed a laugh as she said it.

'You bloody cheeky—' He laughed on seeing her expression. 'Right, have your break and I'll get Victor working for us by the time you get back.' He wheeled himself out of her office.

Relieved to have overcome her dad's objections, she finished her paperwork. She'd considered taking the train, but decided to drive. If she took the Maserati, she could enjoy the trip through the Borders on the A7. She left after lunch and arrived in Edinburgh at dusk, having enjoyed passing through historic towns where the English and Scots had massacred each other not so long ago. It was amazing how quickly people could bury ancient enmities.

The hotel, a Georgian mansion in a country park, stood against the backdrop of Holyrood Park and Arthur's Seat. Her

Maserati looked at home with the other vehicles in the car park. She treated herself to a suite and visited the gym before eating in the Michelin-starred restaurant. She justified the expense by telling herself that if this venture paid off, she and her father would never need to worry about money.

* * *

After a surprisingly disrupted sleep – she kept being woken by disturbing dreams she couldn't remember – she had a light breakfast and visited the pool and spa, being pampered all afternoon. Robertson had suggested a restaurant in the centre, near the castle, less than three miles from her hotel. She took a cab so she could have a drink and looked around her when she got out.

Instead of a view of the castle, a brutalist office block in grey concrete with light grey highlights loomed over her. The entrance to the restaurant – an industrial-looking wooden gate – added to her disenchantment. Where the hell had Robertson brought her? Or maybe she'd got the wrong address, but a Bentley with the number plate AR1 occupied one of the parking spaces on the street. Archie Robertson clearly liked to be noticed, and she congratulated herself on her insistence he didn't come to Manchester for this meeting.

Inside, a waitress showed her into a vast, high-ceilinged room with cast-iron columns supporting huge wooden joists. The aroma of rich sauces and the sounds of a busy restaurant filled the air. The waitress led her to a table at the far end of the room, a rustic-looking object made of wrought iron and heavy boards. Flames danced in a nearby cast-iron fireplace.

She studied the two men at the table as she was led to it. The younger had sandy hair and pale eyes and occupied a wheelchair exactly like the one her dad had just bought. A crescent scar two centimetres across, just below his hairline, spoilt his otherwise conventional good looks. His father, the man she was here to meet, rose to greet her. He stood half a head taller than her one sixty-five. Unblinking pale eyes appraised her, and his beak-like nose added to the impression of being examined by a bird of prey. His well-cut green tweed jacket contrasted with the mustard cords and red checked shirt she recognised as the Robertson tartan.

'Ms Novak, pleased to finally meet you.' His deep voice belied his slim build.

She took his offered hand, a strong but not wince-inducing grip. 'Pleased to meet you, Archie, and it's Judy.' She gave a pointed look at his companion.

'Ah. My son, Hamish.'

The younger man waved at his chair and gave a self-deprecating smile. 'Excuse my not getting up.' Unlike his father, he had no trace of a Scottish accent.

Judy stopped herself from forgiving him and took his offered hand.

Robertson waited until the waitress took Judy's drink order and left them. 'Hamish is learning the ropes in my business with a view to taking over.'

'Oh, right?' That was news to her. 'Is the takeover imminent?'

'I hope—'

'—not for a while.'

They spoke over each other and then laughed, but Archie's laugh sounded forced.

This could be awkward. She wasn't sure if she wanted to partner with a family at war. She didn't have fond memories of the early days when her brothers were taking a more prominent role in her dad's business before he handed over the reins.

'If we are going to work together,' she said, 'I need everyone to be clear on their roles.'

The two men studied her in silence for seconds, then the father spoke. 'Don't worry, we are clear. Just family banter. I'm sure it's the same with you and Alex.'

She wasn't sure, but nodded. 'Shall we order?' She perused the short but interesting menu.

Around her, the hubbub of conversation drowned the background music, and the nearest tables were distant enough to prevent eavesdropping. Robertson noticed her checking.

'There is a private dining room, but I've always found it discreet enough in here. We can continue any detailed discussions in our hotel suite. It's nearby.' He pulled a wine bottle out of the bucket on a stand beside his seat. 'I took the liberty of ordering a Chablis. I hope it suits.'

Judy wasn't a big wine snob, although the finishing school her mum had insisted she attend had equipped her to converse with any she encountered. She recognised the label as one commanding three figures at the wine merchants', and hated to think what they charged here. She held out her glass, and a waiter swished over to relieve Robertson of the bottle and pour.

They ordered and made small talk while they waited for the food. Judy had read little about Hamish, although she knew he was an only son. Robertson, however, seemed to know a lot about her brothers – especially Marko, the younger, which surprised her. He'd had a much lower profile than Milan.

'You've done your research, Archie. Marko would have been flattered that you studied him in so much detail.'

The two Robertson men exchanged a look before the father replied. 'Your brother made a sojourn to our fair city and made himself known.'

Although she hadn't had much to do with them at that time, having embarked on her ill-fated career as a reporter, she remembered some upheaval linked to Marko going to Scotland, and turning up with the icy woman she had never warmed to.

'I hope he didn't cause too much trouble.'

Another silent exchange between them, and he shook his head. 'Nothing we couldn't handle.'

Something about the way he said it made her want to dig further, but the starters arrived. The food, as Robertson had promised, was worth waiting for. Hamish had more than his fair share of wine, and they ordered a second bottle. Judy drank more water than alcohol, keen to keep a clear head.

The dining room had thinned out by the time they finished, and Robertson suggested they retire to his hotel suite. He must have rung ahead because a chauffeur, who looked more like a bodyguard, had brought the Bentley to the front door. He carried Hamish into the back of the car, then stowed his chair in the capacious boot.

The hotel, less than a mile from where they ate, was all dark wood and heavy fabrics. The Robertsons' suite – two bedrooms and a living area – took up the top floor. Archie poured them all whisky from a bottle on the sideboard. Judy could take or leave it, but recognised its rich quality. Something her father would appreciate, and she noted the label. She'd get him a bottle or two. Ease his irritation at her coming here. She imagined his fury if, *when*, he discovered the reason for her visit.

The real negotiations began and, after an hour, Archie stated, 'We think we should be looking at sixty per cent of the project. We've got the plans ready for two hundred and sixteen units, which we know will be passed.'

'Ours are two thirty-six.' Her father had discovered that Glass had received the nod for that many apartments, and she'd already spoken to his architect. 'That's twenty more. An argument for our having the lion's share. We're also the local company, which will appeal to the council.'

'Not with your track record.'

She held his gaze. 'I don't have a track record, as you call it.'

'No, but your family has.'

She hoped that the planning authorities would overlook her family's past and focus on her and the new company. 'So does yours.'

'Not in Manchester, Ms Novak.'

'We've been instrumental in getting rid of the chief competition for this project.'

'You may have, Ms Novak, but we know you haven't the money.'

'You know nothing of the sort.'

'Sixty-forty or it's no go, Ms Novak.'

She'd discovered from talking to Glass's architects that the combined heating system they were planning, a net-zero proposal, gave them an edge over the competition. Although she considered mentioning it to swing the negotiations her way, what if the partnership didn't proceed? She'd have given her plans to a competitor.

'Let's be honest, Archie. Neither of us would be here if we genuinely believed we could handle this project without overstretching ourselves. The difference is we're on the ground and can deal with any difficulties, where you're three hundred and fifty miles away.'

'She's got you there, Dad,' slurred Hamish, who'd been hitting the whisky.

His father gave him a glare, which should have stunned him. 'Don't you think you've had enough?' He took the bottle off the coffee table and to the sideboard. 'Excuse me a minute, Ms Novak.'

Judy waited until the door to the bathroom closed and spoke to Hamish. 'What happened when Marko came to Aberdeen?'

The look he gave her made her fear an attack, then he gave a nasty grin. 'He made a mistake, which cost him his life.' He rubbed the crescent scar on his head.

What the hell did he mean? Did Robertson have anything to do with the death of her brothers? 'How did you get that scar?'

'A loving present from my wife.' He thumped the wheelchair. 'This was part of the same gift.'

'What happened?'

'I made the mistake of saying no to her.'

Judy was putting things together. 'Did she run off with Marko?'

Hamish stared into the distance, vision unfocused.

Before she could ask him again, the toilet flushed, and Robertson returned. Hamish sank into his chair. 'I'm going to bed.'

Judy gave a silent curse, but smiled and said goodnight. They waited until he left the room, and Robertson fetched the bottle back, topping up both their glasses.

'Okay, Judy, we go fifty-fifty.' He held out his hand, and she took it without thinking. 'Here's to a fruitful partnership.' He raised his glass.

Judy did the same.

Was this man responsible for the deaths of her brothers?

CHAPTER 15

As Bowling had forecast, the local CID officers arrived to investigate the break-in and assault on Zofia. At her suggestion, none of us mentioned Mulberry and, once the detectives left, Kasper had driven his still-shaken sister home, and she'd taken the Thursday off, Cleo staying with her.

I'd parked up in the car park and got my head down for a couple of hours before opening the office at seven and washing in our cramped bathroom. The gloomy start to the day matched my mood, and I got stuck into work, catching up with stuff I should have done while I was investigating Harry's death. Kasper arrived while I was having breakfast bagels, and we held the fort.

Exhausted after being woken in the early hours, and upset by the attack on Zofia, wondering if they'd try again, neither of us got a huge amount done, despite my early start. The arrival of the glaziers to replace the broken window didn't help.

We both focused on jobs for the clients who paid our wages. In between, I made a start on tracing the GMC Sierra, which I believed had followed Harry on the night he died.

* * *

On Friday the siblings came into the office together, with Cleo, who seemed to have bonded with Zofia. Oscar wasn't happy about this but brightened up when I pointed out that it meant we didn't need to have Cleo living with us. Kasper's cold, which had shown signs on the Thursday, had got worse overnight. Zofia suggested he take the day off.

'I'll be fine.' His sneeze and long sniff belied his statement.

'Don't be spreading it to us,' I said.

He waved my complaint away. Zofia, who I guessed hadn't slept well, looked like she should take another day off. With the weekend imminent, they should both have time to recuperate. I returned my attention to the list of dealers who sold GMC pickups. I also checked local second-hand car dealers who didn't specialise. The thought that I would also need to check private sales for the previous six months gave me a headache. Zofia heard my sigh of frustration.

'What's up?'

I told her.

'Why do you need to check six months?'

'Because they damaged the van they used to attack me in mid-April and set fire to it two weeks later. I'm assuming they bought the replacement vehicle in the intervening period.'

'Are you sure there have been no attacks since they had a go at you?'

I'd checked all news outlets and double-checked with John and Digger. 'Just one a few days later, then none since they fired the van.'

'So, Harry was the first since then. I'd assume they've not had the pickup long, so start looking at private sales from last week and work backwards.'

That made sense, but it still left a huge amount to do. Kasper's next words brought home how much.

'Have you checked social media?'

'What do you mean?'

'Lots of people sell stuff on social media now.'

'Cars?' I used social media to keep tabs on my daughters, but that was all. I used to use it to post updates on my family, sharing our holidays and milestones with colleagues and friends. Being homeless soon cured me of that habit; 'my latest squat' didn't quite have the ring of holiday snaps from a sunny corner of the world.

Kasper snapped his fingers. 'Earth to Victor.'

'Sorry.'

'I said yes: cars, even houses.'

'Great,' I said. 'That will keep me busy.'

'Aren't John and Craig helping you?' He sniffed and blew his nose.

'Yeah, I'm meeting them at lunchtime. I've got that process to serve in Trafford Park, so I was planning to meet them after.'

'It might be the last one we get for a while.'

'Why's that?'

'We get a lot of that sort of work through the SPI website.'

Zofia frowned. 'Haven't you emailed them yet?'

'I did yesterday. And they've responded, asking what other steps we've taken to return Casin's money.'

I looked on, unsure what they were talking about. 'Is this about the guy who splashed acid on you?'

She nodded. 'We're trying to prove we didn't do any work for him. We need to return his retainer.'

'I can drop the money around to his house.'

'We'd need to prove we've returned it,' Kasper said. 'He told Zofia to sling her hook.'

'But his wife didn't,' Zofia pointed out. 'She offered to take it off me. I could go back and get her to sign the receipt.'

Kasper sneezed, but I could tell he didn't like the idea of her going back there, and neither did I.

'I'll do it,' I said. 'Give me the money and a receipt for her to sign.'

I collected the paperwork I needed, plus the envelope containing the two fifty.

As I put on my jacket, Kasper finished a call and said, 'Where in Trafford Park are you going?'

I was immediately suspicious. 'Why?'

'A divorce I'm dealing with, the guy has claimed he's sold his car for ten grand. His wife says it's worth five times that, and he's been seen driving it. I've found the garage where he gets it serviced. He's collecting it this afternoon at two. I need photos of him collecting it and proof he paid the garage.'

That would take me well past the time I'd agreed to meet John and Craig.

'You can borrow my camera.'

Zofia saw me still hesitating. 'Why don't you tell John and Craig to come here? They can use our computers and Wi-Fi to help with the search.'

I'd planned to park up outside a hotspot and have us work from the van. Not ideal with three of us packed in it. 'Yeah, thanks. I'll tell them to come here.'

I rang and told Craig to come to the office and told him how far I'd got so they could make a start before I got back – he was the computer whiz of the two of them.

My first call was to Casin's house. The lack of a car on their drive was the first sign I'd be out of luck. Nobody answered my ring. I was contemplating checking around back when the neighbour came out to her car.

'Hello, I'm looking for Mr or Mrs Casin.'

She laughed. 'Good luck with that. They've gone on holiday.'

'Do you know when they'll be back?'

'Sorry, no, but more than just overnight, I reckon. I saw them loading several cases into their car.'

I thanked her and reported back to Zofia.

My next call was to serve a summons on the owner of a café in Trafford Park. It was lunchtime, and they'd be at their busiest. He wasn't there often, but never missed Friday lunchtime. I left Oscar in the car and joined the queue at the counter. The delicious aroma of cooking made my stomach rumble.

Three harassed-looking women were doing most of the work, overseen by a man with a sour expression. I'd folded his summons, so the title faced me, and held my phone ready to snap him taking it from me. I dawdled at the counter, pretending to be choosing, until all three women were busy. He came forward to serve me, and I handed him the summons, taking the photo while he was still grasping what had happened.

His furious reaction convinced me to get my lunch elsewhere. I got a sandwich a few streets over and drove with it to the garage, where I had twenty minutes before Kasper's errant husband was due to arrive. I parked where I could see the front and took Oscar for a walk along the Bridgewater Canal while I ate.

Is Cleo staying with Zofia now?

'She seems to be.'

She won't be staying with us?

'Don't you like her?'

She's okay, but we haven't got room. He cocked his leg at a clump of dandelions. ***Do you think Zofia likes her more than she likes me?***

'She needs more attention than you. Her owner's just died.'

Would Zofia like me better if you died?

I looked at the dark water of the canal and veered away. 'It depends if you caused my death.'

He trotted on, deep in thought.

'Cleo will probably go to a kennel once she's finished her medication.'

Is she ill?

'She just needs a bit of TLC.'

Would I go to a kennel if you died?

'Don't be morbid.' I checked the time. 'We'd better get back.'

I didn't have to wait long before a Yaris pulled up outside the garage. With Kasper's wonderful camera, I had no trouble capturing the image of the driver, a younger woman who kissed the passenger as he got out. Through the lens, I recognised him beyond doubt as the errant husband. He walked towards the Mercedes SUV on the garage forecourt and unlocked it. I took a series of photos showing him doing it.

An overalls-clad man came out of the garage carrying a clipboard. He spoke to the man, showed him around the car, pointed out two tyres, and got him to sign a form. The man then produced a wad of notes, which he handed to the mechanic. I got it all on the memory card. Kasper would be pleased.

We returned to the office, arriving just before three. I heard the cacophony before I opened the front door. A high-pitched hysterical barking came from the office, and I charged up the stairs, Oscar ahead of me.

John and Craig had arrived, and the latter held Trixie in his arms. Zofia held a distressed Cleo, trying to calm her.

'I'd better go.' Craig backed out of the door I'd just come in, stroking Trixie's head.

'I'm really sorry, Craig,' Zofia called after him, looking bewildered.

Once Craig left, Cleo calmed down.

'Sorry, Sister,' John said. 'We didn't realise Cleo would be here. She's never got on with Trixie.'

I looked at Kasper and Zofia. 'Why don't you two get off? You both look like death warmed up.' I persuaded Kasper I had all the footage he needed for his case, and I'd upload it to our server so he could send it to his client on Monday, and the two of them and Cleo left.

Craig returned with a still-indignant Trixie, who Oscar comforted, and with one of us at each workstation, we continued our search for the car involved in Harry's killing. After two hours, I was wilting and suggested we take a break. The doorbell buzzed, and John, the nearest, stepped to the intercom.

'Police, Victor.'

Had Bowling got an update for us? I joined John at the screen. Two uniformed officers stood at the door. Behind them, a scowling Lambert.

CHAPTER 16

Lambert stood between the two uniformed officers, obviously picked for their size. If he expected me to be intimidated, he'd misjudged me, although it would have worked not long ago. I'd since toughened up, and I thought he looked like a kid between two adults. The idea made me smile, and Lambert's scowl deepened.

'Where's your boss?' Lambert directed his glower at John and Craig. 'Does she know you let dossers use the office when she's not around?' He made a point of sniffing and screwing up his face.

John ignored him, but Craig half rose to his feet. I gestured for him to stay in his seat and, with a show of reluctance, he lowered himself, making do with a sneer. The tension in the room dropped a notch, but the uniformed officers stayed on their guard.

'What do you want, Sergeant?'

'We've had a complaint about you assaulting someone.'

I considered what I'd done since last seeing Lambert. 'Whoever told you that is lying.'

'Oh yeah? We've got you on camera.'

I shook my head. 'No, you haven't.'

'You calling *me* a liar?'

'I'm saying you haven't got footage of me assaulting anyone.'

'I've got three witnesses, and that's apart from the complainant.'

'As I said, they're lying.' I'd worked out what he was referring to and tried to recall if there were any cameras in the café I'd visited. 'Which cameras am I on, then?'

'We've got your scuzzy van on several traffic cameras in Trafford Park. What were you doing there?'

'My job. What are you doing here?'

Craig stood and walked round his desk.

The three coppers tensed.

'I'm going for a piss.' Craig pointed behind them to where the toilet was, off the reception area.

Lambert and one of the uniforms had to step aside to let him pass. Craig left, closing the door behind him.

'Are you going to tell me who I've assaulted?'

'Yeah.' He named the owner of the café.

I laughed. 'And your witnesses are his three staff, who are clearly shit-scared of him?'

'You think assault's funny?' Behind him, the toilet flushed, and the coppers tensed until the door opened and Craig returned to his desk.

'I think what you're trying is funny,' I said. 'I served him a summons for not paying his bills. The café was packed, and I bet not one of his customers is backing up his accusation. Just the three women he bullies.'

'I've got evidence—'

'Yeah, of my van in the area. I've not denied being there.'

His jaw clenched. 'The gentleman suffered injuries. I've got them on camera.'

'Okay, let's see them.' That he hadn't arrested me yet suggested he had nothing.

He stared at me, then produced his phone and opened the screen. 'Here.' He pointed to a still of a hand with a mark on it.

John, who hadn't moved since the police arrived, leaned over to see it. 'That's a burn mark. Are you saying Victor burned him?'

Lambert reddened but didn't respond.

I picked my phone off the desk and scrolled through to the video of me serving the summons. 'Point out where I assaulted him?'

He swallowed. 'The gentleman made a complaint and had witnesses.'

I addressed the two uniforms. 'You guys happy to be muscle for the sergeant here while he tries to intimidate law-abiding citizens?'

'I'm not trying to intimidate you—'

Craig snorted. 'Good thing. You're crap at it.'

Lambert pretended to ignore it, but his companions failed to smother their smirks in time for them to go unnoticed by their superior. 'I'm investigating an accusation of assault. I'll be lodging this in our records, and your employer will have to address it. The CPS will decide if we're going to take it further. This is a serious complaint. I believe it's the second one against your employer.'

He left, the now embarrassed-looking constables at his heels. I waited until the door to the street slammed and I checked on the screen to see that it was closed.

'Sorry about that, guys.'

'What did he mean about being a second complaint, Brother? Are Zofia and Kasper in trouble?'

'They've upset someone, and he's throwing shit around. Nothing to worry about.' I hoped I was right and checked the time. 'Guys, shall we call it a day? I'm shattered, we can meet here in the morning. Shall we get something to eat, my treat?'

Before they could answer, the door buzzed again. Outside, staring at the camera, stood a guy I vaguely recognised, but not where from.

'Can I help you?'

'I'm looking for a guy called Victor.'

'That's me.' What now? He wasn't police, more like a gangster.

'My boss wants to see you.'

'We're closed. Tell him to come back Monday.'

This seemed to puzzle him. 'Look, I'm asking nicely.'

'Glad to hear it, and I'm telling you nicely.'

'Mr Novak won't be happy.'

'Alex Novak?'

'Yeah.' As if I should have known.

'Where is he?'

'In the car, outside.'

I checked with the others. 'We're just leaving. I'll come and speak to him in the car. Won't be a minute.' I replaced the handset. 'I'll lock up and have a quick word before we get off.'

Craig said, 'If you need to speak to him, let's do the meal another time.'

'It will be fine.' We closed everything down, and I put Oscar's lead on him.

'New harness, Oscar,' Craig said. 'Looks smart. I might get one for Trixie.'

Oscar preened as they led him outside, and I set the alarm. Novak's car sat on the opposite side of the road. The driver's door opened, and the lump who'd rung the bell ran between the traffic and stopped two paces away.

'Mr Novak says you can come too.' He pointed at Craig and John.

I said, 'It's fine, I'll talk to him over there.'

'Says to tell you, you're going for a meal.'

'Why didn't you say?'

He shrugged.

'Okay, guys?' They gestured, *why not?* 'What about the dogs?'

The man's brow furrowed as if I'd asked him to recite pi to two hundred places.

'Never mind,' I said. 'Let's go.' We waited for a gap in the traffic and crossed to the other pavement. I slid open the back door of Novak's car, a smart, black people carrier. His chair occupied the space where they'd removed two seats. 'Alright, Alex.' I'd not seen him since he took Kasper, Zofia and me out for a thank-you meal at a very smart restaurant.

'Victor, you're looking well. Why don't you come in, and your friends?'

To his credit, he didn't react when my unwashed friends clambered into the back, along with the dogs.

'Your friend said we're going for something to eat,' I said. 'Where are we going? Same place you took me last time?' I imagined the consternation of the other diners if we turned up.

'Erm, yeah, I've booked a table for two, but I'm sure they'll accommodate four.'

Craig held Trixie on his lap. 'Will they feed the dogs?'

Novak frowned. 'We can leave them in the car. Billy can take care of them.'

'Not my Trixie, she doesn't like strangers.'

Novak and Craig stared at each other.

John broke the silence. 'If you're happy to go for a curry, we know a place.'

Novak, anticipating a slap-up meal with me in a smart restaurant, hesitated, then agreed. John directed the driver to a side street in the Northern Quarter. I got out and recognised the place as somewhere Craig had once taken me to for breakfast after saving me from thugs who'd been beating me up.

Five minutes later, we sat in a private dining room at the back, the dogs in a corner with bowls of food and water, and the four of us at a large round table.

'Have whatever you want, guys, I'm paying,' Novak said. 'Shall we get a bottle of Pinot?' He noted our reaction. 'Beer, then?'

‘Not for me, Brother. Water will be fine.’

When Craig and I asked for the same, he got the message. We ordered food, and he regaled us with amusing anecdotes while we waited for it. Many seem to require a quote from either Sun Tzu, Machiavelli or Shakespeare to finish it.

He’d just finished one and Craig said, ‘Who said, “If someone’s trying to impress you with their erudition, they’re usually trying to pull the wool over your eyes”?’

The room chilled, and Novak paused a few seconds. ‘I don’t know that one, Craig. Who said that?’

Craig waited a beat. ‘Eddy Price.’

‘I’ve not heard of him. Was he a general?’

‘Not quite, he made lance corporal. My dad. The only piece of advice I remember from him.’

After another silence, Novak gave a strained laugh. ‘I like you, Craig.’

‘You don’t, but you want something from me.’

The food arrived in a cloud of garlic, coriander and cumin, breaking the awkward atmosphere. We tucked in, and Novak, seeming recovered from Craig’s put-down, looked up at me and got to the purpose of the meal.

‘Judy tells me you’ve turned her down?’

John and Craig looked puzzled.

‘I didn’t turn her down. I said I’d consider the job offer.’

Novak laughed. ‘Yeah, that’s a polite brush-off.’

I didn’t deny it.

‘She may not have made it clear that we also want to employ your friends.’ He gestured to John and Craig.

‘As hired thugs?’ Craig said.

‘In a variety of roles commensurate with your abilities, Craig.’ He waved at me. ‘We’re looking at Victor here to be in charge.’

My two friends stared at me, open-mouthed.

'Cheers, guys.' They clearly didn't think I was up to the job.

John recovered first. 'Sorry, Brother. I didn't doubt you. I just didn't think a job in Mr Novak's organisation would suit you—'

'We're changing,' Novak cut in. 'That's why we want Victor here running things. As Sun Tzu said, "A good commander is benevolent and unconcerned with fame."' He continued with the sales spiel his daughter had used on me. He mentioned salaries for the two of them that made both blink, although a fraction of what Judy had offered me. 'And we're also providing accommodation for our staff. You can each have a flat or share. Up to you.'

How many luxury flats did they own? 'On Deansgate?'

'Afraid not, that's for management. These are in Harpurhey.' He mentioned a block of flats, which brought back terrible memories.

'Isn't that where you kept the girls from Eastern Europe?' I asked him.

He reddened. 'I told you, we're pivoting. We're not doing anything like that now. We've done the flats up – new kitchen, bathroom, carpets. I can take you after we've eaten.'

'There's no need, Brother. Like Victor, we'll think about the offer.'

At the end of the meal, we sat full and with lots to think about. Novak waved at the empty bowls and plates. 'I was expecting a gourmet meal at a fancy restaurant tonight, but this was exceptional. How do you know this place, John?'

'First off, I haven't lived on the streets all my life. I once had a home, a job, social life. Second' – he counted off on a finger – 'the guy who owns this place lets customers buy meals for those less fortunate, as well as providing some himself. Craig and I have been fortunate to enjoy his generosity.'

Novak looked embarrassed, but I noticed he added two hundred pounds to the bill when he paid. John and Craig left with Trixie, and while Oscar and I waited for Novak's driver, he asked, 'What were the cops doing at your place?'

I didn't want Novak, even the affable version we'd encountered tonight, knowing our business. 'Social visit.'

'Watch your back. That little shit in plain clothes works for someone you don't want to cross.'

'Mulberry, you mean?' I let him know we had our sources.

'Someone's given you the nod. Piece of advice, Victor: be very careful. There are two types of bent copper. Those who are weak and greedy and who fall into corruption through temptation. They're usually cowards and easy to control. Then there's the other type. Those who are predators who have joined the police to further their criminal enterprises. These are bloody dangerous bastards. Mulberry is one of the latter.'

I suspected he knew what he was talking about. 'Thanks for the advice.'

'I'll give you another piece. As Sun Tzu said, "Pretend inferiority and encourage his arrogance."'

'I'm not sure what you're getting at.' My friends and I were inferior to a senior police officer in terms of the power we had. We didn't need to pretend.

'If you work for me – and my daughter – you don't have to worry about Mulberry.'

No, just you. And I wasn't sure who was the more dangerous. 'Thanks, I'll consider it.'

CHAPTER 17

Zofia woke with a head full of cotton wool. She'd woken a few times, provoked by dreams she couldn't recall but which left behind a residue of unease. A weight on her legs puzzled her until she remembered. She opened her eyes. Faint light leaked in through her red curtains, tinting the room pink. The cone around Cleo's head pointed at Zofia's face, and the eyes within it blinked.

'Hello.'

A thump on her duvet as Cleo wagged her tail.

Zofia checked the time, almost ten. 'We'd better get up, young lady. The day's almost gone.'

A few more thumps and Cleo sat up. Zofia slid her legs out of the bed and grabbed her dressing gown from behind the door. Even on a Saturday, the heating switched off at nine. As she left the room, Cleo followed and, at the bathroom door, she attempted to sneak in with her. Zofia blocked her with a leg and received a reproachful look.

She stopped in the doorway. 'I'm going in there to have a shower. You go back to bed.'

She shut the door, ignoring the pitiful whining. A cold shower cleared her head, but she increased the temperature to wash her hair. Once dried off, she wiped the mirror and checked her reflection. The bruise on her head hadn't gone full rainbow, but the graze had scabbed. She dried it with gentle pats and, wrapping her hair in the hand towel, got dressed and headed down to the kitchen, Cleo close on her heels.

The lingering aroma of toast and coffee told her Kasper had already finished in there. She found him in the living room, lying on the sofa.

'How you feeling, bro?'

'No worse, but no better. I've looked up my symptoms on robodoc.'

'Oh yeah?' He'd once examined his tongue and, using the internet medical site he swore by, convinced himself that his taste buds were symptoms of a dangerous tropical illness. 'What have you got? Ebola, Green Monkey Disease?'

'*Caninus allergia.*'

She deciphered his cod-Latin. 'You mean, Cleo?'

On hearing her name, her tail thumped on the floor.

'Uh oh. Can you keep her out of here?'

'Sure.' She eased the dog out and closed the door. 'Shall I get you some antihistamine?'

'I've taken some. It's eased off the symptoms, but I'm afraid it won't work. Having her here.'

'You were okay with Oscar.'

'I think it's her hair. As Victor kept telling me, Oscar doesn't shed, but she does.'

'Right, okay.' Heavy disappointment settled on her. 'You had breakfast?'

'Thanks.'

She left him with the door closed and returned to the kitchen. Now he'd mentioned it, she couldn't help seeing the myriad thin strands in the air, highlighted in the rays of the wintry sun flooding through the windows. She let Cleo out for a short walk, and fed her, then had breakfast. She realised she had no choice, but the thought of getting rid of Cleo filled her with a sense of loss. The poor thing had been with them for three days, and Zofia couldn't imagine her not being there. She told herself the plan had been for Victor to have her until she was fit enough to go to a kennel, and that's what would happen. Cleo seemed to sense something was wrong and placed her cone on Zofia's lap.

'I'm sorry, girl.' She finished her coffee and picked up her phone to make a call. 'Hi Victor.'

'Zofia, everything okay?'

'Yeah, yeah, I'm fine, fully recovered now. Where are you?'

'At the office. John and Craig are here.'

'Overtime?' A sense of guilt that she wasn't working made her chest tighten.

'It's all tedious legwork, checking internet posts. We finished early yesterday.'

He paused, making her think he wanted to say something else.

'So we're in today,' he said. 'How's Kasper?'

Thank you. 'That's why I'm ringing. He's allergic to Cleo. Her fur, anyway.'

'I'm sorry. Is he any worse?'

'No, I'd say not. Is it okay if I bring her?'

'Of course. I'll see you later.'

Zofia packed up Cleo's stuff, noticing the layer of hair on the flat surfaces of her bedroom. That was what she'd be doing on her return, hoovering and cleaning. She shouted goodbye through the living room door and took Cleo to the car. She stopped off in Longford Park and took her for a long walk, enjoying every minute of what seemed like a brief reprieve.

On the drive to the office, Zofia reminded herself she would see Cleo at work, then realised Victor couldn't bring her in. This was almost too much to bear, and she blinked tears away. *Come on, you've never been this soppy about a dog before.* She considered that it wasn't Cleo she was pining for but the thought of someone else leaving. Zofia dismissed the notion. She and Victor were just colleagues. As she pulled off the main road into the car park, she saw Craig at the door, waiting to be let in. He must have nipped out to get something to eat.

Cleo, although aware of something amiss, recognised where they were and relaxed. In the office, the three men had their heads down, working. Oscar greeted her, but seemed less than enthusiastic on seeing Cleo. Of course, they'd be sharing Victor's tiny caravan. She offered everyone drinks and went through to the kitchen, but couldn't detect any food. Then she realised where Craig had been.

'Where did you take Trixie, Craig?'

'Toff's taking care of her.'

'Thanks.'

Craig looked embarrassed. 'She'll enjoy it. He spoils her.'

'Shall I get something for lunch?'

'That's okay,' Victor said. 'The guys downstairs are doing us a special bucket. I thought we should support them after . . . you know. Their help.'

With a jolt of guilt, she realised that although she'd thanked them on the night, she hadn't been in to speak to them since they'd intervened in her assault. 'Let me pay for it.'

'Already sorted.'

That made her feel even worse, as did Victor's refusal to let her help them, saying they were going to finish when they'd eaten. 'Oh, okay. I'll get going, then. Bye, Cleo, see you Monday.'

'Do you think I should bring her?' Victor asked. 'With Kasper's, you know . . .'

'Of course, I didn't think. What will you do with her?' The reminder she'd never see Cleo again stung.

He shrugged. 'I'll sort something out.'

'Right.' Now even more upset, she said her goodbyes and headed out. Cleo attempted to follow, and Victor gently held her back. Zofia rushed down the stairs trying to block out the dog's pitiful cries. Maybe it would be better if she didn't see Cleo again. Parting each day if Victor brought her in would be unbearable.

An envelope sat in the post basket inside the door. It hadn't been there when Zofia arrived. She opened it and, wishing she hadn't, took it back upstairs.

Cleo's excited yap and hopeful look cut her. 'Do you know anything about this?' She showed it to Victor.

He read it with increasing agitation. 'The bastards. Sorry, Zofia. Lambert came around yesterday after you left. He claimed I assaulted the guy I served a summons on.'

'You didn't?'

'Of course not.' Victor reddened. 'I've got video proving I didn't.'

'Sorry.' *Of course he didn't, you idiot.* 'What happened?'

'We sent him off with his tail between his legs, but he's obviously taken it further.' He tapped the letter. 'Can the police strip us of the process server's licence?'

She wasn't sure. 'They don't issue the licence, but if they object to us having one I suspect the authorities would take notice.'

'This is police harassment. You should complain to the chief constable or the police and crime commissioner.'

'Yeah, I will. Thanks.' She left the letter on her desk. There was nothing she could do with it until Monday.

As she left, Cleo again tried to follow. Her reproachful expression and whimpers followed Zofia to the car, and she set off for home, feeling beleaguered. She glanced at the empty seat next to her, and her eyes filled with tears.

CHAPTER 18

We finished our bucket of chicken, and I realised why our neighbours had queues outside their shop every day. We washed our hands and gathered around my desk so we could each see the screen, Craig at the keyboard.

He pointed at the screen. 'I've set up a spreadsheet listing every dark, double-cab GMC Sierra pickup put up for private sale in a radius of seventy-five miles in the last three months. A few of the adverts mention Quadrasteer, and I've highlighted them at the top of the list. We should focus on them, but I've rung a couple who advertised without mentioning it because they don't see it as a selling point.'

I checked the counter on the left side of the screen. Well over a hundred, and that didn't include the ones John and Craig had already cleared. 'Okay, thanks Craig. I've looked at the dealers within two hours of Manchester. That takes us down to Birmingham, across to Hull, up to the Lakes and across to Bangor in North Wales.'

'That must be a lot of dealers, Brother.'

'A fair number, but because so many are tied to a brand and only sell that make, I can ignore those.'

'What if they part-ex one and sell it on?'

'I'm assuming they unload it through a dealer network, otherwise we'll never finish.'

John's expansive brow furrowed. 'We know the car's in Manchester. Why don't we just look for it?'

'Unlike the police, we don't have access to the camera network. Even for them, without the reg number, it's a huge amount of work.'

'But we've got a lot of eyes on the ground. What if we offered a reward?' John looked at me with a hopeful expression.

I reminded myself we were looking for the men who murdered John's brother. 'I'm happy to put the money up, although I'm not sure how effective that would be. These guys won't be driving around in it day to day.'

'It doesn't matter,' Craig said. 'We should print off a picture of the truck, add our numbers and tell everyone there's a reward. If they find it, great, if not, we've wasted a bit of paper and ink and a few hours. These searches we're doing won't guarantee we'll find them. What if one guy has an uncle in Dover who had an old pickup he didn't want? We'd never find them.'

Craig was right, and a sense of despair overwhelmed me. 'Okay, it's worth a shot.'

It took Craig twenty minutes to design a small poster, and we printed off a hundred. They took half to distribute to their network, and I took the rest to drop off at Digger's. The reward of a hundred quid should be enough to interest people but wasn't enough to attract too many time wasters. John and Craig left at three, leaving me with the two dogs.

I looked at Cleo's stuff in a large carrier bag. I couldn't manage it and the two dogs, so I'd have to take it down first. As I opened the door, Oscar got up.

Where are you going?

'I won't be long.' I ignored further questions and rushed down to the car, returning in under a minute.

Oscar studied Cleo. ***When's Zofia coming back?***

'Monday.'

Who's looking after Cleo?

'Guess.'

Nope, I'm no good at guessing.

I wasn't in the mood for Oscar's games. 'Right, come on, we're going.' Cleo, who'd hidden herself beneath Zofia's desk, made a point of ignoring me. 'Come on, Cleo, time to go home.' I knelt before her and stroked the back of her neck. She gave a desultory tail-wag but didn't look like moving.

Why don't we leave her?

'Because.' *I'll bloody leave you.* 'Come on, Cleo.' In frustration, I attached her lead and picked up Oscar's. 'Come on, Oscar.'

I'll be fine without.

'Don't be difficult. I'm hoping she'll see you coming along happily and copy you. I'm not leaving her, so we either all stay here or all go home. Are you going to help me with this?'

He stared at me, then trotted over so I could clip the lead onto his harness.

'Good boy.'

He bared his teeth but said nothing.

'Cleo, come on.' To my surprise, Oscar nudged her, and she stood. 'Well done.'

With my encouragement and Oscar alongside her, we got her downstairs and into the van. He didn't even complain when I let her on the front seat and relegated him to the back. The late Saturday afternoon traffic meant the journey to Digger's place at the bottom end of Deansgate took longer than I expected. Even in my rush, I admired the magnificent Victorian and Edwardian buildings lining the route. The low sun gave even the modern additions a sheen which made them glow. I abandoned the car at the side of the road and left the dogs in the car, with instructions to Oscar to behave himself. Cleo looked panicked when she realised I was going, but to my surprise Oscar came to the front of the van and stuck his head through the bulkhead, reassuring her. I waved to them and ran into the dining hall.

Digger served breakfast and lunch on weekends and dinner most days. The aroma of the hotpot they'd served at midday lingered, not yet overwhelmed by that from the evening meal.

My friend looked shattered.

'Hi Digger, busy lunchtime?'

'You wouldn't believe it. We've got an hour before the evening shift, but I'm lucky that tonight I've got the Tibetan Kitchen helping.'

I felt guilty piling more work on him. 'You know we're looking for the guys who killed Harry. This is the vehicle they were driving.' I thrust the bundle of leaflets at him.

He read the text and nodded. 'We'll put them on the counter. Harry was popular, I'm sure you'll get lots of interest.'

I thanked him and rushed back to the van, just beating a traffic warden to it. The drive back to the campsite from Digger's place took in a much more picturesque route, and I stopped off in Clayton Vale to let the dogs stretch their legs. Cleo seemed less anxious, and I returned to the van, believing this could work out, but knowing how upset Zofia would be at not seeing Cleo. The pair had bonded with remarkable speed. I wished I could do something to ease her heartache. I'd have to sort something out for Cleo for Monday. I reminded myself that we'd been operating on the assumption that she would only be with us until she was fit enough to go to a kennel.

* * *

Saturday night passed without incident, and I woke to a bright sunny morning. I let the dogs out and fed them outside. It looked like being a fine but chilly day, so I drove towards Delph and stopped at a café and farm shop. The dogs played in the enclosed field next to the café. Cleo seemed distracted, like she was waiting for someone, and each time a woman came near she watched her until sure it wasn't Zofia.

I'd just finished my breakfast when my phone rang. 'Victor?'

I didn't recognise the voice. 'Yes, can I help you?'

'Yeah, I want the hundred quid.'

I laughed. 'I'm sure you do. Why should I give it to you?'

'I saw the car you're looking for. I got a photo.'

Eagerness made me sit up, but I reminded myself not to get too excited. 'Where are you?'

'I'm on Hyde Road, near where it goes under the railway line.'

It wasn't too far from where John and Craig were staying, but it would take me an hour by the time I coaxed the dogs back in the van. I arranged to meet him in an hour and contacted John to tell him to meet me there. On the way through Mossley, I stopped at a cashpoint and took out a hundred, just in case.

As I turned onto Hyde Road, John rang to tell me the meeting was actually at a disused petrol station just *past* the railway line. I saw Craig first and pulled across the road, stopping on the cracked concrete of the service station. John stood talking to a man who could have been forty or sixty.

I reassured Cleo and left the car, approaching the three men. The man who'd rung me was taller than John, but Craig towered over him. He wore his thinning brown hair long and sported a scruffy beard.

'You the guy with the money?' He didn't offer me a hand.

'What have you got for us?'

'Let's see your money first.'

'Come on, Brother. You know me and Craig. You can trust us.'

'But I don't know him.' He jabbed a hand at me.

I took out my wallet and fanned the fresh notes. 'Here. Now, tell me what you've got for me?'

He licked cracked lips. 'I've got a picture of the car you're looking for.' He produced a battered smartphone with a cracked screen.

I looked at the image but couldn't make out what it showed, so returned his phone. 'Can you send it to me?'

'Money first, mate.'

I shrugged. 'If I can't see the picture, you're getting nothing.' I turned to John. 'You guys want a lift?'

'Hang on.' He grabbed my arm. 'You owe me a hundred quid.'

Craig stepped towards him. 'We owe you bugger all.'

He released my arm and stumbled back. 'Right, okay, but I need some juice. I ain't got no credit.' He held his phone up.

John pointed towards town. 'There's a drive-through takeaway about half a mile that way. You can use their Wi-Fi.'

'Right,' I said to the informant, 'I'll take you. John, can I leave the dogs with you?'

'With pleasure.'

I clipped their leads on and let them out.

'I'll come with you.' Craig squeezed himself into the back and the three of us set off.

The stink of cheap booze accompanying the man intensified in the confined space and, despite the chill, I opened a window. I pulled into the car park of the fast-food outlet, close to the building, and picked up its Wi-Fi. Moments later my phone pinged and, checking the image had come through, I drove back.

'When do I get my money?'

I ignored him and pulled back into the forecourt, where Oscar and Cleo flanked John. I put the dogs back in the van before looking at the image, a blurred photo of a pickup leaving the main road and taking the corner of the road opposite where we stood. John and Craig studied it. He enlarged the image.

'It's the right shape,' he said, 'and you can just make out the GMC logo on the grille.'

I took the phone from him. It needed some imagination, but I suspected we could sharpen it up on the big screen. 'You didn't get the number plate?'

'I remember it.'

Three of us looked at him expectantly.

'Well, some of it. The number was fifty-two, my age, and two of the letters were my initials. RD.'

'RD fifty-two?' My voice rose as excitement infected me.

He looked unsure. 'It had R and D in the letters. It was dark.'

And you'd had a drink, I finished for him. 'You're sure about the number?'

'Positive!'

Although disappointed, I reminded myself that we now knew the number and two of the five letters in the number plate. I retrieved the money and handed it over. 'Thanks.'

He almost ran towards town, leaving us on the forecourt. John took my phone from me and studied the image.

'The pickup went that way.' He pointed down the lane branching off Hyde Road. 'Is it worth driving down there in case we see it?'

We all clambered into the van and set off. I drove along a road lined with houses and industrial units until I got to the T-junction at the end and stopped, unsure which way to go.

Craig thrust a thumb over his shoulder. 'We should go back and check the side roads. If he was going any further, he'd have come down Ashton Old Road.'

I had to agree, and we spent ninety minutes traversing the warren of side streets but didn't see the vehicle we wanted. Few of the houses we passed had garages, but most of the industrial units could easily accommodate a vehicle.

John made a suggestion. 'Why don't we come back tomorrow and check all these units? If they're open and look legit, we can discount them.'

I wasn't so sure. 'We're assuming he's keeping it around here.'

'We haven't got a better lead, have we, Brother? And we can carry on with the searches we're doing, plus check the number plate.'

It would involve an enormous amount of work, but we agreed. I bought them both a late lunch and dropped them off before returning to the campsite. I'd parked up and was going to take the dogs for a walk when the site manager came over. She looked troubled.

I smiled. 'You okay?'

'I'm afraid you have to leave.'

'What? Why?' Had I heard her right?

'Sorry.' She kept her gaze on my feet. 'The police came round asking about you. They said you'd attacked a man. I can't—'

'I didn't attack anyone. It was a vexatious complaint. I served him with a writ, and he wanted to retaliate.'

She took a step back. 'I'm sorry, Victor. I don't want any trouble. You've paid until the end of the month, here's what I owe you.' She held out an envelope.

'Seriously, I didn't attack anyone.'

'I don't want to get into an argument.' She thrust the envelope at me. 'Please take this, and I want you gone by midday tomorrow.'

Her husband and another man hovered in the background, and I took the envelope. Where the hell was I going to go now?

CHAPTER 19

A dark shadow spoiled what should have been an enjoyable break in Edinburgh for Judy. Her conversation with Hamish, and the hint that he knew something about the killing of her half-brothers, kept going round her head. Had he or his father been involved in what happened to them? She'd slept in on Saturday, nursing a whisky hangover, and taken it easy until late afternoon when she'd met an ex-schoolfriend. They'd not been close, but one thing they'd learned at the expensive private school she'd gone to was to cultivate contacts.

Her friend, daughter of a prominent family in St Andrews, had already married and nursed a four-month bump, squashing any notion of reliving the debauched skiing trip of their final year. Judy found herself alone in the bar of the Balmoral Hotel as her friend retired to her suite at nine.

What to do? Go back to her hotel and get an early night herself, or head out to a club? In the event, a polite cough led to an introduction, which led to a third option.

A man of about forty, dressed in casual but expensive clothes, stood behind her. 'Didn't I see you last night?' He mentioned the restaurant where she'd met Robertson.

'That's possible. I was there, but I didn't see you.'

‘I’m easily overlooked.’ He gave a smile. ‘If I want to be.’ He offered a manicured hand. ‘Gavin.’

She took it, cool fingers and strong, but he didn’t seem to feel the need to show it by crushing her hand. ‘Judy.’

‘Can I buy you dinner?’ He gestured towards the restaurant. ‘Not quite up to last night’s standard, but acceptable.’

‘No, thanks.’

‘No pressure. Just a friendly gesture from one Mancunian exile to another.’

She studied him. Above average height and slim, he looked harmless, or at least less dangerous than she was, and she didn’t have a better offer. ‘Okay, but we split the bill.’

‘Fine by me.’

She didn’t want another selection of beautifully cooked, but in her opinion over-fussy dishes. ‘Do you know somewhere where we can get a decent steak?’

‘A woman after my own heart.’ He mentioned a restaurant she’d not heard of, reassuring her they did the best steaks in Scotland. They got a cab, arriving at the bottom end of Dundas Street ten minutes later. The restaurant occupied the lower two floors of a grand Georgian townhouse. The staff greeted Gavin like an old friend and led them through into a high-ceilinged, wood-panelled room infused with the aroma of cooked meat and gentle herbs.

As they waited for their food, he asked her about the previous night’s meal. ‘Old friends?’

‘Business acquaintances. Do you know them?’

‘I recognised the older guy. I think I read a magazine article about him. What sort of business, if you don’t mind me asking?’

‘Not at all. Ask away. And what line are you in, if you don’t mind *me* asking?’

He raised his glass to her. ‘Very good. I’m in reputational management.’

'A spin doctor.'

'Of sorts.'

The food arrived, and the steaks were excellent. Gavin told her about himself, his upbringing in a very different part of Manchester to the one where she grew up. She got a sense of the retelling of a curated legend. His questions stayed just on the right side of probing, although he brought the conversation back to Robertson. She deflected again, and he left it. But it reminded her she'd found out little about him.

She tried again. 'You've not said why you're in Edinburgh.'

'Business and pleasure. I categorise this under the latter.' He drained his glass and suggested a malt.

She refused, still feeling the effects of last night's indulgence. The entertaining but empty conversation continued and around midnight, he allayed her worry he might suggest going back to his place – the bloke was over forty, almost old enough to be her dad – by offering to let his cab drop her before taking him back to the Balmoral.

Although she'd enjoyed the evening, a sense of unease wouldn't leave her. Nor would the thought that he'd been at last night's restaurant to check on Robertson. She left mid-morning on Sunday and got back to Manchester around lunchtime to find her dad out, she assumed for lunch with one of his cronies.

She'd moved back in with him after he'd been shot. Builders had come in to convert the house to accommodate his wheelchair, and they'd put a kitchen in what used to be her old bedroom. The house now comprised two apartments, hers upstairs and her dad's on the ground floor. They'd designed it so she didn't need to enter his part, and she took her case straight upstairs.

Around four her dad's car returned, and she waited for his call. It arrived five minutes later, and she told herself not to snap at him.

'Hi Dad. You had a pleasant lunch?'

'Yeah, okay, thanks. I ate at Roger's. His missus always burns the beef and doesn't do proper gravy. How come you're back so early? I wasn't expecting you until tonight.'

'I can always go out if you'd rather. I'm sure Mum would be glad to see me.'

'That's not what I meant. It's that you usually . . . anyway, did you have a good time?'

'Yeah, fine, Dad, thanks for asking.' If he ever – make that *when* he discovered what she'd been doing, he'd be incandescent. And if what Hamish intimated was true, his reaction didn't bear thinking about.

'Now you're back,' he said, 'we'd better look at the candidates for Jerry's job.'

Thanks for bringing me down, Dad. She remembered his proud boast that he'd convince Victor to take the job. 'Did you speak to Victor?'

'You want to come down? One thing Roger's missus does well is cakes, and she's given me some lemon drizzle. I know it's your favourite.'

On one occasion ten years earlier, Judy had told her paternal grandmother that she liked her lemon drizzle cake. He'd given it to her ever since. Every time they had cake. She told herself to be nice and made her way down to his kitchen. He'd made a pot of tea using his best china. He obviously had bad news. Despite her eagerness to hear what he had to say, she waited until he was ready.

'I took Victor and two of his mates for a curry.'

'I thought you were taking him to that new place in Spinningfields?'

'Yeah, well, they had the dogs with them, so . . .'

That had to be Craig, the big ex-soldier with his ridiculous toy dog, so the other guy had to be Brother John, the one who looked like Friar Tuck. 'Nice meal?'

'It surprised me, but yeah, great. We'll have to go sometime.'

'And did you offer them jobs?'

'I'm not sure they're right for the organisation.'

'All of them?'

'As you know, I've championed Victor.'

'Okay, what's wrong with the other two?' During her admittedly short spell living on the streets in her past life as an undercover reporter, she'd heard a lot of good things about Craig and John, with both having legendary status among fellow street dwellers.

'They haven't got the experience—'

'Don't you always say, "Hire character. Train skill."?'

'But you need *some* skill.'

'Craig has military training. You're the one who told me ex-forces guys can offer a lot.'

'It's your decision, but I'd have strong objections if you gave Craig a job.'

What the hell was this about? 'What happened, Dad?'

He focused on topping up his cup.

'Did he tell you to sling your hook?'

'He seemed very unstable.'

'Okay, I'll bear that in mind. What did Victor say?'

'He'll think about it.'

And that's where they were before she went up to Edinburgh. She'd have to look at the other candidates they'd put on a tentative shortlist, but had to face that they both may need to step up and do more. Manage without a front man.

* * *

The next morning, she joined her father for breakfast in his kitchen. Much bigger than hers, they'd extended it onto the garden by adding an orangery, and it overlooked the lawn. As usual, he had the TV on, showing the local news, volume low. She sipped her coffee, glanced at the screen and almost spilled her drink.

'Can you turn it up, Dad?'

He used the remote that lay on the table in front of him.

'. . . I can assure your viewers, this has nothing to do with the death of the homeless man in the disused pub last week. He died of smoke inhalation after setting fire to the building. We believe he started the fire to keep warm. Yesterday's victim fell into the canal while drunk. In neither case—'

A reporter intervened: 'You've determined the gentleman was drunk?'

The interviewee looked uncomfortable for a moment. Then he gazed at her, exuding sincerity. 'Witnesses confirm he'd been drinking, and tests will show this. I can assure our unhoused population that there isn't a serial killer preying on them.' He smiled into the camera.

'Thank you, Chief Superintendent Mulberry.'

Her dad cut the volume. 'He's a smarmy git, isn't he? What are you so interested in that story for?'

She wasn't, but she did want to know what the hell DCS Gavin Mulberry had been doing in Edinburgh, and how come he'd happened to 'bump into her' in the bar of the Balmoral.

Had he been watching Robertson, or her?

CHAPTER 20

In Zofia and Kasper's kitchen, they watched the same footage.

'So that's the guy Colette warned us about,' Kasper said. 'He doesn't look that scary.'

Dressed more like an expensive lawyer than a policeman, his light brown hair was immaculate, and clear grey eyes stared straight into the camera lens. She caught a flash of irritation, which undermined the impression of sincerity he projected. Zofia had enough experience to know not to judge by appearances. Some of the nastiest people she'd met looked the most innocuous. And this one had her and her brother in his sights, an idea which made her most uncomfortable. All because of an investigation they'd already discontinued. She feared that contacting Rudy Glass to say they were no longer investigating him would be counterproductive. How the hell could they get him, *and* Mulberry, off their backs?

She considered what he'd said. 'He's decided Victor's friend killed himself. I wonder what Victor thinks about that?'

'He's probably right. It makes more sense than the idea of a serial killer preying on homeless men.'

Zofia wasn't sure. Mulberry would push the establishment narrative, and the idea these were unrelated accidents would appeal far more than the idea that the police were letting a murderer run amok. She remembered their mum talking about the Yorkshire Ripper and how the police didn't put in much effort while he killed prostitutes and only did so after he killed a student.

'We've agreed to help Victor. Don't forget, he's found the vehicle following Harry.'

'Hmm. A vehicle that *could* have been following him.'

She didn't want to get into an argument about it. Thoughts of Harry reminded her of Cleo and how much she'd missed her. The realisation she'd not see her at work added to her unhappiness.

She only caught the end of what Kasper was saying: '. . . couple of errands, so I'll meet you at work. Shouldn't be long.'

Not wanting to admit she hadn't been listening, she acknowledged him and followed him out of the house. On the journey, she reassured herself she would see Cleo as Victor would have to keep her in the van. She could visit her during breaks and take her for walks.

She arrived at work before Victor, uneasy about being first in. It was her first time opening up since the thug had attacked her. The guys at the takeaway hadn't opened, and she felt vulnerable as she unlocked the main door and reset the alarm. She was working her way through the post when Victor rang.

'Sorry, Zofia, I'm going to be late.'

'Everything okay?'

'I shouldn't be too long.' He ended the call.

Everything was obviously not okay, and he didn't want to confide in her. Stung by this, she told herself he might be in the middle of something, and she'd find out what was troubling him when he arrived. At ten, she heard the door open, and the sound of Oscar's claws on the laminate flooring in the reception told her it was Victor.

His earlier snub still rankled, so instead of asking how he was, she stood. 'Shall I take Cleo out for a walk?'

'She's not with me. Toff's taking care of her today. That's why I'm late, he was still asleep when I got to him. I didn't want to leave her in the van all day. Sorry.'

'Oh. Of course. It wouldn't be fair to leave her alone all day.' She tried to hide her disappointment and told herself off for being short with him.

'I can ask him to bring her over at lunchtime.'

'That's fine, I don't want to put him out.' She'd have to get used to not seeing her, and the sooner she did, the easier it would be for both. 'Do you want a drink while I'm up?' She noticed Oscar's disappointed expression. 'And you, Oscar. Lovely to see you.'

He wagged his tail, but she sensed he doubted her sincerity. She returned with a coffee and a bowl of water. Victor was ending a call.

'No dogs, right,' he said. 'Thanks.' His shoulders dropped, and he nodded a thanks for the drink.

'Trouble?'

'No, I just need . . .' He trailed off, then looked at Oscar. 'It's not just you now,' he said to the dog, then listened and said, 'No. I told you. That's final.'

She waited for him to respond to her. Although she sometimes found herself in what amounted to conversations with the dog, she worried at the extent to which Victor did it.

'Sorry, Zofia. I need to find another site for the van.'

'But I thought you liked that place.'

He gave a bitter laugh. 'I do. It's *they* who don't like me.'

'What happened?'

'Someone told them I was being charged with assault of that café owner. I'm pretty sure it's that shithouse cop, Lambert. I'm reading between the lines, but I suspect he suggested they move me on.'

'Oh, I'm sorry, Victor. You've heard nothing more from the police about those charges?'

'They'd laugh it out of court if they charged me.'

'Hmm. I wouldn't put it past them. Have you saved the footage of you serving him the summons? Email it to me, and we'll put it on our secure cloud server.'

'Yeah, I did that on Friday after he came round.'

She hesitated before giving him the next piece of news. 'Lambert's boss, Mulberry, was on telly this morning. He said they're treating your friend Harry's death as an accident.'

'What?'

'Sorry. He was being asked about another death last night—'

'Of another homeless man?'

'That's what he said.'

'Did they give a name?'

She thought back to the bit of the interview she'd heard. 'I don't think so. Sorry.'

Victor gave a puzzled frown. 'You sure they said last night?'

'Yeah, why?'

'We – John, Craig and I – offered a reward for anyone seeing the pickup which followed Harry. Someone saw it on Saturday night or early Sunday morning and took a picture. We checked, but there were no reports of attacks, so we assumed they'd just taken it for a drive.'

'Or maybe it wasn't the right car?'

'Yeah, well, I'm starting to think that.' He looked even more deflated.

She hated seeing him like this. 'Can you send me the picture?' It arrived attached to an email, and she opened it using their new image-enhancing software. She wasn't up to Kasper's standard with it, but she sharpened the photo enough to confirm the make. She compared it to the image they'd got from the CCTV at the takeaway. 'It's the same car.'

'You sure?' Victor joined her so that he could see her screen.

She pointed to a mark on the front wing in both images. 'That looks like the same dent.'

'It is. Fantastic, well done.' He squeezed her shoulder and then released it as if it were hot.

Her cheeks warmed, and she stared at the screen. 'A shame your friend didn't get the number plate.'

'He got a partial. It's a fifty-two, so the right age, and contained an R and a D.'

'In that order?'

'No such luck.'

She noted the details on a spreadsheet. 'We'll check all dark double-cab GMC Sierras registered as a fifty-two and find those still out there. There can't be many.'

'You might be right, but I'm wondering why they were out a day earlier if they killed the guy last night.'

'I can think of two good reasons. They might have needed to fuel up, or they went hunting on Saturday, but didn't find anyone.'

'You could be right.'

His cheerier demeanour improved her own mood.

'Where's Kasper?' he asked.

She checked the time. 'He said he'd be late, but it's almost eleven.'

As if on cue, the main door opened, and what sounded like a battalion of house movers came up the stairs. Zofia checked what was happening, and her brother staggered up the stairs carrying a box the size of his torso. Victor, who'd followed her into the waiting room, stepped forward to help and took the top end.

'It's not that heavy,' Victor noted.

'I never said it was.' A red-faced Kasper wiped his forehead with his free hand. 'It's just bulky.'

Zofia waited until they'd placed the box in the middle of the office floor. 'What is it?'

Kasper walked to his desk and picked up the scissors. 'A top-of-the-range air filter system. It's powerful enough to change the air in here three times an hour and clear it of contaminants, allergens and odours, including pet hair.'

Zofia's eyes filled up and her throat thickened. 'Oh, Kasper, thank you.' She hugged him until her tears stopped. 'Thank you, bro.' She kissed his cheek.

'Get off me.' He concentrated on opening the box, and within twenty minutes he'd set it up, and it emitted a low hum in the corner by the printer. 'Victor, can you help me reorganise the desks?'

Victor ended his call and helped Kasper move furniture while she focused on work. With a lot of swearing and grunting, they rearranged the office so Kasper could work under the window furthest from the dogs.

The doorbell rang, and Zofia answered it.

Toff made his way upstairs holding Cleo's lead. He'd had his brown hair cropped short and looked like he had another graze on his face. As always, Zofia thought he could do with a wash and a good feed. Cleo looked nervous until she sensed Zofia, then jumped at her, covering her hands, and then her face when she bent down, with kisses and licks. Zofia, her heart full, thanked Toff, who looked embarrassed, but more relieved than anything else. Victor took him downstairs and bought him a bucket of chicken from their neighbours, then returned.

Even Oscar seemed happy to have Cleo back. Zofia kept glancing at her, reassuring her that she was still there.

Victor made more calls until he finally heard what he wanted. 'Great. Yeah, I've got two. They're both well behaved, you'd hardly know I've got them.' He listened some more, nodding. 'I'll be there about six after work.' He ended the call wearing a big grin.

'You got somewhere?'

'Yeah. Near Heywood. And they're happy to have the dogs.'

Zofia, relieved to have got Cleo back at least during office hours, continued her search for the pickup. As she'd predicted, there weren't many fifty-twos left on the road. She was collating the results when Kasper swore.

'Cheeky sods!'

'What's up?'

'The bloody SPI.'

'Have they replied to our appeal already?' She'd hoped they'd reinstate their membership, but it didn't sound like it.

'Have they heck. No, listen to this: "It has come to our attention that one of your staff assaulted a man he was tasked with serving a writ on. This clearly goes against the requirement that you carry out these tasks without coercion, and you may have violated the legitimacy of the service. We will investigate and be speaking to the parties involved before deciding what action to take. In the meantime, please inform me what action you have taken against the employee." Pompous sod. I'm not having this.'

'Kasper, please think before—'

But he'd already dialled the number. She tried to get his attention to tell him to end the call while they passed him through a series of hoops, but he ignored her. She caught Victor's eye, and he shrugged.

'Right, so you're the one who wrote this letter. Who told you one of our staff assaulted someone?' He listened. 'Did the police officer identify himself?'

The voice on his speaker carried to Zofia as a tinny fuzz.

'Okay, I'll tell you who it was. A DS Lambert.' Kasper listened. 'Yes, I know his name because he's got a vendetta against us—' His knuckles tightened on the phone. 'Yes, we will be taking out a complaint. Did he tell you why they haven't charged my employee with assault, or any crime?'

Kasper shook his head and sighed.

'So, although my employee has committed no crime, I have to treat him like a criminal?'

He rolled his eyes.

'I don't need to. He told me he hadn't attacked anyone and showed me a video of him doing his job. He's not an aggressive man.'

Kasper's face reddened.

'Yes, I know, and we've appealed. Thank you.' He ended the call. 'For nothing. Pompous ass.'

Zofia gave her brother a few seconds. 'What did he say?'

'Unless we suspend Victor until we've carried out a full investigation, then they will expel us from the Society with immediate effect.'

'That's not fair. We're not doing it.'

Victor cleared his throat. 'You have to. You can't risk expulsion. I'll take leave. I'm due some, and I'll follow up on Harry's death until this blows over.'

She wanted to argue, but realised he was right.

Her worry though was that this might never blow over.

CHAPTER 21

I left Cleo with Zofia – I was meeting John and Craig, and Trixie might be there – and led Oscar out of the office. Zofia had assured me they'd keep me on full pay, however long this nightmare lasted. But the way they were being attacked, I had to wonder how long they could keep the business going at all, much less pay me for not working.

At least we'd found somewhere to stay tonight. I'd not mentioned I was looking for a long-term pitch; I'd do that once I'd seen how the land lay. Oscar seemed to be sulking as we crossed the main road.

'What's up?'

Why don't they get one of those air-cleaning boxes for Kasper's house?

I'd explained his allergy to Oscar, who interpreted the fact Kasper wasn't allergic to him as a sign of his superiority. 'They'd need one for each room.'

Is there a shortage?

'I've no idea, but they cost a few hundred quid each. And anyway, there's a difference between an office where he spends a few hours a day, and his home.'

It sounds like you're making excuses for him.

'It sounds like you want to be left behind in the van. We're going to see Trixie, are you coming?'

Why didn't you say?

He perked up, and we hurried to Sand Hills, a park on the northern edge of the city centre. The buildings lining the route looked in serious need of demolition or renovation, a stark contrast to those less than half a mile south of us. I knew dozens, including me, who'd jump at the chance of living in one of them if the council did them up.

I considered again Judy's offer. If I took the job, I'd have a fabulous apartment, not the cramped van. Even though winter hadn't set in, I already woke up freezing. And the van hadn't wanted to start this morning.

Then I remembered Novak's black expression when Craig baited him during our meal. And lest I forgot, not that long ago, the man had arranged for his daughter to lure me to a rendezvous so his men could kidnap and then torture me. And my head still contained information he desperately wanted about the bloody fate of his sons – not that I could ever really forget *that* particular night. I shuddered to think what Alex Novak would do to me if he knew my fragile skull harboured that data.

We crossed the River Irk, and a chemical stink came from either one of the units nearby or the less-than-clean-looking water flowing under the bridge. At the edge of the park, I unclipped Oscar. He sensed Trixie before I saw my friends and I trudged up the cobbled path in his wake, to join them on the bench they favoured. A black plastic bag full of dog mess had snagged on the side of the bin and perfumed the air as I passed it.

My friends studied a phone, grim-faced, and John held it out to me without preamble. He'd opened it to a local news page, which detailed the sad demise of the man the police had discovered this morning. The report stated that they believed the body had remained underwater in the canal for twenty-four hours, trapped under debris, before a jogger saw it.

John waited for me to finish. 'You know what that means, Brother?'

'They killed him on Saturday, so they must have been returning the pickup when matey saw it.' They hadn't been fuelling up, but returning from a successful 'hunt'. I felt sick.

Craig's gravelly voice broke the silence. 'I'm certain it's them, and they're hiding the car in the area we searched. If we can use the office, I can get a large-scale map and mark each building and who occupies it. The ones whose occupiers we can't identify will need checking.'

I inspected my footwear. 'Kasper's suspended me.'

'Whatever for, Brother?'

Craig gave a thunderous frown, making me fear for Kasper.

I told them what had happened.

'You still think Bombyx Mori is behind it?' Craig said.

'Who?'

'Our friend's joke, Brother. That's the Latin name for the silkworm, and you know what they eat?'

'Mulberry leaves?'

'Right in one.' Craig scratched his nose with a not-too-clean fingernail.

'I'm pretty sure Mulberry's behind the campaign against KZD,' I said, 'but that slimeball Rudy Glass is the one pulling his strings. Zofia did him a lot of damage with her investigation.'

'I saw Mulberry claiming both Harry and this latest guy died in accidents.'

At Craig's words, John's already grim expression blackened. I couldn't imagine how upsetting he must find the fact that the police had dismissed his brother's death, almost blaming Harry for starting the fire that killed him.

'If we can show him up by proving someone murdered them, we might get Mulberry off our backs.'

Craig snorted a laugh. 'Or make him more determined to nail you.'

I hadn't considered that possibility. 'Do we know who this latest victim is?'

'They haven't released his name, and we haven't heard of anyone going missing. There are so many new people on the streets of late it's hard to keep track.'

John brought the conversation back to my earlier point. 'Does your suspension mean you can't use the office?'

'As far as the SPI are concerned, I shouldn't go near the place, but if I go in when Zofia and Kasper aren't around, they can claim ignorance. We'll have to work outside office hours.'

'We can do that.' John checked the time. 'Do you want to start tonight?'

'I've got to collect Cleo and then drive up to Heywood, check into my new site.' I'd told them I was moving, but not why.

'Do you think it's worth speaking to the police, give them the information about sighting the pickup?'

I thought about my last encounter with Lambert. 'I see little point.'

'You said his boss might be a better bet?'

Grimes terrified me, and I had no desire to speak to him. 'I haven't got his number.' But I remembered an officer whose number I had and rang it.

'Victor, how can I help you?'

That she still had my number stored on her phone threw me. 'Colette, have you got a minute?'

'Anything to get a break from reviewing yet another return. Is it about Zofia's assault? How is she?'

'Physically okay, but she seems to have lost confidence.'

'That's not a surprise. I'd like to get hold of the bastard who attacked her.'

'You and me both.' Although not a violent man, I was prepared to make an exception. 'I'm concerned about the two homeless men killed in the last fortnight.'

'I can chase up what's happened to Zofia because I attended, but I have no involvement in those two cases. Sorry.' She sounded relieved not to be working under Mulberry's direction, rather than sorry.

'I appreciate that, but they're ignoring evidence of a link—'

'What evidence?'

I told her.

'And you've given all that to DS Lambert?'

'Not the latest.' I didn't want to mention that he'd accused me of assault. 'He made it clear he gave any information from me zero priority.'

'Especially as his boss dismissed any connections.'

'Grimes, you mean?' That was news to me – bad news.

She laughed. 'The boss above Darren.'

She had to mean Mulberry. 'Is it worth your having a word with Darr— DCI Grimes?'

'Hmm. Hang on.' She punched numbers, and my phone buzzed. 'I've sent you his number.'

'Right.' I swallowed. 'Thanks, Colette.'

John and Craig, who'd heard the exchange, looked expectant.

'I'll ring him now.' Despite my willing him not to pick up, he did.

'Yes. Who's this?'

'Hello, Chief Inspector, it's Victor. Peter Timothy.' I'd adopted the name Victor Mitchum when I ended up on the streets, promising I'd use my real name once I had a home and job. A tiny rusty van wasn't quite what I had in mind, and I felt I'd grown into the name Victor.

'Mr Timothy. How may I help you?'

I told him about the sightings of the pickup.

'How come I'm only hearing about this now?'

'I emailed some of the info to your sergeant, but not the latest sighting.'

He let out a growl followed by the sound of keystrokes. 'Yeah, the footage is here, but not the report that they'd followed Harry Sanders on a previous occasion.'

Why did that not surprise me? 'Shall I send the latest photos and location of the sighting?' I didn't intend to tell him we were searching for the vehicle in case he told me to stop.

'The chief super has deemed them accidents, so—'

'That's just bullshit! I know they were both killed.'

'If you'd let me finish?'

I imagined his scowl and quaked. 'Sorry.'

'Send me the image and the address where your informant took it. I'll flag it as an anonymous tip-off and check it out to "eliminate" it.'

'Right. Thanks.' I ended the call, hot and shaky.

John, Craig and I agreed to meet at nine the next morning at the disused petrol station where I'd bought the photo of the pickup, and I returned to the office. Although certain Kasper and Zofia wouldn't mind my using the office out of hours, I didn't want my doing so to compromise their chances of clearing their names.

'Would there be a problem if I came in to use my computer out of office hours?'

I waited while they exchanged a look. Zofia said, 'How would we know?'

'Wouldn't the monitoring company tell you if someone disabled the alarm?'

'Yeah, but we often work late, so they wouldn't think anything of it. If they don't tell us, we'd never know. I never check the alarm logs, do you, Kasper?'

'Well, actually, I— No, not unless . . . almost never.'

Zofia's fierce glower transformed into a smile.

Not for the first time, I wanted to hug her. 'Thank you.'

Cleo took such persuading to come with me that Zofia and I didn't say proper goodbyes. The fact I'd not be seeing my colleagues every day didn't sink in until we were on our way. A melancholy settled over me, and even Oscar noticed.

Don't worry, I'll take care of her.

'What?'

I'm assuming you're upset because we've got madam here to look after.

'Yeah, right. Thanks, Oscar.'

Don't mention it. He waited a beat. ***Of course, I will.***

'Of course.'

We left the M66 at Bury and followed the satnav to the new campsite. This was real countryside and, as we neared the site, the road became narrower, surrounded by trees losing their foliage. Signs for the site appeared, and I slowed, then pulled off onto the track leading to the office. Although in an idyllic setting, the site felt remote, especially for someone used to city living. They were expecting me, and a chunky, bald man wearing overalls welcomed me into the office.

He pushed a guest book on the desk to me. 'Get lost?'

'Sorry?'

'You said six.'

I checked the clock on the wall, seven minutes past. 'I missed the turning.'

'Aye, easily done. The first time.' *Don't do it again being the subtext.*

I paid for the three nights we'd agreed, and he showed me to my pitch. He looked at the dogs. 'Why's that got a megaphone on? Does it bite?'

'She's had an operation. It's to stop her licking or worrying the wound until the stitches come out.'

'Right.' He didn't look convinced. 'You sure they don't bark?'

'Rarely, and then only if there's something wrong, like a burglar.'

Or a nosey fat bugger.

I resisted telling Oscar off, and the man left us to it. I fed the dogs and cooked a simple dinner and then took them for a short walk. True to his promise, Oscar helped calm Cleo, and I put them in the front cab for the night, she on the seat and Oscar on the floor. Halfway through cleaning my teeth in the toilet block, a cacophony of barking summoned me out. The feeble lighting hanging from poles along the driveway fought a losing battle with the darkness.

To my chagrin, Oscar was leading the barking, with Cleo's shrill backing. 'What the hell's going on, Oscar?'

Before he could answer, the irate occupant of another caravan arrived, followed by the manager, swinging a powerful flashlight.

'You said they don't bark!'

'I'm really sorry. Being in a new place must have unsettled them. It won't happen again.' I'd bloody kill Oscar.

We all stopped as a car came out of the darkness and crept past, returning to the exit. The driver gave an ironic salute as he passed. Lambert.

CHAPTER 22

Judy was in her office, still thinking about Mulberry's presence in Edinburgh when another bombshell arrived.

'Three weeks, Jerry?'

Jerry Sweeny shrugged. 'I'm owed seven weeks according to my contract, three from last year.'

'I don't doubt it. But I thought we'd pay you for that. You never take your leave allowance.'

He looked embarrassed. 'The missus wants to go on a cruise before I start the new job.'

'For three weeks?' Judy couldn't imagine being stuck on a ship with strangers for a fraction of that time.

'Just two, but we're also babysitting the grandkids during half-term for a week. That's why I need to go tomorrow, so we can fit it in.'

'Grandkids?' She thought he was estranged from his daughter.

He reddened. 'Strictly speaking, they're step-grandkids. My second wife's. But I love them like my own.'

She realised how little she knew of Sweeny's life outside work, and, unable to think of a legitimate reason to refuse him, and embarrassed by her probing, she reluctantly agreed. From tomorrow, she and her dad would have to step up. She checked he was in and made her way to his office. Despite his criticism of her removing Marko's stuff from her office, most of Milan's things had gone from his and, of Marko's knick-knacks, he'd only kept two signed football shirts, one from each team in the city.

He was putting his phone away when she walked in. 'Right, I've arranged to meet Mouseheart.'

She'd never met the senior policeman her father referred to by that disparaging name. 'I don't want Mulberry finding out we've been asking about him.'

'No chance of that. The guy's shit-scared of him. Are you sure it wasn't just a coincidence that he bumped into you at the Balmoral?'

She'd not mentioned Mulberry had also seen her with Robertson. That was something her father mustn't discover, at least until she'd tied everything up. 'It might well be, Dad. But I want to make sure. "Know thy self, know thy enemy. A thousand battles, a thousand victories."' She quoted Sun Tzu.

Alex Novak frowned and then brightened. '"An overactive imagination turns men into cowards."'

'You calling me a coward?'

He reddened. 'No, of course not, love. I just mean, don't imagine enemies where there aren't any.'

'I won't, but I don't intend to bury my head in the sand.' *Bloody hell, find another cliché*. She took a seat. 'Has Jerry spoken to you?'

'Ahh. About the cruise?'

'When did you find out?'

'Just now, he—' He sighed. 'He rang me last night.'

'And you didn't think to tell me?'

'What could you have done? You'd have just worried.'

He was right, but it still annoyed her that Sweeny had told him first. He was still her father's creature. She'd make sure that whoever replaced him would owe their loyalty to her.

Alex cleared his throat and produced a sheet of paper from a drawer and slid it across the desk. 'I've sounded out a couple of people.'

'What?' She reached over and took the paper. He'd scribbled two names in his spidery hand. 'Who the hell are these two?'

'Some guys I know. They're sound. I thought Jerry taking a holiday would give us the opportunity to try them out.'

'Dad, these aren't interns or apprentices. Whoever does Jerry's job will know our business from the inside, and at the moment there are things that can do us serious harm in the wrong hands. They could even—'

'Whoa, whoa!' Alex held up his hands, palms forward. 'These aren't mugs. They're people I trust.'

She glanced down at the paper. The names appeared as blurred letters, and she took a deep breath. 'We won't be employing any of your cronies. Anyone who works for me must understand that I'm the boss. I don't want them running to you first. Is that clear?' By the time she'd finished, she held Alex's gaze.

He broke it first. 'Yeah, of course. I'm just trying to help.'

'Yeah, thanks.' She stood and picked up the paper. 'I'll speak to them.'

Her dad nodded, and she returned to her office. She could have done with a drink, but made do with a strong coffee. To her surprise, both men her father had suggested had significant online footprints, including LinkedIn profiles. More surprises, they held high-profile corporate roles. She parked her prejudices and looked at them with fresh eyes.

How would she feel if they'd applied to a job ad or recruitment consultants had sent their details? She had to admit she'd have interviewed them. She made an internal call.

'Dad, have you spoken to these two?'

'I thought I'd leave it to you.'

'Right, thanks. Where did you meet them, and how much do they know about what you do?'

'I'm a successful businessman, like they are. They belong to the same lodge. They've got lots of contacts, especially if we're going into property.'

'Right, thanks, Dad.' She'd forgotten that he belonged to several business networks. Many of them not open to her.

She needed a more in-depth search of the two potential candidates. There was someone she knew who could do that. But they had links with the man she'd already offered the job to. She decided it wouldn't hurt him to discover he wasn't the only fish in the pool and rang the number.

'Zofia, I've got a job for you.' The contrast with the first time they met, when Judy had been posing as a homeless woman and Zofia gave her a tenner, made her smile.

'Judy. This is a surprise. What sort of job?' Zofia didn't hide her reluctance, despite the fact Judy had helped her to expose Glass.

'I'm looking for a new chief executive and want you to carry out background checks.'

'Okay, that's a straightforward assignment.' She hesitated. 'Is this the job you offered Victor?'

'Will that be a problem?'

'No. And obviously he won't be involved in this investigation.'

Judy would rather he found out. 'I'm sure that if Victor were to learn of this investigation, he'd be professional enough not to sabotage—'

'Of course, that wouldn't happen. What I meant was, we don't want any suggestion of impropriety.'

'Of course not. What *I* meant was, I have no concerns about Victor learning we're looking elsewhere.' Was that a bit too on the nose? 'Can I have your findings this week?'

'No problem.'

Judy ended the call, almost certain Victor would discover she was looking at other candidates. Her phone buzzed with a call from her father.

'You ready? We should go soon.'

She checked the time. 'Give me five.'

They took the lift down, and Billy had the converted people carrier waiting at the back entrance. The drive to the meeting venue took ten minutes, and they pulled up around the back of the pub, which lay just outside the city centre. Built in the Victorian era, when terraced houses lined the surrounding streets, it now stood in isolation on a street corner.

The mean houses it once towered over had gone, replaced by modern blocks of apartments soaring above it. Her father had used it to meet informants in an upper room but, without a lift, that was now impossible. The odour of stale beer attacked Judy's nostrils as Billy helped manoeuvre her dad's chair through a narrow corridor into what she took to be the manager's living room on the ground floor.

Judy had plans for the place, and they didn't include keeping the existing management team. She settled into the threadbare armchair next to her dad while Billy hurried off to collect their 'guest'. Her father's irritation at having to be helped showed in his face and body language.

'Dad, calm.' She reached across and gripped the back of his hand.

'Yeah, yeah, don't fuss.'

Billy returned alone. 'He's not here, Boss.'

'Where the hell—'

'We're a bit early, Dad.'

'What?' He checked the time. 'Yeah, s'pose so. Send him through when he arrives.' Billy left them, and her father cleared his throat. 'I've been thinking about the two names I gave you. They're not right for us.'

'What do you mean? I looked them up, and they seem excellent.'

'Don't get me wrong, they're good lads, but a bit corporate, you know. Not sure they'd fit in.'

She had got that impression, but assumed her dad had sounded them out. 'I've already asked Zofia to do a background check.'

''Ave yer?' He looked pleased.

'I can tell her to drop it, but I thought it might get back to Victor . . .'

He chuckled. 'You're a real chip off the old block, aren't you?' A note of pride deepened his voice.

She wasn't sure how much of a compliment she saw it as. 'So who do we get instead?'

'I'll have another go at Victor.'

'I thought you didn't like his mates?'

'Well, that's his mates. Anyway, it was just Craig. And I've been thinking about it. I saw me arse because he stood up to me, but that's the sort of guy we need. If a little squirt in a wheelchair intimidates you, you're not much of a man, are you?'

Bloody hell, Dad, all it took was a bullet in the spine and you've become philosophical. 'Yeah, you're probably right.'

A soft knock and the door opened. The man who entered on her father's terse response had to duck beneath the doorframe. He looked the part of a heavyweight, but something about his eyes didn't convince. Judy wondered if her father's disparaging comments, as well as the nickname – Mouseheart – he'd given him, had influenced her judgement.

She signalled for him to sit and, after checking with her dad, he sank into a similar chair opposite hers, his solid bulk leaving him lower. His attempt to make himself taller made her smile.

Her father gestured to Judy. 'My daughter, Judy, who's taking over the firm.'

'Pleased to meet you, Ms Novak.'

She ignored his half-offered hand and nodded a greeting. 'My father assures me you won't discuss anything we say in this room.'

He smiled. 'Do I look like an idiot?'

She glared until the smile slid away.

'Of course.'

'What can you tell me about Mulberry?'

A look of panic crossed his face, and he regarded her father, who retrieved a brown envelope from inside his jacket and handed it to him.

'Our friend likes his money upfront.'

Mouseheart glanced at the contents and put the envelope away. 'What do you want to know?'

Judy wanted to give this man as little information as she could. 'Why would he be interested in what I'm doing?'

'He might be investigating your family—'

Her father slapped the arm of his chair. 'We're not asking about his official investigations. What are his extracurricular activities?'

Mouseheart blinked. 'How would I know about that?'

'Because you're a senior copper in the same force as him. Now, what's he involved in?'

He swallowed. 'There's a rumour he's working for a property developer.'

'Name?'

'It's just a rumour.'

Judy could see the effect her father had on the man and leant forward, cutting off her dad's next intervention.

'Is it someone local or from Scotland?'

He nodded. 'Scotland. Yeah, that's what people are saying.'

A nasty taste filled Judy's mouth. Was Robertson stringing her along while manoeuvring behind her back?

CHAPTER 23

The fact Mulberry's lackey Lambert had already tracked me down to the new site kept me awake, and my alarm found me exhausted, my eyes sore and head full of straw. I stumbled out of bed into the freezing rain and hurried to the toilet block. Despite persuading him the unknown intruder had alarmed the dogs, the site manager had made it clear I – more specifically, the dogs – were on probation and one more outburst would lead to expulsion.

I had lots of bridge-building to do before I could even ask to extend my stay past the three days I'd paid for. The shower delivered a dribble of lukewarm water and, still chilled, I ran back to the van. Neither dog wanted to leave the dry but cold van, so I put the heater on while I fed them. A cup of tea with my porridge warmed me up, and I worried about Lambert's next step.

Had he known where to find me, or had he searched the caravan parks until he did? Either way, the development wasn't good. Would I return tonight to discover I'd have to move on again? The manager would need little persuading to chuck me out. I decided not to worry about it, but it was easier said than done. I took the dogs for a short walk in the nearby woods, Cleo reluctant to leave my side while Oscar ran off exploring.

Despite the joy of seeing him happy, a darkness settled over me on our way to meet John and Craig.

A call from Zofia alarmed me. 'Everything okay?'

'Yeah, fine. How's the new place?'

'Great—'

Liar!

I gave him a glare in the mirror. 'Very rural, but Oscar loves it.'

Don't you understand the concept of making the most of your situation? It's something you could do with adopting.

I ignored him. 'How can I help you?'

'I presume you're working with John and Craig. You said Trixie doesn't get on with Cleo?'

I voiced an idea I'd been toying with: 'Could I leave her at the office?'

'That's what I was going to suggest.'

'Great.' I'd just joined the M60, so indicated to come off.

Funny how a phone call can change your mood.

'What do you mean?'

A minute ago, you were ready to drive into the central barrier. Now you're ready to go dancing.

'Have you ever seen me dancing?'

Stop deflecting.

'I'd been worrying about Cleo and Trixie, this solves my problem.'

Yeah, okay, I believe you.

I ignored him, irritated that I was so transparent that a dog, admittedly a bright one, could see through me.

I'll never understand humans.

Although I knew I'd regret it, I decided to bite. 'In what way?'

If I meet another dog, we sniff each other's bottoms, decide if we like each other and then we're either friends or not. You obviously like Zofia, and she likes you.

'How do you know?'

Sheesh! You don't have to be particularly observant to see it. Anyway, you're always pushing her away.

'No, I'm not.' I didn't like the way this was going.

Okay, let's pretend I'm wrong.

I felt the need to defend myself. 'It's complicated. She doesn't want to be tied to a homeless failure.'

It hasn't bothered her, from what I can see. But I'm only a dog.

'There's also Carol. Don't forget I'm still married.'

In name only. She's got a boyfriend. Helen told us all about him.

I still wasn't sure how I felt about that. To my relief, we'd arrived at our destination, and I could extract myself from this conversation. 'You be alright in the van while I take Cleo up to the office? I won't be long.'

Whatever. Zofia barely notices me now Cleo is around. Nobody does.

Was that true? I hadn't ignored him, had I? But I'd make sure he got plenty of attention. As we pulled into the car park at work, Cleo, who'd been lying on the front seat, sat up and let out a bark. The rain had eased off, and after attaching her lead, I let her out and decided to take Oscar.

'You coming, Oscar?' I opened the rear door.

Don't mind me, I'll just wait here.

'Okay.' I closed the door and walked two paces before returning. 'Come on, Eeyore.' I clipped his lead on, and he almost leapt out.

To his and my delight, Zofia made a big fuss of him; she must have realised she'd neglected him. Despite the underlying tension, I soaked up the comforting companionship and even stayed for a coffee, putting off having to leave. Kasper fretted as the clock approached nine, and we left, promising to collect Cleo at the end of the day.

John and Craig waited under the shelter of the canopy at the disused petrol station. Both carried takeaway coffees and looked to be wearing their best clothes. Trixie wore a purple ribbon and barked a greeting as we got out. Craig had a rolled-up map of the area and a writing pad in a carrier bag. I opened the rear of the van, lowered my bed, and we spread out the map upon it. We gathered around the opening, creating a makeshift windbreak.

Craig traced a rough rectangle on the map, starting from where we were. 'If we use the railway line, Hyde Road, Pottery Lane and Ashton Old Road as the boundary, that's the area we need to search. Here' – he placed a large hand in the southeast corner – 'is mostly housing, so, unless they have a garage, we ignore them. You should check those, Victor, as you'll be quicker in the van. For the bigger premises, we need to note who occupies them, if we can, so that will be slower. You can drop me here.' He pointed to a road junction near an industrial estate before moving his finger. 'And John, here. When we finish our sections, we report back and help whoever's struggling. Make notes on these.' He ripped sheets from the pad and handed them out. 'Obviously, if we find the car parked on a drive or in a car park, we're laughing. Questions?'

As usual, Craig had summarised what needed doing. He rolled up the map and returned it to the bag while I folded the bed away. Craig sat in the front seat while John stayed in the back with Oscar and Trixie. I dropped them off as directed and let Oscar join me in the front while I carried out my reconnaissance. As Craig had suggested, my job consisted of driving up and down roads and confirming none had somewhere to hide a vehicle.

Most of the roads around there were dead ends, and I did a lot of reversing and turning around. Although most of the houses didn't have a garage at the front, I discovered some people had put gates in their back fence so they could drive into their back yards. Most were made of open bars or had gaps so you could see the vehicles. One had heavy black steel gates, and I stopped beside it.

I saw nobody in the narrow back lane and got out. There were no gaps between the uprights and the gate, nor at the centre where the two halves met. The gates stood over two metres high with metal spikes on the top. I grabbed two, shoulder-width apart, and pulled myself up.

'Oi! What do you think you're doing?' A dreadlocked man, his bare shoulders and arms swathed in tattoos, glared at me from inside the yard and lowered a kettlebell the size of my head to the ground.

I dropped onto the road as he dragged open one of the gates. As he did so, a large black dog leapt through the gap, teeth snapping.

CHAPTER 24

Once Victor had left that morning, Zofia took Cleo to the huge pet store where Victor had bought Oscar's harness. She bought Cleo a coat, having noticed her shivering. The poor animal was already thin, being half *galgo* – a breed she'd never heard of until Victor told her about them – and half springer, but she'd also been underfed. Once she'd put her coat on, Zofia took her for a walk, mainly to spend time with her, and give Kasper respite. She'd noticed him sniffing yesterday, even with the filter on. Cleo seemed much less timid and even let a dog approach her without seeking the shelter of Zofia's legs. So far, she'd only let Oscar near her.

By ten thirty, she felt guilty at being out for so long and returned to the office. Kasper had something to say, but as usual he didn't come out with it. He did as she brought the coffees.

'I don't think we should see Victor when he brings Cleo.'

'He had a coffee today, but it's the first morning.'

'I know, but we're claiming we don't know he's coming to the office.'

She realised he was right. 'Okay. I'll wait until he arrives and tell him.' It made sense, but she'd rather she didn't have to do it.

Cleo sat under her desk, despite it being closer to Kasper than her bed. He didn't complain, so Zofia let her, enjoying her proximity. She'd been thinking about the campaign against them.

'You got a few minutes to talk?'

'Sure.' Kasper came towards her and then sneezed and stopped.

'Shall we go into the boardroom?' She told Cleo to stay and followed him into the separate room they used for meetings, closing the door behind her. A snuffle and scratch on the door told her Cleo wasn't happy being left alone. She dismissed her concern for the dog and focused on what Kasper was saying.

'Okay, I assume it's about what's happening to us.'

'Yeah.' She nodded. 'We hurt Glass once, by exposing his corruption, and he thinks we're still investigating him, so he's trying to stop us by setting Mulberry on us.'

'We can't prove any of this.'

'I know, but do you think I'm wrong?'

'Nope.' Kasper steepled his fingers. 'But how do we take on a senior police officer everyone seems shit-scared of?'

'I don't know. But if he's acting on behalf of Glass, we need to get Glass to back off.'

'How do we do that?'

'I've told the news site paying us to investigate him we've done all we can and aren't doing any more. I'm hoping the message will get back to him—'

'How long's that going to take?' Kasper looked despondent. 'Why don't *we* tell Glass we're not investigating him?'

Much as she wanted to reassure her brother, she didn't think this a good idea. 'What do we say? "We know you've got a corrupt relationship with Mulberry and are using him to attack us, but please stop, because we're not investigating you?"'

'Of course not.' He frowned. 'But there must be something we can do.'

'We need to find a link between Glass and Mulberry. If we can show a corrupt connection, we can use it as a lever to get them both to back off.'

Kasper exhaled and scratched his right earlobe. 'What if we find something, and they don't back off?'

'Then we put it out there, like we did with Glass last time.'

'And just piss him off even more. And Mulberry.'

'What do you suggest, then? We roll over and die like cowards?' She regretted saying it as she spoke. 'Sorry, I didn't mean that.'

They sat in silence for a long moment.

'You're right, sis. We need to fight back. Let's look for something and, if we find it, assess how damaging it will be. To them and us. In the meantime, we try to get the assault charges against Victor dropped. Then address the issue with Casin and get our SPI membership reinstated. If we can get those cleared up and Glass leaves us alone, I'll be happy.'

'And let him get away with it?'

'They always do. We just need to make sure we're not crushed beneath their feet.'

She wasn't sure if hearing him say this depressed her more than her knowing he was right. They returned to their desks, she letting Cleo sit at her feet while she worked.

The first thing to do was get them to drop the charge against Victor. Part of her suspected there wasn't one and the police would never charge him with the offence Lambert accused him of. She contacted Stretford station, assuming that's where the investigating officers came from, and posed as his solicitor. They didn't have any record of Victor being accused of a crime, let alone being charged.

Frustrated by the lack of information, she contacted Bowling and told her what had happened.

'They haven't charged Victor for the café assault yet?'

Zofia was sure he'd have said something this morning. 'Not yet.'

'Hmm. You said it happened on Friday, so they could be gathering evidence before deciding to charge him.'

'But wouldn't Stretford at least have a record of his being accused?'

'There should be a report, but they may not have it on the system yet. You said Lambert told you about it, so until he enters the details, it won't show up.'

'We can't prove that Victor isn't being charged?'

'What you need to do is gather any evidence you have to refute the accusation. Be ready to fight back. Have you got a decent solicitor?'

'I'll contact them. Thanks, Colette.'

She put the phone down and realised she hadn't asked about the investigation into *her* assault outside the office in the early hours of last Thursday, but surely Bowling would have said if there was news. The mark on her forehead had almost gone, and she wanted to forget about it. Although the thought of the man who'd attacked her still being free made her uneasy.

'No joy?' Kasper studied her with a questioning look.

She brought him up to date and emailed their solicitor. She'd send the footage of the incident Victor had recorded later.

A call from Judy caught her out. 'Sorry, Judy, I haven't finished the investigation—'

'That's okay, Zofia. I'm ringing to tell you to cancel it. Send me an invoice for whatever you've done.'

'Is Victor taking the job, then?' She held her breath, waiting for the reply.

'We're no longer considering the two candidates. Thanks, Zofia.' She ended the call.

'Was that Novak's daughter?'

'We should call *him* Judy's father. And yes, it was. She wanted me to investigate two candidates for the job she offered Victor, but she's now told me not to bother.'

'Does that mean he's taken the job?' A rising inflection showed Kasper's disappointment.

'She wouldn't say, but I suspect Judy wants Victor to know they're looking elsewhere.'

'To what end?'

'I'm not sure. To make him decide sooner rather than later?'

'You going to tell him?'

Was she? 'I'm not sure I enjoy being manipulated. He'll make his own decision.' And she hoped it would be the right one.

The solicitor replied, and Zofia sent Victor's footage, then arranged a meeting the next morning. Kasper worked on Mulberry's career, tracing his impressive rise through the ranks and cataloguing the high-profile cases he'd worked on, especially during his three years in fraud. Zofia, conscious they'd done no fee-earning work today, took Cleo out for an hour.

When she returned, Kasper had clearly been working himself up to say something. 'Okay, spit it out, Kasper.'

'I know you've agreed that we mustn't see Victor when he comes in, but I don't think that's enough. We need to tell him he can't use the office—'

'No!'

'Yes!'

She blinked. Kasper never contradicted her. 'You think the way he's been treated is fair?'

'Of course it isn't. But we've got to think about ourselves. We've built up a good business, let's not risk—'

'Thanks in a big part to Victor.'

'I'm not disputing that.' He took a deep breath. 'It's pretty obvious, even to an unobservant PI like me, you're attracted to each other.'

'No, we're not. We're just colleagues.'

'Yeah, right.' He snorted. 'But you're not colleagues. You and me are his employers. We may have to let him go.'

'No!'

'It may not come to that. He may even leave of his own volition. But if he doesn't, and this campaign against us doesn't end – or it does and we're so damaged we can't afford to keep him on – we'll need to consider all alternatives. And now is the time we ought to get ahead on that consideration.'

Though her heart was pounding, Zofia, who'd always seen herself as the practical one in the partnership, realised her brother was right. 'Yeah, okay. But we can't stop him from using the office. They're looking for the men who killed John's brother.'

'If you believe their claims.'

'And I do. Kasper, this isn't negotiable.'

He glanced at his hands. 'Okay, he uses the office. But we mustn't see him, and we must prioritise our survival.'

And whatever that entailed. 'Yeah, of course.'

'Sorry, Zofia. I know things are tough, but we need to stick together. Family is everything, don't forget that.'

How could she? Kasper was her brother, and she'd promised Mum she'd look after him. No matter what.

CHAPTER 25

The dreadlocked man thrust out a large hand and grabbed the collar around the black hound's neck. Despite the man's muscular frame, he struggled to hold the animal, but after he spoke to it in soothing tones, it calmed down.

I waited until my pulse slowed. 'Hi. I'm looking for a car that almost ran me off the main road early Sunday morning.'

'And you think that was me, do you?' The dog glared at me with a baleful expression as though seconding his master.

My mouth dried, and I swallowed. 'I've no idea until I see the car. *Was* it you?'

'No, it bloody well wasn't.' He came closer, bringing the dog with him. It panted, an eager glint in its eye. I could almost smell its breath.

'Glad that's cleared up.' I edged past the open gate and glimpsed the back of a bright metallic green saloon. 'See you, then.'

I'd gone three paces before he said, 'What car was it?' He'd retired his angry tone and his dog, now looking bored, sat in the open gateway.

'It's a GMC Sierra pickup with—'

'An extended cab?'

My pulse jumped with excitement rather than fear. 'You seen it?'

'Yeah, the arsehole almost took my wing off. Must have been the same night he did you.'

'Where was this?'

'Over there.' He pointed north, the direction I'd dropped John.

'You don't remember which road?'

'Sorry, mate, I was with me girl. A bit distracted.' He winked and showed a collection of white and gold teeth.

'No problem. You've been a great help, thanks.'

'When you catch him, give him one from me.'

I waved and got back in the car.

I was ready to come to your aid, but you'd locked me in.

'Not to worry. I'm saving you for when I really need help. Maybe if it's another dog, like Tyson.'

Great, thanks.

His show of coolness was well short of convincing. My mention of the fearsome, aggressive dog of a neighbour in our halfway house had had the desired effect. He looked so worried, I laughed.

I rang Craig, who answered with his usual grunt, and told him what I'd discovered.

'Okay, that's useful, but we need to be systematic. Let's finish what we're doing now and then focus on the area he mentioned for phase two.'

We've got a phase two? 'Yeah, no problem.' It made sense, and I continued my traverse of the side streets.

I was congratulating myself on making good progress when I drove into a street of new townhouses with built-in garages. Each had the gates closed, so I couldn't tell what was behind them. I drove to the end of the street and turned around. A curtain twitched in the end house, so I stopped, got out and approached it.

I called up the image of the truck on my phone and rehearsed my story as I waited for an answer to my ring. An older guy with grey stubble and glasses opened the door.

'Hi, I wonder if you can help me.' I told him the story I'd used on the man with the dog and showed him a picture of the vehicle on my phone.

He took it from me and peered at the screen. 'That will be the lads at number eleven.'

'Are you sure?' My voice went up.

'Yeah, they got one of them. They're always coming home in it late, blaring loud music. I've told the council, but they've done nothing.'

'What time do they usually come home?'

'Eleven, midnight, sometimes later.'

'They're not home now?'

He stepped out onto the pavement. 'Nah. Can't hear any music.'

'Thanks.' I took my phone off him and returned to the van to report to Craig, who again told me to finish the task at hand.

An hour later, we met at a mobile canteen parked at the entrance to an industrial estate. After getting sandwiches and chips, we exercised the dogs and carried out a catch-up. The rain, which had eased off, returned with a vengeance, and we squeezed ourselves into the back of the van, wishing we still had use of the KZD offices.

Craig produced his map, damp at the edges despite the plastic bag. 'Where was this house where the bloke told you there's a pickup?'

I got my bearings, found the street and pointed. 'It's the one in the middle.'

'That's not near where the other guy said he'd seen it.'

'Which of the two seemed the most reliable witness, Brother?'

I considered. 'One was sure about his vehicle, but the other looked like a neighbourhood watch type.' I told them what he'd said.

Craig frowned. 'Playing loud music's not how I'd expect these two killers to behave. They'd be keeping a low profile.'

'What do you suggest?'

He shrugged. 'We need to check both.'

We finished our takeaway teas, and the rain eased. I drove to the area the man with the dog had directed me to, and we split up. The neighbourhood contained many small industrial units, often without signage. We'd almost finished our survey when the rain returned with biblical intensity. We returned to the van, filling it with a fuggy, wet-fabric stink.

John checked the time. 'Can we use the office now, Brother?'

It was almost six, and the heavy cloud made it seem later. 'I'm sure we can. Shall we call it a day here and collate the information we've gathered?'

Neither objected, and I drove to the office, relieved to find Zofia's car still there. We left the dogs in the van, edged past the queue at the chicken shop, and I unlocked the office. Zofia greeted us with her coat on.

'You going?' I couldn't hide my disappointment.

'I'm not supposed to know you're using the office.'

'Oh, of course. Sorry.' At least I'd see her tomorrow morning.

'Where's Oscar?'

'Keeping Trixie company.'

'Right.' She bit her lip. 'In the morning, you can leave Cleo here and go before we arrive?'

'Has anything happened?'

'Nothing to worry about.' She turned away from me, said goodbye to Cleo, and then the three of us before leaving. Cleo tried to follow, and I held her back, stroking her until her pitiful cries stopped.

Once Cleo realised Zofia wasn't coming back, she quietened, and I held her, understanding how she felt.

'You alright, Victor?' Craig said with surprising tenderness.

I stood. 'Tea or coffee?'

We printed three new maps using Kasper's A3 printer. Then, using a laptop so we didn't leave a footprint on the desktops, Craig transferred all the information from the notepad pages to a spreadsheet while John and I annotated the maps. Around eight we ate from the takeaway downstairs and, exhausted from my broken sleep, I called it a day. The others didn't object.

The rain had stopped, and a bright moon sat in a clear sky. Trixie bared her teeth at Cleo when she tried to enter the van, so Craig removed her, and he and John walked into town.

Oscar stared at Cleo's jacket. ***Can I have one?***

'No, you've got plenty of fur and fat.'

How dare you! That's relaxed muscle.

'Whatever it is, is keeping you warm enough.'

I started back for the campsite, then felt guilty about not checking the house where the men with the pickup lived. I'd drive past and see if they'd come home yet.

The lights were out, so I drove past, turned around and parked on the opposite side of the road. I felt exposed when I realised there were no other cars on the road. Before I could move, the loud rumble of a powerful engine came from the far end of the road, and high-beam headlights blinded me. Then, I heard the music. The vehicle stopped, and someone got out.

I couldn't see much past the lights, but the beams swung round as the driver reversed towards the garage door. I started my engine and put on my headlights. The driver stopped reversing and stared at me. A young Asian lad and the vehicle was a Nissan. I drove past, ignoring his glare, overcome with a mixture of relief and disappointment.

Can we go home now?

We weren't far from the last few units we'd yet to check on the final industrial estate. It wouldn't take long at this time of night. 'Soon.'

I parked where we'd finished that afternoon and got out. No streetlights showed. 'You want to come with me?'

Are you scared of the dark?

'You coming?'

Keep your hair on.

Cleo wasn't interested, so I took Oscar and checked the final few units. The last three were round the corner from the van, and I noted the phone number of the occupiers of the only one with signage outside. Oscar grew agitated as we returned.

'What's up, boy?'

Then I saw them. Two men in dark uniforms shone a lamp into the van. I assumed they were police and came up with my story. But I saw their vehicle and realised they weren't coppers, but private security. I'd had awful experiences with private security operatives.

'Alright, gentlemen?'

Two torches shone into my face, then one focused on Oscar.

'This is private property.'

I shielded my eyes with a forearm. 'I'm just taking the dog for a walk.'

'You cleared up after your mutt?'

The voice brought back terrible memories. 'He just needed a piss.'

'I know you, don't I?'

'I don't think so.' The last time I'd met him, I'd been on the streets with a matted beard and stained clothes. He wouldn't recognise me now.

The other one spoke. 'Yeah. I know your dog. Mate.' He infused the last word with a world of menace.

'I've not had him long.'

The second man circled me so he came alongside and shone his torch into my face. 'You was the cunt spying on Milan Novak's place just before he got killed. You got the same voice.'

Shit!

CHAPTER 26

The next morning, as Zofia sat in her kitchen, gathering her energy to face a day at work, her mood as dark as the weather outside, a call arrived from Victor. She snatched up her phone, but it cut off before she could answer it. She called back, but it rang out.

'Who was that?' Kasper buttered another slice of toast.

'Victor, but he's not answering.'

'Probably a pocket call.' He bit a corner off the slice.

'So why doesn't he answer?' She tried again and got the same result. A sense of panic infused her, a certainty that something had happened to him. 'Where did you say he was staying?'

'Somewhere near Rochdale. Why?'

She opened her map app and checked caravan sites. Two showed up, and she read out their names.

'The second one. You're not thinking of going?'

She finished the dregs of her coffee and stood. 'I am. Can you go to the solicitor's? You know what to say.'

'Hang on, what are you going to do?'

'I'm going to see what's happened.'

'You remember what happened last time we panicked because we couldn't get hold of him? I got shouted at by his landlord, and we found out he'd been in bed with the phone off.'

'Yes, but he rang me first and the phone's not off. He's not answering it.'

'I told you. It will be a pocket call, and he's on the toilet or something, embarrassed to pick up.'

She tried again with the same result. So did Kasper. She stepped into the corridor. 'You satisfied now?'

'I'll come with you.'

'You see the lawyer. I'll ring you once I get there.'

The wind flung rain at the windows, and she wrapped up in her winter gear before going out. Her satnav told her the journey would take forty-seven minutes. She took the motorway, cursing when she caught the traffic around Stockport. Spray and rain reduced visibility, and her wipers struggled to keep up. A sense of panic gripped her insides and made her want to drive too fast.

She left the motorway at Bury and, after traversing narrow lanes lined with houses, she was out into the countryside. Trees and hedges on the verge crowded the road, and then she saw the sign for the caravan park, almost missing the turning and earning an angry blast from behind as she slammed on the brakes, skidding for a heart-stopping second. She gave an embarrassed wave and took the sharp bend at walking pace.

The narrow, twisting lane passed farms, and the trees opened up to reveal fields. The road narrowed, and she feared she'd taken the wrong turning and would end up in a farmyard. Then she saw the entrance. Blue lights reflected off trees, and her pulse jumped. She raced into the campsite and followed the road around. A fire engine, lights flashing, blocked her way. Beyond it, surrounded by firefighters and civilians, was a corner of Victor's van. On its side. She slewed to a stop, threw off her seat belt and jumped out.

CHAPTER 27

During my last encounter with the two thugs masquerading as security guards, I'd been watching a warehouse where a monster had murdered two women. Fed up because Kasper had made me walk across town to change a battery in a hidden camera, I'd insulted both. This time, I'd hoped that a humbler persona, and my tidier appearance, would persuade them I wasn't the same man. But they'd refused to accept my claim that Oscar was a recent addition to my family.

'That's my dog.' I pointed at Cleo. 'We just got this one from an animal shelter.'

The larger of the two, a bearded figure with a scar across his cheek, peered into the van. 'Why's she got a megaphone on 'er 'ead?'

'It's stopping her from biting her stitches. I had to get her spayed when we got O— Ollie here.' Did I call Oscar when they last saw me, and if I did, would they remember his name? It hardly seemed likely.

They stepped away and held a quick confab. I didn't dare look at Oscar. They returned, and I could tell it wasn't good news.

'Mr Novak is offering ten grand for that dog.' He pointed at Oscar.

I fought the urge to run. 'Alex? You're joking. We were with him the other day.'

'Fuck off! You don't know Mr Novak.'

I retrieved my phone and rang his number.

'What you doing?'

'I'm calling him.' I willed him to answer and turned on the speaker.

'Victor?' He sounded surprised.

'Hi Alex.'

'Why are you ringing me at this time?'

'I've got a couple of lads here who're giving me a hard time and are keen to speak to you.' I held the phone to the nearest, who took it as if I was handing him a live grenade.

'Hello. Are you Mr Novak?' He spoke like someone who'd never used a telephone.

'What sort of question's that? Who the hell are you?'

'They call me Ox.'

'Do they? Is it for your intelligence?'

'No, it's—'

'That's what you call a rhetorical question, Ox. It means you don't have to answer. This next one isn't. Why the fuck you giving my mate Victor a hard time?'

I wished Novak would tone it down, but it seemed to have the desired effect.

'Yeah, sorry, Mr Novak. We're just doing our jobs.'

'Yeah? Well, do it somewhere else, and if I hear you've given Victor any more grief, you'll be joining all the other bovines at the abattoir.'

'Right.' He swallowed.

'Put Victor back on.'

He handed my phone back, and I took it off speaker.

'You got an answer for Judy?'

I could barely hear because of the whooshing in my ears. 'Thanks, Alex, have a great evening and I'll see you tomorrow, usual place.' I ended the call before he could respond.

The two men sidled off back to their car, heads bent and shoulders hunched. I tugged on Oscar's lead and returned to the van, fighting the urge to run. Once back in the van, I started the engine. The headlights of the security men's car came on, almost blinding me, and they shot past, engine revving in fury.

I set off for home, my legs shaking and sweat pouring down my neck.

Ollie?

'I couldn't think of anything better on the spur of the moment.'

You got me from a shelter, did you?

'I'll happily put you in one.'

So, you and madam can live without me?

'At least thugs from our past won't recognise me and attempt to hand me in for a bounty.'

I knew it would be my fault for being too good-looking. I've told you to get rid of me many times. Don't let me stop you now.

Too tired to argue, I made my way to the campsite, almost going off the road twice when I dozed. I took the dogs for a short walk and, after a quick wash, fell into bed. A troubled sleep peopled by monsters from my past, including a man with a red snake tattoo, lasted until my alarm woke me. Still clumsy from sleep, I dialled Zofia while trying to stop the sounder.

'Shit.'

I killed the call and, pulling my raincoat over my head, scurried out through the downpour. The ringtone blared in the van behind me, but I ignored it and splashed to the toilet block. I was first in today and, despite the icy cold, I forced myself into the shower. As I'd hoped, hot water surged out of the faucet, and I stayed under until it warmed me. As I dried myself, a crash came from outside.

I froze, then pulled on my undies and slipped shoes and the coat on, before running out.

I stared into the rain, unable to believe what I saw. My van had been overturned. Shadowy figures ran from it, doors slammed and a vehicle sped away, engine silent but tyres hissing on the tarmac. I chased it, but then heard pitiful barking. I stopped and rushed to the van.

Lights came on behind me, followed by alarmed voices. Then, torches illuminated the van. It lay on its side, the vehicle's body distorted by the impact. Chips of glass from the windows scattered on the ground. I ran to what had been the driver's door and peered into the space. A man with a torch joined me, and I took it from him.

At the far end of the cab, in a tangle of limbs, lay Cleo. I saw the cone she'd worn for a week at an impossible angle. 'Shit!' I peered into the rear compartment. 'Oscar!'

I'm in the back.

He sounded okay. I ran to the rear of the van. The doors bulged, deformed and wedged together. 'Where are you, Oscar?'

On your bed, near the back door.

I shone the torch into the hole where the back window had been and saw his legs. 'Are you okay?'

I think so. My head hurts.

'Don't worry, boy. I'll get you out.'

The manager appeared behind me. 'I've called the fire brigade.'

'Have you got a crowbar?'

'A pickaxe?'

'That will do.'

He ran to fetch it, and I reassured Oscar. Did he know Cleo was dead, I wondered? I'd have to tell Zofia. I hoped the poor animal didn't suffer.

The manager returned with a pickaxe and, handing the torch to him, I shoved the pointed end into the seam between the two doors. Once I had it in firmly, I grabbed the handle and pulled. Nothing happened, and then one of the other residents joined me.

With both of us pulling, the metal groaned and bulged, then the spike slipped out and we fell back, landing on the muddy ground. The door had moved but stayed shut. I inserted the spike into the wider gap we'd created, and when it bit, the two of us pulled again. The handle bowed and then, with a sudden screech, the doors flew open.

Something hit my forehead, but I rushed to the van. The nearside door lay on the ground. I knelt on it and stuck my torso in the opening.

A warm tongue licked my face, and I buried my head in his fur. 'Are you okay?'

I've been better. Can we get out?

'Sure.' I held him in a gentle grip and reversed, rising to my feet when I cleared the van.

'Is he okay?' the manager said.

'I think so.' I held Oscar up, and someone took him.

'Come on, boy,' someone said to him. 'Let's get you in the dry.'

Where's Cleo?

I couldn't tell him. I took the torch and shone it along what remained of my bed. At the far end, in the opening in the bulkhead separating the van from the front cab, light glinted off the cone. I took the lamp and crawled forward. The vehicle groaned, and sharp objects attacked my knees as I passed over them. In the distance, a siren sounded.

I pressed on and reached the bulkhead. The stink of coolant and engine oil came from the engine under the front seats. The cone lay in the opening, and I gripped one edge. Using two fingers, I pulled, and it moved, too light to be her body. I dropped it as if it were hot, and vomit surged up my throat. With an effort, I swallowed it down. My hand shook, and I wiped my clammy forehead.

A low whimper came from ahead.

'Cleo?'

Movement in the torchlight, then a familiar thump.

'Cleo, you're okay?' I didn't know whether I expected her to speak to me. Her brown eyes glinted in the torchlight.

I reached my free hand through the opening and stroked her body. A warm tongue greeted me. I tried to check her for injuries, but could feel nothing obvious, and she didn't cry out. The sirens came closer.

I wedged the torch to one side and passed both arms through the opening. I gripped Cleo's torso and with gentle encouragement pulled her to me. She used her back legs, and before I knew it, her head lay on my shoulder. I backed out, holding her tight, and using my elbows to propel me.

I cleared the van and straightened. Strong hands took Cleo, and the siren stopped, in its place a powerful diesel engine, then the hiss of air brakes. Blue lights strobed as people helped me to my feet.

'You've cut yourself.' A finger pointed at my forehead. I dabbed at it, and my hand came away wet. Firefighters arrived, and one wanted to lead me to the fire engine. I made sure Oscar and Cleo were okay before I let her take me.

In the lights of the back cab, she made me sit and examined me. 'That's a nasty cut. It might need stitches.'

'Can you bandage it? I can't leave the dogs.'

'What breed have you got?'

I told her.

She sprayed disinfectant on the wound, making me wince, and used three butterfly stitches to close the wound before covering it with a bandage. As she finished, a car raced up, and a door slammed. A woman cried out, and I thought I was hallucinating.

'Zofia?' I stumbled out of the cab.

Zofia spun to face me and ran to me. 'Victor!'

We held each other, me conscious I wore little under the raincoat.

'Where are Cleo and Oscar?' she asked, untangling herself and looking at the van.

'Safe.'

But whoever had done this was sure to return, and next time . . .

CHAPTER 28

The first morning without Sweeny couldn't have gone any worse for Judy. She'd arrived at the office by nine and had fielded questions and dealt with problems since she walked in. Every time someone knocked on her door, she hoped it would be the stick-limbed accountant saying he'd changed his mind. Most of the issues were low-level, but each required a decision, and by eleven thirty, when her dad arrived, her head was buzzing. If it wasn't for Keira Foley, who'd managed the office for her brothers, Judy would have gone under.

It was Keira who told her of her father's arrival, and Judy burst into his office before he'd settled. 'Dad, we agreed you'd pull your weight while Jerry's away.'

'I had my physio. Do you want me to atrophy?'

'I need you here.' She pointed at his desk. 'Not farting about in the gym. You can do that in your own time.'

'My own time?' He spoke through gritted teeth. 'It's all *my own* time.'

She wouldn't back down. 'No, it isn't. You've committed yourself to working here. If you want to swan about doing your own thing, fine. You can retire. There's the door.'

Her dad's face reddened, and he gripped the arms of his chair with white knuckles. Then he took a deep breath. 'You're right. I apologise. What needs doing?'

'Keira's got a list. I'll be in my office.'

She returned to her desk feeling drained, elated and saddened, all at once. The latter at the change in her relationship with her dad. He'd always been the big beast in their family and, even when the boys ran things, he'd still had the final say. Now, she did, which was scary and exhilarating, but she hated the fact it came at such a cost to her father. She'd treat him to something nice, like a weekend in Edinburgh. Or possibly not, after her last visit.

A call on her mobile made her look at her door but, almost certain her dad wouldn't be popping in unannounced, she took it. 'Archie, a pleasure to hear from you.'

'Likewise, Judy. I wanted to follow up on the weekend's events. Are you ready to go ahead with what we agreed? Fifty-fifty on the project with a breakdown of responsibilities as outlined in the email you sent yesterday?'

'That was quick, Archie. I wasn't expecting such a rapid response.'

He hesitated. 'Once Hamish and I decided we'd be happy to work with you, we didn't see any reason to prevaricate. That's our primary consideration when looking at partners, a personal connection. You're a woman we can do business with.'

Did he feel he'd agreed too quickly? 'Of course, I agree.' Then she worried he was trying to rush her. But whether he was, she needed to address an issue before they went any further. 'Did I tell you I met a senior Manchester police officer on my visit?'

'You did not.'

'He seemed to know you.'

'Know me, or *of* me? I'm reasonably prominent north of the border.'

'The former. Do you know anyone like that?'

'I know many people, Judy. It's an advantage in business to cultivate acquaintances.'

She hadn't wanted to ask him directly, but she needed to know: 'Is Gavin Mulberry one of your acquaintances?'

He chuckled. 'He's someone I know *of*. Was he the one you met?'

'I wondered what he was doing at the bar where I met my friend, and imagine my surprise when I discovered he'd also seen us at dinner.'

'Is that so, Ms Novak?' He paused. 'That coincidence convinces me of the need for swift action on our parts. Mr Mulberry has links to a certain Rudy Glass. As I'm sure you're aware, Glass is interested in developing the same property we are going for. I appreciate he's been removed as a potential developer by the council due to certain . . . difficulties he experienced, but political decisions can be reversed. If Mulberry followed you to Scotland and saw us meet, we need to get moving.'

There he was again, rushing her. 'I'd heard Mulberry had links with a Scottish property developer?'

'Yes. Glass is from Stirling.' He paused. 'You didn't think it was me?'

She wasn't going to admit that was exactly what she'd been wondering. 'I didn't think anything, Archie.' She woke her monitor and googled 'Rudy Glass'. There it was on his profile page, born in Stirling. How the hell did she not know that?

'Ms Novak. Trust between partners is paramount. Without it, we don't have any basis to work together.'

'I agree, Archie. Which is why I told you about my encounter.' *Idiot, you might as well have accused him of setting Mulberry to spy on you.*

His reply took so long coming, she feared he'd be backing out. 'I'm glad you did. As I've said, it underscores the necessity for speed. I'll get my lawyer to draw up a standard contract in line with the heads of agreement you sent over yesterday.'

Relieved, but still unable to dismiss the sense of being rushed, Judy ended the call. She spoke to her father, who seemed to have recovered some of his normal ebullience but rebuffed her suggestion that she take him away for a break. He obviously needed longer for his ego to recover.

A message from her solicitor just before she finished for the day told her the contract had arrived, and she arranged to see him in the morning.

* * *

Soon after nine the next day, she drove into the car park off Spinningfields looking for the reserved spots her solicitor kept for clients. She found the firm expensive and stuffy, but her father said they gave them gravitas and impressed the establishment. She wasn't sure, preferring a firm where they were a significant client and would get preferential treatment. She found a space and drove into it.

An older guy in a shiny red Porsche with an oversize spoiler appeared behind her and beeped his horn at her. She ignored him and got out, taking her soft leather briefcase with her.

'Excuse me, young lady, these spaces are for their clients.' He pointed at the sign above the space.

'Yes, very good. I imagine their clients can read and don't need someone to point it out to them. But if you give me your name, I'll be sure to mention what a good job you're doing.' She walked away.

'Hang on!' He got out.

She ignored him.

He grabbed her shoulder. 'I'm talking to you.'

She brushed his hand off and spun to face him.

He pointed at her car. 'I need that space.'

'You need to learn some manners. You touch me again, and you'll be wearing that spoiler up your arse. Sideways.'

He reddened, but she recognised he'd do nothing else. She continued her journey, and behind her he muttered something, got into his car and screeched off, leaving half his tyres on the concrete. Her mind returned to her reason for being there. Was Robertson hurrying her for some nefarious reason or, as he claimed, did he just want to get cracking?

On any other matter, she'd ask her dad's advice. She could ask the solicitor, but she'd never met him. She'd asked to see a different partner to the one her father usually dealt with.

The office reception rose through two floors, and an enormous vase of flowers scented the space. On closer inspection, she realised they weren't real, and neither was the scent.

An immaculate receptionist, a bit older than her and wearing a power suit comparable to Judy's but by a different designer, led her to the partner's office as Porsche-man came into the reception, his bad mood not helped on seeing Judy and having to wait while the receptionist saw to her. Judy focused on the upcoming meeting and followed the receptionist into the corner office. One window overlooked the open-air bar she frequented in warmer weather and the other, Manchester Crown Court.

A man behind a vast desk stood to greet her. Tall, with thinning hair, he wore heavy-framed glasses and a traditional suit, tailored to his chunky frame. She guessed him to be in his thirties, and he dressed older to put more traditional clients at ease. She didn't care. If he was good enough, he was old enough.

He led Judy to a seating area overlooking the courts and sent the receptionist to fetch the pot of coffee they'd opted for. Two bound documents with coloured markers sticking out of their edges sat on the table. He made small talk while they waited for the drinks. A rich coffee aroma accompanied their arrival, and once they were alone he led Judy through the document.

She recognised most of the clauses from her email, although they were now in legalese. One, she didn't recognise.

'What's this?'

'It's standard in this sort of agreement. If either party pulls out, they're responsible for the costs incurred by the other.'

'What costs are we talking about?'

'Legal fees, for example, if Mr Robertson backed out, you would reclaim my fees. The project requires substantial funds, and this clause covers whatever costs you incur in arranging those. Typically, on a project this size, it involves significant six-figure sums.'

'I'd hate to lose that if he pulled out. Leave it in.'

They completed reading the document, and she examined the signature page, which already bore Robertson's autograph.

'Mr Robertson seems keen.'

'It's normal in a case like this to move fast. You need to secure the deal before someone beats you to it. Our conveyancing department is ready to go on your signal.'

That was reassurance of sorts. 'That's good to hear.'

He studied Judy. 'I assume you've done your due diligence. We did a quick check to ensure he's solvent, but it's not comprehensive. We can carry one out. It will take a day or two, and I can give you an estimate of costs.'

She'd carried out a credit check and had considered using Zofia to make background checks, but she wanted nobody to have an inkling of this deal until she signed it. 'That won't be necessary.'

She signed the paperwork and returned to her car. Her next meeting was with their banker, a man who'd become friends with her father, but she was relying on his professional discretion. His office lay off Portland Street, less than a mile away and only a short walk from hers, but she didn't want her dad to guess where she'd gone.

She left the car in a brutalist concrete multi-storey car park and hurried along Chorlton Street. In spite of the rain, she slowed to admire the elegant former warehouse on the corner of Portland Street. Its Victorian owners had built each floor in a different style, and, despite being occupied by a mediocre hotel, it still outshone the newer buildings around it. That they had created such a building for use as a warehouse still amazed her. Nothing she could remember going up in the city during her admittedly short life could match it. The thought that anything she built would struggle to come close to its splendour gave her pause for thought.

She hurried on and arrived for her appointment late and hot. An assistant showed her into the wood-panelled office, where the smell of mothballs and old cigars greeted her. She exchanged pleasantries with the man she'd first met at a barbecue when she was twelve, then settled back in her chair.

'I reiterate, this must remain confidential, and you mustn't discuss it with anyone.'

'Including your father. I'm aware of that, Judy. I acted for your brothers when they ran the company, don't forget.' He studied her with his watery blue eyes.

'Sorry, of course. I gave you an idea of the sums we'd need.'

'Yes, it surprised me. But I'm relieved it's half what your father was talking about.'

'We've taken on a partner.'

'Can you tell me who it is?'

'Someone from out of town.'

He waited for her to continue and gave a thin smile when she didn't. 'I'll have to be happy with that.'

She pulled out a bound document she'd produced with the help of the architect they planned to use. Sweeny had produced the cash-flow forecast for her dad, but she'd used his template and halved the figures before printing them out. She waited, tension making her vibrate, as the banker read it.

'So, you're looking for seven mill to start and eighteen by the time you've completed in two years.'

She nodded. 'That's all.'

'We've already advanced you three million on Beswick Street.'

'That's secured on the property.'

'It's a shell. We've allowed one point two on it. The rest is coming off your overdraft.'

She was sure Sweeny had said the bank had lent two and a half on the property. 'That leaves us three point two on the overdraft?'

'One point two.'

'What? The OD is five.'

'Was five. It's now three.'

'Since when?'

'Since your turnover dropped.'

She was sure it had returned to former levels and even increased. 'I've not brought those figures with me. I'd assumed they'd be no problem.'

He stared at his screen and punched keys. 'They're here.' He spun the screen towards her. 'As you can see, there's a significant drop in turnover and an even bigger drop in profit.'

She'd known they laundered some money from their sex club through the casino, but hadn't realised how much. 'We want to secure the rest on the site—'

'Half the site.'

'Sorry?'

'You have a partner, Judy. They will own half, which leaves you with half.'

She took a deep breath. 'Okay. The casino is worth—'

'Mortgaged.'

'What?'

'Your brother borrowed three million just before he . . . earlier this year.'

How the hell had that happened? 'Do you have the—'

He produced a document, which he slapped on the desk. 'That's Milan's signature. Marko also signed it.'

She recognised the scrawl. 'Okay, as you can tell, that's news to me.'

'Maybe you should rethink this project.'

'I can't.' Her pulse raced. 'How much can we have?'

He blew out his cheeks. 'With the overdraft and a small amount I can advance on the casino, two million, plus maybe three on your half of the site, once you get planning permission.'

That left her two mill short. And that was just to start. 'Do you know what the boys did with the three mill?'

'Marko was boasting about an investment with huge returns, but Milan shut him down. To be honest, I didn't want to know.'

'Right. Can you get the paperwork ready for a second mortgage?'

'Of course, Judy.'

She stood, head light, and swayed. He took her hand and led her to the door. An odour of mints mingled with the mothballs.

'Give my regards to your father.'

She nodded and made her way to the creaking lift, which took her to the ground floor. Outside, she stepped into the alleyway down the side of the building, leant against the brickwork under the metal fire escape and threw up.

CHAPTER 29

Despite sunup being over an hour earlier, there was no sign of it when the firefighters righted my van. Its contents crashed as it bounced and then settled on its wheels. The rear doors, distorted when the vandals overturned my van, now swung open, twisted further by my attempts to open them. I stuck my head in to check the damage.

My bed had come free of its brackets, as had half the kitchen cupboards, the items they'd contained scattered on the floor where they mixed with the contents of the water tank. The rain, blown in through the broken windows, joined it. The sliding doors of the under-bed cupboard refused to budge, and as I leant in to get more leverage a voice summoned me.

'Mr Mitchum?'

A young constable stood behind me, water dripping off her cap.

'Yeah, that's me.'

'Can we get a statement?' She gestured towards the site office, and I led the way.

I shivered, although I now wore my clothes under my raincoat. A two-bar electric fire took the chill off the room where Zofia sat holding Cleo, Oscar at her feet. The odour of wet dog overpowered the plug-in air freshener, which exuded a chemical-floral scent.

She looked from the policewoman to me. 'Do you want me to go?'

'No, you—'

'If you don't mind,' the constable spoke over me.

Zofia placed Cleo on the floor and stood. 'I'll wait in the car.' She led the dogs out and closed the door behind her.

I took the seat she'd vacated, and the constable sat at the desk in the opposite corner. She wrote my name in her notebook. 'Can you tell me what happened?'

I recounted what I could recall, and her disappointment reflected mine.

'You didn't see the car?'

'It was pitch-black and chucking it down. It sounded electric; I didn't hear an engine over the rain.'

She noted this. 'Do you know anyone who might have done this?'

I'd thought of little else since I'd rescued Cleo. Had Novak sent someone to make me reconsider my reluctance to work for his daughter? Making me homeless would increase the attractiveness of her offer. He'd seemed surprised when I rang him last night. Had he arranged for someone to overturn my van at the time I was being hassled by the security guards? I'd also suspected them. Had they followed me last night? I'd been so tired I'd not kept alert for a tail. My third suspect, Lambert, seemed the most likely. He knew where I lived, but why destroy my home?

'Mr Mitchum?'

'Sorry. I can't think of anyone. It was probably vandals.'

'We don't get many out here. So, nobody you've fallen out with?'

I could imagine her reaction if I accused my prime suspect. 'Sorry.'

'Okay, if you think of anyone, let us know.' She handed me a card.

I found Zofia in her car, the dogs on her back seat on a rug. She rolled the window down. 'How did it go?'

'I saw nothing, and my suspects are Novak or a policeman, so I said nothing.'

'Do you want to get in? I'll take you back to our office. You can stay the night at ours.'

'What about Cleo and Kasper?'

'Bugger! I forgot.'

I'd been thinking about what to do. 'Don't worry, I've rung Digger, and he's coming with a recovery lorry for the van. I'll salvage what I can and take it with me. You get off to work, take those two, and I'll ring you.'

'Where will you sleep tonight?'

'I'll sort something.'

I watched her leave to join Kasper at the office, rain dripping off my hood, and returned to the van. The site manager joined me.

'I'm sorry about what happened,' he said, 'but it's not our fault.'

'I'm not blaming you.'

'You're not? What did you tell the police?'

I told him.

'How will you get this off-site? You can't drive it.'

'A mate's picking it up.'

'Oh, right.' He stood in silence for a moment. 'One of the statics is empty tonight. You'll have to make sure you clean up after the dogs . . .'

'That's very kind. Thanks.' I'd have to borrow a car, but at least I'd have somewhere to sleep. I found a roll of bin liners in the kitchen drawer and bagged my belongings. My clothes were fine, but none of my crockery or glasses had survived.

The growl of a diesel engine announced Digger's arrival in a recovery vehicle, the livery of the rescue service it had belonged to still visible under the cheap paintwork covering it. The rain had eased, and he pulled up alongside the van.

'Victor, you've been in the wars again?' He gestured at the bandage on my forehead.

I brought him up to date, and we put my undamaged belongings in the empty caravan I'd been offered before he reversed up to the van and dragged it onto the load-bed. I joined him, and we set off for Manchester.

Once on our way, I jerked a thumb at the back of the vehicle. 'I'll claim on the insurance for that.'

'No point. Once they deduct the excess, they'll pay next to nothing, and you'll have a claim on your record.'

Even though I insisted, he refused.

I let John and Craig know what had happened and we dropped the van at a scrapyard, where Digger had once met me on our way to rescue Zofia.

'Where to now?' he asked.

'I'd better collect Oscar and then I'll meet John and Craig.'

Kasper stared at me when I let myself into the office. 'You can't be here, Victor.'

'Don't be silly,' Zofia said. 'Of course he can. I'm not throwing him out on the street.'

'But . . .' Kasper left off, recognising the futility of arguing.

'It's okay. I won't be long. Did you get them checked out?'

Zofia said, 'I took Cleo to the vet you told me about. She removed her stitches and checked them both out, said they were okay.'

Only because I didn't complain.

'Great, I'll take Oscar with me, then.'

I'm fine, thank you. Warm, dry and fed.

'I'll buy you a coat.'

Hmmm, coat and wet streets, or no coat and warm office? Guess what I'm leaning towards.

'And booties?'

That's decided it. I'm staying. There's no way I'm poncing about with those on my paws.

'Don't be difficult.'

Zofia took pity on me. 'He'll be fine here, Victor. Did you sort the van out?'

'Yes, and the guy at the site said I could use one of the static caravans. But I'll need—'

'Of course you can borrow my car. I'll share Kasper's until you're sorted out.' She retrieved her keys and handed them to me.

I could have hugged her, and my mind returned a few hours to the time I had. It had been wonderful, almost worth losing the camper for. But who was I kidding? Not only was I a married, homeless loser, but she was much too young for me, closer in age to Helen than to me. Closer even to Em. I dismissed my idle fantasy and focused on Kasper.

Conscious of his agitation, I said, 'I'll collect the dogs about six. I'll wait until you've left.'

Don't hurry back on my account.

I borrowed the laptop we'd used the night before and arranged to meet John at a café I had frequented during the time I'd lived in a tower block nearby. The lunch crowd had gone, and I ordered a coffee before commandeering a corner table and fielding questions about my cut and why Oscar wasn't with me. I powered up the laptop and logged into the Wi-Fi while I waited for the others to arrive.

I'd updated the spreadsheet with the addresses of the places I'd checked on my way home last night, before my run-in with the security thugs, and sent two emails to estate agents before John and Craig joined me. We ordered a late lunch and, while we ate, they quizzed me about what had happened.

'You've no idea who it could have been, Brother?'

I put my cutlery down and counted the three suspects on my fingers.

'And which one do you think is most likely?'

'The only one who knew where I was is the copper, Lambert.'

Craig pointed with a sauce-smeared knife. 'The fact they did it while you were having a shower suggests someone who didn't want you hurt.'

'Novak, you mean?'

'You know my opinion of him.'

'I think Lambert is the more likely suspect. But would a serving cop risk my getting injured or worse? There's a world of difference between vandalism and hurting someone. They're hardly going to throw resources at an investigation into the damage to a van worth a few hundred quid.'

'The question is, what are we going to do about it?'

'Much as I want to know who attacked me, my priorities are finding somewhere to live and hunting down Harry's killers. Don't forget, they're still active and killed someone a few days ago.'

A waiter clearing a nearby table must have overheard me and gave me a sideways look before scurrying away with a rattling pile of dirty crockery. Once we'd eaten, I showed John and Craig the updated spreadsheet, and we identified the premises with no obvious occupiers.

Craig marked up the three maps we'd printed off and devised a route for the three of us to follow so we could check each one in person, speak to an occupier if we could, and a neighbour if we couldn't. 'We'll make a start, and you join us after you've looked for somewhere to live.'

'I've already done that. We'll focus on finding Harry's killer.' How could I slope off to find myself somewhere to live when my friends had nowhere to call home?

The rain had almost stopped, and we piled into Zofia's car before making our way to the area we suspected Harry's killers had stored their vehicle. Craig directed me, and we dropped John off. Next, I dropped Craig and drove on to the last section. I parked up outside an industrial estate, which had once been a large factory and was now divided into myriad small units.

Several signs on the external wall advertised the occupiers, and we'd already identified which units they related to. I folded the map Craig had marked so I could refer to it and stepped through the brick pillars flanking the entrance. Large metal gates hung off each pillar, and I wondered what time they locked them, if ever, and who had the keys.

Craig had marked seven premises on the map, and someone answered the bell at the first two I tried. The suspicious way they greeted me suggested they didn't want anyone to know what they did there. I armed myself with a tale that I was looking for work, and my bedraggled appearance, a result of my bandaged cut and my still damp clothes, lent it credence.

Three more had neighbours happy to discuss the business of the occupiers. I made my way to the back of the estate and discovered another entrance. This one had no gates protecting it. The last two unidentified premises lay in this area. One had an estate agents' board above the entrance, and I stood outside and rang the number on it.

The enthusiastic manner of the man who answered changed when I told him which unit I was interested in. 'That's not available, sir. I'm sorry.'

In order not to raise his suspicions, I asked if he had any similar, but he didn't. I'd spotted something that piqued my interest. The edge of a fresh patch of oil peeked out from under the roller-shutter. It must have dripped onto the ground with the shutter up. The weathered agents' board suggested it had been there a while, a fact confirmed by a neighbour.

I asked him if he'd seen anyone in there. His unit stank of hot metal, and he was working on an ornate wrought-iron gate.

'Now you mention it, I was 'ere Saturday, working late.' He frowned. 'No, it was Sunday morning. Had a rush job, and I heard a car, so stuck me 'ead out. A car was reversing in, so I assumed they'd let it and went back to work.'

'What time was that?'

He blew his cheeks out. 'Two-ish. I finished at half past. Me missus had been ringing, asking if I'm ever coming 'ome.'

With a sense of excitement, I showed him a picture of the front of a GMC Sierra.

'Yeah, that's the one. They not nicked it off you, have they?'

My hand shook as I opened the phone and rang John.

CHAPTER 30

Worrying about what could have happened to Victor if he'd been in the van when they overturned it distracted Zofia as she attempted to focus on work. Victor had shared his theories about who could have been behind it, and she couldn't believe he'd not told her about Lambert tracking him down to the site. He'd said he didn't want to worry her, but that he hadn't confided in her hurt. The policeman gave her the creeps, and she was sure he'd been behind it.

Kasper's thoughts seemed to be following the same lines. 'Who do you think vandalised Victor's van?'

'Lambert is favourite.' She told him what Victor had said.

'Bloody hell! You reckon he'll come for us?'

Maybe Victor was right not to worry them. 'I'm sure he won't.'

Kasper ruminated for a while. 'What about Alex Novak? I know you quite like Judy, but do you trust her father?'

'But Victor saved Novak's life.'

'Yeah, he did. But he'd ended up paralysed from the waist down. He might resent the fact and wish he'd died.'

'And blame Victor? No way. Anyway, his daughter wants to employ him, so why would he want to hurt him?'

'You can never tell with a psycho like him.'

She had to concede that Kasper might have a point. Talk of Judy reminded her she'd not invoiced her for the background checks on the two men Judy claimed she wanted to interview for the job she'd offered to Victor. Although they'd not completed it, she'd spent a few hours and paid to use a database they usually accessed through their membership of the SPI.

Judy had been keen for Victor to know she was considering other candidates, and Zofia suspected it might have been a ruse to hurry him into taking the job. But why cancel it unless he'd taken the job? The thought that he might have accepted Judy's offer without telling them disappointed her. But why shouldn't he? It was a fantastic opportunity to improve his lot, however much it would hurt her *and* her brother. She produced an invoice and emailed it to Judy.

Judy's response arrived within half an hour, as Zofia's phone rang. 'Everything okay, Judy?'

'Yeah, I got your invoice, and we've paid it.' Judy hesitated. 'What did Victor say when he discovered you were doing a job for me?'

'He doesn't know. He's taken a few days off.'

'Oh, right.' Judy sounded disappointed.

The realisation Victor hadn't taken the job made her light-headed with relief. 'If that's all?'

'No, I've got another job. I need this to be kept confidential—'

'Of course, we treat everything you tell us in strictest confidence.'

Judy hesitated. 'I need a financial health check on an Archie Robertson.'

Zofia gave an involuntary gasp.

'Sorry?'

'I beg your pardon, Judy. My dog just put her nose somewhere she shouldn't.'

'Is that Oscar?'

'No, Cleo.' As she said the name, Cleo got up and wandered to her desk.

'Okay. I'll send you what I've got on Mr Robertson. Can you put a rush on this?'

'Will do.' Zofia ended the call and sat thinking.

'Judy Novak?' Kasper's question made her jump.

'Yeah. She's . . . She asked me to check up on Robertson.'

'What, the Robertson who . . . ?' He didn't need to finish.

'The same.'

'Bloody hell!' He thought for a few seconds. 'Shit! What does she want to investigate him for?'

'I didn't ask, but it's a financial health check. Would she be going into business with him?'

Kasper didn't answer for a long moment. 'Why would she?'

'I don't know. She's going into property, and her dad was looking at the site Glass *and* Robertson were interested in. If she goes into business with Robertson, that's one rival she doesn't have to worry about.'

'You could be right. That would be a disaster for us.'

'Don't be melodramatic, Kasper.'

'Melodramatic? What if he lets slip about . . . what happened on Riverpark Road?'

Zofia, even though certain they were alone, and Kasper had swept the office for bugs, looked around and lowered her voice. 'You expect him to say, "By the way, my men shot your brothers, and Kasper and Zofia helped them"?'

Kasper sniffed and gave an exasperated sigh. 'Of course not, but what if he lets something slip, and she gets thinking? She's no mug.'

Zofia couldn't ever see this scenario playing out. 'Are you suggesting I make up some negative findings, so she backs off?'

'No. But if there's anything negative there, don't underplay it.'

Zofia didn't need her brother's advice and thought he was being alarmist. But she couldn't dismiss her unease at the possibility of Robertson going into business with Novak. The further he stayed from Manchester, the better.

After lunch, the rain eased, so she took Cleo out for a walk. She couldn't put her in her brother's car, so they visited the nearest green space. She spent the afternoon carrying out a deep dive into Archie Robertson's finances.

An article threw up a familiar name. Robertson was one victim of a serious property fraud, which had snagged several wealthy investors. The Manchester-based con man had promised investors good, but not unrealistic, returns. Zofia checked why she'd seen the name and found the link.

Mulberry had been on the team investigating the scam. Zofia had thought that was where he'd probably crossed paths with Glass, one of the other victims. The thought Mulberry might have also met Robertson made her think.

'Look at this, Kasper?'

He joined her but sneezed twice, and Zofia moved a reluctant Cleo back to her own bed, near the printer in the far corner of the room.

'What am I looking at?' Kasper's voice had taken on a nasal quality. He read the report, his lips moving as he did so. He finished reading and pulled a chair over from Victor's desk. 'You think Robertson is the one pulling Mulberry's strings?'

'I still think it's more likely to be Glass. He was the one we'd hurt with the revelations of his links to a corrupt official and his murder, and he thinks we're still investigating him. I thought you agreed with me.'

'I did until I discovered Robertson's expanding his interests into Manchester, and especially if he goes into business with Novak, what we know can derail that.'

He had a point, but she had her doubts. 'Robertson, as we've seen from close range, has a more direct style. If he wanted to get rid of us, he'd use permanent means. Why would he risk letting a senior police officer know he had a beef with KZD if he was going to end up getting rid of us? Mulberry might be corrupt, but would he cover up multiple murders?'

Kasper considered her words. 'Maybe Robertson is just warning us off.' He pointed at the screen. 'What will you do with this information?'

'Give it to Judy. I don't think he's the one behind Mulberry.'

Kasper stuck his lower lip out. 'When is she expecting your report?'

'I've not given her a time, but she wants it quickly. I've got a couple of requests coming back in the morning, so I'll let her have it once they've come in.'

'So, you're going to carry on looking for links between Mulberry and Glass?'

'The fact Mulberry investigated a scam in which Glass was a victim isn't enough. There were dozens of victims, and we don't even know if they met.'

Kasper returned to his desk, not hiding the fact that he disagreed with her. Unable to progress the report on Robertson until the next day, Zofia returned to her investigation of Mulberry's background. Apart from the fraud case, which also involved Robertson, she'd found no other links between the policeman and Glass.

Oscar stood and barked, then the front door opened. She checked the time, five thirty. Victor was early, and Kasper didn't hold back in telling him.

'Sorry, I'm looking at some houses from six and didn't want the dogs to be alone for too long.' Victor looked stoked.

'That's fine,' Zofia said. 'You look pleased with yourself, Victor.'

He gave her a smile. 'I've found out where they're keeping the pickup used to follow Harry.'

'Have you told the police?'

'Not yet. I don't trust Lambert to do anything and would rather have more before I take it to Grimes.'

At the mention of Grimes, Kasper winced. 'Good idea. What more were you hoping to find?'

Victor frowned. 'We're planning to follow them and catch them red-handed.'

'And how are you going to do that?'

'Do you still have those tracking bugs you used on me?'

Zofia's cheeks grew hot. She'd put one in Victor's jacket without his knowledge, and it had contributed to saving his life. She'd apologised afterwards but still felt embarrassed.

'Sure,' Kasper said. 'I'll bring one in tomorrow. If you're attaching it to their pickup, I'll bring one with a magnet.'

'Right, thanks. I'd better get going. Come on, Oscar and Cleo.'

Victor turned to Oscar as though he'd said something to him.

'The jacket was if you came with me this morning,' he said to him. 'It's too late now. The item's no longer on the table.' He attached the leads to both dogs. 'Yeah, life's unfair, and then you die. Come on, we'll be late.'

'He's getting worse,' Kasper said and shook his head as the door closed.

The office seemed empty without them, and Zofia considered what Victor had said. 'Do you think their plan is wise?'

'Why not? They need evidence. Otherwise, the police won't do anything.'

'But these are violent men who, if Victor is right, have killed several men.'

'Yeah, but they'll have Craig with them.'

'I still think it's dangerous. What if the men give them the slip and kill someone?'

'They'd do that if Victor did nothing. I'm sure he's considered the risks. You're the one who's always saying to trust him.'

She couldn't deny that and returned to her work, pleased when Kasper said, 'Shall we finish in fifteen? Get a chippy tea tonight?'

'Great idea, I'll finish soon.'

A search of Mulberry's name linked to the term 'police' had come up with many hits, most to do with cases he'd worked. She'd listed them all with their links and had two left to check. She opened the next link, but instead of the story of another police investigation, this story concerned a golf tournament. Mulberry had won the nearest-the-pin competition, and a photo showed him receiving the trophy.

The man presenting it to him looked familiar, and she enlarged the image, but it pixelated. However, the caption identified him as the sponsor, Rudy Glass.

CHAPTER 31

How come she gets a jacket, and I don't?

'I've told you. You could have had one if you'd come with me this morning. Now pipe down, I'm looking for somewhere to park.'

Oscar peered out of the back window of Zofia's car. ***What are we doing here anyway?***

'I'm meeting the estate agent.'

Oh God, is it going to be like last time?

'I hope not.' We'd been shown a selection of depressing hovels before Oscar scared off the estate agent for disrespecting me. 'Now take care of Cleo. I won't be long.'

Can't I see it? I'll have to live there.

'Let me check them out first. I wouldn't want to waste your time.'

Good point.

I slammed and locked my door. Red-brick Victorian terraces lined both sides of the narrow street. They'd have once housed the workers from the nearby cotton mills, which were now either converted to business spaces or flats. From the looks of the houses, the landlords who owned them rarely maintained them. Most had a row of wheelie bins outside their front windows, the overflowing ones scenting the air with rotting garbage. The estate agent's car sat outside a house six doors up from where I'd parked. A young man in a suit with shiny lapels and elbows got out to meet me, a tablet and a sheet of paper in his left hand.

'Mr Mitchum?' He offered a limp hand. 'I'll give you the details.'

The sheet of paper, wilting in the damp atmosphere, showed an image of one of the surrounding houses.

'This is number eighteen.' He pointed to an off-white uPVC door with eighteen scrawled on it using permanent marker. It opened directly off the pavement. He produced a key and opened the door. A ferocious barking greeted us. He retreated, and the door slammed as a large body crashed into it.

Loud voices, including the accusation, 'Did you forget to lock the effing door?', more barking, and the sound of a struggle came from inside and then the door opened a fraction.

'Yeah, what?' A large man with an unkempt mop of brown hair and a ferocious expression stood in the narrow gap.

The agent glanced at his tablet. 'Mr Harrop?'

'Who wants to know?'

'I'm from the estate agents'. The house is supposed to be empty.'

'Yeah, right.' His belligerence evaporated. 'We're going tomorrow. They couldn't find anywhere for the dogs. The social won't let us keep them in the next place.'

'Is it okay if I show Mr Mitchum around?'

'Yeah, whatever.' He stepped back and waved us in.

'What about the dogs?'

The man waved a hand. 'They're locked in the back room.'

The estate agent stepped in, and I followed. The ripe odour of unwashed dog overwhelmed me. We were in the living room. The furniture – a worn black leather sofa and mismatched armchair, facing a screen bolted to the chimney breast – bore the signs of large teeth.

The estate agent led me up a narrow, steep staircase to a small landing. Clothes and other belongings lay scattered around the two bedrooms, and I saw no signs of packing. The bathroom washbasin had a corner smashed off, and the shower curtain hung on half its loops. The thought of living here filled me with horror.

It must have shown on my face because the agent said, 'Of course, we'll get it professionally cleaned before you move in.'

I made a noncommittal noise and followed him back down.

'Can we look at the kitchen?' He pointed a nervous hand at the door leading to the back of the house.

'I'll get the missus to put the dogs out.'

I stopped him. 'No need. What have you got?'

'Two Staffies.'

'You said you couldn't find anywhere for them?'

'My cousin said he'd have them while we find somewhere.'

'Good luck.' I shook his hand and stepped outside, taking a gulp of evening air, and waited for the agent to join me.

'Shall I take that as a no, Mr Mitchum?'

I nodded. 'Why's he moving out, do you know?'

'Can't afford the rent. His wife's in a wheelchair, so the council has found them a small flat, but they can't keep the dogs there.'

I felt even worse. 'Right, where to next?'

He checked his screen. 'Three streets that way and then we've got one over the other side of the main road, opposite the park.'

'That sounds more promising.'

'I wouldn't get your hopes up. This place' – he jerked a thumb at the house behind him – 'isn't the worst we're looking at.'

After four more viewings, I realised he wasn't exaggerating. I set off for the caravan park, a depression settling on me. The houses we'd seen didn't look too bad in the pictures the agency showed on their website, but the owners had obviously taken the photos a few tenancies ago, when the decor was clean and the furniture new.

While looking on the letting websites, I'd seen a flat in the tower Judy had taken me to. Smaller than the one she'd shown me, it was three grand a month, far more than I could afford.

I stopped at a chippy in Heywood, and the mouthwatering aroma of fried fish, chips and vinegar accompanied us on the last leg of the journey. The static caravan we were staying in that night felt like a palace compared to what I'd been looking at. The manager wasn't around, but in the morning I'd ask him if we could stay longer.

Once we'd eaten, I took a torch and led Oscar and Cleo out for a walk in the woods where we'd gone on our first day. Cleo, now more comfortable with Oscar and me, followed him as he explored in the pitch-black, the dogs rustling as they wound their way through the undergrowth. My thoughts returned to the people whose house I'd looked at. The thought of their losing their dogs left a hollow in the pit of my stomach. And even though I knew they had to move anyway, I couldn't take their place.

Oscar returned to me, Cleo at his heels, and I bent down to hug them.

What's up with you?

'Just pleased to have you two around.'

I thought she was only staying for a few days.

'Don't you like having her stay with us?'

She's okay.

They chased each other back to the caravan and waited for me at the door. I noticed the doorbell camera and checked the area it covered – Zofia's car. I walked towards the plot where we'd spent the previous night.

You going to let us in?

'I'm checking something.'

How about letting us in first?

'Just wait, I won't be long.' I reached the empty plot. A piece of glass glinted like a diamond in the beam of the lamp, and I picked it up. Digger and I had cleared it, but we must have missed a bit. I looked back towards where I'd parked Zofia's car. It was near where I'd heard the getaway car. With a growing sense of excitement, I returned to the caravan.

Can we go in now? Poor Cleo is shivering.

'Yeah, sorry.' I unlocked the door and let them in.

Great, my happiness is of no account, but as soon as madam is uncomfortable . . .

'I thought a tough boy like you, who'd lived on the streets, wouldn't be worried by a slight chill.'

I'm not worried, I just don't like it.

'Soft bugger.'

I topped up their water and pulled out their bedding. We had far more room than my tiny van had afforded us, but it wasn't palatial. I examined the camera and looked for a screen like we had for our office intercom but didn't find one. My excitement at discovering the camera covered the area used by the getaway car turned to frustration.

I retrieved the laptop from the boot of Zofia's car and logged in to the site's Wi-Fi. Ten minutes later, I'd downloaded the app onto my phone but couldn't get it to link to the camera. In frustration, I rang Craig and told him my problem.

'You've got the software on your phone and set up an account?'

He talked me through it and then tried to connect the camera but failed again. After a frustrating half hour, he talked me through removing the memory card. I put it into my wallet and fell into bed, hoping it showed something I could use to find my tormentors and get them off my back.

CHAPTER 32

After leaving the bank, Judy had driven to Dunham Massey park and walked out amongst the deer. She'd come here with her mother throughout her childhood and still visited whenever life became too challenging. She focused on her surroundings, the autumnal colours and the elegant deer who stopped to watch her as she walked past.

An hour later, she returned to the car and drove back to work. She arrived mid-afternoon, feeling like she'd already done two days. She'd been thinking and had ideas to deal with her problems. But first, she needed to discover the extent of their financial problems. Her father arrived, closed the door and wheeled himself to her desk.

'You okay?' he asked.

'I've been better. I drove to Dunham Massey as I needed to clear my head.'

'Alright for some of us to swan around. And you had the cheek to quote Churchill at me? I'll give you one of his quotes: "The price of greatness is responsibility." You think it's responsible to go lazing about with what we've got on?'

'Dad—' She was going to tell him to 'sit down', but caught herself and grew hot. 'I was trying to sort out the funding for the project on the Rochdale Canal.'

'I've already started that ball rolling.'

'And what have you secured?'

He broke eye contact. 'It's in the early stages. I wanted you on board before we signed anything. It's your baby now.'

'Okay. I'll tell you what I've discovered.' She told him what the bank manager had said and how much they had available. Nowhere near enough.

'No, that's not right.'

'So, he's lying?'

'No, what I meant is . . .' He took a deep breath. 'Have you checked what he told you?'

'I'm doing it now.' She nodded at the screen. 'Did the boys tell you what they did with the three mill?'

He looked embarrassed. 'I didn't even know they'd borrowed it. If I had, I'd have stopped them.'

'Do you think Jerry knows?' She'd been thinking about his glib assurances about the funding for Beswick Street being in place. He'd not mentioned that they'd used most of their overdraft to pay for it. Could she trust anything he'd told her?

'He must do. He's our accountant.'

'But not for much longer.' Was he leaving because he was jumping a sinking ship? Did he know where their money was?

'You think he's stiffed us?' Her dad seemed to have shrunk.

'Let's not jump to conclusions. I'm going to spend the rest of the day tracking our assets. I'll need your help to list any properties or investments you can remember from the time you ran this place.'

'That was a few years ago, love.'

'You're telling me you've forgotten them?'

He winced, recovered. 'Right, I'll make a start.' He stopped at the doorway. 'Remember, Churchill said, "Difficulties mastered are opportunities won."'

'Thanks, Dad. Didn't he also say, "If you're going through hell, keep going"?'

'He did.' He chuckled and let himself out.

Judy let herself into Jerry Sweeny's office, reminding herself she still had to find his long-term replacement, especially as Victor seemed to be ghosting her. She logged on to his computer and opened the accounting software. It looked identical to the one on her machine – a mirror copy.

A search of his folders disclosed a set listing various properties. Again, this looked like the folder she had on her desktop but hadn't looked at since Sweeny had shown her the system. She opened each and, as she had recalled, they contained details of each property, including who lived there and who owned it. They used several proxy companies to hide the ownership. Under each company name, she listed the details of the properties they owned.

A sub-folder within the maintenance folder of the last property she checked caught her attention. It contained details of several properties she didn't have records of. Since she'd taken over, she'd visited each place they owned. She locked Sweeny's office and rushed back to hers. The sub-folder didn't exist on her version.

'Shit!'

She returned to Sweeny's office and checked which company owned those properties. She'd never heard of it. No point in checking at Companies House. The reason they used these proxy companies was so nobody could trace the owners. Not without a lot of difficulty. A folder in her safe contained the details that enabled her to control these companies. She checked it, but couldn't find the new company.

What the hell was Sweeny up to? Her suspicion that he wasn't coming back to work his notice after his holiday ended deepened. Exhausted after a tough morning, she called it a day, telling her father she was going. He looked as shattered as she felt and, deciding she didn't need to tell him her suspicions of Sweeny tonight, she left.

On a whim, she took a detour, going past Sweeny's house. She saw the 'For Sale' sign long before she reached it. She drove past it, uttering a series of unladylike oaths.

CHAPTER 33

The next morning, I woke early, exercised the dogs and showered, relieved when I returned to find my home undamaged. I wanted to get going but had to wait until eight thirty, when the manager arrived, and I asked him about the camera.

'The old guy who stayed there before you put it in. I know nothing about them, sorry.' He sat behind his desk and switched on his laptop.

'How long was he there?'

'Three months, why?'

'I'm looking for somewhere longer term.'

'Sorry, mate. I've got someone until the beginning of December, and then we have to leave it empty for two months. It's in the terms of our licence. We can't allow permanent residents.'

'Right, okay. Thanks for letting me have it last night.' I trudged towards the door.

'Hang on.' He checked his screen. 'The guy moving in won't be here until Sunday. I want you out by Saturday morning, and make sure your dogs don't make a mess. Forty quid a night, cash.'

I rushed back to the caravan with a swagger and picked up the dogs. On the way, I rang Kasper.

'A memory card reader? Of course, why?'

I told him why I needed it.

When I reached the office, he didn't complain about my being there during office hours. I gave him the memory card and chatted to Zofia. We moved to the kitchen and made coffee. Our hands brushed as I passed her a mug, and I felt a shock up my arm. She seemed to feel it too and snatched her hand away before focusing on pouring our drinks. Or had I imagined that? I remembered what Oscar had said about her being interested, but he was just a dog, and I was still a washed-up old man who was going to be homeless in two days. A shout from Kasper made the dogs jump and interrupted my descent into self-pity.

'What you got?' I hurried to his desk.

'Got 'em.' The image of the rear of a car filled his screen. Even I, a car ignoramus, recognised the distinctive emblem of a Tesla, then he zoomed in to the number plate. Blurred, but clear enough to trace it, and with that, the owner.

Zofia sat at her desk and checked the time. 'You'd better go, Victor. You're not supposed to be here. Kasper and I will track the owner and let you know how we get on.'

'Yeah, you're right.' The fact that she seemed as unhappy about it as I did made me feel a bit better.

I collected the tracker Kasper had brought from home, checking he'd given me one with a magnet so we could attach it to the pickup we'd traced, and set off to look at more houses, this time in a different part of the city. Today, Oscar agreed to join me, claiming he'd found yesterday with Zofia and Cleo boring, but I suspected he didn't like that Cleo got more attention than him.

Although the houses we saw were marginally better than those I'd seen yesterday – the better weather helped – none appealed to either me or Oscar. We finished the final viewing and returned to the car, fed up. Although we had two more days' grace, I wasn't sure it was enough time to find somewhere.

I bought a late lunch and stopped off at Queens Park. The autumn sun illuminated the trees in various states of undress as they shed their leaves. I sat on a bench alongside the tree-lined avenue, which led to the red-brick mansion at the centre of the park. Despite the surroundings, a depression settled on me.

Almost two years of homelessness, more than half spent on the streets, had lowered my resilience, and a fear that I'd never get back on my feet wormed its way into my mind. Even with the job I had, not the worst paid by a long way, I couldn't hope to get a decent home. And with the problems assailing KZD, I may not even have that job much longer.

Oscar nuzzled against my leg. ***You okay?***

'I've been better.' I stroked his back.

What's up?

'I'm just fed up we've got nowhere to live.'

We'll find somewhere. You always do.

Thankfully, he seemed to have forgotten the time we'd lived on the streets. 'It won't be easy this time.'

What about that flat in the sky? I could have my own room. And so could Cleo.

'I can't afford it.'

Why don't I get a job like that dog on the TV? You know I'm good at finding people in fires. I'd even wear those booties they made her wear.

I wasn't sure how much they paid fire search dogs, but suspected it wouldn't be enough for a decent house. 'That's a good idea, but it won't be necessary. Come on, let's go.' I screwed up my rubbish and deposited it in the bin.

I'd arranged to meet John, Craig and Toff at dusk. We planned to break into the unit where the two men stored the pickup and plant the tracker on the vehicle. We needed some tools. I'd wandered around the back of the unit, pretending to be lost. A narrow window above a bricked-up doorway provided the only access. Rusted screws secured the grille covering it to the frame. I needed a set of screwdrivers, wire cutters in case we couldn't remove the rusty screws, spray-on rust remover and lubricant, and brackets to reattach it if we had to cut it. The tracker had a powerful magnet, but I also bought a roll of duct tape.

My worry was that, once we'd replaced the grille, it would be obvious we'd broken in, but from the state of the alley behind the unit I suspected nobody ever used it. Infected with an excess of caution, I bought the items in different shops, using cash, and throwing in two pairs of gloves and a small but powerful torch at one DIY warehouse. The sight of couples buying items for their homes reminded me I didn't have one, not that I needed reminding.

I'd bought everything and was driving to the rendezvous when a siren got my attention. Blue light flickered in my mirror. Police. I pulled over and stopped the engine. Two officers got out of their car and walked towards me, one on each side of the vehicle. The one on my side arrived first, and I lowered the window before he ordered me to.

'Is this your car, sir?'

I tried not to smile at the old cliché. 'It belongs to my employer, Zofia Dąbrowski.'

'And does she know you've got the car?'

'She gave me the keys.'

'Can you tell me what you're doing around here?'

'Minding my own business.' I shouldn't have said that, but the guy's attitude was getting up my nose.

His companion had joined him. 'What my colleague means is it's neither near her home, office or your home.'

How the hell did they know that? 'Are we restricted to where we can go now?' I told myself to calm down.

'When people get defensive about what they're doing, we get suspicious.'

I didn't respond. That I was on my way to break into a garage unit made sweat run down my spine. Then I remembered that apart from the tools, which had innocent uses, I also had a tracker on me.

'What you got in the boot?' the first one asked.

I knew I could refuse, but they were already suspicious and would give me a hard time. I had an idea and hoped Oscar would play along. 'Let me show you.' I got out, and Oscar tried to follow. 'Stay, boy!' I used a stop gesture.

He hated that and snarled in response.

'Shit!' I jumped back and slammed the door, stepping away from the car. 'It should be okay to check the boot. He's only got over the back seat into it once.' I paused a beat. 'Twice. Sorry, but the guy shouldn't have been trying to steal Zofia's shopping.'

'Is that her dog?'

'He comes with the car. He's okay once you get to know him.'

Oscar placed his nose against the back window and bared his teeth.

'Okay, we'll let it go this time.' Although we'd discouraged them from looking in the boot, they still checked the tyres and the lights before deciding to stop harassing me.

They walked off and, as I congratulated myself and Oscar, one of them stopped. 'Adie Lambert sends his regards.' He winked and returned to his car.

I got back in mine, watched them drive off and sat for several minutes, shaking and soaked in sweat. They, or someone like them, would be back. I retrieved my phone and punched in a stored number with trembling hands.

'Victor?'

'Hi Judy. I've thought about it. Is the job still open?'

I held my breath, worried she'd say no, and released it when she said, 'When can you start?'

'Tomorrow?'

'Don't you need to give Zofia notice?'

'She'll be fine.' I wouldn't tell her I'd been suspended. After agreeing to see her tomorrow at midday, I ended the call.

Instead of elation – I'd have a great salary, a car and a fabulous apartment, and, if Alex Novak was right, the police would leave me alone – a sense of sadness overwhelmed me. I didn't know who I feared telling most – Zofia and Kasper, or Craig and John. But that could wait. Tonight, we needed to attach the tracker to the pickup.

More bad news. Oscar put his head between the seats.

'No, boy.' I stroked his head. 'We'll be moving into the flat in the sky.'

He withdrew his head and spun on the back seat, howling at the roof. ***Can we go now?***

'Maybe tomorrow. Now we've got to pick up Cleo, and then we've got work to do.' Although I wanted to see Zofia, part of me hoped she'd not be there so I could put off telling her my news.

CHAPTER 34

When Victor took the tracker Kasper had brought and left with Oscar, the office felt empty. Zofia thought back to when they'd made coffee. She was sure he'd felt something when their hands touched. She had.

Although keen to find ammunition to use against both Mulberry and Glass, she wanted to focus on the people who'd attacked Victor's van.

Kasper stared at his screen with a frown.

'What's up?'

'The image of the number plate isn't brilliant.'

'I thought you'd got a clear image.' Typical of Kasper to give an over-optimistic initial assessment.

'Even cleaned up, one letter could be a B or an R and another might be a D or an O, or even a Q.'

'That's only six combinations.'

'Hmm, this end one is even dodgier.'

'Let's see.' She joined her brother and peered at the image. The last letter showed as a blurred blob. 'I see what you mean. We can rule out several letters it *can't* be.' She listed them.

His shoulders slumped. 'That still leaves eighteen it could be.'

Even more typical of her brother: first underestimate an obstacle, then overreact once he'd discovered it was bigger than he first thought. 'That's just over a hundred combinations. We know the car's a Tesla, so it should cut that down significantly.'

'Yeah, you're right.'

'That shouldn't take too long.'

She returned to her desk and opened the database linking car number plates to their registered keepers. She made good progress, eliminating many because of the make of car. Halfway through the list, only two cars matched the make, but a run of five from the same dealer took her up to seven. Then, Kasper let out a cry and jumped up.

'What's wrong?'

'My appointment with our solicitor,' he said. 'She's fitted me in at lunchtime after letting me down yesterday.' He rushed out, slamming the door behind him.

Zofia fetched his list of the numbers checked and added them to hers. With her brother out of the office, she could have Cleo under her desk.

Half an hour later, she took her out to the local park. Cleo had gained weight, so she no longer looked skeletal, and with the fur growing over the shaved patch, she looked far better than when she'd arrived. People stopped to admire her and, although still lacking in confidence, she no longer cowered behind Zofia.

Back in the office, Zofia finished the list and now had eight names and addresses. She opened a map and marked them off. Three were over a four-hour drive away, so she put them to one side, focusing on the other five.

None had an obvious connection to their prime suspect, DS Adrian Lambert. She realised they should have a more open mind; after all, they still didn't know who'd been behind the attack. According to Victor, the most likely candidates were Lambert, Novak and the unnamed security guards he'd had a run-in with.

The outer door opened, and Kasper clattered up the stairs. Zofia moved Cleo to her bed at the far end of the office and made him a coffee.

'How did you get on with the solicitor?' She placed the mug on his desk.

'A waste of time. She said that it depends on the SPI rulebook. Although the police haven't charged Victor, the SPI could take a credible report that the police are investigating him as grounds to suspend our membership.'

'What about the fact we've suspended *him*?' Which still rankled with Zofia.

'That's in our favour. She recommended we carry out an independent investigation into the incident.'

'There was no *incident*.'

'I told her that, and she said my attitude illustrated why it had to be independent.'

'Let me guess, she offered to get her firm to do it.'

'For a fat fee, yep.'

'How have you left it?'

'She's agreed to write a letter on our behalf, outlining what we've done and emphasising that the police still haven't charged Victor.'

'Fat lot of use that will be.' The unfairness of the situation infuriated her.

'We have to do something.'

'I know, and I'm not blaming you. Let's focus on looking for some leverage to get Glass to back off.'

'I mentioned the fact Lambert has been harassing Victor, getting him chucked out of one site and following him to another.'

'What did she say to that?'

'Do we have evidence?'

She jabbed a hand at her screen. 'If we can link the attack on Victor's caravan to Lambert, that's plenty of evidence.'

'Can we?'

'Not yet.' She gave him the five names she thought most likely to be involved. 'Can you check their social media to see if they're linked in any way? I'd focus on Lambert as the prime suspect.'

She returned to her investigation, and an email arrived, a response to a search on Robertson. It listed his investments. The man had the sort of wealth that would make most people happy. Although there were no overt questions about the source of his money, the notes at the bottom suggested he may have been involved in low-level money laundering, but Police Scotland didn't have enough proof – or couldn't be bothered to look for it. They listed three senior police officers linked to him, which suggested the latter. She carried out searches of the officers and saw one was in Manchester, but it wasn't Mulberry.

Zofia added the information to the report she'd already started. She didn't think the rumours of money laundering would bother Judy. She'd mention it in the executive summary, but she wouldn't say anything about his relationship with the police officers. It was outside the remit of their brief, and would be useful to keep back in case he ever did decide to come after them, once he'd gone into business with Judy.

The other agency she'd spoken to hadn't replied, so she sent a chase-up. The search through the online footprints of the five car owners took the rest of the day, and they still hadn't finished when Kasper sat back with a long sigh.

'Shall we finish?'

She checked the time. 'It's early.'

'Gone five.' He cleared his throat. 'Our solicitor made it very clear that Victor must not come to the office while suspended until we or the police clear him. We need to get out before he comes by for Cleo.'

She closed her eyes and drew in a breath. 'Right, give me five.' She made a fuss of Cleo before leaving, but the poor dog's pitiful cries as they locked her in followed Zofia to the car.

'Victor won't be long.' Kasper squeezed her shoulder and walked around to the driver's side.

Zofia looked back towards the office, unable to dismiss the feeling that something bad had happened.

CHAPTER 35

Judy's dream of her throwing Sweeny over the side of a cruise liner and watching the bloody froth in their wake after the propeller finished with him lingered as she woke the next morning from a troubled sleep. She didn't need a soothsayer to interpret that dream, and she ground her teeth as she grabbed her first coffee of the day.

At nine, she rang the estate agent selling Sweeny's house. He assured her that the house wasn't in a chain, so he wasn't waiting to sell it before moving out. It confirmed her fear that he'd run off. She probed, hoping to find out where Sweeny was moving to, but the estate agent grew suspicious, and she ended the call. She decided not to say anything to her father about her suspicions and drove in to work to continue her search for their assets, in particular, the money her brothers had taken out of the casino by mortgaging the building.

Her father's driver had collected him before she left the house, but he wasn't at the office when she arrived. She was sure she'd discovered everything on Sweeny's computer, and she made a start on the paperwork. As she returned the contents of another filing cabinet drawer, her dad appeared in the doorway.

His expression told a story. 'What's up, Dad?'

He closed the door and approached Sweeny's desk. 'You'd better sit down.'

She did. 'Okay, what's happened?'

He struggled to get the words out. 'I think Jerry's done a runner.'

Relief that it wasn't a fresh disaster made her light-headed. 'Yes, I drove past Jerry's house, and he's selling it. The estate agent intimated he's not buying anything else.'

'Oh, yeah. He told me about that. He's downsizing, he owns a nice flat in Bowdon. No, I went to see the accountant he's supposedly working for when he leaves. He plays golf with a mate of mine, and he said Jerry's not spoken to him about a job.'

Her insides fluttered. 'Right.' She took a deep breath. 'Do you know who he took the cruise with?'

'Sorry, no. But Keira might.'

She called her PA in. Could she trust her? 'Keira, did Jerry say who the cruise was with?'

Keira frowned. 'I can't recall the cruise line, but he always booked through the same agency. I teased him about paying extra for something he could have got on the internet, but his friend runs it.'

'Yeah, I know who you mean,' her father said. 'Thanks, Keira.'

Judy suppressed her irritation as Keira closed the door behind her. She'd wanted to question Keira about what she'd found on Sweeny's computer, but maybe it was best to do it without her father present. She'd tell him when she had something more concrete. He was making a call at the moment, so she returned to the filing cabinet and opened the next drawer.

Her dad ended the call. 'Fucking bastard!' He threw the handset onto the desk. 'Sorry, love, I hate foul language.'

She returned to the chair and waited for him to elaborate.

'The bastard booked a cruise, but didn't show up in Southampton. He's set us up.' Alex clenched his fists and slammed them on the arms of his chair. 'BASTARD!'

Judy glanced at the door. 'Okay, Dad. Let's keep this quiet. We don't want rumours to start. And you know we discussed taking on Jerry's daughter to keep him in line once he'd left? Let's forget that idea; that's well and truly flown.' Once they'd got through the current crisis, they'd find another way to deal with him.

He glared at her and then subsided. 'Yeah, you're right. I've got the list you asked me to compile. I'll email it to you.'

'Thanks, Dad. We'll get through this.'

She paused in her checking of Sweeny's filing cabinets and returned to her office, partly to give herself a break from scanning paper files, but also because she had plenty of other work to keep on top of. The most pressing problem was replacing Sweeny. Whoever came in would need to get to grips with it on their own, as Sweeny would clearly not be doing a handover.

A call on her mobile stopped her in her tracks. 'Victor?'

'Hi Judy. I've thought about it. Is the job still open?'

Taken aback, she hesitated. Had Zofia told him about the other candidates? Whatever the reason, she was grateful. 'When can you start?'

Did that sound too eager? Did it matter? She was giving him the job, so she was clearly keen. His being able to start the next day was a big bonus. She ended the call with a sense of relief. She went to her father's office to give him the good news.

'Something made him change his mind,' she said.

He grinned. 'I think I know what that might be.'

'Oh yeah? What have you been up to?'

He tapped the side of his nose. 'What you don't know can't hurt you.'

She wished that were true. Plenty of things she didn't know seemed to be hurting her now. Still, it was with a sense of positivity she hadn't felt for a while that she returned to Sweeny's office to work through his files. By ten that night, she still had one cabinet to check, but went home, exhausted and frustrated.

CHAPTER 36

When I got back to the office, Zofia and Kasper had left, and although it meant I could put off telling them, I hated not seeing Zofia. Much as I knew she'd be disappointed at my leaving, part of me was desperate to share my good news with her. Cleo, relieved when we arrived to collect her, shared the back seat with Oscar, and I set off. I arrived at the rendezvous point, the disused garage where we'd met the man who'd photographed the pickup. Craig got in the front and John joined Toff in the back. Toff was the youngest and fittest and should fit through the window at the back of the unit where I'd hoped to find the pickup. Oscar wasn't happy to be squashed up with Cleo but, excited about the move, didn't complain too much.

Are you going to tell your friends the news?

'Not yet.'

Craig gave me a puzzled look but realised I was talking to Oscar and ignored me. We drove past the industrial estate, but several units near our target had lights on. I carried on and we stopped to get a takeaway at a drive-through. We finished eating and returned to find fewer lights, but still too many. While I drove, I worried the police would stop us. They must have the car's details and would be looking out for it to harass me.

At ten thirty, we found the site in darkness and, turning my lights off, I stopped by the narrow alley leading to the back of the unit. Craig and Toff put the gloves on and got out, carrying the items they needed in a carrier bag. If we got stopped now, we had no excuses. I drove around to the front of the unit and parked in the shadows where I could see the entrance without being noticed.

* * *

Round the back, Toff followed Craig, who used the narrow beam of the torch to light their way. They followed Victor's directions and found the mark he'd scratched on the back wall of the target unit using the corner of an old brick. Craig handed the torch to Toff and pulled out the can of spray-on lubricant. The noise of the spray echoed in the alleyway, and the stench of oil and chemicals filled the air.

Craig retrieved the screwdriver set, found the right one and attacked the screws. Toff took the tape out of the bag and stuffed it in a pocket. Accompanied by a series of grunts and much muttered swearing, Craig removed six of the screws securing the mesh and handed them to Toff. He then used the wire cutters to free the last two while Toff held the mesh in place. The biggest screwdriver made quick work of the lock on the window.

'You ready?' Craig whispered.

Toff could only nod. He gave the screws to Craig, who placed them in his pocket, cupped his hands together and boosted Toff up to the opening. With his shoulders inside the opening and legs supported by Craig, he swung the torch beam around the inside. The pickup almost filled the unit, which was not much bigger than a domestic garage. It left a gap of fifty centimetres between the pickup and the back wall.

Toff held the torch in his teeth and reached down to the rear of the pickup, pushing with his legs. At the tipping point, he slid forward, breaking his fall and landing with a thump in the load-bed.

'You okay?' Craig's hoarse whisper carried from outside.

'Yeah, sound.' He rubbed his ribs where they'd caught against the roll of tape and lowered himself to the floor.

Craig had talked him through where best to place the tracker, showing him a picture on his phone, and he inspected the underside of the vehicle. Dried mud coated the steel beam Craig had identified, and he used the torch to chip away at it. Once he'd cleared a large enough patch, he retrieved the tracker and attached it to the top of the beam with a satisfying clunk.

He pulled out the roll of tape, found the end and pulled off a strip. The sound filled his ears, and when he stopped pulling, his phone vibrated. Before he could check it, the roller-shutter clanked upwards.

Shit!

CHAPTER 37

Zofia had taken her laptop home and intended to continue her investigation of the five Tesla drivers. After they'd eaten, she remained at the kitchen table with her laptop and cup of tea. At around ten, as she considered packing up for the night, she found a picture of one of the drivers on the website of a football team. The driver, Lyndon Bennett, stood to the left of the team photo, and behind him, a face she recognised.

With a sense of excitement, she carried out a check of Bennett's social media. His LinkedIn profile listed his employer, and she investigated them. Once she'd got the information she needed and come up with a plan, she called her brother.

He stuck his head into the kitchen. 'Yeah?'

'Look at this.' She spun the screen so he could see it.

He peered at the image. 'Bloody hell, that's Lambert.'

'Unless he's got a twin.' She pointed at Bennett. 'And that's the guy who parked his car at Victor's caravan site the morning someone wrecked his van.'

'But we're not sure, are we? He owns one of the five cars it could be.'

'You think it's a coincidence he knows Lambert?'

'Yeah, okay.' Kasper fetched the remains of the beer he'd been drinking and sat next to her. 'What do you want to do?'

She'd been considering her next steps since she began the search. 'We should contact the driver and tell him we know he took part in the attack on Victor's van.'

'But we can't prove it.'

'He doesn't know that. But if we get the police to investigate, I'm sure they'll find his car on one of the local ANPR cameras. He won't have signed up for a police investigation. I bet Lambert told him it was just a prank and would be a laugh.'

'You think the police will investigate it?'

'They will since I contacted the local animal charity and explained about the two dogs being in the van.'

'You could be right.' But Kasper made it clear he didn't think it would work. 'How will you get hold of him?'

'I'll ring him at work tomorrow. He works for a PR company. They won't be impressed if one of their staff is involved in an unprovoked attack on two dogs. The guy who runs the company is a dog owner himself. His company sponsors a charity looking after strays.'

'And then what?'

'We use it to get Lambert to back off.'

He nodded. 'You going to tell Victor?'

'Of course. Blast, not tonight – he's planting the tracker.'

CHAPTER 38

John and I swivelled in our seats and watched the car drive towards us, slow and cautious with no lights, just like we'd done. We kept still and held our breaths until it passed us. It slowed, the flaring brake lights blinding us. Had he seen us? But no, he stopped outside the unit and got out. I picked my phone off the dashboard and sent Toff a warning. John did the same to Craig.

Were they going out so soon after their last attack? But the driver had parked blocking the exit, and only one man got out. I peered at the car but couldn't see anyone else in it. I lowered the windows, letting in icy air, then checked my phone for a reply from Toff. We didn't even know if he'd got in yet, or if he'd finished and they were reattaching the grille.

The heavy-set and shaven-headed man placed the padlock on the ground and lifted the roller-shutter.

I leant across to John and whispered, 'If he finds Toff, we go in and sort him.' When had I become this tough guy?

John nodded. We'd lose any chance of catching them with evidence, but our friend's safety trumped that.

Almost at once, a car door slammed, and the man came out carrying a piece of fabric. He stuck it in a pocket, lowered and locked the gate and drove off. We waited in silence for a moment, then John's phone vibrated.

A text from Craig: All okay, coming out.

Relief flooded through me, and I bumped fists with John before closing the windows. The next message from Craig saying they'd finished seemed to take an age coming, and we drove around to meet them at the end of the alley. While we waited, John got in the back, Oscar grumbling because he had to move. Toff appeared first, almost dancing with exhilaration, with Craig, his usual placid self, following.

The doors slammed, and I drove off, eager to escape from the scene of our crime. 'What happened, Toff?'

'Bloody hell, I almost pissed meself. I was just taping the tracker to the cross beam like Craig said, when the shutter started opening. I pulled me legs under the truck and prayed, but he just opened the car door, then shut it and left.'

'He collected some clothing.'

John leant forward. 'You noticed he wore gloves?'

'I was memorising the number plate of his car.' I should make a note before I forgot it.

'I reckon they're making sure there's nothing linking them to the pickup. He must have left something he'd worn behind.'

Toff said, 'There was a funny box welded next to the spare wheel.'

'What do you mean?' Craig asked.

'You showed me a picture of the underside, but someone had added a box – like a money box, a kind of safe, with a lock on it.'

I filed this information away. 'Craig, are you picking up the tracker?'

'Yeah, I checked before we left. Nice powerful signal. And you said we can pick it up from anywhere, so I don't need to stay local?'

'That's what Kasper said, and the battery should last.'

Relieved that we'd succeeded without serious mishap, I dropped my friends off and arrived at the campsite at around one in the morning, wondering what the hell was in the box under the vehicle.

CHAPTER 39

Judy got in early and finished the final filing cabinet. She'd still found no paperwork relating to the new company she'd found in the hidden folder on Sweeny's PC.

She needed to get hold of two million before they could move ahead on the project. Most of the properties they owned were mortgage-free. She'd have to get them valued and see what they could borrow. She rang their bank manager to discuss the best way of doing it.

'We wouldn't extend a mortgage to a company registered in a foreign jurisdiction.'

Bugger! She hadn't thought that would be a problem. 'How can we get around that?'

'We don't get "around" it. You must transfer the properties into the ownership of the company. There will be tax implications, and I'd suggest you speak to a specialist, but it could be a very lengthy and expensive exercise.'

She didn't like the sound of that, and she didn't have time for a *lengthy* process. 'Is there another way you can do it?'

'You could sell them. But you'd have to account for the money to the taxman.' He paused, letting that sink in. 'Your brothers owned their own homes outright. Milan's is going to his wife, but

Marko's is still going through probate. Do you know who he's left it to?'

He'd not left a will, but their father was his next of kin. An idea occurred to her. 'I've got three flats in the tower. They're each worth at least a million—'

'I doubt that.'

'What do you mean?'

'One of my other clients has just sold one very much like yours. The issues with leaks, lifts breaking down and structural concrete needing repairs meant he got less than six hundred.'

This hit her like a punch in the gut. 'I'll get them valued.'

She ended the call feeling sick. Although she would get them valued, including the one she'd offered to Victor, she suspected the bank manager was right. He had a finger on the city's financial pulse, which is why they used him.

Unless she could raise another two million, and sharpish, she was in deep trouble.

CHAPTER 40

That morning, Zofia and Kasper drove in early. Kasper had an appointment with a client for nine sharp, and they needed to keep them happy, especially as they'd not had a single new enquiry since the SPI took them off their website. The office felt lonely without Cleo or Oscar.

When Victor hadn't shown up by nine, she began to worry. Had things gone wrong last night?

She resisted the temptation to chase him up and instead called up the number of the employer of Lyndon Bennett, the man she'd identified as the driver of the car near Victor's van the night it had been toppled. Zofia claimed to be working on behalf of the news outlet she'd given the Glass story to. A story about a corrupt copper victimising a former homeless man was perfect for them to run, and Bennett would have no doubt she worked for them.

'Hi, Lyndon Bennett here. I've worked with you before.' He mentioned the reporter Zofia had dealt with.

'Yeah, she'll be involved with this story.'

'Great, say hi. How may I help you?' He had a faint Canadian accent.

'You've not had your Tesla stolen, have you?'

'My car, no, why? It's downstairs in the parking garage.'

Great! You can't claim someone took it. 'We're doing a story about people attacking pets.'

'Pets? What's this about?'

'A couple of days ago, a gang of thugs attacked two dogs—'

'That's awful, but what's it got to do with me? I assumed you had some work for us or wanted a favour.'

'The dogs were in a minivan, and someone pushed it over on its side.'

He didn't reply for an age, but Zofia heard his breathing.

'Nothing to say, Mr Bennett?' This time she let the silence build.

'Nobody mentioned the dogs,' he said very quietly. 'Are they okay?'

'One's traumatised, but physically they're not too bad.'

'Good.' He paused again. 'Look, I've got nothing to say to you.'

'You've just confessed you did it by telling me you didn't know the dogs were in there.'

'No, I haven't.' He sounded like a petulant child.

Zofia couldn't help laughing. 'We've got footage of your car, and you've just confessed.'

He didn't respond.

'Apart from the police, who admittedly may only do you for criminal damage, how do you think your boss will feel about you hurting those dogs?'

This last threat did the trick.

'Look, the guy said—' He swallowed. 'I just know him through the soccer team.'

She waited for him to continue.

'We just did it as a favour.'

'A favour?'

'Yeah, Adie's a cop, and he'd done a favour for one of us, getting him off a speeding ticket, so he asked us if we'd push this van over. It was meant to be a prank.'

'Adie. Is that Adrian Lambert?'

'Should I be talking to my lawyer?'

'If Sergeant Lambert misled you into thinking the van was empty—'

'Yeah. He told us to wait until the guy went for a wash.'

'So it *was* Adrian Lambert?'

'You won't mention I gave you the name?'

'Of course not. We never disclose a source.'

He hesitated, and she held her breath.

'Yeah, it was.'

CHAPTER 41

I woke late and took the dogs out before having a shower in the toilet block. The thought that I'd soon have my own unlimited supply of hot water helped me bear the irritation of being left with lukewarm water.

By the time I'd driven to the office, though, trepidation had overtaken me. I toyed with the idea of not telling Kasper, and especially Zofia, that I'd agreed to take the job with Judy. They'd suspended me, after all, so wouldn't notice if I didn't come in to work. I tried telling myself that getting rid of me would make their lives easier, but couldn't make it stick. If Mulberry was indeed targeting them, my leaving would only send him off in search of another, perhaps more destructive angle.

My search for some way to soften the blow produced a strategy I was at least somewhat happy with by the time I pulled into the car park. With any luck, Zofia would have traced the car of the people who'd attacked my van. I'd give her the number of the car we'd seen last night, and then I'd drop my bombshell.

Oscar studied me as we approached the front door. ***What's up with you?***

'Nothing, why?'

You're like you were the day before we got chucked out of our home in Bristol.

That was a day I tried to forget. I'd come clean to my wife about the fact that the company I'd worked for had sacked me several months earlier. She'd not taken it well, especially when she received photos of me with a female colleague in a wine bar. The meeting had been completely innocent – I'd met her to discuss how we could save *her* job after she'd embezzled money from our employer. And then, no good deed ever going unpunished, she'd ended up accusing *me* of the crime, and they'd believed her.

That was the start of the worst eighteen months of my life, until I met Kasper. And then I met Zofia. And while I'd not exactly been floating from triumph to triumph since then, the general thrust of my fortunes did seem to be climbing.

Well, most days. Or at least with increasing frequency? I'd settle for that.

Well? Oscar pressed. ***I'd rather not be surprised. Are we doomed to another string of disasters?***

'Don't be so dramatic. Come on, let's go in.' I opened the door and let him and Cleo precede me.

Zofia's affectionate greeting of the two dogs weakened my resolve, but I pasted on a smile and followed them into the office. She was on her own, so I didn't have to endure Kasper's disapproval at my being there in office hours. It also gave me an excuse to have a coffee and delay telling them my news. I needed both there when I did, I told myself. And besides, Zofia obviously had news of her own.

'What have you got?'

She gave a big smile. 'We've tracked down the owner of the Tesla you found on the doorbell camera.'

'Bloody hell! That's brilliant. Have you told the police?'

'Not yet.' She told me about the links between the guy who'd turned my van over and DS Lambert.

'What does Kasper say?'

'He doesn't know yet. I spoke to the guy ten minutes ago. I was going to use the information to pressurise Lambert into backing off.'

It seemed like a good idea, but I had concerns. 'What if Lambert forces Bennett to withdraw his claim? You recorded him without telling him, isn't that illegal?'

She grimaced. 'Not unless we share it, and it also depends if they see it as a business call, or if I can claim I was doing a friend a favour. I don't think it will come to that. We're not planning to prosecute them, are we? We just want Lambert to back off.'

That meant the people who made me homeless would go unpunished. I didn't like that, and now I was leaving KZD Lambert wasn't a threat.

'How did you get on last night? Did you attach the tracker?'

'Yeah, no worries.' Although I doubt Toff would have agreed; he'd looked shaken by the experience.

I gave her the number plate I'd collected.

'Whose car is this?' She opened her database and typed in the figures.

'It belongs to a guy who took something out of the pickup I saw following Harry.'

'You think he's involved in Harry's murder?'

I could only shrug. 'If nothing else, he's got questions to answer.'

It didn't take long to find the owner. 'It's registered to Ryland and Co. They're commercial estate agents.'

That clicked for me. 'They've got a board outside the unit where they're keeping the pickup. I rang, and they told me it's not available. The guy must be senior if he can keep a unit unoccupied. It's a clever ploy. If it's ever discovered, they don't own or rent it, so the people working at the estate agency might not get investigated.'

Zofia punched some more keys and turned the screen so I could see it. I moved closer and caught a hint of her subtle perfume.

I tried to ignore it and forced myself to focus on the screen. A page of the estate agents' website showed headshots of several people. I studied them and, with growing excitement, pointed at the manager.

'That's him.'

Zofia turned the screen back and read the name, Merkul Akimov. 'I know that surname.'

'Yeah, that's the same one as the guy you and . . . The guy who died when . . .' I didn't want to say, 'the guy you and your brother killed', but that was the size of it: either she or Kasper, or both of them, *had* killed a man with that surname.

'Yes,' she said, her eyes glistening, 'that's him.'

I wanted to comfort her – tell her the man would have killed her, and me – but instead, considered the implications. 'They must be related.'

She focused on the screen as her fingers caressed the keys. 'Three Akimovs in the UK, two in London and one in the North West.' She typed some more. 'A year ago, there were two up here.'

'The chances are he's the brother or cousin of the one . . . who died.'

Zofia studied me. 'What are you thinking?'

'The security guys I ran into the other night knew a man with a dog had been watching the Novak boys and their men, including the dead Akimov, in the days before they were all killed. If they knew, then Novak's people probably knew, and this guy, the brother, cousin or whatever, might think I had something to do with his relative's death.'

'And he's targeting homeless men with dogs because he's looking for you?'

Typical of Zofia to reach a conclusion in moments, which had taken me days. 'I think so.'

'But Cleo looks nothing like Oscar.'

Not all dogs can be as handsome as me.

'If this guy just has a description of an older homeless man with a medium-sized dog, he could be targeting *any* homeless guys with dogs.'

'Thank God you're no longer homeless.' She reddened. 'I meant . . . it's another reason to be grateful.'

I gave her a smile. 'I know what you mean.'

'You said there were two of them. Do you know anything about the other one?'

'Oh yes. I got hold of his work ID card—'

Who got hold of his ID card?

'—Oscar got the man's ID card, and I traced him to a firm of accountants based in Spinningfields.'

Thank you.

'High end, then. You got the name?'

'Miles Colby.' I'd never forget that name. 'Kasper compared his photo to one of the men in the pickup and said there's an over eighty per cent chance it's the same man.' I'd convinced myself it was a hundred.

'The firm he works for?'

'Sorry, Ash and Caulk. He's still there. I checked the other day.'

'I've heard that name before, and I'm wondering why.' She typed it in. 'I thought so. They work for our old friend Rudy Glass.' She punched more keys, and Colby's familiar face appeared on the screen.

'Did you know you were doing that?' Zofia asked.

'What?'

'It was like a cross between a snarl and a growl.' My face grew hot, and she laughed. 'I'll take it as confirmation he's the other man you're looking for. I'll carry out background checks on him and the estate agent.'

An email arrived with a name I recognised in the title, and Zofia spun the screen away so I could no longer see it.

'Sorry, Victor, I need to respond to this, it's urgent.'

Why was she getting an email with Archie Robertson's name in the title? Had he been back in touch with her?

I moved away and jotted down Merkul Akimov's name. Part of me wanted to stay to discuss the best way of dealing with Lambert. Even though he'd soon not be a threat to me according to Alex Novak, he remained one to Zofia and Kasper.

On the other hand, if I left now, I could avoid telling them I'd be leaving.

Before I could make my escape, Kasper returned. He didn't look happy I was there, but said nothing about it. Nor was I pleased, as his arrival removed any excuse I had to delay telling them I was leaving. Though I could just sneak off while Zofia was busy and send them an email, couldn't I?

No. I couldn't do anything that cowardly.

While I exchanged strained pleasantries with Kasper, Zofia finished what she was doing.

'While Victor's here, Kasper, why don't we discuss what to do with Lambert?'

'What about Lambert?'

Zofia brought him up to date about finding the link between the owner of the Tesla and Lambert.

Kasper punched his left palm. 'We've got the bastard.'

'The question is, how best to deal with him.'

Zofia turned to me. 'What do you think, Victor?'

I'd been watching the discussion, feeling I was outside my body. Now I froze for a moment, then to my relief my mind's gears engaged. 'It would buy you only a temporary reprieve. Your main tormentor is Mulberry, and Lambert is just the tool he's using. It won't take him long to find another.'

Kasper slumped in his seat. 'You're right.'

Zofia looked exasperated. 'Yes, of course, we keep working on Mulberry and Glass, who is ultimately the instigator of all this. But getting Lambert out of the game means you can come back to work. We can threaten to expose his part in wrecking your van and get him to withdraw his threat to charge you with assault, and once he does that the SPI won't demand your suspension.'

It was now or never. I had to tell them.

Zofia misunderstood why I was hesitating. 'If you're worried about this investigation into Harry's killers, you can have as much time as you need.' She stilled Kasper with a gesture.

'Thanks, that's very generous.' I took a deep breath.

Just tell them, will you? Don't be a coward. Oscar had left Cleo by the window and joined me.

I just blurted it: 'I'm going to have to resign.'

'What are you talking about?' Kasper demanded.

I'd kept my attention on Zofia, and watched with a pang as comprehension bloomed across her face. 'You've accepted the job offer.'

'I've got nowhere to live, Zofia. The thought of being homeless again or living somewhere like the shitholes I've looked at in the last few days . . .' I took another breath. 'I just couldn't do it. This way, my daughters can stay with me—'

'What's going on?' Kasper's voice rose.

Zofia, eyes brimming, shook her head. 'I understand. You don't need to explain yourself to us.'

But I did.

CHAPTER 42

I left the offices of KZD in the back of a black cab, Oscar at my feet. The expression of hurt in Kasper's eyes when he realised what was happening had almost surpassed the pain in Zofia's. Wretchedness and gloom enveloped me. Anyone observing me would imagine I was on my way to get sacked, rather than being transported to a job and a dream flat.

'Bad news, mate?' The cabbie studied me in a small rear-seat mirror.

'No, not really.'

He digested my reply. 'Gambling isn't the answer.'

'What?'

'You're going to the casino. There's only one thing people go to do there.'

'Right. No, I'm not going gambling. I've got a job interview there.'

'Ah. Well, if you don't mind me giving you some advice, I'd cheer up.'

'I do mind, actually.'

This bounced off him. 'People don't come to the casino to see a miserable sod. I don't, I could get that at home.' He shook his head. 'I was miserable when I married me missus, and I thought it was because I was hiding my true self, so when I came out, I thought I'd be happy. I was, for about a month. But then . . .'

I tuned him out, but at base he was right. If I presented her with a miserable sod, Judy could withdraw her offer. No, I'd need to impress her for a few months until I became indispensable. I realised I'd not considered this as a long-term move, but a stepping stone. Whatever it was, I needed to shine.

'That's better.' The cabbie gave me a thumbs-up.

My scowl returned until we drew up outside the casino, when it deepened, as the driver, seeing a homeless woman across the square, made a derogatory comment ending in, 'Bleeding beggars.'

I used my card to pay. 'You don't mind if I give your tip to that woman over there?'

I slammed the door behind me, cutting off his expletive-laden response, and made my way across to my old spot in the alley where Oscar and I had spent many months. The woman who now occupied it studied me with suspicion until I pulled out a fiver and handed it to her.

Her smile lit up her face. 'Oh, cheers, mate, that's very generous.'

I returned across the square, wishing I could do more than give her a few quid.

The casino wasn't open yet, so I rang the doorbell. A large man in a suit opened the door. 'We're not open for another five minutes, mate.' He noticed Oscar. 'If he's not a guide dog, he's not coming in.'

'I'm here to see Judy. Name's Victor.' I'd stick with my street name, for a time anyway.

His manner changed. 'Oh, right. Mr Mitchum, isn't it? I'll take you straight up.' He still gave Oscar a scowl.

You can call me Mr Wilde III. Oscar adopted a swagger and walked alongside me as I followed the bouncer upstairs and through a door marked 'Staff Only'.

Judy stood as I entered her large office. She nodded a thanks to the bouncer and gestured to the visitor's chair.

'Welcome, Victor, glad to have you on board.' She glanced at Oscar. 'And you, Oscar.' She looked tired, and dark smudges discoloured the skin beneath her eyes.

I made the usual response, ensuring I infused my voice with enough enthusiasm. 'Sorry about Oscar, I came in a cab.'

'No worries.' She talked me through my role, giving me a manual which I suspected she'd produced since I'd accepted the job.

For the first time in almost two years, I'd be managing people and have a job with serious responsibilities. The thought energised me, and by the time she showed me round – leaving Oscar in her office – I wasn't faking it.

During my tour of the offices, she'd ignored two doors opposite each other and then taken me down to the casino and kitchens. The delicious aroma of cooking reminded me I'd not had a proper breakfast. I tried to memorise the bewildering array of names as I met all the staff. We returned to the offices, and she took me to the first of the two doors. She knocked and waited for Alex Novak to invite us in.

Judy gestured for me to go ahead, and the scent of a powerful aftershave mingled with older odours as I entered an even bigger office. Judy had made it clear she ran the operation, so I suspected she'd let her father have the bigger office to assuage his ego. Trophies more fitting for a younger man adorned the walls and surfaces. Were these left by his sons? That I'd been involved in their deaths, however tangentially, made my insides tremble. He must never find out. Even the fact that I'd saved his life wouldn't spare me from his wrath.

'Welcome, Victor.' He crushed my hand. 'A great Buddhist teacher said, "There are three essentials to leadership: humility, clarity and courage." I know you have the first.' He winked.

I waited for him to continue, and Judy filled the silence. 'What Dad means is he's looking forward to working with you. It was he who talked me into offering you the job.'

'And I'm sure I won't regret it, will I, Victor?' He studied me with his deep-set dark brown eyes.

'I'm sure you won't, Alex.' I held his gaze.

Again, Judy broke the silence. 'I'll take you and Oscar to your office.'

I nodded goodbye to her dad and followed her. We collected the handbook and Oscar from her office and made our way to the last door.

'I'll make other arrangements for Oscar.'

What arrangements?

'I'll put him in doggy day care.' With my new salary, I'd have the money to do it.

Why don't you have me put down?

'There's no need,' she assured me. 'He'll be okay, but don't let him enter the kitchen or dining area.'

Judy opened the door to a decent-sized office, not anything like the one her father occupied, but bigger than the one I'd had in Bristol. The chemical stink of a plug-in air freshener lingered. Oscar wandered around the room, checking the corners. In the final one, he cocked his leg.

'Oi, no!' I stepped towards him.

I was joking. You've got no sense of humour. He lowered his leg and trotted on.

'He thinks it's funny.'

Judy didn't look amused. 'I'll let you get used to your office. All your passwords and instructions are in that.' She nodded at the handbook and left us to it.

'You trying to get us thrown out?'

Even you must have noticed the funny stink.

I approached the window, which looked out over the back of the building. Novak's office must overlook the square. I found the number for the kitchen and ordered a sandwich and something for Oscar. I'd have to get him bowls and a bed. Over the next two hours, I searched through the filing cabinets and got to know the computer system.

Keira Foley, a smartly dressed woman in her mid-thirties with a no-nonsense chestnut bob and square, tortoiseshell glasses, was Judy's PA and office manager and seemed on top of the admin. I suspected I'd be relying on her until I got to grips with the systems they used.

Around four, Judy joined me and placed two sets of keys on my desk. 'These' – she touched the first set – 'are for your flat. Shall we go there and get your car? It's in the underground car park.' She pointed at the other set of keys. 'These are for the offices. I'll talk you through the alarm system.'

I memorised the code and the doors each key opened. Judy led us to her car and looked dubiously at Oscar. 'Shall we get a cab?'

The bright blue Maserati didn't appear to have a back seat. 'Good idea.'

Excuse me for not being good enough to get into her car.

We took a black cab waiting outside the casino for the brief journey to the tower block where we'd now be living. Oscar sulked until we entered the light-filled apartment. It contained everything we'd need apart from a bed for Oscar and my clothes. Judy showed us around, explaining the appliances and air control systems until a text from Zofia reminded me I had to collect Cleo.

We took the lift down to the basement car park, and she led me to a shiny Range Rover. 'This belonged to Marko, my brother. It's only got six thousand on the clock.'

With a shock, I remembered the identical car his older brother Milan drove. I'd left it full of bullet holes and surrounded by the bodies of the brothers and their men. The fact I'd not fired the guns didn't make it easier to forget what I'd seen.

'You okay, Victor?'

'Sure.' I clicked the doors open and let Oscar into the back. The odours of leather, polish and aftershave escaped.

I drove Judy back to the casino and, before she got out, she opened her handbag and handed me an envelope. 'Here's five grand. An advance on your first month's wages. Get yourself some decent clothes before you come back in. I want you to look the part before you meet the evening staff. See you at eight o'clock tomorrow night.'

I thanked her and set off for KZD's offices. A faint glow came from the front window, telling me Kasper and Zofia had gone home. With a sense of disappointment, I pulled into the car park and made my way up to collect Cleo. I supposed I should return my keys, but then, I told myself, Zofia would have to stop seeing Cleo, which would be unfair to both of them. A subdued Cleo got up and greeted Oscar when we walked into the office. I turned out the lamp they'd left on, set the alarm and led the dogs to the car.

Cleo hesitated when I opened the back door of the new car. Thinking it was because it was higher, I helped her up, but she didn't like the smell.

We arrived at the caravan park in darkness and, exhausted after a challenging day, I was tempted to spend a last night there. Then I thought of walking to the toilet block in the morning.

It didn't take long to pack all my belongings and clean the caravan. Lost in thought, I drove towards work, and it wasn't until I approached the shopping centre where I'd bought Oscar's harness that I realised my error. I continued along Cheetham Hill Road, and in the distance, the distinctive tower block I now called home rose above the bulk of the AO Arena. It disappeared as I passed between glass towers – changing the look and character of the city – and got closer to the stadium.

On Deansgate, cars like the one I now drove ferried their well-heeled occupants out for the evening, to the theatre, perhaps, or upmarket restaurants. I reminded myself I had five grand in my glove compartment and could join them. The city looked very different now that I had money. Once we'd arrived in the underground car park, I put the envelope in my jacket and grabbed my clothes. My bedding and other belongings could go to Digger to give to people who needed them.

Cleo found the car park intimidating and trembled as we entered the lift. The pungent perfume of a previous occupant filled the chamber. I knelt and reassured her as we rose forty-two floors. In the flat, Oscar showed her around while I put my meagre clothes in my bedroom's huge walk-in wardrobe.

Judy, or someone working for her, had filled the fridge, freezer and larder, including food for Oscar and Cleo. I fed them and opened a beer while my dinner heated in the oven. The view from the enclosed balcony took my breath away. I retrieved my phone and made a call.

'Dad! Is everything okay?'

'Hi Helen, of course.' Guilt that I didn't speak to my daughters often enough tempered my pleasure at hearing her voice.

Our initial awkwardness quickly wore off as I caught up with her news and came to the reason for my call. 'How would you and Em like to spend half-term up here?'

'With you, in Manchester?'

'Yeah.'

She was going to say no. I could imagine her mum and Al, the boyfriend, had arranged an exotic holiday.

The squeal almost burst my eardrum, and she shouted for Em to join her. Their excited chatter as they asked about Oscar and if we could go to Blackpool filled me with joy. An awkward conversation with their mother ended with Carol agreeing to let them come if I showed her the flat via a video call. The view almost settled it, but once they saw Cleo the girls would have defied their mother if she'd said no.

I ate and turned in, feeling that this made up for the sense that I'd betrayed Zofia and Kasper.

A call from John dragged me awake.

'Victor, the pickup's on the move. Come and collect us.'

CHAPTER 43

For half an hour after Victor left, taking Oscar with him, neither Zofia nor her brother spoke. She vacillated between a sense of anger that he'd betrayed them, to understanding he had to do what was best for his family. He owed them nothing more than his labour for the hours they paid him.

She focused on completing the report on Robertson. She was sure Victor had noticed his name, but they'd done plenty of work for the Scottish businessman, so he'd assume they had another job for him, if he thought of it at all. She finished her report and sent it to Judy.

'Coffee?' Kasper stood at her desk, a mug in his hand.

'Yeah, thanks.' When she returned her attention to the screen, she was surprised to see Lambert's name on it.

He'd targeted Victor, and now that Victor had left, she was sure he'd come after her or Kasper. A surge of anger banished her sense of weariness. She brought up Lambert's contact details and stared at them, thinking of the most effective way of dealing with him.

Kasper returned, accompanied by the rich aroma of their drinks, and placed an overfull mug on the corner of her desk. 'What do you want to do about him?' He jerked his head towards her screen.

'I'm going to ask to see him.'

'And then what?' Kasper took his mug to his desk, leaving a trail of drips on the floor behind him.

'I'm going to ask his advice.' She laid out what she planned to do.

Kasper expressed reservations, but he could tell she wasn't to be put off. He pretended to work while she phoned Lambert.

'I'm pretty busy, Ms Dąbrowski.'

'Of course, but I don't think anyone else can deal with it.' He agreed to meet her near the police station on Northampton Road.

'Has he fallen for it?' Kasper said when she'd hung up.

'I knew he couldn't resist an appeal to his ego.'

'I'll come with you.'

'There's no need.'

'I'd feel happier.'

An hour later, she arrived at Moston Vale and took Cleo for a walk. Now that she had her car back, she could take Cleo with her. Ten minutes before her appointment with Lambert, she made her way to the pop-up café in the park, five minutes from the police station he worked out of. She glanced towards the bench behind some shrubs about eighty metres away. As agreed, Kasper now occupied it, his long-lens ready. She could just about see him, but someone not knowing he was there wouldn't notice. So she hoped.

She tied Cleo's lead to an outdoor table in Kasper's field of view and entered the café. It still bore traces of the changing rooms it had once been, but the young woman running it had tried to make it a welcoming space by using bright colours and decorative hangings.

Zofia took her drink to the small seating area outside and put it on the table with her phone alongside it. Soft rugs lay draped over the backs of the aluminium chairs, and she placed one on her legs. Cleo's nervous yap warned her of Lambert's approach.

'Parky out 'ere. You fink you're going to show a suvern sooftie up?'

'Sergeant Lambert. Can I get you a coffee?'

'Shall we get on wiv it?'

He moved the rug off the seat opposite and dropped it on the ground.

Zofia picked it up and placed it on a nearby chair. 'We've found out who was in the pickup seen following Harry Sanders.'

He frowned. 'You said you had a line to whoever killed 'im, but that's just speculation. In fact, we're pretty sure the dozy plonker killed himself. Did that ex-tramp put you up to this?'

'Nobody put me up to it. I make my own decisions.'

He studied her. 'Yeah, you probly do.'

'Since you mentioned Victor, did you know someone wrecked his little caravan?'

'Did they?' He laughed, a genuine sound, but his surprise was confected.

She waited for him to stop. 'Unfortunately for them, they parked outside a caravan with a doorbell camera.'

'Oh yeah?' His shock, covered up in an instant, didn't escape her notice.

'Yeah. And the guy who owns the car has admitted everything.'

'Has he? He given a statement, then?'

'Not yet, but I recorded his confession.'

'And you told him that beforehand?'

'No.' She smiled. 'As a private eye, I record all my conversations, just in case.'

'In that case, he can deny it all.'

'He even told me who put him up to it.'

Lambert was shaking his head before she finished speaking. 'None of that will stand up in court.'

'My solicitor disagrees. I've sent him a transcript of our conversation.'

Lambert considered this for a few seconds, his jaw working. 'You try that, and you'll regret it.' He jerked his index finger at her like a pistol.

'You threatening me?' Her pulse raced, and Cleo stood, teeth bared.

'Me?' He scoffed. 'You fink it's me behind this? I'm just following orders.'

'That excuse didn't work out so well for the Nazis.'

He looked about him, but they were alone. 'I like you, Zofia, so I'll give you a warning. I don't know what the fack you've done, but you've upset someone powerful. They've told my boss to give you a hard time, so I've done it. I'm sure if you're determined to use this recording, it will make my life awkward for a while, but I'm protected. You're not.'

'You're saying Grimes is behind this?'

'That facking clown? Nah, much higher.'

'Mulberry, then?'

Again, shock registered on his features for a second. 'Goodbye, Ms Dąbrowski.' He stood and walked away.

'Thank you for confirming that a senior police officer is harassing us.'

He stepped back and snatched up her phone. 'You recording this?'

'Please put my phone down.'

'Recording me in a public place without my knowledge. Oh dear, oh dear.' He scoffed again and studied the handset.

'I'm not using my phone, I've got a bug on my jacket. It's all uploaded to the cloud, and you knew I was recording you. I told you I record my conversations.'

He stared into the distance and then lunged at her, stopping centimetres from her face. Despite herself, she yelped and cringed. Cleo stood and barked a warning.

He gave a nasty smile. 'Have a lovely day, Ms Dąbrowski.' He sneered at the dog, daring her to do anything, before walking away.

The man's spittle spotted Zofia's chin, and she waited until he'd walked away before wiping it, then calmed Cleo.

Kasper ran towards her, his camera in one hand. 'You okay?'

She waited for her heartbeat to slow. 'Yeah, thanks.'

'You get him to confess?'

'We've got enough to get him off our backs, but he didn't name Mulberry.'

'It looked like he'd head-butted you. I've got photos, and if we can link them to the recording, we'll have an excellent case.'

'Yeah.' But she was thinking of what Lambert had said. She'd got Lambert off their backs, but had she disturbed a hornet's nest?

Back at the office, Kasper produced an audio-visual presentation showing stills of Lambert talking to her, synchronised with the soundtrack. She had to admit, it looked compelling, especially when he said she'd regret it and the last scene, which made her flinch even in replay. It might not be admissible in court, but it should support a complaint to the police authority.

'What do we do now?' Kasper said.

'I don't know. Despite his bravado, I think we've done enough to make Lambert back off, but Mulberry is still after us. We need to continue looking for dirt on him and Glass.'

Kasper looked uncomfortable. 'I'm going to tell the SPI that we've dismissed Victor.'

'That's as good as admitting we believe he was guilty.'

'What do you think we should do?'

'Get the police to admit he did nothing wrong. Don't forget, we suspended him, and that's made no difference. It will look like we're sending staff out to break the law and then sacking them if they get caught.'

He took a deep breath. 'How do we get the police to admit he's innocent?'

'I'll speak to Colette.'

Temporary Inspector Bowling answered straight away. She stopped Zofia before she could tell her too much. 'Of course, Ms Dąbrowski. I'll find out what's happening with the investigation into your assault and get back to you.'

'Oh, okay, thanks.' Zofia ended the call. Bowling must have been unable to talk freely.

Zofia spent the afternoon carrying out background checks on the two men Victor suspected of killing Harry. He might have left them in the lurch, but his friend deserved justice.

Bowling didn't ring until five. 'I can talk now. I spoke to the detectives looking into the attack on you. They don't appear to have made any progress—'

'You mean they haven't investigated?'

'I didn't say that. They've done what I would have, but sometimes there's no trail to follow.'

The thought that the man who'd assaulted her was out there, free to do it again, made her angry more than afraid. She carried a tube of bright dye and a rape alarm, wary of carrying anything more offensive while she had Mulberry and his goons gunning for her.

'I've got something I wanted to run by you.' She told the policewoman about her meeting with Lambert.

'Are you going to give the number plate info to Rochdale police?'

'What do you recommend?'

Bowling sighed. 'It would give Lambert a headache, and I, plus most of my old team, including the DCI, wouldn't be upset by that. But as he said, you won't get to Mulberry.'

The idea of hitting back at Lambert, and getting justice for Victor, appealed. 'Right, I'll send it to them.'

'You've made the right decision, but be careful. It wouldn't surprise me if Mulberry sends someone else your way.'

She thanked Bowling, ended the call and updated Kasper, omitting the warning at the end. He'd only worry.

Cleo made her way to her desk and nuzzled against her leg. What the hell would happen to the dog now Victor wasn't coming back? She texted Victor, who replied, confirming he'd pick her up later. Concern tinged her relief. What would happen next week?

Having to leave Cleo alone in the office again filled her with guilt. Part of her looked forward to the weekend. A short break would do her good, but she had so many things on her mind, she doubted she'd relax.

They got a Chinese takeaway and shared a bottle of wine. A call from a friend offering Kasper a ticket for Sunday's United game at Liverpool raised his spirits. Despite her concerns, she fell asleep almost at once.

* * *

She woke at two, the banging at the front door sounding like someone intended to break it down. A sleepy Kasper met her on the landing as she pulled a dressing gown around her. He went ahead of her, down the stairs as another volley of banging shook the front door. She squinted when he put the hall light on and joined him beside the door. Blue lights flickered through the pebbled glass. They exchanged a look before he opened it.

'Miss Zofia Dąbrowski?' Two uniformed constables stood on the doorstep. Behind them, two more stood on the pavement in front of a marked car and van blocking the road, their lights illuminating the street in a blue wash.

'Yes?'

'You need to come with us.'

'What's this about?'

'A hit and run. Your car hit two blokes and drove off.'

'I've not been out since I came home.'

'Oh yeah.' He stood aside and shone a torch towards her car, parked on the pavement outside, highlighting the crumpled nearside wing and broken headlight. He sniffed. 'You been drinking?'

'Yes, but I've not been—'

He grabbed her arm. 'I'm arresting you on suspicion of drink-driving, failing to stop . . .'

His words faded out.

CHAPTER 44

Oscar spotted John and Craig before I did, and I pulled up alongside them. They studied the imposing, almost new SUV suspiciously until I slid the window down.

'Do you want to get in?'

Craig threw a holdall into the front footwell. Its contents clinked, and he followed it in as John climbed in the back. Doors slammed, and the car settled onto its springs.

'Where are they?'

Craig studied the screen of his phone. 'They've stopped just off the A6 in Levenshulme.'

I punched in the address on the satnav, and the powerful car surged forward. Within seconds we were breaking the speed limit, and I eased my foot off the accelerator, wary of getting stopped. Neither passenger said anything, but their unasked questions about where I'd got the car settled on its inside like an added weight.

As much to break the tension as anything, I said, 'Have they moved?'

Craig checked the time. 'Not for seven minutes.'

The sense that we'd be too late to stop them made my insides quiver. We hit the A6 in Longsight. Discount stores, restaurants and takeaways lined the road. Silhouettes of lingering diners dappled the windows of the few still open at this hour, and streams of cars travelled in both directions. We drove towards Levenshulme, an area of the city I didn't know. The lights at the next junction changed, and we stopped.

They seemed to take an age to change, and I imagined Harry's killers taking another life while we waited at these lights. The atmosphere in the vehicle told me the others felt the same. Even when the lights changed, none of the cars moved for what seemed like minutes, then we were on our way. I resisted the urge to race past cars seemingly happy to potter along. The shops finished, replaced by houses, most in darkness, then more shops and restaurants.

Craig checked his phone. 'They still haven't moved.'

I checked the satnav, which told me we'd be there in two minutes. It told me to take the next left, and I slowed. The map showed I'd be heading into a maze of narrow streets in a rough grid pattern.

'Keep going and take the left after the supermarket.' Craig's tone brooked no argument.

On our right, the car park of a huge restaurant disgorged a stream of cars onto the main road. I took the left and, stopping the satnav, let Craig direct me through a maze of narrow streets lined with red-brick terraced houses. Although apprehensive about what could transpire, especially if they were armed, the thought that we could be close to catching Harry's killers made the blood surge through me.

'Stop!' Craig's sharp order made me slam on the brakes.

'What?'

'They're on the next street.'

'How far?' I asked him.

John stuck his head between the front seats.

Craig passed me the screen, which showed a flashing dot halfway down the next street, about seventy metres from the junction.

I returned it to him. 'Is that where they've been since they stopped?'

He nodded.

At least that meant they'd not finished what they came to do.

From the rear, John said, 'I'll walk down the street, make out I'm a drunk on the way home and come back down the alleyway behind the houses and let you know what they're doing.'

It made sense, but I had a concern. 'What if they're attacking someone?'

'I'll shout.' He slid out of the back door. 'Stay, Oscar.'

'John,' I whispered, 'take him, it will look more convincing.'

'Good idea.' Oscar jumped out. John pushed the door shut with a quiet click and walked around the front of the car, Oscar at his heels.

Seeing him with Oscar made me realise I'd made him a target. They disappeared around the corner. I told myself the men we were after were clearly here looking for someone they'd already identified. Before I could articulate my concerns, Craig bent to collect something from his bag, then handed me a soft bundle. Gloves and a ski mask. I placed the mask on my knee and put the gloves on while he retrieved a rounders bat and placed it between our seats. My pulse rushed in my ears, and my mouth had dried.

Leather squeaked as he pulled on his gloves and retrieved another club. In the back, Cleo, likely sensing the tension, fidgeted. I lowered the windows, then tried to picture where John and Oscar were. The noise of traffic from the main road carried to us, and a late-night plane on the way to the airport flew over. As its sound faded, a car engine started, making me jump.

Craig clutched his phone. 'They're on the move.'

'Where the hell's John?' *And Oscar.*

'The car's left the street.'

I started the engine and roared round the corner, taking it too fast, and almost wiping out a car on the opposite side of the tight bend. My lights illuminated a narrow street with a few cars parked on each side, none of them pickups. I couldn't see anybody moving. I raced to the end.

'Which way did he go, Craig?'

'Right.'

I stopped at the junction, aiming right.

'Go left!'

A police car stood half on the pavement. Next to it, Oscar. A policeman sat in the back with someone. Another sat in the driver's seat. I turned the wheel and pulled up in front of the patrol car. As I got out, Craig followed, and the police driver did the same.

'Everything okay, Officer?'

'That's a Novak car.' He pointed at the SUV I'd come out of and gave Craig a nervous glance.

'Yes, I'm Victor Mitchum, their new general manager.' I ignored Craig's questioning glare. 'Anything wrong?'

The policeman's attitude changed. 'We're just questioning this gentleman about what he's doing here.' He pointed at John in the back seat.

'He's taking my dog for a walk. Oscar, come here.' After hesitating for a moment, he trotted to me.

'He works for you?' The officer didn't hide his incredulity.

'Of course.'

He opened the back door, and following a brief exchange, they let John out. He bade goodnight to the coppers and took Oscar to our car.

'Someone beat up one of the guys who lives in the hostel there last night.' The officer I'd spoken to pointed down the street where the pickup had been parked.

'Do you know who did it?'

'Some drunks. Unfortunately, it happens too often these days.'

I remembered Miles's assault on me with shame. I exchanged a look with Craig. 'Are you sure?'

'Yeah, we're sure.' His attitude hardened. 'What do you know about it?'

'Nothing.' I didn't want him paying too close attention to what we had in our car. 'I hope you catch the bastards.' Craig and I got back in the car. I drove away, watching them in the mirror. 'Where to, Craig?'

He checked his screen. 'They're going back to town.'

I followed his directions.

I hope you're suitably grateful for my obedient dog act.

'Of course I'll reward you, don't worry.'

I would think so, and Cleo?

'Of course.' I glanced at John. 'What happened?' I feared the men had cut and run because they'd seen John and realised we were following them.

'I walked past them. Oscar sniffed their wheels and relieved himself on the front one. I think he did it on purpose to mess with me, didn't you, boy?'

I did not! Obviously, I relieved myself on purpose. I'm not incontinent, but I wasn't messing with you. I just saw the wheel, and you know . . .

'I'm sure he did, John. Is that why they left?'

Thanks for standing up for me.

'The cop car passed the end of the street and stopped. I was deciding what to do when the pickup scarpered. Then the cops pinched me.'

'What's this about you working for Novak?' Craig's voice held an edge of steel.

'Shall we sort Harry's killers out first?'

Craig didn't seem sure.

'He's right, Brother.'

Craig, whose glare I could feel melting the side of my face, returned his attention to the screen. 'They're back on Hyde Road.'

John leant forward and grabbed Craig's headrest. 'You think they're going back to put the pickup away for the night?'

'Or they're looking for more prey.'

I followed Craig's directions, and we returned to the street where they kept the vehicle. I killed my lights and pulled up at the place from which we'd watched the unit while Toff had planted the tracker. The pickup stood outside, the two men at the rising shutter. Then, one of them stepped inside. In a few moments, a car inside the unit started, and he drove it out. It was the vehicle Zofia had traced as belonging to the estate agent whose board hung on the wall above the opening. The other one reversed the pickup into the unit, they locked up and drove away.

Before they did, I saw the other man. 'It is Miles!' The confirmation of the other man's identity felt like a vindication.

'You know him, Brother?'

'And he knows me. He's the one who beat me up, and Oscar attacked.'

I knew it would be my fault.

'Nobody's blaming you, Oscar.'

That's not what it sounds like.

'I say, well done, Oscar.' Craig reached into the back seat and patted him.

Most people appreciate my qualities.

John yawned. 'Can you drop us off?'

'I'm going back to the hostel they were watching. We need to warn the man they beat up.'

'The police will have spoken to them.'

'They're dismissing it as a group of drunks. The guy's life is in danger.'

'Yes, sorry, Brother. I'm not thinking straight.'

We retraced our steps and pulled up outside the house the two men in the pickup had been watching. The street lay in darkness, and Craig accompanied me to the door. Nothing much happened when I rang the bell, so Craig thumped the door with a huge fist. The thunderous banging echoed off the houses opposite, and a light came on upstairs. A dog began barking. Shortly, light showed around the door, and it was snatched open.

'Who the hell are you?' A muscular, bare-chested man of about thirty, wearing nothing but stained jogging bottoms, glared at us. The stink of weed wafted from his long hair.

I pointed at an older man behind him holding the collar of a medium-sized mongrel. 'I need a word with your mate.'

'He's not my mate. I'm the night warden. These guys are temporary residents.'

I'd experienced living in temporary accommodation and hadn't liked it one bit. 'However you think of him, I need to speak to him.'

'Residents aren't allowed visitors. Especially at this time of night.' He squared up to us. Two more men had appeared in the corridor behind him and, like the man with the dog, had the underfed look of street dwellers.

As I had Craig beside me, I ignored the aggressive warden and addressed the man with the dog. 'Did you see who beat you up?'

He came closer and stood under the light. His nose looked swollen and lopsided, and a variety of bruises covered his face. 'A big bastard with a beard.'

'On his own?'

He looked embarrassed. 'I think so.'

'Posh voice?'

'How d'you know that?'

I exchanged another look with Craig. 'You were lucky. He normally goes out with another guy, and they kill people. They were outside the house tonight, waiting for you.'

His suspicion turned to concern, and he swallowed.

The warden addressed the man with the dog. 'I don't want you bringing trouble here. You'll have to move out.'

Craig growled, and the warden took a step back.

The man with the dog looked beaten. 'I was thinking of leaving, anyway. I've got a brother in Bolton. I'll stay there a few days.'

Reassured he'd be safe at his brother's, we left and returned to the car, bringing John up to date.

'What do you think happened, Brother?' he asked me.

'I think Miles came across him while on his own, and had a go. Then, he and his oppo found out where the poor guy was staying and came back for him. He's had a lucky escape.'

They agreed, and I dropped them off at a less than salubrious-looking squat before driving to my luxury flat. We'd been lucky they'd not finished him off, but we couldn't rely on luck forever.

CHAPTER 45

Zofia's thoughts returned to the humiliation of being bundled into the back of the police car in full sight of her neighbours, many of whom had been friends of her mother. At least the police had allowed her to get dressed and hadn't cuffed her. Although the young woman PC had been keen to do so. The breathalysing and taking of a blood sample at the local police station hadn't seemed as intrusive as that moment.

She and Kasper had given statements, and the police had removed her car. Her solicitor arrived, but she didn't recognise him. The lawyers she dealt with at the firm weren't specialists in criminal law.

Zofia had been in an interview room before, but she'd been there as a witness, not a defendant. The one Grimes had questioned her in had been a newer and bigger version of the cramped space she found herself in with just her solicitor. The smell of fresh beige paint overwhelmed the aftershave he'd put on before coming out in the early hours.

The police had given him the details of the charges, and Zofia listened in silence.

'These are quite serious, Ms Dąbrowski. You're looking at up to two years in prison.'

'I was in bed. It wasn't me.'

'So, you're denying the offences.'

'Of course I'm denying them. I know who's behind this.' Even to herself, she sounded hysterical.

He studied her through his black-rimmed glasses. 'You think someone is carrying out a vendetta against you?'

'Against us, me and my brother. And anyone who works for us.'

He studied her as if she were unhinged. 'These are serious accusations.'

She swallowed. 'I know, and I don't make them lightly.'

'Who is behind this campaign?'

She hesitated, unsure how much mentioning her suspects would increase the lawyer's incredulity. 'The person behind it is Rudy Glass—'

'The businessman?'

'Yes. We exposed his links to a corrupt council planning officer, who was murdered.'

'I recall reading about it. He was cleared in the investigation, as I recall?'

'Technically. The police decided not to investigate. But he—' She had to be careful what she said. 'It *appears* he may have been involved in further illegal dealings. We were being paid to investigate them.'

'Who by?'

'You know I can't tell you that.'

He shrugged. 'You're saying Mr Glass is waging this campaign to stop you investigating him?'

'We have stopped, but the message doesn't seem to have reached him.'

'And how is Mr Glass manipulating the police to get at you?'

His sneering tone made her teeth grate. 'He's using a senior policeman, Chief Superintendent Mulberry, to attack us.' She gave a quick outline of what had happened.

'You've got the recording of the detective who threatened you?'

She nodded.

'But nothing on the chief super?'

'Just his links to Glass – he was the officer who dropped the original investigation – and his link to Casin, the man who led to our suspension from the professional body.'

'How so?'

'He investigated a fraudster who targeted Glass last year and also received an award from him at a golf event Glass had sponsored. Mulberry also arrested Casin a few years ago.'

'A few?' The solicitor's eyebrows rose.

'Mulberry was a sergeant.'

'So, more than ten years. Any recent contact?'

'Not that I've found.' Zofia's voice faded as she said this.

He'd been doodling on a notepad and continued doing so while humming, then put his pen down. 'Right, I think we should just deny these charges for now, and work on a defence once you're back out. I can't see them remanding you in custody.'

She hadn't even considered they would, but the idea took root and filled her with foreboding. Her solicitor transcribed her statement as she explained she'd been in bed at the time her car struck the two cyclists. He informed the officers they were ready and returned to take the seat alongside her. The two constables who'd arrested her trooped in, and one read a caution, then recited the charges against her: 'Driving while unfit through drink or drugs or with excess alcohol, dangerous driving, failing to stop after an accident and failing to report an accident.'

Her irritation with her solicitor had distracted her from her predicament, but hearing the charges put to her by a uniformed officer made them much more real, even though she denied each one. Her solicitor read out her account of what she'd done the previous evening until the police had woken her.

'Your car shows no sign of being tampered with, which suggests that whoever drove it, had a key. How do you explain that?'

She'd taken back the key Victor had borrowed, and both keys had been in the house when the police arrived. 'I can only conclude someone has cloned my key.'

The constable looked sceptical and finished writing her statement out. 'Your brother's given a statement' – he paused for a few seconds – 'and his corroborates what you've said.' He slid the document across for her to read and sign, then regathered the pages. 'I'm going to release you on police bail.'

He relayed the conditions, but such was her relief she didn't take it in. Her solicitor did, and he led her out of the room. Kasper sat in a moulded chair in the reception area and rose to meet her. His breath smelt of the wine they'd both drunk, and she hoped he'd not driven, but wasn't going to say anything in the police station. Their lawyer checked they both understood their responsibilities, explaining those Zofia had failed to take in, and left them.

They hurried out of the station into the autumn rain. It was still dark, and chill seeped into her bones as Kasper led her to an unfamiliar car. The lights came on as they approached, and they clambered into the back of a mercifully warm taxi for the brief trip home.

Although exhausted, she doubted she'd sleep and made herself a herbal tea. Kasper poured a glass of water and joined her at the dining table.

'I spoke to one of the officers from the van,' he said, 'outside the house. She said a speed camera picked your car up just after it hit two cyclists—'

'Do you know how they are?'

'Both at Trafford General, but not life-threatening or changing, she said.'

'At least that's one thing. They said someone used my keys, but both sets were at home.'

'It's easy enough to clone. I thought nobody would target our cars, but stealing them isn't the only reason they would do it, as we've found out.'

The thought that someone was prepared to injure two strangers to get to her made her shiver. 'Do you think Lambert's behind this?'

'I suspect he's told Mulberry about you unmasking him, and his boss is retaliating. Showing you he's not to be messed with.'

'Nor are we.' Flushed with determination to hit back at the man, she finished her drink and returned to bed.

CHAPTER 46

I slept through, waking at nine to find two dogs desperate for a walk. Bleary-eyed and unwashed, I crossed Deansgate and took them to the local park where they explored the Roman ruins. I considered what had happened last night and the fact we'd not found the pickup that had been outside the hostel for at least fifteen minutes. Plenty of time to have killed someone.

A message arrived from John, saying almost the same thing. I closed the message, considering how we could get early warning of the pickup being on the move. I noticed an email from Zofia, sent the previous evening. Without opening it, I speculated on its contents, fearing it would be something negative. *Come on, coward, open it.* To my surprise, she'd sent me the details of the two men we'd followed last night, Miles Colby and Merkul Akimov, including their home addresses. Colby lived in Heaton Moor, not too far from the hostel we'd visited last night, supporting my conclusion that he'd spotted the man he'd attacked while out on his own.

Zofia confirmed Akimov was the brother of the man we'd encountered, and the summary of his criminal record made me pause. He'd been inside for five months for assaulting a man in a pub brawl. That explained why the attacks had paused. But how had he landed the senior job at the estate agency so soon after coming out? That needed to be investigated, and I sent Zofia a quick request after thanking her for what she'd done. I spent a few moments considering the tone of my reply before deciding to reply as if nothing had changed.

Once I'd done it, I fretted that I'd made a mistake, but it was too late. I tried to focus on the information she'd sent me and considered what to do with it on our walk back to the flat.

What's up? Oscar, as usual, picked up on my mood.

I didn't want to discuss my concerns as I was sure he'd mock me again, so told him about the information Zofia had sent.

Why don't you watch their homes? Next time they go out, you'll have early warning and get there sooner.

That made sense, and we had an army of homeless people who could do it. But I had a new job, which I suspected would be full-on. 'We'll be out every time they go anywhere.'

You only need to do it at night, and then only if both leave their houses.

He had a good point. 'Great idea.'

Don't sound so surprised.

I waited until we returned to the flat and had breakfast before ringing John with Oscar's suggestion.

'Great idea, Victor. I'll organise people to watch the houses. Can we offer them anything?'

I almost suggested twenty-five pounds a night – enough to pay for a stay in a hostel – then remembered being furious with Kasper for offering me a derisory sum because I was homeless. I agreed to pay two people minimum wage for six hours each night and ended the call.

Oscar watched me as I ended the call. ***I knew you'd claim the credit for the idea.***

'We're a team, Oscar.'

He wandered off muttering. I sent another email to Zofia, asking if she fancied helping me choose my new clothes. To my disappointment, but not surprise, she declined, and I spent a couple of hours buying clothes for my new job in the city centre shops. Memories of being chased out of the Arndale Centre by its security guards made me avoid it and go to King Street and Market Street, but I didn't feel ready for the designer outlets near the cathedral. The last time I'd done this, I'd been with Carol and the girls, who'd been tiny, but Helen still shared her opinions on what I was buying.

I spent just over a thousand, full of guilt, and although I gave generously to everyone who asked me for money, I couldn't meet their gazes and, to my relief, I saw nobody I knew from my time on the streets. Yet again, I considered how different the city looked when I had money. Exhausted by the ordeal, I decided to save the rest to go shopping with the girls.

The thought of seeing them cheered me up, and I took Oscar and Cleo out to Knutsford, parking just off a different King Street and going on a long walk in the grounds of Tatton Park. Walking through the huge stone gateway made me feel we were entering another world and reminded me of the smaller, but more elaborate entrance to Ashton Court, where I took the girls. The smell of pine, grass and animal dung filled the air.

Once inside, Oscar wandered off to explore, but Cleo stayed by me, seeming happy to do so, although she looked hopefully at any women who passed. I was focused on her when Oscar suddenly let out a yelp and ran out of the stand of evergreen shrubs he'd been exploring. Then I saw why. A small herd of red deer emerged from the undergrowth, at its head a magnificent male with an impressive rack of antlers.

He stopped ten paces away and stared at me. My heart raced as I recalled a recent spate of attacks on walkers by stags. I could smell his musk, and his nostrils flared as he smelt me. Seeming satisfied I wasn't a threat, he turned and led the herd back into the undergrowth. Oscar, who watched from between my legs, let me attach his lead without protest, and we continued our way towards the lake.

Cleo seemed more relaxed than at any time I'd seen her, and I felt sad she'd not been able to visit places like this with Harry. The thought that we were on the trail of his killers made me feel better. We left before sundown and returned home, Oscar having rewritten the incident with the stag to make him the hero on the journey back. At seven thirty, I changed into my new clothes and set off for Sackville Square. Manchester's streets teemed with revellers, and I drank in the atmosphere, feeling part of it rather than an observer, as I had been when living on the streets. I turned off Portland Street onto the quiet of Abingdon Street.

The lights on the stretch leading to Sackville Square weren't working. I hurried, feeling suddenly vulnerable. A large dark car sat in the shadows ahead of me and, as I neared, the doors opened. Two bulky men got out. In the illumination from the courtesy lights, I recognised Miles Colby and his sidekick Merkul Akimov, a flash of red from the tattoo at his collar.

I froze.

CHAPTER 47

My surprise that the two men we'd been hunting a few hours earlier had nodded a greeting as I walked past, instead of battering me, increased when I met them in the casino. Colby's reaction when Judy introduced me as the new general manager gave me another surprise. She explained that she'd interviewed him for the job and told him it had gone to someone else, but he obviously hadn't expected to see me in the post so soon.

I'd have sworn he didn't recognise me, but I saw something shift in the eyes of his friend, whose tattoo stuck out above his collar. He was now giving me a frankly puzzled look. He'd stared into my face after chasing me in their van a few months earlier. It had been dark, and soot stains covered my face, but he must have seen enough to raise a question in his mind, but not enough to remember where he'd seen me. I avoided them for the rest of the evening and didn't outwardly react to Judy's suggestion that we consider Colby for the role of group accountant, a job my predecessor had done.

I went home at three in the morning, exhausted, then took the dogs out before collapsing into bed. Although I woke to exercise the dogs, I returned to bed and spent the Sunday morning there. My internal clock would need reprogramming. My body told me I couldn't do this every night, and I had the girls coming to stay. In my excitement at the prospect of seeing them, I'd not considered that I'd be working long hours.

At midday I received a call I'd expected with a sense of dread. Craig was his usual taciturn self. 'We need to talk.'

I suggested we meet for lunch at a restaurant with a heated outside terrace near the Rochdale Canal. It had been sunny but not warm when I'd taken the dogs out earlier. In my eagerness to get off the phone with Craig, I'd forgotten to ask if Trixie would be coming – she still didn't like Cleo – but didn't want to ring him back. I could leave the dogs in the flat together for a couple of hours.

I arrived before my friends and commandeered a table at one end of the terrace. Despite the heating, only me and a couple had braved the chilly weather. John and Craig arrived, and the waiter intercepted them at speed, but following a brief exchange with John, he led them over. I stood to greet them. Although they'd put on their best clothes, an earthy odour accompanied them.

'No Trixie?' I gave Craig a smile.

He didn't return it. 'I thought you'd have your whippet with you.'

'She's half *galgo*, half springer.'

'A Spanish hunting dog, Brother?' John used a conciliatory tone, took my hand and sat opposite.

Craig sat next to him without further greeting. The waiter gave them each a menu and scurried away.

'Hang on, mate.' Craig held his menu towards the young man. 'I'll have prawn cocktail to start, the roast beef, pink, with extra roasties, and a second Yorkshire. Plenty of gravy and horseradish. Is it hot?'

The waiter nodded.

'Good. Then, apple crumble and custard. Make that two of them.'

The panicked waiter looked at me and John. 'Are you gentlemen ready to order?'

I'd already decided before they arrived, and we gave him our orders. An hour later, we'd cleared our plates and sat drinking coffee.

Craig leant forward. 'I thought we'd agreed. You don't work for Novak.'

'You decided *you* won't work for him.' My pulse thrummed in my ears.

Craig clenched his fists, and John placed a hand on his forearm. 'What Craig means is we're all at risk if' – he checked nobody was in earshot – 'our part in what happened to his sons comes out.'

'I'm the one at risk. And Kasper and Zofia. We're the ones who worked for Robertson.'

A low growl emanated from Craig's throat. 'You think he'll draw a distinction? He'll want to take revenge on everyone who was there, all of us' – he gestured around the table – 'plus me mates who helped us out.'

I looked to John for support.

'Craig's right, Brother.'

'But my working for them makes us safer.'

'How do you work that out?' John asked.

'From there, I can monitor what they're doing. Until now, we've been in the dark, worrying about what Novak or Robertson are doing. Now, I'll *know* what they're doing.' I hesitated before making the next claim, which was a guess. 'Novak's planning to do something with Robertson.'

John's eyes widened. 'How do you know?'

'Zofia was investigating Robertson for Judy Novak.' This was all conjecture, based on seeing the heading of an email about Robertson, but why else would Zofia be investigating him?

John frowned. 'And you'll be able to tell us what Robertson's doing down here.'

'Exactly. And if he does anything to compromise us, I can warn you.'

They exchanged a look. Craig hesitated, then nodded. 'Make sure you keep us apprised.'

'Of course. But why don't you join me? We need reliable staff, and there's accommodation included.'

'Don't push it.' Craig stood.

John joined him. 'We've got someone watching those two addresses between ten p.m. and four.'

To fund these efforts, I'd brought five hundred of the money Judy had given me in an envelope, which I handed to John with a sense of sadness. Something had ruptured between us. I suspected that once we'd caught Harry's killers, we'd drift further apart.

CHAPTER 48

After a troubled weekend, Zofia woke on Monday and found a bleary-eyed Kasper in the kitchen. The aroma of toast and coffee made her stomach rumble. She'd spent the remains of the Saturday and Sunday looking for ammunition she could use to attack Mulberry and Glass, frustrated that she couldn't get hold of information at the weekend. She had a list to attack once they got to the office.

A text while they were driving to work diverted them to the car pound in Longsight. A security guard in a too-generous uniform led Zofia to her car, and she examined it. She'd need to get the light fixed, but otherwise it would drive fine. Inside, she couldn't see any signs of an investigation.

'Aren't you going to fingerprint the steering wheel and gear lever?'

The security guard who'd brought her to the car shrugged. 'I've no idea what they've done. All I've been told is that you can take it.'

More than ever convinced that the police had no intention of carrying out a proper investigation, she got in the car and checked the lights. To her surprise, the damaged sidelight and indicator worked. She drove out of the pound and waved to Kasper, parked outside waiting for her. He fell in behind her car, and they drove to work in convoy.

On Great Ancoats Street, a food delivery rider lost his balance and crashed to the ground a car length ahead of her. She slammed on her brakes. The car slid on the wet tarmac and then slewed to a stop. Someone screamed. Zofia sat shaking, her heart thumping, before forcing herself to move. Was this another one of Mulberry's traps? On shaking legs, she stood beside her car and looked at the front.

Behind her, Kasper had stopped and joined her. 'Wait, Zofia!' He bustled past her and looked at something in the road. 'You okay, mate?'

A man gave an embarrassed laugh. 'Yeah, just lost me balance there.'

Relief flooded through her, and she joined Kasper. A man in cheap bike leathers with a high-vis vest over the top sat up. Next to him, an e-bike, its rear wheel distorted and caught under her front bumper. On seeing he was unhurt, the rubberneckers moved on. Kasper helped him to his feet, and he limped a few steps before massaging his knee.

'You going to be alright?' she asked. He looked exhausted, and she suspected he'd fallen asleep.

'Yeah, I'll be fine.' He bent to pick his bike up and dragged it to the pavement.

Behind them, cars tooted, and, checking again he was okay, she got back in her car and drove off. Something caught under her shoe, and she slid it to the side, picking it up at the next junction. She recognised the tracker they'd been looking for before Kasper found a new one to give to Victor.

She lost Kasper at the lights at the bottom of Cheetham Hill Road and arrived first, taking the tracker with her up to the office. Cleo barked an excited greeting, and Zofia bent to hug her, receiving a face wash in return. She gave silent thanks to Victor; she'd not arranged anything with him, but had hoped he'd bring Cleo to the office.

Kasper arrived as she poured out the coffees, and she placed the tracker on his desk next to the mug. 'What's this?' He picked it up.

'It's the one you were looking for last week. It must have got jammed under my seat and shot out when I braked for that cyclist.'

'Are you okay?'

'Yeah, a bit of a scare. So relieved he was unhurt. Poor guy looked shattered.'

'Yeah, they work stupid hours.' He brandished the tracker. 'I told you it was in your car. You put it there after Victor had it in his jacket pocket.'

'That was six months ago. Do you think it's still transmitting?'

He blew out his lips. 'Unlikely. It's linked to your phone, isn't it?'

She retrieved her handset and opened the app. She had to log in again and feared it was because the tracker battery had died. But she found her password, and it hadn't.

'I've found it.' Her voice rose.

Kasper joined her as she dialled back the date to Friday evening, 10 p.m. The tracker didn't move until midnight. Then it set off, travelling along Kings Road to Moss Side. It turned off Upper Chorlton Road and stopped.

Kasper pointed at the screen. 'What road's that?'

She opened her desktop and brought up a map of the area. 'Shrewsbury Street. It's the house nearest the church.'

She returned to the app on her phone. Her car stayed there for seven minutes before moving off. It turned left onto Ayres Road, moving fast, and then into Seymour Grove and then back, seeming to quarter the surrounding streets in an aimless pattern.

Kasper leant forward. 'They're looking for someone to hit.'

The knowledge chilled her, and then the car slowed.

He pointed at the screen. 'That's where they hit the two cyclists, the policewoman told me it was on Seymour Grove.'

The car accelerated, then drove through Chorlton before returning to their house.

Kasper straightened. 'The speed camera was in Chorlton.'

Zofia sat in stunned silence. Someone had used her car as a weapon to injure two people, just to get at her. Up to that point, she'd told herself it was probably an accident, and they just wanted her done for speeding, or drink-driving if they were lucky. But you couldn't argue with what they'd seen.

Kasper had to repeat what he said: 'I'll find out who lives at the house they stopped outside.'

'Unless they went into one of the other houses. It's a terraced street.'

'Oh yeah.' He sighed. 'I'll check them all.'

Her first instinct would have been to contact the police, but after her recent experiences she rang another number. 'Zofia, I saw your name on the log,' said Bowling. 'How are you doing?'

'Okay, thanks, Colette. Are you working out of Stretford nick now?'

'No, but . . . look, after what you told me, I asked around on the QT, and you're on a shit-list. So's your brother.'

And Victor, she thought. He'd said something about being stopped in her car, but she'd assumed he'd done something wrong and had been too embarrassed to admit it to her. She flushed with shame. 'I know that now. I wanted to run something past you.' She told her about the tracker and the car's movements it had recorded.

'Have you got the address they stopped at?'

She gave it.

'Leave it with me.' The police officer ended the call.

Despite Bowling's confirmation that they were on a list to be harassed by corrupt officers, at least she was keeping an eye out for them. The feeling that they were fighting back, and they weren't alone, lifted some of the gloom that had been infecting her.

CHAPTER 49

On Monday morning, I dropped Cleo at KZD, disappointed nobody had arrived yet. I swung by the pet hypermarket and bought Oscar new feeding bowls and a bed to install in my office. I'd not discussed it with Judy but, should the issue come up, I was sure one of her father's quotes about asking for forgiveness rather than permission would cover it.

She'd not arrived at the office, so I set Oscar's space out in a corner by the window and got to grips with my paperwork. I couldn't believe I'd only started on Friday. Thoughts of how to spend time with my daughters next week had kept me awake, so I made a phone call.

'This had better be important.' Novak sounded out of breath.

'Morning, Alex. I need a favour.'

'Yeah?' His tone suggested he'd say no to whatever I asked.

'My daughters are coming to stay next week. I've not spent much time with them for two years.'

He didn't answer for a long time. 'And what do you want?'

'Can you cover for me some of the time?'

'What does Judy say?'

'I've not told her.'

He chuckled. 'As Churchill said, "It's easier to ask for forgiveness than permission."'

Right on time. I smiled and didn't correct him. 'Exactly.'

'Let me know when you need me. I wish I'd spent more time with my girl as she was growing up.'

I believed him. 'Thanks, Alex.' Had I misjudged him? Then I remembered him directing his henchmen to escort me to a torture chamber, a visit interrupted only because a rival had attacked him and Zofia had called in the cavalry. No, I'd best remain vigilant.

With a lighter heart, I returned to my work. I had access to my predecessor's computer and wanted to reconfigure it. He used a different email client to the one I preferred. I checked he hadn't already downloaded the app. A search suggested he had, but I couldn't find it on the hard drive.

Intrigued, I looked through the apps, but couldn't find it listed. I was scratching my head when a warning flashed up: Unable to back up. D drive missing.

D drive?

I found a screwdriver in the top drawer and removed the side of the tower. An outline in the dust showed where the hard drive had been. There was a third hard drive in the casing, but it wasn't listed on the computer, and after replacing the side panel, I carried out a search in the settings until I eventually found it. Whoever had configured it didn't want it found, and if I hadn't seen it, I'd never have looked for it. It contained several folders and the email client I was searching for.

There weren't many messages, but one mentioned a familiar and frightening name. Before I could investigate further, Judy arrived. A sense of unwarranted guilt made me close the client and open the one she'd shown me on the main drive.

She stared at Oscar. 'Hello, Oscar. You seem to have made yourself at home.'

You want me to sleep on a wooden floor?

I fought the urge to apologise and ignored her disapproving tone. We'd already discussed where he could go. 'Can we have a chat about my hours?'

'Hours?' She sat in the chair facing my desk.

'It's half-term next week, and I need to have time to spend with my daughters.'

'This is your first full day, Victor, and you're already asking for time off.'

'I'm asking not to be working twenty-four-seven. I'm happy to put in the hours, and I'll do extra this week and after they've gone home.'

'We'll have to see.'

'Alex is happy to cover for me.'

'You've spoken to him?'

'Yes.'

Her frown deepened. 'I thought you understood. *I* run things.'

'Of course. But I wanted to make sure he was happy to do it before I bothered you.'

She held my gaze. 'Okay, I'll speak to him and coordinate dates and times.'

I let out a silent sigh of relief. We discussed my day's tasks, and, impatient to get back to checking the emails I'd found, I rushed through the questions I had for her. Once she'd left, I opened the second hard drive and returned to the emails. The familiar name belonged to a senior police officer, our nemesis – not mine anymore, I reminded myself – Mulberry. He seemed friendly with my predecessor, Jerry Sweeny.

Before I could check them, a call came in and soon I'd become embroiled in the minutiae of my new job. I returned to the messages as time allowed throughout the day and found more emails between them. Sweeny had deleted some, but left them on the server. On the surface, the messages were innocent. They related to a charity for rehabilitating convicts. The emails discussed how to help them and mentioned the ex-cons by name. One name stood out: Nirmal Casin, the man who'd posed as a customer of KZD and led to their being suspended by the SPI for working for a criminal.

I resisted the urge to ring Zofia. It was almost five; I could go round to collect Cleo and give the siblings the news. After telling Judy I was taking a couple of hours and would return at eight, I drove to KZD's office with a sense of excitement, partly because of the link I'd discovered between Mulberry and my predecessor – although I had no idea what it meant yet – but also, the thought of seeing my friends, especially Zofia. The sight of her dented car concerned me, and I wanted to rush up and check she was okay, but reminded myself to ring the bell. I still had the keys, so I could collect and drop Cleo off, but I wasn't part of the team anymore.

Zofia let me in, seeming unhurt, and gave Oscar a warm greeting, but Kasper soon put a dampener on my visit. 'You shouldn't be here.'

'Good to see you as well.'

'Don't mind him, Victor. Drink?'

I accepted and took a seat at my old desk, ignoring Kasper's disapproval. 'What happened to Zofia's car?'

'I'll let her tell you.'

'Someone stole my car while we were asleep on Friday night, Saturday morning, took it for a joyride and hit two cyclists.'

I listened with growing concern as she told me about being arrested and the subsequent questioning. 'Are you sure Lambert wasn't behind it?'

'I think we'd scared him off.' She told me about her meeting with the detective sergeant at the outdoor café in Moston Vale. The fact I'd have been there had I not left them made me feel an outsider after just three days.

'So, Mulberry has another person to do his bidding.'

Zofia grinned. 'I've got the name of the person we think took my car. Theo Cook, who's got convictions for aggravated burglary, car theft and ABH.'

I'd seen the name Theo Cook recently, but couldn't immediately recall where. 'How did you identify him?'

Kasper joined in. 'Do you remember the tracker she put in your jacket when you had dinner with Novak?'

'As if I could forget.' It was the reason I was still alive.

Zofia said, 'Yes, well *I'd* forgotten about it, and it's been in my car since. The battery's still working, and I tracked him to his flat.'

'Bloody hell. What an idiot! Do you know why he did it?'

'To pick up his girlfriend. She's a piece of work, with convictions for wounding with intent amongst others.'

'To go joyriding?'

'They activated a speed camera and, if I was supposed to be driving it, they needed a woman. They were both masked, but it could have been me driving. She has similar hair.'

'How did you get all this?'

Kasper said, 'A friend of Colette's at Stretford nick.'

'I've seen Theo Cook's name on an email.' The memory had returned, and with it a frisson of excitement. 'He's one of the people Jerry Sweeny, my predecessor, discussed with Mulberry in a secret stash of emails I found on his computer.'

Zofia grinned. 'Yeah? Well, Mulberry, as a lowly inspector, arrested Cook.'

I gave them my other discovery. 'You know who else Mulberry discussed with Sweeny? Nirmal Casin.'

'Really? That's fantastic.' She gave me a hug, and we held each other until a cough from Kasper separated us. 'You know what that means. Mulberry not only arrested two criminals who've been tormenting us, but he'd been keeping track of them.'

I didn't know how we'd use this information, but it felt like a breakthrough.

CHAPTER 50

Judy had wondered if giving Victor the job had been a mistake when he started talking about his working hours. He got a big pay cheque, a car and a flat so he would put the hours in. She also had second thoughts about letting him bring the dog. Her misgivings faded when he'd returned from his evening break without the dog and had worked through until two the next morning.

He'd also made suggestions for improving things at the casino, including several that would save money. While these were of course welcome developments, they did remind her of her weak financial situation: if she couldn't come up with the funds for her half of the Rochdale Canal project, she'd not only have to pay Robertson a six-figure compensation, but would lose face, something far more dangerous in their world.

She could raise just about enough to start the project, but it would leave them vulnerable. She had some time to find the money for the later rounds of work, but she'd been hoping to use the still-unfinished project itself as collateral for some of it. As a joint project, both partners would have to agree to this, however, and Zofia's report on Robertson had made her doubt he would agree.

Although he didn't have the funds to handle the project on his own, he had more than enough to pay his half. She assumed he'd be doing a similar investigation into her family's finances. From the outside, it looked like she had the money for *her* half. It was possible his finances were in an equally parlous state, but he didn't have brothers who'd bled the company dry, leaving it a shell.

On Tuesday morning, she took her laptop and a sheaf of papers from her study at home and visited her father in his kitchen.

He put his protein drink down. 'Alright, love. How's Victor doing?'

'Okay. I wasn't happy when he asked for time off, but he put in a long day yesterday and has been in since half eight, according to Keira.'

'I can't fault a man who wants to spend time with his daughters.'

Unlike you, you mean? 'No, you're quite right, Dad.'

'As they say, "A daughter is a treasure and a cause of sleepiness."'

She smiled. 'Isn't it sleeplessness?'

'That's what I said.'

'Here's something to make you sleep.' She sat at the kitchen table, placed the laptop on it and opened it to the cash flow she'd been working on for most of yesterday and this morning.

He wheeled himself alongside her. 'What am I looking at?' He tapped the screen with a manicured fingernail. 'What are these figures at the bottom?'

'That's how much we're short for the Rochdale Canal project.'

He whistled. 'What about the money from selling the flats on Beswick Street?'

'That's here.' It hardly made a dent in the row of red figures. 'And that's assuming we sell them all.'

He stared at the screen. 'I don't understand this. Jerry showed me some figures and, though we had a few months where we needed a bit of finessing to sail through, we had it covered. You sure we got this right?'

She knew he'd spoken to their bank manager, who wouldn't have sugar-coated it. 'You know I have.'

'Okay.' He took a deep breath. 'So we forget about the Rochdale Canal?'

'It's not like you to give up.'

'I'm not giving up. We need to fight the battles we can win.'

'We can win this. If we can find a partner to share the cost—'

'And the profit?'

'Of course, we'll have just half of it. But if we don't do it, we'll have nothing.' *A lot less than nothing once I've paid Robertson.*

'I don't like it. We've never had partners.'

'We've done nothing this big.'

He shook his head. 'Having partners is too risky.'

'Didn't Machiavelli say, "Never was anything great achieved without danger"?' She tapped the keys, and the screen changed. 'This is the same cash flow if we have a partner.'

Alex opened his mouth to object, then studied it. 'What's this figure?'

She'd hoped he wouldn't notice. 'It's the money from mortgaging this house and the one in Abersoch.'

'Whoa! Where the hell do you get off mortgaging *my* houses?'

'This project will secure our future as a family. We either pursue it or we hide in a corner, too scared to take any risks, and see everything we've worked for seep away.'

'What about the place I gave you in town?'

'That's already committed.' She pointed to the line in the seed capital of the project.

'Hang on, I paid twice that.'

'Yeah. It looks like you overpaid. I've had two estate agents price it up.' She listed the faults that had come to light in the block.

'Fuck!' He wheeled himself towards the coffee maker and banged about as he put on a pot. 'You want one?'

Did she? Not really. But it would help build bridges if they shared a drink. 'Yes, please, Dad.'

Half an hour later she'd got his reluctant agreement to sound out a partner. *Way ahead of you, Dad.* She drove in to work, speaking to the architect on the way. Now that she'd persuaded her dad to accept they needed a partner, she wanted to move things on.

'Ms Novak,' said the architect, 'I've heard the planning committee is looking for a bit more of a commitment to social housing.'

'In what way?' This was all she needed.

'More units and closer to the city centre.' He cleared his throat. 'I was wondering about Beswick Street. We can squeeze six more units into it if we're using it as social housing. That should blow any competition out of the water.'

'How much would that cost us?'

'Half a mill.'

Another half million to find. 'I'll think about it.'

She cut the call and realised Robertson would need to find half of the shortfall. In fact, as they'd already bought the land and started the build, if it became part of the main project, Robertson would need to stump up half the money they'd already spent. She arrived at work feeling more positive than she had in a while.

She'd ring Robertson to tell him, but first she needed to speak to her contact on the planning committee to check what the architect had told her. It wasn't long before an item of news from that contact punctured her good mood.

'The new bidder seems to be well in with the council.'

'What are they offering?'

'The bid's like yours except they've offered more social housing and closer—'

'We'll be increasing our offer.' She told her about Beswick Street.

'That sounds very promising. But they've got someone on the board with a keen interest in helping the homeless community.

They're talking about a hub for the homeless at the site of the social housing. Apparently, he's also keen on helping ex-offenders.'

'My new chief executive was living on the streets before he started here, and so were some of our staff.'

'That's interesting. We're organising a meet-and-greet in a week or so. Would he like to join us?'

'I'm sure Victor would love to.' She ended the call and asked Victor to see her. 'No need to look so concerned.' She told him what she wanted. 'You be happy to go?'

'Yep. I might have the girls with me if it's next week.'

'Let's worry about that once we've got a date.' The idea of a homeless hub had got her thinking. 'What would most homeless people want? Top of their list.'

'Easy. Somewhere decent to live where they're treated like humans.' He said it as if he meant it.

'Okay, we can't provide that, but if we could provide a hub for homeless people, what would you want us to include?'

He frowned. 'I appreciate you're trying to make me feel I belong, but how does this fit in with your core business?'

'Aren't you interested?'

'I'm more than interested, but I . . . I don't see the Novak family as friends of the homeless. I'd have thought they'd be more likely to exploit them.'

She laughed. 'You don't hold back, do you?'

'It's best to be honest.'

'I agree. And one thing I want to change is our company ethos. Make social responsibility a key area of our offering.'

'Does that include giving jobs to homeless people?'

'Dad mentioned he'd spoken to two of your friends. We can offer one of them—'

'Not Craig, eh? I suspect he'd tell you where to stick it, and so would John. No, I spoke to the young woman who sleeps across the square. She used to work in a kitchen.'

'Tell her to come in.'

'Great.' He grinned. 'And I'll think about what you can provide to help the homeless. Is there a budget?'

Bugger all, she wanted to say. 'Let me have your thoughts and we'll assess the practicality.' With the affordable housing and something for the homeless, she had a good feeling about winning the project.

'Okay.' He sat looking as if he wanted to say something. 'You may need to rethink the practicality.'

'What do you mean?' A chill nibbled away at her optimism.

'I'll show you.' He stood, and she followed him to his office.

He sat behind his desk and turned the screen so she could see it. 'Did you know you've got more than one hard drive in this thing?' He pointed to the tower.

'Yes, a backup. It also backs up to a server in the basement in case of fire. Jerry didn't trust the cloud.'

He laughed. 'Yeah, that figures.'

'What's the problem?' Her unease increased.

'The backup has gone.'

'Jerry's taken our financial information?' Her father had warned her when Sweeny wanted to leave.

'I don't think that was the intention. There's a third drive in the case. It's hidden on the computer, so you can't see it on the list of drives. I found it only because I'd seen it and knew it was there. I think he meant to take that and got the wrong one.'

Her stomach trembled. 'What's on it?' Was the hidden folder she'd found on the other drive a decoy, to stop her looking further?

'I've not checked all of it, but it looks like he was ripping you off. I found details of an investment scheme which had three million in it but is now empty.'

She felt sick. Although she'd guessed he'd taken *some* money, she'd assumed they'd eventually track down the money her brothers had siphoned off, either during probate or using specialist forensic accountants. It seemed Jerry had conned it from them, and that wouldn't be happening.

Victor gave her a sympathetic look. 'There's an email client, and I've been going through the messages. A few you need to be aware of, but these two are the most urgent.'

He opened two emails from HMRC. The first, a penalty for late filing of Value Added Tax, and the second, chasing a Corporation Tax payment.

She tapped the screen. 'We paid the tax and the VAT. I countersigned the cheques.'

'Cheques? You've got direct debits set up.'

'How do you know?' She hadn't given him access to the bank accounts.

'I checked the statements. You paid by DD until the last ones.'

'Shit!' The bastard Sweeny must have altered the cheques and taken the money. 'How much are we short?'

'Together, about seven fifty K.'

Acid filled her throat, and she swallowed it back down.

CHAPTER 51

On Wednesday, Zofia arrived at the office early, but Victor had already been, and a relieved Cleo greeted her. Zofia knew he worked late and hoped he wasn't overdoing it – although she still felt betrayed by his decision to leave, especially as he'd given them no notice. That he hadn't discussed it with her was what hurt the most. But seeing his joy at the prospect of spending a week with his daughters almost made her forgive him. Almost.

She got down to work and finished the email to her solicitor, updating him and giving him another link between Mulberry and the people who'd been giving her a hard time. Bowling had told her she wasn't aware of any recent contact between Mulberry and Theo Cook, the man who'd stolen Zofia's car and used it to knock two cyclists off their bikes. The emails Victor had discovered gave them evidence of that contact. Before she could ring Colette, the policewoman contacted Zofia.

'You've saved me a call, Colette. We found a link between Mulberry and Cook.'

'Have you now?'

Zofia gave her the link, but not how she'd discovered it.

'That's interesting, thanks, Zofia.' Bowling paused in thought. 'I've two more names for you, but you need to keep them quiet.'

'Of course.'

'Gideon and Gabriel Myer.'

'And who are they?'

'They're the men who attacked you outside your office after they threw a brick through your office window.'

Zofia thought back to her terror and anger at the attack. She'd almost given up on the police tracking them down. 'How did you find them?'

'Your neighbour in the chicken shop. He punched one of them, and the detectives I called out swabbed the graze on his knuckles. The blow scraped off the skin of one of the brothers, enough to give a profile. They're identical twins, so the best we can say is that the sample is probably Gideon's, but there's a long record showing that the two always work together. Our guys should be picking them up about now.'

'That's fantastic news.' A surge of relief made Zofia realise how much the fact that her attacker was still out there had affected her. 'Are they linked to Mulberry?'

'Sorry, he's never even arrested them. But I'll check if this "charity" of Mulberry's you mentioned has helped the other ex-cons.'

'I'll ask Vic— I'll check with my contact.'

'Great, let me know if you find anything. And say hi to Victor.'

Her cheeks burning, she ended the call. She checked the Myer brothers' records and realised she'd had a lucky escape. With a record like theirs, they'd be unlikely to give them bail.

Kasper arrived before she could ring Victor, so she sent him an email.

While she was updating her brother, Victor rang back. 'I've sent you an email,' he said, 'but Mulberry helped both Myer brothers when they came out of Wakefield. It looks like he's recruiting ex-cons for his own crooked schemes, under the guise of helping rehabilitate them.'

'I agree.' How many others could he turn on her and her brother? 'You've got evidence of his meeting them?'

'I've got an email where he discussed them with Sweeny, my predecessor.'

She opened her emails and found the one to her from Victor.

'I'm assuming Mulberry's not emailed sanctioning the attack on me?'

'Nothing so obvious, but they discussed the brothers in an email at the end of September. It looks pretty innocuous, but the timing suggests it happened around the time the campaign against KZD started.'

She read the email. 'Do you know the other people named?'

'I assumed they were ex-cons that he had other plans for. I'd imagine he's got other schemes running.'

'I'll check if they've got records. Thanks, Victor, this is a massive help.' She told him what Bowling had told her.

'Have you got enough to get Mulberry?'

'I'm not sure. I'll send this to—'

'Sorry, I've got to go. Speak later.' He ended the call, but not before Zofia had heard Judy speak in the background. She sounded stressed, and Zofia wondered what issues Victor was having to deal with. It wasn't her problem, and she had plenty of her own.

She brought Kasper up to date, left a voicemail for Bowling and updated her solicitor. His last response had suggested he was taking her claim about a vendetta more seriously. This should strengthen her case.

At lunchtime, Kasper received an email that made him laugh. 'Too late.'

'What?'

'An email confirming they're no longer investigating Victor for assault. It doesn't help us much, as he's already left.'

'I'm sure he'll be relieved to find that out.'

'Yes, sorry, you're right. I'll let him know.'

'Does that mean the SPI will lift our suspension? It's a pain not having access to their databases, not to mention the cost of using the others.'

'Yeah, I'll chase them up.'

He didn't get a reply until gone four.

'What's up?' Zofia could tell he'd received bad news.

'Bastards!'

She waited for him to calm down.

'Not only are they not lifting our suspension, they're considering additional sanctions.'

'What?' She got up and joined him at his desk.

'They're claiming that because the police have charged you with several "serious offences", they may have no option but to expel us.'

She leaned over his shoulder and studied the email, growing angrier as she read. One step forward, three steps back. Would this bloody nightmare never end?

CHAPTER 52

Following a troubled night, Judy arrived at work on Wednesday determined to sort out the problems Sweeny had left them with. After being kept on hold for what felt like hours, she spoke to someone about their Corporation Tax. She explained what had happened, but they wanted evidence of fraud, including a police report. Judy got them to halt enforcement action while she gathered the information they wanted. She left the VAT call for another day. The thought of going through the same soul-destroying process filled her with gloom.

If the police got involved, she wanted to make sure that none of the officers she knew would hear of it. They'd pounce on any sign of weakness. She checked the police website to discover the names of the officers in charge of investigating fraud. To her relief, Mulberry, the officer who most worried her, wasn't part of the team. But that didn't mean he wouldn't hear about it.

She could do with someone to use as a sounding board. She'd have considered their bank manager, a man she instinctively trusted, but he mustn't find out. If she told her dad, he'd be even more determined to kill Sweeny, but she didn't want to worry him. He adopted a tough persona, but she could see it being chipped away by these revelations. And to cap it all, he was the man who'd trusted Sweeny for so long.

She had to deal with this on her own. The next call promised to be no easier. She wanted to start the call to Robertson with positive news, but she'd already intimated to him that her father was on board with their partnership, so announcing that he now actually *was* wouldn't help her credibility.

She double-checked her figures before ringing him. Robertson reacted precisely how she'd feared he would.

'You're asking me to pay half for a project you've already started?'

'We're sacrificing the project so our group can win the bid for the Rochdale Canal development. They want more social housing and nearer to the city. The alternative is to make one in five units of the new development social housing.'

'Don't be ridiculous. You know that won't fly.'

She counted to five. 'Which is why I've suggested we sacrifice our existing development on Beswick Street. That's costing us seven hundred grand.' No harm in exaggerating her losses.

They argued some more, Robertson suggesting the path she proposed for them was being too generous and her countering that she was more worried they could lose out by not being generous enough. Somewhat to her surprise, he eventually agreed, and that's when she dropped the next bomb.

After a long pause, Robertson said, 'So, this Victor Mitchum. He'll be taking your seat on the joint board, or your father's?'

'Neither. He'll chair it, but won't have a vote.'

'How come you've not mentioned him before?'

Not wanting to say, 'Because he only started last week', she opted for, 'I've been trying to persuade him to front this development for a while, and he's only just agreed. His experience is exactly what you need to get this project over the line.'

'And what is that experience?'

'He's been intimately involved in working with the homeless community in Manchester, something our mayor, and therefore the council, considers important.'

'I seem to remember Mr Glass, our erstwhile rival, had credentials for working with the homeless, but look where he is now. Blacklisted by the council.'

'Rudy Glass talked the talk. Victor walks the walk.' God, she couldn't believe she'd just said that. 'And Glass's demise is down to his link to corrupt officials. Something I'll have you know I helped expose.'

'Did you now? I'll need to watch you.' Robertson chuckled. 'And we'll have to make sure we don't make the same mistake.'

'Quite. So I can go ahead with putting Victor on the board, and you're agreeing to share the costs of Beswick Street and putting it as our social housing contribution?'

'No. I want all the figures, and I want to meet this Victor before I agree anything.'

'Okay, I'll arrange a Zoom call if you send me your availability. Sooner rather than later.' She didn't want it to drag into next week.

'I don't enjoy being railroaded and—'

'I'm not railroading you. Things are moving fast. We need to react, or we'll lose the project.'

'Don't lecture me on business protocol. And I'd appreciate it if you didn't interrupt me, Ms Novak. I've not made anything of your inexperience, giving you the benefit of the doubt, but it's showing. Good afternoon.'

She stared at the dead handset for a long time. 'Fuck you!' She slammed it onto her desk. Who the hell did he think he was, lecturing her? Part of her wondered if she was indeed out of her depth, but that only plunged his barb deeper.

Her email pinged. Robertson, saying he'd speak to Victor this afternoon, or not at all.

She had plenty on this afternoon, but he was obviously asserting his authority, like a schoolyard bully. She made herself a herbal tea, hoping it would calm her, and drank half before going to see Victor.

Still irritated, she barged in. 'Victor, I need—' She stopped.

He ended the call he was on. 'Why don't you come in and sit down?'

She bristled but calmed herself and sat. She'd been the one to barge in, and he wasn't the person who'd annoyed her. 'We need to prepare for a Zoom with Archie Robertson.'

He looked like he'd have a heart attack. 'Do we?'

She gave him the background, trying to work out why he'd reacted like that.

'Okay, I think I can manage that. It's just that my last Zoom was the one where my employer in Bristol sacked me. So obviously . . .'

'Yeah, sure. Shall we do a couple of run-throughs with Keira and Dad? He hates doing them as well. Just as a rehearsal, and then us two will take Robertson on.'

'Sure.'

In the end, Victor handled Robertson just right, and by the time they finished the call, the latter's belligerence had disappeared.

'Well done, Victor,' Judy told him.

'Thanks.' He checked the time. 'I'll just take Oscar out and drop him home. See you about eight.'

'Sure.' She waited until he'd gone and, taking a formatted hard drive with her, logged into Sweeny's computer, relieved Victor hadn't changed the passwords.

She used his instructions and opened the files on the hidden hard drive. After copying them, she closed everything down. She would spend whatever free time she had going through the material, hoping it would hold the secret of where their money had gone. The three million might have disappeared, but there should be more. If she failed to find it, everything her family had worked for could come crashing down.

CHAPTER 53

Zofia stood at Kasper's desk, trying to get her head round this latest blow. An incipient headache threatened.

Kasper picked up his phone. 'I'm not putting up with this.'

She stayed his hand. 'Let's wait until we're calmer.'

'I don't want to be calmer. I want to give the bastard who sent this a piece of my mind.'

'Yes, I know, and so do I, but we need to consider what we want to achieve. The way we feel, we'll say things we can't row back from. We need to think about what we're going to say and not lose our tempers.'

Kasper sat, his jaw working.

'Please, bro.'

He put the phone back on his desk. 'Okay.'

She worked on a reply, toning the language down with each pass through until she had a version she believed had the best chance of getting the SPI to reconsider their action. Kasper read it and agreed with her. They sent it, hoping to get a positive reply tomorrow. She was getting ready to leave when Victor rang.

'Have you had your car repaired?'

'I've not had the time. It's legal to drive.'

'I've got a guy who reckons he can do it overnight.'

She'd not heard from the insurance company and suspected she'd have to pay the excess – a few hundred pounds she didn't want to spend until they had the business back on track. 'Thanks, Victor, but I'll leave it until I hear from the insurers.'

'He'll do it free of charge.'

'What's the catch?'

'No catch. He rents his premises off the Novaks, and I've done him a favour. He wants to repay it.'

She wasn't precious about her car, but she hated seeing it dented. It was like it had a sign on it, that she didn't care about it. 'That's really kind.'

She and Kasper waited for Victor to arrive. He arrived with Oscar, looking troubled, and, remembering the exchange she'd overheard on his earlier call, she said, 'Is everything alright at the Novaks'?'

'Not really. Did you investigate Robertson for them?'

The question threw her, but she couldn't speak about it. 'I can't discuss client information.'

'Of course not. I saw the header on the email you got last week. And I know—' He laughed. 'I shouldn't be betraying confidences either.'

Zofia had come to her own conclusions. 'Are they going into business together?'

'You remember that school where Toff got attacked, the one where Judy set fire to the security guard?'

'You mean the one Robertson was interested in?'

'Yeah, well, they're developing it together, and Judy's asked me to front the company.'

Both Kasper and Zofia stared at him open-mouthed.

Kasper recovered first. 'You've been there a week.'

Victor spread his fingers. 'She's obviously recognised my talent.'

Zofia had a horrible thought. 'Or she needs someone to take the fall if it goes wrong.'

Victor smiled. 'My first thought, but it's something far more prosaic. A rival bid is offering support for the homeless, and they think having me onboard – with my history – gives Judy and Robertson an advantage.'

'You've met him?'

'Zoom.'

'And?' Kasper didn't hide his curiosity.

'Do you remember Basil Rathbone, who used to play Sherlock Holmes in the old black-and-white films?'

Kasper laughed. 'Did he wear a deerstalker and smoke a pipe?'

Zofia joined in: 'What about a kilt?'

'I only saw his top half. Tweed jacket and old school tie.'

'What was he like? We've all been terrified of him.'

Kasper said, 'Only because his men shot and killed six people on the streets of Manchester.'

Victor gave a rueful smile. 'There was that. He wasn't happy when I Zoomed with him. I think he and Judy had had words about something else before the meeting. He seemed to think she'd tried to pull a fast one over something else, so by the time he met me, he wasn't exactly being welcoming. I'd be very wary of falling out with him, even if I didn't know about his tendency to murder people he doesn't like.'

'But he still agreed to your fronting the company?' Kasper asked.

'I have one non-voting share and zero share in the profits.'

'That doesn't sound like a great deal for you.'

Victor shrugged. 'I negotiated a generous bonus for attending meetings.'

'I'm really pleased for you,' Zofia said. 'Well done.' She meant it, although she worried Judy had a hidden agenda that could cause Victor trouble.

'Thanks. If I'm getting your car repaired, shall we swap keys?' He produced his car keys.

'I was going to go with Kasper.'

'Oh, right. I'd rather not leave mine here all night.'

Zofia wasn't sure she felt comfortable driving such an ostentatious car, and Kasper, noticing her hesitation, stepped in. 'Can I drive your car?'

Victor shrugged. 'It makes no difference to me. It's insured for any driver. Just don't get caught speeding.' He looked at Zofia and reddened. 'Right, I'd better go. You've got the keys?'

He took her car keys and led both dogs out. Cleo didn't seem too upset at being separated from Zofia, causing her a pang of disappointment. It felt like she was losing her. They locked up, and Kasper roared off in Victor's SUV while she got used to Kasper's temperamental gearbox. He arrived home long before her and had swiped the last parking spot near the house.

She parked down the street and walked back. He was holding court with the lads from next door. Two teenagers obsessed with cars, and one of their mates.

'Yeah, sure, I can take you for a spin.' He turned to her. 'I won't be long, we'll just nip down to the ring road.'

The three lads, almost unable to contain their excitement, clambered into Victor's car. She couldn't help smiling at their enthusiasm, even when Kasper set off too fast. She let herself in and, after changing, made a pasta sauce. He hadn't returned when she'd finished, so she set it on a low heat and took a shower.

He still hadn't returned when she came back down. She'd been home almost an hour. She picked up her phone, but realised he didn't have hands-free in Victor's car. And she could imagine his embarrassment if he got a 'where are you' call from his sister. Thirty minutes later, she heard someone at the door.

Her relief turned to panic when the visitor banged on the door. Two grim-faced policemen stood outside.

CHAPTER 54

Early Thursday morning, I dropped Zofia's car back in the office car park, deep in thought about what the mechanic had told me. She'd had a lucky escape this time, but they'd try again. I'd speak to her when I collected my car that evening. The cab dropped me on Sackville Square, and I glanced towards my old shelter. Sophie, the woman who now occupied it, sat up, wrapped in a patchwork of stained blankets and duvets.

I walked across to her, warm in my new coat. 'Morning, Sophie. I missed you yesterday.'

She laughed, and the scar running from her lip to her right ear widened. 'I got a night in a hostel. I feel almost clean now.'

'You said you worked in a kitchen.'

'Aye, I was the pastry chef in a fancy hotel near Peebles, but I did all sorts. Cooking, cleaning, washing up. Whatever.'

'You fancy a job at our place?'

'What, there?' She inclined her head towards the casino.

'Yes.'

'Doing what?'

I remembered what the place had been – not just a casino, but also a sex club – and my cheeks grew hot. 'In the kitchen.'

'You serious?'

'Yeah.' I told her who to ask for. 'She starts at ten, so you've got time.' I pulled out a hundred pounds and gave it to her.

'Wot's this?'

'An advance. Get some clean clothes. You know Digger's place?'

'Aye.'

'He'll be open at eight. Grab breakfast and a shower and get ready.'

'Aw, ah don't know what to say.' Her green eyes filled with tears.

'You don't need to say anything.' I set off towards the casino.

'Thank you, thank you, thank you.'

I waved and continued.

'Ah, mister?' she called after me.

I turned. 'Yeah?'

'Ah'll need somewhere to live.' She looked embarrassed, and waved a hand to encompass the scrappy cardboard mattress under her, and her two bags of belongings.

'Of course. We'll sort that. I told you, I was in your place a year ago, so I know what it's like.'

With another wave, I resumed my walk to the casino, more thanks ringing in my ears. I returned to my office and continued getting to grips with my new job. In between that, I'd been exploring the hard drive Sweeny had used. I'd copied its contents onto a new drive, air-gapped, just in case Sweeny realised he'd taken the wrong one and got a hacker to wipe it.

Judy, busy with the new construction project, had tasked me with checking the drive, and I was reporting to her each time I finished a folder. I'd found two encrypted, but hadn't mentioned them to her after considering what Sweeny might have hidden. If I'd been him, I'd have kept evidence I could use as leverage if ever Novak turned nasty. It wasn't a bad idea for me to have similar leverage.

A copy of both encrypted folders sat on the memory stick in my pocket. I intended to ask the best computer guy I knew to have a look at them. But Craig and I hadn't parted on the best terms. Judy's question about what homeless people wanted had also got me thinking, and I'd carried out a check of the Novaks' property portfolio. An idea occurred to me, and I printed off some information and made calls while I waited for her to come in.

She arrived late morning with Alex, and I requested a meeting with both. We held it in his office.

'Come in, Victor, what can we do you for? You're not asking for more leave, are you?'

I put my folder on the boardroom table and sat opposite father and daughter, counting to three before I replied. 'Not before Saturday, when I'm picking up my girls.'

'We've been thinking about that.' He gestured to Judy to continue.

'What time did you finish last night?' she said.

'Almost four. I've been putting in the hours.'

'Nobody said you haven't.' She used a conciliatory tone. 'If you're going to drive to Bristol on Saturday, I don't want you here until the early hours. You can finish at ten on Friday.'

'Right, oh, thanks.' I worked out I'd already done forty-nine hours this week, and I'd do another twenty-five, even if I finished at ten on Friday. But I still felt grateful.

But I didn't sound grateful enough for Alex, who scowled. 'What did you want?'

'I've been thinking about the Rochdale Canal project—'

'You think you should get a share, do you?' Novak's face reddened.

'Dad, let him finish.'

'Thanks. The strength of our bid is the helping-the-homeless angle. Besides a hub, which our rivals are also offering, we could offer accommodation.'

Alex wagged a finger. 'Hang on, we're already selling Beswick Street off cheap.'

'I'm not talking about any of your developments.' I retrieved the sheets I'd printed and passed one to each of them. 'You own several low-value properties in tough parts of the city. From what I can gather, you used them for' – I was going to say, 'to house the trafficked women who worked in the sex club', but thought better of it – 'staff accommodation. But many are empty. Why don't we offer them to homeless people as a halfway-house?'

'And have a load of junkies wreck 'em?'

'They'd only be available to people who were clean, and we'd have staff to check up on them.'

'How much will that cost?'

'We can get funding from the council. I've printed off some stuff they sent me. All it costs us is the income on a few houses and flats, which we're not even renting out. And I've asked about housing benefit, so it might not even cost us.'

Judy had a question. 'How do we make sure we don't get any junkies?'

'I've got people who can check that.'

Alex fixed me with a stare. 'Your mate Craig, you mean?'

I wanted to lie and say no, but it was best not to. 'Amongst others.'

Judy shuffled her papers. 'Can you give us a few minutes to think about it?'

I was sure Craig's involvement would scupper it, but they were both smiling when they called me in.

Judy gestured for me to sit. 'Yes. It's a good idea, but *you* need to make sure it happens. You'll be on your own. I can't spare any staff.'

Despite thinking, *how the hell do I fit it in?* I grinned. 'Great, thanks.'

An hour later, as I finished a meeting with someone from the council, Zofia texted asking if I wanted Kasper to drop the car round. I thanked her and told him where to park it, intending to speak to him when he left it. A text told me she'd arrived in it, and I put on my jacket to go and meet her.

Judy met me outside my office door. 'Where are you going?'

'I lent Zofia my car while hers was being fixed—'

'Tell her to leave the keys at reception. Robertson's demanded a Zoom, now.'

'Right.' What the hell did he want?

CHAPTER 55

Kasper had returned home from his joyride in Victor's car while the police were looking at each other like lost souls. He stood behind them with a questioning expression. Zofia, who'd recovered from her terror that something had happened to him, wanted to tear a strip off him.

She resisted the impulse. 'These officers wanted to fingerprint my car,' she told him.

'Yes,' said the officer who'd done the talking to her. 'We needed to check it out.'

Kasper said, 'But I thought you'd done all that. What about the chain of evidence? We've had it back since Monday.'

They ignored him and returned to their cars.

'Miserable sods. Why have they got a dog?'

Zofia hadn't noticed. 'I thought they'd come to tell me you'd wrapped Victor's car around the central barrier.'

'Oh, yeah. Sorry about that. One of the lads wanted to go to Heaton Park—'

'Round the motorway?'

He nodded.

'That's miles.'

'Yeah, well, we did the ring road.'

She looked at him incredulously. 'All the way round?'

'Yes, I've fuelled up. It bloody guzzles it.'

She hoped he'd not picked up any speeding tickets, but he looked so delighted, she forgave him.

The next day, her car was already at work, not a trace of the dent. It had seemed strange that the police had returned to take fingerprints days after she'd collected it. Although they hadn't said that was what they wanted, she'd assumed. They'd looked panicked when she told them the car was in a garage getting repaired. They must have worried about the garage valeting the car, but it didn't look like they had. She was just grateful to have the repair done.

In the office, Cleo leapt up and ran to her. Zofia made a fuss of her until Kasper sneezed and she returned her to her bed by the window.

Zofia contacted the officer investigating the drink- and dangerous-driving charges against her. He was surprised to hear from her, and even more so when she mentioned the other officers' visit to her car, reassuring her they didn't need to inspect it. She told Kasper.

'You know what these big organisations are like, left hand doesn't know what the right is doing.'

He was probably right, but something seemed off. Once it became obvious Victor wasn't coming for his SUV, Kasper remembered several errands he needed to run and spent much of the day out in it. At two, she texted Victor, offering to drop the car at work, and he agreed, sounding harassed.

Because they had to take Cleo in the car, Kasper reluctantly let her drive it, and he followed in his. A concert at the Arena meant traffic was a nightmare, so they decided not to return to collect Zofia's. It should be safe overnight. Victor didn't respond to her text saying she was outside, so she took Cleo and the keys to the receptionist in the casino, said goodbye and joined Kasper in his car.

Halfway home, Bowling called. 'Bad news, I'm afraid, Zofia. Our guys didn't pick up the Myer twins.'

The realisation that the men who'd attacked her outside her office were still free hit her like a blow. 'What do you mean? You said they'd picked them up.'

'I said they were *picking them up*. Unfortunately, it seems someone tipped them off, and they've disappeared. Sorry.'

'Who tipped them off?'

'We're investigating.'

'Mulberry?'

'We're investigating.'

Zofia suddenly felt vulnerable. 'Thanks for letting me know.'

'We will get them, I promise you.'

Yeah, before they get me?

CHAPTER 56

In the event Robertson was civility personified and he even apologised for his language at our first meeting. It still meant I missed seeing Zofia. I finished at three the next morning, and after four hours' sleep, dropped Cleo off at their office.

I was so busy on Friday, I almost forgot to collect her in the evening, but I finished at ten. Tomorrow, I'd be picking my daughters up. My luxurious sleep lasted until my phone went off at 3.07 a.m.

Craig, with his usual succinctness, announced, 'They're both on the move.'

Despite my exhaustion, I jumped out of bed and dressed, remembering to wear dark clothes. I gave thanks I was in a warm flat as rain lashed against the windows. At the door, I remembered the torches I'd bought after our last excursion. I hadn't intended taking Oscar, but he insisted on coming, and so did Cleo. At ground level, rain fell, but as gentle precipitation and not the stormy deluge I'd experienced forty-two floors up.

It wasn't until I saw Craig and John on the pavement that I remembered Trixie, but she wasn't with them. As before, John joined the dogs in the back, and Craig sat in the front with his holdall. I handed him the bag of torches.

'Have they moved?' I asked.

'Not yet. We got the call when the guy with the tattoo, Akimov, set off.'

'You've called me because one of them went out?'

'At three a.m.'

'He could be going to the all-night garage for cigarettes.'

'He isn't—'

John grabbed Craig's shoulder. 'We also got a call to say the other one, Colby, was up and about, Brother. I've just had confirmation that Akimov's picked him up.'

'Oh, right, okay.'

Craig and I, annoyed at each other for different reasons, seethed in silence. As we neared the unit where they kept the pickup, the tension in the vehicle grew thicker until I could almost touch it. We turned off Gorton Road, and I peered into the darkness. Ahead, a faint light shone on the side of the road.

'Lights out and pull over where we hid last time.'

Craig's instruction made me jump and, as I'd already been about to do as he suggested, it annoyed me. I extinguished the lights and drove into the shadow of the nearby warehouse.

A hundred metres away, lights shone out of the storage unit we'd broken into when we'd bugged the killers' pickup. The vehicle stood half on the pavement, pointing away from us, and the car they'd arrived in was in the unit. Craig distributed the gloves and ski masks. As before, I put the gloves on and put the mask next to me, ready. The weapons in his holdall clunked as he got them out, passing one to John and leaving mine in his footwell.

The car's lights died, and the roller-shutter fell. We waited for the two men to finish securing the building and make their way to the pickup. The relief that they were on the move mixed with apprehension about what was to come. They got in the pickup, and it set off, emitting a cloud of evil-smelling exhaust. We waited until they disappeared around the bend and wouldn't see my lights. With the tracker, we could afford to stay back.

Craig checked his screen. 'They're going right onto Hyde Road.'

We followed the vehicle onto the Mancunian Way and into Hulme. 'They've changed their hunting ground.'

Craig grunted.

Then, their quarry took a right towards Old Trafford. We were heading towards Zofia and Kasper's home, and for a moment I feared that was where they were going. Had Akimov discovered the part they'd played in his brother's death? But even if he had, how would he know where they lived?

They turned off at the next lights, no longer going towards my friends' house. My relief lasted until Craig announced, 'They've stopped.'

'Where?' I asked.

'At the next junction.'

'*At* the junction?' That seemed a strange place to park.

'Stop,' he barked.

I slammed the brakes on.

'I can't see them,' Craig said.

'Where have they stopped?' I could smell their exhaust, so we weren't far.

'There.' He thrust the screen at me and pointed at the map.

It looked like they'd stopped at the next junction, but none of us could see them.

John stuck his head between the front seats. 'Drive up to it. They might be in that alley beside the post box.' He pointed to it.

I rolled up to the crossroads, the three of us peering at the road ahead.

I needed new glasses, but Craig had excellent eyesight. We got within twenty-five metres, and he pointed. 'There!'

I peered into the mouth of the alley John had suggested they'd gone down, but saw only darkness.

Craig got out and ran. I grabbed the club he'd left for me in his footwell, looked around for a target and opened my door. He stopped at a pothole at the junction, picked something up and ran back. 'Bloody tracker's fallen off.'

I stared at the dripping, tape-wrapped device in his hand. We'd lost them, and in the next few minutes they would kill someone. Dread set my insides churning.

CHAPTER 57

On Friday afternoon, Zofia's solicitor rang with news that the police wanted to interview her on the Monday morning.

'What have you done with the details of the incidents of harassment we've been receiving?' she demanded.

'I don't think we can characterise what happened Wednesday night as harassment. They have a duty to carry out a thorough investigation.'

'What about the links between Mulberry and the criminals who've targeted us?'

'I'll be frank here, Ms Dąbrowski. If we make wild, unsubstantiated accusations, we risk coming across as unhinged.'

'Unhinged? They attacked me, wrecked an employee's home, stole my car and ran two men over in it.'

'But there's no evidence—'

'I thought you were on my side.'

'I am. If you don't feel I've given you the level of service you expect, feel free to find another solicitor.'

She took a deep breath and checked the time. Almost five. 'What time on Monday?'

'Nine thirty.'

Would she find another solicitor over the weekend? 'I'll see you there at nine.'

She put her phone down and did something she should have done earlier. A search of Mulberry and her solicitor's names came up with an image. The two men wearing dinner jackets and bow ties sat at a large round table at a fundraiser for a local cancer charity, heads together.

'Shit!' She slapped her desk.

'What?' Kasper studied her with concern.

'They're pals.' She made an angry gesture at the screen.

'Who?' He came over and looked over her shoulder. 'Bloody hell! No wonder he kept prevaricating about naming Mulberry. What will you do?'

She was exhausted by it all. 'I don't know. I'll think about it tomorrow. Tonight, I'm having a large G and T.' She smiled. 'Make that two.'

Again, they left before Victor came to collect Cleo. Would it be long before he stopped bringing her? Zofia hoped that wouldn't happen. On the drive home, she wondered if Victor would bring his daughters to see them. She'd met Helen, his eldest, when they had rescued her from a predatory couple outside the casino he now worked in. She'd like to see her again; she seemed a nice kid.

A car cut her up on Chester Road, and she had to pump her brakes to avoid hitting it. They'd been soft since Victor got the car repaired. She'd get them checked tomorrow and finished her journey driving more cautiously.

For a change, there wasn't a police car on their street. Kasper, who'd insisted on following her 'just in case', pulled in behind her and waved to the neighbour's boys, who looked disappointed he was back in his own car. She limited herself to one *very* large G and T, and they ordered a Chinese to be delivered.

As she was loading the dishwasher, someone banged on the door. Her pulse raced as she rushed to answer it. Outside stood the same two police officers who'd arrived while Kasper was joyriding in Victor's car.

'Yes?'

'We've got a warrant to search your car.' The younger officer proffered a sheet of paper.

'Warrant? Aren't you here to check for fingerprints?'

'Do you have the keys?'

'Sure.' She stepped back into the hall where Kasper now stood. 'They're here to check the car.' She scooped her car keys out of the bowl on the hallstand and handed them to the policeman.

Kasper took the sheet of paper off her while she slipped her shoes on and stepped outside. The night had chilled, and she shivered. As last time, they had a dog van, and an excitable spaniel stood near her car. The officer with her keys pointed them at her car, and the lights flashed. The dog handler opened the door, and the dog leapt into the back.

Kasper came alongside her and slid her jacket over her shoulders.

'Thanks.' She slipped her arms into the sleeves. 'Have you seen? They've brought a dog again.'

'Yeah, drugs.'

'What?'

'Didn't you read the warrant? They're looking for drugs.'

What? A sense of panic seized her. The dog came out looking subdued, though, and its handler shook his head. The officers had the same look of puzzlement they'd had two nights ago, when they'd discovered she hadn't got her car with her.

Zofia watched them as if in a trance. One of them stepped away and made a call. He ended the call and spoke to the others. The dog handler got back into the car and emerged a minute later carrying something, looking like he'd won a prize. His colleague bagged it, and the two who'd come to the door returned.

'Ms Dąbrowski,' said the older one, 'I'm arresting you for possessing a controlled substance with intent to supply. You do not have to say anything. But . . .'

Zofia listened without hearing and let them cuff her, telling Kasper not to worry. As soon as Kasper mentioned drugs, she guessed what had happened. Now that they'd found the drugs they must have planted, a sense of fury came over her, and with it an unexpected calmness. They took her to Stretford, and as she sat in the back of the car, she decided not to call their lawyer. By the time the duty solicitor arrived, Zofia was almost asleep.

The young woman breezed into the dingy interview room with a cheery, 'Hello, I'm Sylvia Akinwale.' She placed two covered takeaway cups on the table and took Zofia's hand. 'Neither has sugar, I'm afraid.'

'That's fine, thanks.' Zofia slid one towards her and removed the lid, releasing the rich aroma of coffee. She sipped the dark liquid as the lawyer read her notes.

The young woman's smile faded as she read and, once she'd finished, she gathered herself. 'I won't sugar-coat this. You're in the shit. They claim to have found one point two kilos of cocaine hidden in your car. That's a minimum of seven years.'

CHAPTER 58

I stared in panic until Craig said, 'Go left at the junction.'

It made sense, so I did. Side roads led off, right and left. I took the first left. Terraced houses with cars outside lined each side of the narrow lane.

From the back, Oscar barked. ***They didn't come down here. I can't smell the exhaust.***

I found a gap between the parked cars and steered into it.

'What's up, Brother?'

'They didn't come down here. I can't smell the exhaust.'

Typical, you take the credit for my olfactory superiority.

I made a turn, returned to the first junction, and took the right. I checked with Oscar.

They came this way.

I peered into the darkness, and we hit another junction. I made a quick decision. 'This way, Oscar?'

I think so.

'You think so?'

They're around here somewhere.

'Even I guessed that.'

Craig, although used to my talking to Oscar, gave me a sharp look.

'They're near here.' I hoped I was right.

Two turns later, I slammed the brakes on. A paved area edged with concrete bollards divided the road. Cars on both sides made turning impossible. I reversed.

'THERE!' Craig shouted, and I stopped.

The dark shape of the pickup stood halfway down a narrow lane. I pulled into it and cut the engine. There wasn't enough room to drive past. Just on the other side of the vehicle, an alley cut across a passageway, giving us three directions to check.

'We'll have to split up.' Craig thrust a torch into my hand. He had his ski mask on. 'You take the right branch and John, take the left.' He jumped out, and John opened the back door.

I left my glasses on the dashboard, picked up my ski mask, grabbed the club and got out. Craig and John were already at the pickup. Oscar had followed John out of the vehicle and waited for me. I opened the back door and pointed. 'You stay here.'

How are you going to find them without me?

'Okay, but stay out of the way.' Cleo cowered on the back seat and whined when I closed the door but didn't look like she wanted to follow. We left her and set off. The distinctive stink of its exhaust confirmed we had the right vehicle.

I ran awkwardly to the pickup, club in one gloved hand and torch in the other as I pulled the ski mask over my head. The engine ticked as I passed it. The other two had already disappeared. I took the right fork. A mixture of moonlight and streetlights gave enough illumination to make out obstacles, so I didn't need to use my torch. Oscar ran ahead, and I hoped that meant we were going the right way.

He stopped and waited for me. The alley opened out. We were at the back of a low industrial building. I stepped closer. Mesh or plywood covered the openings. This had to be where their target was dossing down. I took a chance and rang Craig.

'They're down the right branch,' I rasped between laboured breaths.

'On my way.'

Before I could call John, a cry came from our right. My pulse spiked. I found John's number and pressed Call before putting my phone in my pocket, confident that John would hear me and investigate. Someone needed my help, but the knowledge I was alone made me hesitate. Then, the terrified yelp of a dog galvanised me. I ran towards it.

Halfway along the building, an opening in the wall led into a courtyard. Not daring to use the torch, I stepped through it and stood in the pitch-black, listening.

In my pocket, I heard a tinny voice, then it stopped.

There. Oscar was looking towards the far corner of the courtyard. ***Smoke.***

I could smell it as well. Flames flickered behind a window, and another cry rang out. The flames silhouetted a bulky figure in the courtyard, his back to me. Something about the way he stood told me it was Colby. I charged, almost tripping on the uneven cobbles. He spun around at the last moment, but I was in range and already swinging. A sense of satisfaction temporarily overcame my fear as my club smashed into his head with a pleasing thunk.

He fell to his knees with a surprised cry of pain. I hit him again, and this time he collapsed forward onto his face. Breathing hard, I stood over him and looked around with my club held aloft. Where was Akimov? I peered through the window into the flames. Pale and flickering, they hadn't fully caught hold yet. The dog I'd heard before yelped again. Where was it? Then, from a doorway to the right of the window, a man stepped out.

No longer worried about being heard, I shouted, 'CRAIG, THIS WAY!'

The man and I faced each other. Through his ski mask, his teeth glinted in the flame light. It had to be Akimov. With a shock, I saw the pistol in his hand.

CHAPTER 59

After relieving Victor on Friday evening, Judy considered how his first week had gone. His plan to use the empty properties for the homeless had appealed to her. She'd realised during her short spell of living on the streets how many people just needed somewhere to live for it to improve their lives significantly. She'd not expected her dad to go along with it, but the way Victor sold it as a way to bolster their chances of success in the bid swung it. He clearly knew how to handle her dad.

She'd had limited experience of seeing managers up close: Colin the creep, who'd been her editor at the paper, and her dad and brothers. She'd known enough to realise she didn't want to emulate any of them. Although she'd had limited experience of Robertson's style, she'd thought it one she might copy, but on Wednesday he'd been little different to her dad, bullying when thwarted. At the end of the Zoom, it was Victor who'd got what he wanted.

The second Zoom with Victor and Robertson went even better, starting with a sincere apology from the Scotsman. Victor, despite having limited time to prepare, seemed on top of his brief, which reassured Robertson. All in all, she felt she'd made the right decisions.

She checked the time. The casino wouldn't be busy for at least an hour. She spent it at her desk. Victor had sent her a stream of emails letting her know what needed doing while he was away.

None were urgent, so she returned to checking Sweeny's hidden hard drive.

She clicked on the next file and cursed, thinking there was something wrong with her laptop until she realised she'd found an encrypted folder. Then she found another. Why hadn't Victor mentioned them? Maybe he hadn't found them? He'd told her everything else he'd found.

If Sweeny had hidden anything of great value, these new folders were where it would likely be.

She'd have to think of how to get into them. In the meantime, she continued until she found a cache of emails. They were between Sweeny and someone calling himself Alba. She guessed he was Scottish. Robertson? She read the messages, more convinced it was Robertson the further she read. Sweeny had been feeding Alba all the information about the Rochdale Canal project.

But if it had been Robertson, why did he need to partner with her? She'd be sharing all this information with him. He wouldn't need to buy information from Sweeny.

Then, a message that didn't belong: an exchange between Alba and Sweeny about an ex-convict. She opened Sweeny's email client and found the name in there. He'd been discussing the same man with Mulberry. A quick internet search told her what she needed to know. *Morus alba* was the Latin name for white mulberry.

'Fuck!'

A conversation she'd had with her council planning contact came back to her. A rival developer bidding for the same project had links to both homeless *and* offender rehabilitation charities. That one had worried her. Mulberry made no secret of his interest in both causes. A senior police officer wouldn't have the money to fund a project like that, not legitimately and with money-laundering checks; he'd not get away with using any dodgy funds. He had to be fronting someone, and what was the betting it was Glass?

And Sweeny had been feeding them all their information, giving them a heads-up about every decision they'd made. At least he hadn't passed on information about anything they'd done in the last ten days. Unless Sweeny wasn't the only one in their pay?

She told herself not to be paranoid, pulled herself together and, smartening herself up, made her way down to the casino. One thing her dad had impressed on her was to keep up a strong façade and glad-hand the punters. The one weakness she'd spotted in Victor.

At around midnight, a punter tested her façade. 'Evening, Gavin. We don't see you here very often.'

'Judy, delighted to see you,' Mulberry said. 'I'm here with my lodge.' He swept an arm to include a group of older men in dinner jackets, most of them at the bar, but some risking small piles of chips at the gaming tables.

He introduced her to a few, and she memorised their names, another thing her dad taught her. As she said goodbye to Mulberry, she couldn't resist adding, 'I hope we can meet up in Alba again, Gavin.'

Mulberry almost controlled his reaction, but she'd got through. Good, let the creep know she was on to him. She didn't see him again before he left, and she got home after three. In bed, on the edge of sleep, she remembered a message her dad had given her to pass on to Victor. Not wanting to forget to give it to him, she began a text, but fell asleep.

A dream of drowning woke her, but her face was wet. So was her top. She shook her head and opened her eyes, squinting as the light hit her like a slap. A masked man stood by her bed, a pistol in his hand. She closed her eyes, but he was still there when she opened them.

'Wakey, wakey.' He prodded her with the barrel.

She slid her legs out from under the duvet. He stared at them as she sat up. He seemed disappointed she wore a vest.

'Come on.'

Her brain, sluggish a moment ago, now worked at speed. Her phone lay on the floor by her bed. 'Can I get my slippers?'

''Urry up.'

'They're under here.' She bent over, giving him an eyeful, and tapped a quick message while pretending to search for her slippers and struggle to get her feet into them. She pressed Send and straightened while coughing to disguise the sound, hoping Victor would have his phone on.

CHAPTER 60

My pulse raced as I stared at the pistol. In his other hand, Akimov held a powerful torch, which he shone in my eyes. I shielded them with my left forearm and lowered the club.

'Drop it!'

Colby groaned and moved.

'Get away from him.'

I stepped to my right. The flames through the window grew brighter. Smoke poured out of the top of the open doorway that Akimov had come through, stinging my eyes. A faint cry for help came from the opening and ended in a cough.

I nodded towards the doorway. 'That's not the man you two want. Let me get him out.' I kept my left arm up, hiding my face. He'd seen me at the casino and even with my mask on, I feared he'd recognise me.

'How do you know who we want?'

The dog barked in panic. Oscar, who'd been standing over the prone Colby, shot past the window and disappeared through the doorway. Even in the dark, the smoke seemed thicker and caught at the back of my throat.

Akimov swung the torch to follow Oscar, but brought it back to me before I could move.

'Let me get him,' I said. 'At least I can get the dog.'

He dismissed this with an angry shake of his head. 'You said that wasn't the man we wanted. Why?'

'You're looking for whoever killed your brother.'

He straightened his arm. The barrel of the pistol looked black against the flames behind him. 'How the hell do you know about my brother?'

'He was killed on Riverpark Road, along with the Novak brothers.'

'Ha. That was on the news.'

The dog's cries grew fainter. And Oscar was in there. 'Please, the dogs—'

'Shut up about the fucking dogs!' He looked down at Colby, who groaned and stirred. 'So, my brother. What about him?'

'I know that, unlike the rest of them, he wasn't shot.' Where the hell was Craig?

Colby lifted his head off the ground.

'Help him up.'

I hesitated. Once Colby recovered, they'd escape – likely after shooting me or throwing me into the flames.

'Do it!' Akimov jerked the pistol.

His increasing agitation chilled me. I stepped towards Colby and bent to get a grip of the fallen man.

Then a light shone from the gunman's left side. Another appeared on his right, moving fast. Akimov fired a shot. Then came a cry. The gunman's torch landed on the ground, bounced once, and died. I threw myself to the ground, much too late. Several blows landed, then stopped.

In between heavy breaths, Craig told us it was over.

In the distance, sirens. Someone must have called the fire service. But how far away were they?

I struggled to my feet. John stood a few paces away, holding a club, his torch illuminating the scene. Akimov lay face down at Craig's feet.

'We need to get the man they were attacking out of there.' I pointed to the room behind the fallen Akimov.

'Do you know where he is?' Craig asked.

'In there somewhere.' The flames had got a good hold, and I hesitated.

Oscar appeared in the doorway he'd disappeared into. ***I know where they are.*** He ran back inside.

'OSCAR, WAIT!' I bent low and followed, Craig behind me.

Even down near the floor, the smoke attacked my eyes and throat, blocking out the orange glow of the flames. Ahead, a dog yelped. Not Oscar. Then Oscar barked twice, and we headed for the sound. Heat attacked my skin, even through the ski mask, and flames danced near the ceiling. I crawled as fast as I could and almost collided with Oscar. He stood near a man on the floor.

'Craig! I've got him.'

He crawled up to me, his shoulders filling the corridor. We each grabbed an arm and pulled, but the man didn't move.

'There's something holding him.' Craig crawled past me and checked the man over.

Smoke scoured the back of my throat, and I fought not to cough. Sweat trickled down my neck. *Come on, Craig.* Then with a grunt he crawled back to my side.

'The bastards had him zip-tied to the radiator. Let's go.'

This time the man moved, and we crawled out, dragging him.

I stopped. 'He's got a dog. Take this.' I thrust the arm I held towards Craig.

He grabbed it, and I crawled back inside, my eyes streaming and throat burning. Oscar barked from my right, and I quickly reached him. A mid-sized dog lay on its side next to him. I lowered my lips to floor level, took a deep breath, picked up the dog, then ran, bent over double. Oscar scampered behind me, and we emerged into the cool darkness of the courtyard. I ripped off my smouldering ski mask, straightened and faced the sky, letting cold rain wash over me. I supported the dog on one arm and placed my cheek near its muzzle. The warm stink of its breath confirmed it was still alive, and I lowered it to the ground.

The sirens were much closer now, and blue lights reflected off the clouds.

'Let's go.' Craig took the ski mask off me, picked up the weapon he'd dropped and scooped up the pistol Akimov had fired.

I looked at the man and his dog. 'No, I'll stay.' I pulled out the car keys and thrust them at him. 'I'll ring you.'

He didn't argue, and he and John disappeared seconds before the firefighters arrived. I greeted the officer and pointed to the homeless man and his dog. 'We've just pulled these two out of there.' I gestured at the burning building.

'"We" being . . . you and your friend here?' He nodded at Oscar.

'That's right.'

'What about these two?' He indicated Akimov and Colby, heaped like discarded laundry against the far wall.

'They started the fire.'

'Did they? And what happened? They fell over and bumped their heads?'

I shrugged.

'Right, thanks, leave it to us. But stay around. There'll be questions for you.' He shouted instructions, and two of his crew tended to the fire victims. Two others stood guard over the thugs after first checking them over.

I stepped back and let them deal with the casualties. Colby had almost recovered, but Akimov wasn't moving, so they put him in the recovery position.

In the corner, away from the action, I bent down and hugged Oscar. 'Well done, boy.' I buried my face in his smoke-stinking fur.

He licked my face. The firefighter treating the dog I'd rescued removed the face mask he'd held over its snout. The animal coughed, then vomited and struggled to its feet, looking for its owner. Paramedics arrived and took over the man's treatment. When he sat up moments later, relief flooded through me.

Police arrived and, after a discussion with the fire officer, one came towards me. Although I wanted to run, someone had to tell them what Colby and Akimov had been up to.

'The fire officer tells me you got the man out of the fire.'

'Me and my dog.' I pointed at Oscar.

'What about those two?' He pointed at Colby and Akimov.

I told him a version of what had happened, telling the truth about what I'd done to Colby, but claiming I'd surprised Akimov when he emerged from the building, while not mentioning he'd had a gun. I also didn't mention my two friends being there.

More police arrived and took the two men away after the paramedics examined them. Colby was by now able to walk unaided, but Akimov still appeared groggy. I shivered and watched the scene as I waited for the detectives to arrive. I ran through what I'd say. In the event, I didn't have long to wait.

'Well, well. If it isn't my favourite private detective.' Grimes looked down at Oscar. 'And me favourite mongrel.'

Oscar bared his teeth.

My heart sank as I looked around, expecting Lambert to join him. 'Don't they have other detectives in Manchester?'

'They do, Mr Timothy. But I'm investigating a series of attacks on homeless people. Someone tipped us off about a particular vehicle parked around the corner.' He jerked a thumb towards the pickup. 'I got the heads-up when it triggered one of our cameras.'

'Oh. So you took me seriously?'

'I take everyone seriously, Mr Timothy.' Like most of his colleagues, Grimes used my real name. 'We need a long chat about what happened here.'

He summoned two constables, who drove me and Oscar to his station. One of them took Oscar to get a bowl of water and stuck me in an interview room. I'd been there several months before, and it sorely needed a refresh. The stink of bleach couldn't quite disguise the eau de vomit.

I didn't have to wait long before Grimes arrived along with a detective I didn't recognise. She had spiky blonde hair and glasses. She crinkled her nose as she caught a whiff of the smoke I'd become desensitised to.

'Where's Lambert?' I asked.

Grimes's colleague answered. 'Adie's been—'

'We ask the questions in here,' Grimes cut across her. They gave me the usual spiel and began recording the interview.

Grimes started the questioning. 'You want to tell us what you were doing at the fire?'

'We suspected the two men you arrested had been attacking homeless people who own dogs. By the way, how are they, the man and his dog?'

His sergeant – I'd caught her rank but not her name when she introduced herself – answered. 'They're both recovering and should be fine. Thanks to you and your dog.'

Grimes scowled. 'Now that we've got the welfare check over with, can we return to my question? How did you know they'd be where you found them? And don't tell me you were just out taking your mutt for a walk and bumped into them.'

'We've been monitoring the two men, and I followed them.'

'Who's we?'

'A network of concerned homeless people.'

'But you're not homeless anymore, Mr Timothy. Anything but, from what I hear.'

How did he know? I reminded myself that he was a shrewd and well-connected detective. 'I haven't forgotten my recent past.'

'Who were they?'

'I don't know their names. They just rang me.'

'Why didn't you call us?'

'Your other sergeant, wherever he is, made it clear you needed more evidence when I told him about these men following Harry Sanders before they killed him. I assume you're going to reopen his death and treat it as a murder.'

'As I told you, Mr Timothy, I took you seriously, and we haven't closed that case. We will be questioning the two men we brought in about it.'

I remembered what Toff had said when he'd fixed the tracker. 'Have you got their vehicle?'

'It's in the pound, being inspected. Why?'

I guessed they'd find the metal box Toff had seen attached to its undercarriage. If they didn't, they'd get an anonymous call pointing them to it. 'I wanted to make sure you haven't missed anything, in case there was evidence in or *under* the vehicle.'

Understanding replaced the fleeting blaze of anger in Grimes's eyes. 'Don't worry, Mr Timothy, we won't. Going back to my question, how were you going to get the evidence we needed?'

'I'd catch them red-handed.'

'On your own?'

I swallowed. 'If necessary.'

'And it was indeed necessary, it would appear. Were you armed?'

'No.'

'You don't know anything about a shot being fired? Someone rang us and reported one.'

'Sorry, no.'

He grinned. 'I'm finding it difficult to believe that an intelligent man like you would tackle two bruisers on his own. Unarmed. I'm not being rude, but you're not exactly Superman. More like Clark Kent. By the way, where are your glasses?'

'They fell off in the fire.' I lied without hesitation.

'Of course they did. And what can you tell me about the injury to Mr Colby?'

'I was defending myself. He saw me and reached for something in his pocket. I thought it might be a gun and hit him with a stick I picked up.'

Grimes exchanged a grin with his sergeant. 'He must have been going for that sharp pen we found in his pocket.'

'I wasn't going to wait to find out.'

'Did he turn away just before you hit him?'

'Now you mention it, he did. No idea why.'

'And it was bloody lucky, you finding a rounder's bat just lying there on the ground. What do you think, Sergeant?'

'I think Mr Timothy was very lucky indeed.'

They asked me more questions, seeing if they could catch me out, then at six let me go. I had to drive to Bristol in a few hours. I turned my phone on, and the notifications beeped. Top of the list, a message from Judy.

Dad said if

help gunman home no pigs

CHAPTER 61

I jogged the two hundred metres from the police station to the rendezvous I'd arranged with John and Craig after receiving Judy's message. I reached the junction and ran towards the silhouette of the car. The driver's seat was empty, but two heads poked up above the rear headrests.

'Alright, Victor. Smart wheels.' The cheery Scouse tones of Toff greeted me as I clambered into the driver's seat and caught my breath. The smell of smoke lingered on Craig.

I looked in the back. 'Where's Oscar and Cleo?'

John said, 'We took them to Digger's place. Wasn't sure when, or if, you'd get out of the cop shop.'

The thought that they were safe was a relief.

'What's this about Novak?' Craig asked.

'I got a message from his daughter. I think they're being held by gunmen.' She'd only mentioned one, but there must be at least two, one to deal with Alex, who was still a dangerous man.

'So?'

I'd naively thought risking our lives to rescue a homeless man would have built a bridge between us. 'I'm going to help her.'

He folded his arms. 'Like a good lapdog?'

'Like a decent human.' My glasses were still on the dash, and I put them on.

'I suppose your job depends on keeping her alive.'

'Feel free to leave me to it.' I knew that without Craig my chances of success weren't great.

John leant through the gap in the front seats. 'Surely that's a job for the police, Brother.'

'She said, no police.'

Craig hadn't finished baiting me. 'Afraid of what they'd find.'

'She probably suspects a senior copper's behind it.' I checked the time. 'I'm setting off now. Anyone who doesn't want to come can get out now.' I held my breath. I needed their help, and they knew it.

Three sets of seat belts clicked locked and Craig sat back. 'I've programmed Novak's address into the satnav. That's where you said they were?'

I nodded, hoping I was right, and a mixture of relief and irritation filled me as I started the car. The satnav told me we'd be there in thirty-three minutes, but I thought I could cut that on a Saturday morning. But I'd have to do it without getting stopped. The thought of Judy in the hands of gunmen made my insides churn.

Craig studied his phone and, halfway there, he put it away. 'Give me your phone.'

'Why?'

'Is it registered in your name?'

'Yeah.' I gave it to him and, after switching it off, he gave me another, its cracked case held together with yellow tape.

'It's got my number on it,' he told me.

I slipped it into my pocket.

'The house is on a corner,' he said. 'The road runs along two sides, and they've got high fences on both. Along the western boundary is a cricket club. You two' – he pointed at me and Toff – 'go through that fence.'

'And do what?' Toff asked.

'Find out where they are. They should be on the ground floor, easier for them to get out when they've done their job.'

I had a question. 'How do we go through the fence?'

'There's a good chance that's where they got in, so look for their opening. If you don't find it' – he bent to retrieve something from his bag and passed a pair of wire cutters to Toff – 'use these.'

'When did you pick those up?'

'I brought them and a few other tools, in case we needed them to tackle the two clowns we took down.'

I didn't want to think about why he'd need wire cutters, or the other tools.

He continued with a quick briefing, outlining his plan.

I wasn't sure it would work, but it was the only one we had. We drove through Hale, passing houses big enough to accommodate a dozen or more people. To our left, the sun was brightening the sky. We had about thirty minutes before it became too light, but by then, it would all be over.

I still had my gloves on, and Craig distributed ski masks. He'd also brought a couple of extra surprises for our confrontation with Colby and Akimov, items we hadn't used because we'd almost lost the two killers and things progressed too fast.

We passed the house, huge like its neighbours and still in darkness, and pulled up at the cricket ground. Toff and I got out, carrying what we needed. John jumped into the driver's seat. We clambered over the low gate to the cricket ground and scrambled towards Novak's house. Although we had torches, we didn't want to attract attention. We checked the perimeter alongside the house.

A thick hedge almost three metres high separated the house from the pitch. Through the bottom of the hedge, you could make out a wire fence. The trunks of the hedge stood half a metre apart, leaving room to squeeze through.

''Ere, Victor.' An urgent whisper from Toff summoned me to the rear corner of Novak's garden.

The gunmen had made a hole almost a metre high in the fence. We squeezed between two trunks, clambered through it and came out alongside a smart wooden shed. Lights blazed, most coming from an orangery jutting out of the rear. The patio surrounding it bled into the extensive lawn. They'd be invisible from any of the surrounding houses, and it was the part of the house furthest from neighbours or the road.

'Shit!' Toff stared at the windows.

I could just make out some figures inside the orangery. 'What?'

'They've got the woman tied to a chair, and the old bloke.'

'He's in a wheelchair.' I could now see what Toff meant. Two men stood over the seated figures.

One of the standing men raised an arm and brought it down with vicious force. Was that a cry? I felt sick, but if we were to save them, I had to overcome my squeamishness. 'Can you see anyone else?'

Toff scanned the windows we could see. 'Do you want me to check?'

Why would any of them be anywhere else? Unless they were on lookout at the front. In which case, checking for them meant risking alerting them. I made a decision. We were forty metres from the back of the house.

'Wait here.' I slipped back out of the opening onto the cricket pitch and rang Craig. 'We've found them.' In a low whisper, I explained what we'd found.

'Stay there, we're coming.'

Conscious of the ordeal Judy and her dad were enduring, I waited. I heard John approaching across the grass, but Craig was at my side before I realised. I summoned Toff, and Craig asked him a few questions, then imparted the amended plan to us. We found a spade in the shed.

On Craig's command, Toff and I took the spade and crawled over damp grass to a pair of French doors ten metres past the orangery. I doubted whoever was inside could see much in the dark, and shrubs in beds and the garden furniture on the patio outside the orangery gave us cover.

Then a floodlight came on, filling the back lawn with harsh light. I lay still, my heart thudding. I should have shut my eyes when it came on to preserve my night sight, but I wanted to see what they did. From the corner of my eye, I saw someone come to the window and peer out. Then, a fox scampered across the patio. A curse and a harsh laugh came from inside. I moved my head. The man had turned back to his prisoners and, signalling to Toff, we moved on.

The light died, plunging us into darkness. We reached the French doors and stood panting, then used the spade and the wire cutters to lever the two doors apart. The creak of the timber as it distorted sounded too loud, but we couldn't help it. Then, when I thought the glass would shatter, the door swung out.

We pulled our shoes off and slipped in. Sweat coated my neck and head under the ski mask. We were in a library of some kind, its polished floor slippery under my socks. We headed towards the back of the house and the orangery. A wide carpeted corridor led to a door. I opened it a crack and stopped.

Voices, and sobbing. We were at the right place. I stepped back out, texted Craig and set my alarm for ninety seconds. We sneaked back into the kitchen, sliding across the floor towards the orangery. The spade, which I carried at waist height, scraped against the granite worktop.

The voices stopped, and then Judy let out a shrill scream. 'You bastards! I'll make sure you suffer for this.' She spat, and a slap rang out.

'Dirty bitch!'

My alarm sounded and, with it, a loud bang from the back. Toff threw the flashbang Craig had given him, and it exploded between the kitchen and orangery. Expecting it, I closed my eyes and covered my ears, but it still almost deafened me. The brightness after skulking in darkness made me squint. Acrid smoke filled the room. A smoke alarm wailed. I screamed and, with spade raised high, burst into the orangery.

One of the men had come towards the kitchen to investigate the noise I'd made, and stood two paces inside the orangery. Even squinting, I recognised the man who'd attacked Zofia from his mugshot. I swung the spade with everything I had.

Hot liquid splashed my eyelids, and my hands stung with the force of the blow. He dropped like a felled tree. Through the smoke I saw him again, but this time further away and pointing a gun at me. I froze and stared. A shot rang out. I flinched, but his head exploded. Before I could take it in, John and Craig appeared, the latter holding a pistol.

Craig took over and gave instructions. He crouched over the one I'd hit, and another shot rang out. I looked around in panic, but Craig stood, calm as you like.

'Gunshot residue.' He winked.

The man I'd attacked now had a pistol in his hand.

Alex Novak and Judy looked in a bad way. Both had bloodied, swollen features.

Novak's head lolled, and his left hand looked a bloody mess. John had cut Judy free, and Craig whispered in her ear. She replied at the same volume. Craig grabbed my shoulder and pointed back the way we came.

'We can't leave them,' I said.

'We have to. Now, come on.'

'Victor!' Judy's voice sounded hoarse. 'Take my phone. It's under my bed.'

'What?'

'I messaged you. The police will know you've been.' She told me where to find it, seeming to grow stronger by the second.

I found it and followed the others, scrambling through the hole in the fence. John sat in the driver's seat, and I threw myself in the back. To my surprise, Craig sat next to me. Someone had placed a sheet of polythene on the back seat. Where the hell had that come from? Then I remembered who'd owned the car before me.

Craig had bloodstains on his sleeve, and I remembered the aftermath of hitting the man with the spade. My top and ski mask must be covered. I pulled the mask off and scrunched it up, inside out. I left my gloves on.

The satnav gave instructions, and John followed them. Dawn had broken, and we stopped. I recognised where we were. Digger's diner.

Craig hurried me through the doorway. The aroma of coffee and bacon made my stomach rumble, but Craig pushed me to the showers. I stripped off and got into the first cubicle. The water cascaded over me, and I closed my eyes, trying to forget what I'd seen. When I came out, my clothes had gone and, in their place, the worn but clean items Digger handed out to his clients.

'Coffee?' Digger summoned me to the serving counter and gave me a mug, plus a huge bacon butty containing half a pig.

My mind dwelt on the sound the man's head had made when I hit it.

Oscar nudged my leg. 'Hello, boy. Am I glad to see you.' I bent to hug him, then gave him a piece of bacon and ruffled his fur.

Cleo stood a pace away, her head lowered.

‘Come on.’ She trotted to me, tail wagging. I gave her a rasher and held her.

With a clank, Craig placed my phone on the table. I wiped my fingers with a piece of kitchen towel and switched it on. It beeped with a slew of notifications. Most from Kasper. With a sense of dread, I opened the latest message.

The police are holding Zofia.

CHAPTER 62

Since they'd taken her to a cell, Zofia had lain on the thin mattress on the narrow platform staring at the flaking ceiling, unable to sleep. When she considered her predicament – facing years in prison and, even after release, being unable to continue with the job she'd grown to love – a sense of helpless panic paralysed her. But she focused on her fury at Mulberry and the man behind him, Glass. She would bring them both down.

The door opened, and a constable summoned her out. She followed him to the interview room, conscious of the second officer at her heels. Did they imagine her to be a hardened criminal ready to overpower them and escape? Despite her predicament, the thought made her smile.

Sylvia Akinwale, already in the interview room, rose to greet her. 'Good morning. You seem happy?' The duty solicitor had again brought a coffee for her client.

'Prospect of a decent coffee.' Zofia sat and raised the cup, inhaling the aroma, as the door clicked shut behind her.

'I've got something else to make you smile. I spoke to your brother, and someone called Victor.' She looked embarrassed. 'I'm afraid I shared details of the charges you face, only because your brother—'

'No problem, I trust both of them.'

Akinwale looked relieved. 'He had some information that should get the police to release you. I've spoken to them and requested an urgent interview.' She outlined what she'd told them and called the officers in. Zofia considered the new information and what it meant for her chances of getting out of this unharmed.

Instead of the officers who'd arrested her, two detectives arrived, introducing themselves as an inspector and constable from the drug squad.

The inspector started by reading a statement from his tablet. 'After receiving a request from your solicitor, Ms Akinwale, we've weighed the drugs—'

'Excuse me, Inspector.' Akinwale raised a finger. 'Did you ascertain the package contained drugs?'

'We're in the process of doing so. If you'd let me continue, we've determined that the quantity of dr— substance we recovered from your car is nine hundred and seven grams, not one point two kilos.'

'So, you're dropping the charges?' Akinwale pressed.

'That's still a significant quantity of drugs.'

'If it *is* drugs, the quantity means the charges are less serious. And the doubt—'

'There is no doubt.'

'You've already admitted you're in the process of testing the compound, which suggests doubt.'

He reddened but didn't respond.

'How did you make such a crass error in the quantity of product? It wasn't just a few grams out.'

His colour deepened. 'We're investigating.'

'In the meantime, you've remanded my client for no reason.'

'We've charged her—'

'With possessing one point two k, which you admit you no longer have. Do you want to progress this and see what a judge says?'

He stared at his tablet. 'Ms Dąbrowski, I'm releasing you on police bail. You must surrender your passport and return here for an interview on Monday morning at eleven.' He looked at her.

'Yeah, fine, you can have my passport.' She couldn't believe they were releasing her.

Half an hour later, she was in Akinwale's car on the way home. A fine rain fell, but the morning sun was fighting to break through.

'Do you want me to represent you on Monday?'

'Yes, please, Sylvia.' She remembered her other case. 'They've also accused me of some motoring offences, including drunk and dangerous driving. Can you do that one as well?' She gave her the details.

'Yeah, sure. Who's done preliminary work?'

Zofia told her.

'Right, I see why you're jumping ship.'

'He's got a rep?'

Akinwale gave a rich laugh. 'Far be it for me to disparage a fellow member of the bar . . .'

'I dropped him because he's friends with Chief Superintendent Mulberry.'

Akinwale raised her eyebrows. 'I'd heard rumours of something like that. It explains why some of his clients seem to get a much easier ride than others.'

Zofia let herself relax, feeling confident this young woman would have her back. Akinwale refused the offer to come in and left Zofia on her doorstep.

Kasper let out a whoop and hugged her as she entered.

She powered up her phone, which beeped with notifications. She ignored them and jumped into the shower. Once clean and changed, she followed the delicious aroma of cooking to find Kasper making her an omelette.

As she ate, Zofia checked her messages. One from Victor asked if she was up for minding his daughters tonight as 'something had come up'.

She responded, saying she'd be delighted, and turned to Kasper. 'Did you speak to Victor apart from when you both spoke to Sylvia?'

'I did.' He produced a set of house keys from his pocket. 'He asked me to give you these and this.' A Post-it note had an address and some instructions on it.

'Do you know what he means?' She pointed at the end of his message.

'Yeah, both Judy and Novak are in hospital. Two intruders held them prisoner and tortured them. The police think it was a home invasion that went wrong. The men are now dead.'

'Oh, God. And Judy?'

'Victor seems to think she'll be okay.'

'Her dad?'

Kasper shrugged. 'Victor couldn't say.'

'Poor woman.'

'You need to worry about yourself.'

'I'm fine.'

He scoffed. 'You're still facing two serious charges. Have you got the tracker app for the device you left in your car?'

'Yeah, why?'

'Can I check it?' He held his hand out, and she gave him the phone.

He spent a few minutes fiddling with it and put the screen in front of her. The footage played, and the dot moved a small distance, returning a few minutes later.

'What's this?'

'That's when they planted the drugs in your car.'

'Drugs. So, it is drugs. Sylvia suggested it might be something else.' The optimism infusing her since her release evaporated.

'It's not drugs now. But this' – he pointed at the frozen image – 'shows a copper planting the original package.'

She tried to comprehend what he meant. 'You'd better explain.'

'Sorry. At sixteen twenty-three, while City were playing Everton, a copper needed to get access to a car in the pound.'

'My car?'

'The car behind it. Yours was in the way, and normally the guy on duty would have moved it. He's a big City fan, so when the detective offered to move your car, he accepted. He gave him your keys, but the detective didn't appear on the log as having possession of them.'

'How do you know all this?'

'Victor found the drugs – or Oscar did – on the way to the garage to get your bodywork done. Apparently, he told Victor there was something unusual-smelling under the back seat.'

'Good old Oscar.'

'You think he actually spoke to Victor?' He shook his head. 'Anyway, Victor told the mechanic to check under the seat, and *he* recovered the drugs and told Victor, who asked him to substitute two pounds of baking powder—'

She laughed much more than the revelation warranted. She dried her eyes. 'But how did he know about the guy planting it?'

'We weren't a hundred per cent until I saw this, but he spoke to someone who knew the guard at the pound. They asked him if anyone could have tampered with your car. He admitted a detective sergeant came to look at a car.'

'That detective sergeant got a name?'

He grinned. 'Lambert. I spoke to Colette about it, and she's making sure they carry out a thorough investigation. I'll send her this.'

Although relieved, Zofia was still unsettled. 'So, if Victor hadn't taken my car, and Oscar hadn't found the drugs, I'd still be in jail?'

'Possibly. But they did find them. The mechanic said your brakes would need new pads soon. He didn't have any in stock, otherwise he'd have done it.'

'Yeah, I've found out. Did Victor say what he did with the drugs— God! No wonder they were so confident it was one point two kg. That's how much they planted.'

'He said he's found a good home for it.'

What did that mean? Was Victor selling drugs?

CHAPTER 63

I'd responded to Kasper's *The police are holding Zofia* text, reassuring him I had it all under control and asking him to arrange a meeting with Zofia's solicitor. We left Digger's place with the Saturday morning rush in full swing. By that time, at least three people had passed through each shower cubicle we'd used, and our clothes had gone into the incinerator. The smell of polish and car cleaner confirmed someone had valeted the car while I'd been inside. I don't know if I would ever scrub the memory of hitting the man with the spade.

I stopped to drop them off, and Craig said, 'What are you doing now, Victor?'

'I'm seeing Kasper, Zofia's got a problem I need to sort out, then I'm driving to Bristol to collect my girls.'

'When?'

I checked the time. 'I need to leave at twelve. I told Carol I'd be there at three, but it will be nearer four by the time I get there.' Despite fighting it, I yawned. Now that the adrenaline had left my system and as the fear of getting killed or caught had receded, fatigue gripped me.

'Pick me up at twelve. I'll drive.'

'There's no need.' I wasn't sure I wanted to spend seven or eight hours with Craig in a car.

'I've been sleeping through the day while we've been waiting to catch those two bastards, so I'm less likely to wrap the car, and your girls, around a lamppost.'

He had a point.

To reinforce his case, from the back, John spoke up. 'Craig was a specialist driver in the forces, Brother.'

'Thanks, Craig. I'll collect you at twelve.'

I arrived at the KZD offices before Kasper and walked the dogs. When Kasper arrived, I explained what I'd discovered in Zofia's car and then we told her solicitor. I liked her; she seemed young but switched on. I'd not received a reply to the request I'd sent to Zofia to watch the girls that night, but took a chance and gave Kasper my keys to the flat, deciding to get the spares from Judy's office.

There weren't many people at the casino, but I bumped into Sophie. 'Are you working here now?'

'Thanks to you, started yesterday.'

'Great, can you make me a couple of sandwiches to take with me? I'm driving to Bristol and won't have time to stop.'

'My pleasure. I'll do something special.'

I collected the spare flat keys from Judy's office and let the senior staff know that she and Alex wouldn't be in, but I'd be back later. Sophie came to my office with a delicious-smelling bag. I had time to return to my flat and change into some of my new clothes. I wanted to look my best to collect my daughters and, if I was honest, when Carol saw me.

Craig, despite my misgivings, was entertaining and forthcoming in a way I'd never seen. The bag of sandwiches, which scented the car with its contents, survived until Stoke. I made a note to get my food from Sophie whenever I could. Zofia rang to thank me and confirm she'd be at the flat when I got back with the girls. At Stafford, I fell asleep and woke as we stopped.

I rubbed my eyes and wiped drool off my chin. 'Piss stop?'

'That's up to your missus, isn't it?'

Then I recognised the houses. We'd stopped two doors from where I'd lived with my family for seven years.

I got out and stretched. A neighbour I recognised nodded as he walked past. Before I reached my house, the door opened and Helen shot out, barrelling into me. In the three months since I took them camping, she'd grown, but Em, now twelve, had almost caught up with her. She waited until Helen released me and gave me a fierce hug.

She stepped back and studied my car. 'Where's the cute van?'

'Don't you like the new one?'

'A bit boring. Very corporate.'

Although not a car nut, I felt an unwarranted disappointment, then laughed at myself. I introduced them to Craig, and Carol invited us in for refreshments.

'How about Oscar and Cleo?'

'It's Oscar's home, of course he can come in.' Helen ran to the car and opened the back door. 'Oscar, give me a kiss.' He jumped out, and she bent to hug him, burying her face in his fur. Then she saw Cleo. 'Wow, she's adorable. Hello, Cleo.'

I'm still here, you know. Your beloved Oscar.

Em made her way to the car, trying to appear cool, but not wanting to be left out.

Someone with discernment. Hello, Em.

She walked past him and stroked Cleo, who revelled in the attention.

Have I become invisible?

'Welcome to the club.'

We filed into the house, Craig bringing up the rear.

It felt strange to be a guest in a house that had been my home for so long, and was still home to my children. It was the longest I'd spent with Carol since our separation, and I realised there was no way we'd ever get back together. Even assuming she was still interested, I'd changed too much. I didn't see her new bloke, but she had the contented appearance of a woman happy with life, and I was glad.

Forty minutes later, we were on our way, the boot containing four cases, three belonging to Em. At Craig's suggestion, I sat in the back, between my daughters. Despite my joy at being with them, I fell asleep in the sunlight as we passed Dursley, to wake in darkness as we passed Manchester Airport. The girls were leaning forward, listening to Craig with rapt attention.

'Anyway, yer dad's awake. You'd better pretend to be interested in what *he's* saying.' He winked at them and returned his attention to the road. As we approached the bottom end of Deansgate, the girls pressed their noses against the windows.

'Wow, it's like New York,' Em said.

'More like Guangzhou,' Helen corrected her.

'Whatever, it's fab.'

We parked in the underground car park. Craig said goodbye and left us on the ground floor. Zofia opened the door as I fumbled with the key. Helen had met her before and loved that Zofia greeted her like an old friend. By the time I'd had a shower and changed for work, they were three friends on the enclosed balcony, staring at the city spread out below, while Zofia pointed out landmarks.

'Right, girls,' I said, 'do what Zofia tells you, and I'll see you in the morning.'

They barely acknowledged me.

Welcome to the club, a disconsolate Oscar said from the living room.

Zofia left the girls with Cleo and joined me at the door. 'Aren't they delightful?'

Remembering a tantrum when the hot water ran out at a campsite we'd stayed at in the summer, I made a noncommittal noise. 'You be alright with them?'

'Of course.'

I sensed her unease. 'You'll be fine with all the legal stuff.'

'I'm not worried. Not about that.'

'What, then?'

'The guy who attacked me. Colette said they'd not picked up him or his brother. They're on the run.'

'You don't need to worry about them.'

'Oh yeah?'

I didn't know if the police had released their names yet, but I took a chance. 'They were the two who attacked Judy and her dad. They're dead. Judy told Craig that she'd let slip to Mulberry that she knew what he'd been up to. He must have decided to shut her up.'

'Oh, God!' She covered her mouth.

'You don't have to worry about them anymore.'

'But if the police had picked them up, Judy and her dad wouldn't have gone through that ordeal.'

And I wouldn't have had to hear and see the spade smashing his skull. 'He'd have found someone else to do the dirty work. Anyway, I'm sure they'll be fine. Alex and Judy are both tough cookies.' She looked so distressed, I wanted to hold her, then Helen and Em came to the door, and the moment passed.

'Sorry, Dad,' said Helen, 'we were just enjoying the view. Goodnight, and see you tomorrow.'

I hugged them, winked at Zofia and strolled towards the lift, my heart full.

CHAPTER 64

Judy's headache jabbed at her each time she made sudden movements, and the wounds on her face hurt all the time. She'd taken some pain-killers yesterday, but they'd made her woozy, and she wanted to be sharp. She watched the blanket on her dad's ribcage rise and fall. They'd put him into an induced coma, reassuring her he'd be fine afterwards. But the fear he'd not wake – or if he did, would be a hollow shell of the man she loved – sat like a ball in her chest.

Those men had had no intention of letting her or her dad live. They'd not even tried to disguise themselves or hide who they'd worked for. She realised she'd pulled the trigger with her childish jibe about Alba, letting Mulberry know she'd discovered his correspondence with Sweeny. A lesson, if she needed it, that actions have consequences.

'Sorry, Dad.' She held his right hand. The other was swathed in bandages. 'Thank God for Victor.'

But besides gratitude, part of her felt anger that he'd deprived her of her revenge by killing the men responsible. But, however much she hated them, they were mere tools, and she would do whatever she could to bring down the man who'd wielded them.

She checked the time and realised she had to go. She stood, grimacing as her bruises complained, and leaned over her father's head, kissing his swollen and bloodied cheek. 'Bye, Dad, I'll be here in the morning—' Oh shit, she needed to make a statement. 'Lunchtime tomorrow.'

Billy, her dad's driver, waited outside with one of their other men, and she let him escort her to the minibus and drive her to the flat she'd moved into. In the same block as Victor's, it was smaller and needed a refurb. The house was still a crime scene, but they had let her take some clothes this afternoon. She changed, and Billy dropped her at the casino.

'Go back. I want two of you with Dad all night.'

Despite her admonishments, Victor was at the casino. 'I told you I'd be here. Now get off with your girls.'

'You don't look ready.'

'I'd have thought a man your age, especially with a wife and daughters, would know not to tell a woman she looks terrible.'

He reddened. 'I meant, you should be with your dad.'

'Yeah, but it just makes me furious. When that bastard shot him in the spine six months ago, I knew the gunman got what he deserved. But this time, the person responsible is still out there.'

'Yeah, for now. Karma has a way—'

'Fuck karma. That shit doesn't work—' She'd been about to say look at her family, but her brothers had suffered violent deaths and her dad, already in a wheelchair, looked like he might be in an even worse state. Was this payback for the lives they'd ruined?

'You sure you're okay, Judy?'

She smiled. 'You've done more than enough, Victor. Go.'

'Okay, but I'll do tomorrow night.'

'We'll discuss it.'

'Yeah, okay, and don't worry about Mulberry.'

What the hell did he mean?

She took a tour of the casino, greeting everyone, pretending not to see their shocked expressions at the state of her face, and thanking them for their kind words. Somehow, she made it through the night, and with four hours' sleep, was ready to face whatever copper she had to see.

She met her lawyer at his office and discussed what she'd say, rehearsing the evidence she'd gathered. As he drove her to the cop shop, a terrifying thought occurred to her on the way. What if Mulberry had inserted himself into the investigation? Then she recalled Victor's comment and felt reassured.

In the event, she saw the familiar bulk of DCI Grimes, but he had a new assistant. She'd found the last one intimidating, and Grimes even more so. But she'd grown up a lot in the six months since he'd investigated her dad's shooting. This version of Judy was harder to intimidate. 'How come you're investigating this?'

'Major Crimes. And I'm pretty sure this' – he tapped a folder in front of him – 'meets the criterion.'

Her solicitor objected when Grimes cautioned her, but she waved it away.

Grimes studied her. 'Can you talk me through what happened in the early hours of Saturday morning, Ms Novak, in your own words?'

She kept to the truth, omitting her message to Victor.

'Did the men say what they were looking for?'

She looked him in the eye. 'They made it very clear they wanted a hard drive containing emails between Detective Chief Superintendent Mulberry and Jerry Sweeny, who used to work for me.'

'Did they now?' Grimes didn't look surprised, but she recalled his poker face from last time. 'And what was the nature of these messages?'

'I've no idea, because I don't know where they are. But since Jerry left, we've uncovered embezzlement and other criminal activity.'

'Really? I'm not aware you've reported this to us.'

Bugger! She needed to be careful about what she said to him; he was a lot brighter than he looked. 'We're checking the extent before filing a report.'

'I'll keep an eye out.' He made it sound like a threat.

She continued with the truth, until the moment the rescue party arrived. 'The two men started arguing. One wanted to let us go, while the other wanted to kill us. They had a big row, and the one who wanted us dead stormed off. I needed the toilet, and the other one let me go.'

'On your own?'

'No, Dad was unconscious and strapped to his chair, so the gunman came with me. Then on our way back, a crash came from the orangery. He ran towards it, and I stopped. I stood by the French doors in the dining room, and they were open. I waited a few seconds and then stepped out, intending to get help.' She took a deep breath. 'Then, I heard a shot.' She thought she'd be alright, but her mouth dried and her hands trembled.

'Are you okay to continue, Ms Novak?' her solicitor asked.

She sipped some water. 'I'll be fine, thanks. I stopped, thinking he'd shot Dad. The spade lay beside the back door, so I picked it up and went back inside.'

The sergeant, a delicate-looking woman, spoke for the first time. 'You didn't see where the gunman was when he shot his brother?'

'I was outside, and by the time I went in, one of them lay on the floor on the other side of Dad, dead, and the other had his back to me.'

The sergeant exchanged a look with Grimes, seeming to ask permission. 'What happened then?'

'He still had the gun in his hand, and he raised it towards Dad. He was about to shoot him, and I shouted, no! Or something like that. Then I heard a shot, and he turned to face me. I hit him with the flat of the spade.'

'He didn't defend himself or attempt to shoot you?'

'He didn't have time. I lifted the spade when he aimed the gun at Dad.' Her eyes filled and she closed them. 'I thought he'd kill both of us, so I just hit him with all my strength.'

They asked her to clarify different sections of her story, but she didn't falter. They mentioned the forensic evidence. She'd made sure to 'check' both bodies, so their blood had covered her hands and clothes. Blood had splattered her when Craig shot one brother and when Victor hit the other. She'd worried the police would want to know how that had happened, but they were twins who shared DNA, and she'd hoped this would muddy the waters. In the event, Grimes seemed satisfied and told her the evidence supported aspects of her story.

Grimes studied the notes he'd been making. 'You accused a senior police officer of being behind this attack, but have offered no evidence.'

'I believe I can help.' Her solicitor opened his briefcase. 'Mr Novak had a virtual assistant, and he had the presence of mind to get it to record the first twenty minutes of their ordeal. Unfortunately, at that point, the device complained it hadn't heard one of my client's replies, leading to their attackers discovering and disabling it. I believe they intended to wipe it once they'd killed my clients because they mention who'd paid them to carry out the attack on two occasions.' He placed a small iPad on the table. 'I'll play it if you'll let me. I must warn you, it's distressing.'

The only thing Judy disagreed with her solicitor on was that the interruption was unfortunate. It saved Victor and his friends from being dragged into this.

The recording started, and she was back in the orangery, her dad beside her. His belligerent replies became more subdued as he took a terrible beating. Then they started on her before, mercifully, the recording ended. Tears ran down her cheeks.

'Thank you, Ms Novak,' said Grimes. 'That was indeed genuinely distressing, but there's no doubt in my mind that Mulberry was behind this attack. It may hearten you to know that he's already under arrest. After a tip-off, we found one point two kilos of cocaine, stolen from a huge haul we made over the summer, in a briefcase in his car. May I thank you for your help, and we'll contact you when we next need to speak to you.'

CHAPTER 65

I approached the entrance to Southern Cemetery along Barlow Moor Road and indicated to turn right, waiting for a gap in the traffic.

You could have gone then, Oscar piped up from the back.

'Once you've got a driving licence, you can comment.'

We're going to be late.

'Thanks to you, insisting we get you and Cleo matching black harnesses.'

Well, it's an important day for her. You told me we're saying goodbye to Harry. She's not seen him for ages and wants to look her best.

'Harry won't be here—'

How do we say goodbye to him if he's not here? I've told Cleo he will be.

I sighed with frustration. 'He will be *here*, but he won't see Cleo.'

Why not?

A gap appeared, and I raced through it.

Whoa! Oscar slid across the seat. ***I almost got thrown out of the window. No need to go mad.***

'Don't be dramatic.'

The parking spaces inside the gates were all occupied, so I drove further in. The North Chapel was straight ahead, but a row of bollards blocked my way. I took a left and followed the elliptical drive looking for somewhere to park.

What do you mean he won't see Cleo?

'Can we leave it? I'll explain later.'

No need to snap.

The bright autumnal sunshine cast the shadows of the naked trees that lined the driveways onto the rows of limestone gravestones. To my relief, I spotted Zofia's car parked on the side and pulled up in front of it. I got out and opened the back door.

'Come on, let's go.'

Keep your hair on. Oscar jumped out, and Cleo followed.

I had to admit, they looked smart, and so did I. I knew many of the people attending Harry's funeral wouldn't have good clothes, and I didn't want to stand out. After much prevarication, I'd rung Zofia for advice, and she told me to wear the new suit she and Helen had helped me choose. Although I'd offered to get one for John, he'd declined.

Zofia, who'd been waiting at the entrance, gave us a relieved smile and mouthed, 'You look gorgeous.' She winked. 'And you look nice, too, Victor.'

We followed her into the packed chapel, where she'd saved us seats on the back row. John, in a classic suit, sat in the front row with people I assumed were his family. A commotion as the service started announced Judy and Alex's arrival – him in a powered chair, still bearing the marks of his beating.

After a short but affecting service, we trooped out behind the coffin, with John and a woman I assumed was his sister immediately behind it. The tears that had accompanied his eulogy had dried on his cheeks. All our friends from the streets were there, including Craig, with Trixie, who again wore a black ribbon. We followed the horse-drawn hearse towards the new section of the cemetery, passing the graves of the workhouse inmates, buried eight to a plot, before crossing Nell Lane. At least Harry would have his own grave, thanks to Judy's generosity.

After the burial, the dogs, Kasper, Zofia and I found ourselves next to Grimes and Bowling.

'Glad to see you've got your hair cut,' Grimes said to Oscar. 'It suits you.' Oscar looked surprised, and then preened.

'That was Helen's doing,' I said. 'My daughter insisted he had it done before she returned to Bristol.' My girls had only been gone two days, but I missed them like hell.

'Clever lass.' He checked who was nearby. 'A quick word.' He indicated Kasper, Zofia and me, then nodded away from the other mourners before marching towards some shrubs, Bowling at his side.

We three followed until he stopped twenty paces away, an evergreen shrub shielding us from the others.

'Goes without saying that this goes no further. Right?' He fixed each of us with his gaze, and we each nodded in turn. 'The two guys you caught have coughed to nine murders. Once we found the box under the pickup with pictures of their victims, they wouldn't shut up.'

A mixture of horror and relief made my insides tremble. 'Did they say why they had the box of photos there?'

'They kept them as souvenirs and thought nobody could link the pickup to either of them so they'd be safe to leave them there.' He stared at me. 'They mentioned something about you having two people with you when you took them down.' I swallowed. 'But they were both concussed, so I'm putting that down to confusion.'

I tried to hide my relief. 'Did they say why they did it?'

'Yeah. As though he couldn't imagine what all the fuss was about, Colby essentially admitted to just enjoying humiliating people, and as homeless people didn't fight back or complain to the authorities, it didn't put his nice accounting job at risk.' His expression showed his contempt. 'Except one did fight back and humiliated him in public. He couldn't have that.'

I bent to stroke Oscar's head, credit where it was due for biting the bastard when we'd confronted him in a café soon after he'd attacked me when I lived on the streets.

Grimes continued. 'The other guy, Akimov, claims his brother was being spied on by a homeless man with a dog in the days before he was killed. He said his original plan was to find the man and make him tell him who he was working for, so they targeted a homeless guy outside the casino in Sackville Square where his brother worked. But he didn't know what the hell they were talking about, so they beat him to death.'

Zofia gasped and covered her eyes with her hands. I squeezed her shoulder. I'd known the poor man, and the confirmation that I'd been the target when he'd been killed filled me with guilt *and* anger.

Grimes continued, 'Akimov was the real driving force, which is why they stopped when he was sent down, but they both just got a taste for it. Just twisted fuckers looking for an excuse to kill people.'

'But . . . nine murders?' Zofia said. 'How could that have gone unnoticed?'

Grimes scowled, then checked himself. 'Fair question. Colby's uncle, a chief superintendent currently being investigated on drug charges—'

'Mulberry!' I blurted out.

Bowling nodded. 'He made sure we never fully investigated the deaths and, to our shame, the senior brass let it slide. The victims didn't matter to them.'

'But *you* investigated.'

'I spoke to Darren about what you told me. And we agreed to reopen all the cases.'

'Aye, on the QT,' Grimes said. 'We didn't know who we could trust. We were gathering evidence, but then you went and caught them, all on your own.' He winked at me.

Kasper said, 'What will happen to Mulberry about that?'

'It will go on his charge sheet with all the other shit he's done. Don't expect to see him outside a cell for a long time, if ever.' He glanced over my shoulder. 'I'll let you join your friends. I believe Judy's closed the casino and is hosting the wake.' He exchanged a look with Bowling. 'I suppose we'll be picking up the pieces through the night.'

'You don't need to worry,' I said. 'It's an alcohol-free bar.'

'Aye?' He looked at the mourners. 'Makes sense.' They nodded their goodbyes and left us.

Without a thought, I put my arm around Zofia's shoulders as we watched them walk back to their car. She took my hand as we returned to the other mourners. A small knot had separated from the others at the back. Alex's chair had got stuck in the soft grass, and Craig was helping his minder free it and carry him to the hardstanding. As they put him down, Alex offered his undamaged fist to Craig, who bumped it, wearing a smile.

Zofia squeezed my hand.

ACKNOWLEDGEMENTS

I'd like to take this opportunity to thank those who've helped me on my journey to get this novel published.

I've again taken a few liberties with the geography of Manchester, in particular Sackville Square, which doesn't exist, yet.

Despite this being my eighth published novel, my family and friends have been as unstinting in their support, and I want them to know I never take it for granted.

As usual, I read early versions of this to my writing group, South Manchester Writers' Workshop. Despite the fact that I've never finished reading one out before it's sent to my agent, they never complain and continue to give me constructive advice on my writing.

My agent, Clare Coombes, from The Liverpool Literary Agency, continues to guide and support me and be a powerful advocate for my work.

The team at Thomas & Mercer, without whom this book wouldn't have been published. Although Maisie Lawrence has overseen the day-to-day progress of the novel, the entire team has contributed.

David Downing, of Maxwellian Editorial Services, Inc., who made editing this novel as pleasurable as the last five. His continued wisdom and insightful feedback give me great confidence that my novel will be in the best possible shape.

Ian Critchley, who copyedited the manuscript, is still picking up my verbal tics and embarrassing errors, while suggesting further improvements.

Sadie Mayne, who proofread the final version to eliminate those errors that always slip through and threaten to undermine all the work that has gone before.

Dominic Forbes, whose excellent cover makes the book stand out.

Thank you also to Nicole Wagner, Dan Griffin, and their respective teams for all their hard work in making this series a success.

If your heart was in your mouth as Victor and Oscar raced to find their friend's killers, then you'll absolutely love *A Long Shadow*, starring journalist Antonia Conti. In this dystopian vision of London, public safety is in private hands – and nobody is beyond the reach of the 'law'.

Available now, or read on for an exclusive extract.

CHAPTER 1

Antonia winced as the shorter woman ploughed through her blonde opponent's jab and landed three blows to unprotected ribs before catching her with an uppercut. The blonde fell to one knee, blood streaming from her mouth. The amateur recording of Antonia's next opponent wobbled, but even through the TV screen Antonia could sense the shorter woman's fury. She imagined the same fists ripping into her ribcage as Milo paused the footage.

Milo waved the remote at the screen. 'See her lining up the uppercut? She dropped her left.'

'A right hook and she's history,' Darius said. 'And she so telegraphed it.'

'You'll take her easy, Antonia,' Milo assured her. 'She's only one-seventy, so you've got height and reach on her.' Light glinted off his shaved skull, a huge brown cannonball. 'We got three weeks to sharpen you up.' He grinned and winked at her.

Her mouth dry, Antonia didn't reply. It was easy for them; most of the Dekker brothers' opponents gave up when they saw either of the monsters across the ring and spent the fight keeping out of their way.

Milo killed the screen and Darius said, 'Want a lift home?'

'I'll walk.' She rose out of the shabby armchair in the small TV room at the side of the gym, picked up her backpack and headed for the door. 'Thanks, guys.'

The empty gym smelt of sweat and liniment. Darius had lowered the lights and the heavy bags cast long shadows across the wooden floor. Her trainers made no sound as she reflected on what she'd watched. Despite the brothers' reassurances, Antonia wasn't sure she'd prevail against her unbeaten opponent. Although she'd sparred hundreds of rounds, she'd never fought someone fuelled by so much anger. The memory of a coachload from the gym going to support one of the other fighters in his first bout still mortified her. Despite showing promise in training, he'd frozen at the first bell and had never since visited the gym. The fear she'd do the same haunted her.

Outside, she hesitated. Normally high on the endorphins after a workout, tonight a sense of dread weighed on her. Only the brothers' battered silver Land Cruiser remained in the gloomy car park and she paused beside it. She could say she'd changed her mind.

Don't be a wuss, Antonia. She shouldered her backpack and set off for home.

The familiar route seemed different tonight, the darkened industrial buildings lining it appearing sinister. She shivered and hurried between the pools of light surrounding the scattered lamp posts. Icy air infiltrated layers of clothing and she promised herself a mug of hot chocolate when she got home. Cheered by the prospect, she walked faster.

Instead of fading, the sense of unease grew stronger. *The fight isn't for three weeks. Forget it and pull yourself together.*

Angry voices called out ahead and she faltered. The sounds came from an opening on her left. She glanced up at the nearest camera, for the first time welcoming its intrusive surveillance. As she approached, she saw that the opening led down a narrow potholed lane. In the shadows, thirty metres away, two jeering men bent over a bundle on the ground. One of them kicked it. An old man cried out in pain.

Antonia stepped towards them, shouting, 'Leave him alone!'

The men spun round, seeming unsurprised to see her, and she hesitated. Ignoring the old man, they advanced towards her. Chests thrust out and arms bent, they looked huge, and hostility flooded out of them. *Oh hell, you've done it now.*

Ten metres from her, the men halted. In their mid-twenties, both stood over one-eighty and although not athletes, looked like they could take care of themselves.

The one at the front leered. 'Leave him alone, or else . . . ?'

A gust of wind carried the odour of beer and curry from them. If she ran now, she'd get away, but she couldn't abandon an old man. Although the same height as the one who spoke, she was half his bulk. A sudden movement from the other one made her heart jump until she realised he was pointing behind her.

'Cameras, Arkady,' he said, frowning.

The man called Arkady glared at the camera and then at her as he raised his palms in a gesture of appeasement. 'Come on,' he said and edged past her towards the main road. His small, mean eyes appraised her, making her skin tingle. His principal emotion as he passed Antonia confused her. She expected anger, but she sensed satisfaction, as if he'd achieved something. His companion followed, a scar from his mouth to his ear giving him a macabre grin.

When they reached the corner, Arkady stopped and turned back to her. Her stomach tensed. 'See you around,' he said, blowing her a kiss, and Scar-face laughed.

They left, and she exhaled. Their victim, an unkempt old man, crouched in the gutter retrieving his belongings and she went to help him.

'You okay?' she said, rescuing a grimy, fluorescent-pink sleeping bag from a puddle of filthy water.

A claw-like hand snatched it from her grasp. 'Get your thieving Black hands off!' She recoiled as the old man straightened, his toothless mouth twisted into a sneer. 'Unless you want to give me a gobble,' he said, cackling and spraying spittle.

Cheeks burning, Antonia turned away from him, then stopped. Arkady had reappeared, and now stood between her and the main road along with half a dozen others, the hostility emanating from them like a physical barrier. Her insides fluttered and she checked behind her, along the lane. She didn't even know where it led. The old man, seeming unhurt by the kicking, scurried away and vanished into the darkness.

She remembered what Scar-face had said about the camera. If she stayed within range of surveillance cameras, she should be safe. She set off down the lane away from them. *Don't run, and don't look back. They're just trying to scare you.* The men's heavy steps echoed off the buildings.

Determined to stay calm, she checked the nearest camera. It hung broken, the letters ASL sprayed on the wall under it. Anti-Surveillance League. Although sympathetic to their cause, she cursed them. *Keep calm, there's another one ahead.* She got closer and saw the black paint across the lens. Time slowed. Her pulse raced and the men's steps grew louder. She ran.

She'd pushed herself in the gym and her legs felt leaden. Angry shouts followed her. Heavy footwear thudded on to the road. Images of what they'd do to her filled her with terror. *Save your energy, concentrate on running.* The freezing air scoured her throat. She groped for the mental exercises Milo made her rehearse to block out her fear. The straps of her backpack slapped her shoulders with each stride on the uneven roadway. The sounds of her pursuers grew fainter and she risked a glance behind her. Two men trailed in her wake but she didn't see the others. In a few minutes these last two would give up.

She saw the pothole too late and her foot caught the edge. Her ankle gave way and she stumbled, flailing her arms. Her other foot smashed into the kerb and pain ripped through her knee. She staggered two steps, almost going down. Her pursuers let out yells of triumph. Antonia gritted her teeth and ran.

The knee stiffened with every step but she forced her legs to move, hoping it would ease. The men sounded closer. She must think. If she stayed in the lane, they'd catch her, but if she left it, they'd wait for the others. On her right lay an alleyway. She swerved into it, ignoring the pain as she changed direction, concentrating on keeping her footing.

A shout told her they'd seen her. A distant reply followed a few seconds later, then silence. The path split and she took the left branch. The alley opened out and in front of her lay a stretch of inky water, slick in the faint light. City Road Basin; she'd doubled back on herself. She hesitated, unsure which way to go.

A shout in the distance sounded forlorn. They'd lost her. She relaxed and listened. A yell in reply, much nearer, jolted her into action. She ran left, along a lane bounded by a wall and the water. Each step on the uneven ground jarred her knee. Voices echoed over the water, closer than she expected. They were gaining on her.

A few yards in front, a darker shadow in the wall led to an opening. She plunged through it before skidding to a halt. She found herself in an enclosed courtyard lined with large steel bins. Paralysed for a moment, she turned back, but the men were almost on her. She hobbled to the furthest container and threw herself into it. The stench of rotting garbage made her heave, but she eased the lid shut. Had they seen her? Her pulse pounded in her ears as she listened. When she didn't hear anything for several minutes, she began to hope they'd passed her.

Then a roar of anger and a voice said, 'Where the fuck's she gone?'

She gulped, gagging again at the stink of putrefaction.

'You sure she came down here?' another voice panted.

'Where else would she go?'

'She's probably carried on along the path,' the uncertain one said. 'Come on, Pavlo, we'll soon catch her.'

'What if she *did* come down here?'

'What if she *didn't*?'

She held her breath, willing them to go. A bin lid clanged, sending shockwaves through the soles of her trainers. Plastic rustled and bottles clinked. *Blast!*

'You going to fucking help, or what?' Pavlo said.

'Waste of time,' the other man mumbled, but another lid clanged.

Antonia swallowed. Should she wait until they discovered her or jump out now, surprise them? Would her knee let her?

'Come on, Pavlo, I'm going back.'

'Don't you want the money?'

What does he mean?

'The others might have caught her.'

'Those fat fuckers. No way.' Pavlo's voice came closer.

She could almost taste his anger and she prepared herself, tensing her muscles and inhaling. Bad knee or not, she would do serious damage to whoever found her. Another bin opened, the lid striking the side of hers. She bit back a cry.

'Come on, search under those bags,' Pavlo ordered.

'Shit, it's all over my hands. What the fuck's this stinking crap—'

'Don't be a pussy.'

'Fuck off!' A lid banged shut.

'Where the fuck you going?' Pavlo demanded.

'We don't even know she came down here.'

'Hang on . . .' Something smashed into her bin, making it reverberate. The sound faded and Pavlo muttered a frustrated, 'Shit!'

Their voices grew faint but not daring to hope they'd left, Antonia waited. Her thighs trembled with the effort of keeping her out of the vile-smelling sludge at the bottom of the bin and a chill leached into her weary body. After what seemed an age, she lifted a corner of the lid and drank down the freezing air.

Silence greeted her, so she straightened, easing the cover back against the wall. She flexed her legs, massaging them and grimacing as her circulation returned. Once sure they worked, she grabbed the side of the bin and clambered out. Something made her hesitate; a sensation of danger still close. A dog barked in the distance and a lorry laboured up an incline, its engine complaining. The everyday sounds calmed her and she set about retracing her steps.

Pavlo's words raced round her mind as she tried to make sense of them. *Don't you want the money?* They must have thought she was an illegal. She remembered the outcry when the new company running homeland security suggested offering a bounty for each illegal immigrant handed in. She hadn't realised they'd gone ahead. The stretch of water lay in front of her and she stepped into the open.

A noise like a large animal scratching at the floor made her turn. A bulky figure was almost atop her, charging her with a cry of, 'Got you, bitch!'

Pavlo.

He drove his lowered shoulder into her, hitting her mid-thigh and jarring her teeth. Caught off balance, she flew backward, screaming until icy water engulfed her.

The shock of entering the freezing water paralysed Antonia. Pavlo seized her legs, dragging her under. Foul liquid entered her mouth and nose and she fought not to retch. The numbness faded and she kicked out, twisting her hips. The grip on her thighs loosened, so she kicked again and he released her legs. She struck for the surface but a fist thudded into her shoulder, spinning her. Hands closed around her neck, squeezing. She tore at the fingers digging into her flesh, but couldn't dislodge them. She lashed out, aiming for his head. But the water dragged at her arms, slowing her punches and robbing them of power.

Energy drained from her with each blow she attempted. Her lungs caught fire but she clamped her mouth shut, resisting a desperate need to breathe. A roaring filled her ears and bright lights flashed in front of her. Then anger seized her. How dare this man end her life? After everything she'd survived. She pushed her exhausted body into a final effort. Thrashing feet struck a solid surface and she pushed against it. Her trainers slipped before gripping on a rough patch and she propelled herself through the water. As she emerged from the icy liquid, she gulped for air.

Still blinking to clear her vision, she lashed out. When her hand hit solid flesh and caused him to grunt, she struck again. Encouraged by a cry of pain, she pulled her fist back. Before she could throw the punch, he seized her in a powerful bear hug, pinning her arms to her sides. She fought to free them as he crushed her against his body. The grip intensified, squeezing air out of her lungs. Panic made her mind go blank. Then a small voice told her to stop struggling and let her body go limp.

Pavlo pushed her under the water. As it closed over her, she made herself stay calm. Her feet found the bottom and scrabbled for purchase on its slimy surface, but she kept her upper body limp. After long seconds his hold relaxed. She drove with her thighs, shooting out of the water and smashing her forehead into his face. Bone crunched, and he cried out.

Before he could react, she hit him in the throat. With a strangled cough, he fell back. She made for the bank, scrambled out and lay on the side, panting, muscles screaming for rest.

Come on, don't stop now. With an effort she pushed herself to get up and crawled away from what had almost been her grave.

A hand seized her ankle and Antonia's heart somersaulted. With the last of her strength, she jerked her leg, attempting to free it, but the grip tightened. Then he pulled her towards the water and an involuntary whimper escaped her lips.

ABOUT THE AUTHOR

Photo © 2021 Steve Pattyson Photography

D. E. Beckler writes action thrillers populated with well-rounded characters. Born in Addis Ababa in 1960, Beckler spent his first eight years living on an agricultural college in rural Ethiopia where his love of reading developed. After dropping out of university he became a firefighter and served nineteen years before leaving to start his own business.

Beckler began writing in 2010 and uses his work experiences to add realism to his fiction. Beckler lives in Manchester, his adopted home since 1984. In his spare time, he tries to keep fit – an increasingly difficult undertaking – listens to music, socialises and feeds his voracious book habit.

Follow the Author on Amazon

If you enjoyed this book, follow D. E. Beckler on Amazon to be notified when the author releases a new book!
To do this, please follow these instructions:

Desktop:

1) Search for the author's name on Amazon or in the Amazon App.
2) Click on the author's name to arrive on their Amazon page.
3) Click the 'Follow' button.

Mobile and Tablet:

1) Search for the author's name on Amazon or in the Amazon App.
2) Click on one of the author's books.
3) Click on the author's name to arrive on their Amazon page.
4) Click the 'Follow' button.

Kindle eReader and Kindle App:

If you enjoyed this book on a Kindle eReader or in the Kindle App, you will find the author 'Follow' button after the last page.